The Life of Olaf Waniglia

Body Whisperer

I0601922

Disclaimer

This is a work of fiction. The characters and situations presented herein are not real and are not based on any living person or event. This book is solely for entertainment and the overall enrichment of the soul.

Printed in the United States of America

First Printing, 2018

ISBN 978-1-7326174-0-7

Orsa LLC
3009 Wells Fleet Circle
Willoughby, Ohio 44094

www.orsa.com

www.thelifeofolafwaniglia.com

Contents

Dedications

This book is dedicated to my wife, who inspired my creativity in a way that allowed me to write this story.

This book is dedicated to our children, who allow me the extraordinary privilege of being in their lives.

This book is dedicated to my grandmother, my mother and my aunt—each a teacher—who showed me how powerful and special language can be.

This book is dedicated to my father, who has always encouraged me to let my mind wander.

Hello, dear Reader. My name is Olaf Waniglia, and I am a body whisperer.

A body whisperer, you ask?

Yes—a body whisperer I am. I hear conversations plainly from a person's body, whether they are conscious or not. I couldn't tell you from where this voice originates. I can only say I did not presume to understand how truly special life is without hearing it. My practice has extended for a few decades now, and though I often think I have heard it all, I am surprised constantly to this day. There are those who come to see me because they feel something is amiss and feel I can provide solace. Others present themselves to me when they don't realize they need to. There have been many cases where a body is sick, becoming sicker, and cannot leave its care to its owner to resolve. There have been cases of abuse where the individual was too frightened or ashamed to say anything, but their body was anything but. There have been cases where a person is alone either physically or mentally and the weight of being alone becomes an issue for one reason or another. In each case, I often hear things which are known to an individual, but simply not accepted. In others, I hear a voice who desperately wants to be heard. Every conversation I have—from the hilarious to the tragic—proves we are so much more than we will ever consciously observe.

"Olaf," you may ask, "what do you hear when a conversation begins?"

This is a wonderful question, and one I get quite a lot. The plain fact is, I oftentimes hear two conversations at once until I implore of the voice without lips to wait its turn through what I've learned as a universal form of communication—a single, loud clap. I'm not sure if this stuns the body, but it works. I've gotten quite good at reading lips, but I'm nowhere near perfect and oftentimes have to "have the talk," as I call it, to clarify two conversations are happening. This of course makes for an interesting, albeit strange, bit of dialogue. Imagine, if you will, speaking to a man who randomly claps as you are talking, and then out of nowhere asks you to refrain from speaking such that your body can make its point? I've been slapped, punched, and scoffed at more times than I care to remember through the years, but people are much less shocked now when I have such a conversation. My client pool spans multiple generations and a few continents at this point.

The voice I hear from a person's body is something I struggle to understand when I really think about it. I hear a voice noticeably lower in timbre than the person's voice, and always in the dialect or language of the possessor. The one constant—every body begins its first conversation with me the same way, by saying very simply, "Hello, Olaf." This is not the case as subsequent conversations occur, however, which can be tricky from time to time. There are times it's hard for me to discern from whom a conversation is originating. Remarkably, though I do not know many of the people who I inevitably meet, their body's voice always knows my name. I learned just a short while ago how this was possible, and it is my sincere hope you too will see just how magical this life of ours is as I reveal that lesson. I should, at this point, make reference to the phrase that I have used for most of my career to describe this, I suppose, "inner voice," as I will be using it from this point forward. That phrase, simply, is a semi-formal representation of the Latin phrase for "their body's voice:" vox corporis. This is pronounced core-pore-eese, if you may be curious, dear Reader. I say "semi-formal" as the true Latin syntax of that phrase is vox eorum corporis. I found it is much simpler to eliminate the formality and simply use vox corporis as my key phrase for this voice. No doubt, there will be Latin scholars who frown on this, and truthfully, that's okay by me. I've found this to be the easiest way by far to speak to those I help to describe this voice, to give it identity, and to be mostly accurate in its rightful description.

I am often asked whether I am a doctor. I am not; I gladly left said distinction to my father. I have worked with many doctors through the years, but in the beginning, it highlighted the darker sides of the human spirit. I often would tell doctors a patient they were treating had something very particular wrong with them. If they were unfamiliar with my work, and asked how I knew such a thing, I would take a deep breath and relent, "Their body told me." I was callously— dare I say violently—ushered out of several hospitals in the early days and was even committed at one point. These days, I am much more welcome in medical facilities. A decent amount of my time is spent in hospitals, but I've also had an independent office for many years and see patients by appointment. I used to travel quite a bit for my appointments—often overseas—but as that has become harder as I have aged, I bring people to me now. I converted my parents' house to an office and have done most of my appointments there for quite some time. My father's orchard, which he took such pride in for all of his adult life, is still very much alive and producing delicious fruits. It provides such a wonderful backdrop for anyone who is nervous, and for those who get news of all kinds. I've found beautiful scenery, a doting or sleeping pup, and calm sensitivity makes all conversations easier to bear.

What I have learned by honoring my ability is, our bodies truthfully communicate what we often don't wish to admit. In some cases, this is some personality trait we have but don't internalize properly—something as perpetual as depression, or something as random as an inability to look in the mirror due to fear. In quite a few cases, what I hear is about one's health. I've both felt extreme joy and suffered profound sadness in this realm. It's an amazing thing to consider, that human beings are so much more than what we know. Should you feel I'm nothing more than a buffoon in my assertions, consider this: your heart has its own magnetic field (akin to the Earth's, and for that matter every planet and star known to mankind...) researchers have studied for decades. Don't believe me? Use one of those search engines that are all the rage and see for yourself—you need only feel your heartbeat to confirm, in fact, you have a heart. I apologize to those whose hearts are artificial. Though your heart may not be original, what sustains you in this unseen realm has something eerily similar to that with which you were born. Take what you will from science and that heart of yours, and understand you are more than a bag of bones. Should you really want a challenge, take a nice deep look at your life. I know I have learned so much in doing so as I've written these pages.

I must say the following, though it pains me to do so. Whisperers, as a lot, are often misunderstood as loons. This is true of whisperers of all kinds: ghost, dog, cat, horse, tree—we all suffer the same end. While some respect our ability, many others scoff at it and cast us aside as misfits. Still others, unfortunately, respond to our talents with violence. Many whisperers have chosen to hide their talent for fear of their and their family's lives and well-being as a result. I did not make such a choice, and have witnessed everything from tears of joy, to confronting my own mortality as a result.

Make no mind—I am a loon. Thing is, I am a body whisperer and my status as a loon is quite unrelated. "But Olaf, you speak to bodies," you say with a tinge of condescension in your voice. Yes, dear Reader, I do—and in so doing, I improve and often save lives.

I've included in this memoir many notable interactions I remember for people—some I never actually met—but all whose stories are incredible. How is this possible, you ask? Continue reading. The answer shall become clear in due time. I've had a remarkable life, and it is now I share my story. Won't you walk with me down a road of both intrigue and tragedy? I promise you will laugh, you will cry, and you will perhaps view your own physical self differently for the rest of your life.

Let us begin, dear Reader.

My Childhood... A Comedy of Confusion

Our family's heritage included a commingling of both Irish and Italian cultures. I've been told my paternal great grandfather came to America from Italy, seeking a better life for his family. Apparently, he greatly confused the citizenship officer who received him when he first arrived. You see, dear Reader, our name is pronounced differently than it is spelled, and this was hard for the officer to understand. The story goes, my great grandfather was so stubborn in that conversation that he almost was returned to Italy in chains. The issue simply was the spelling of our last name. The officer kept spelling it "Waneelia" on the citizenship papers. My great grandfather would look to the sky, say something tender and apologetic in Italian, look back at the officer, and say something much less tender and apologetic in Italian. This prompted his wife to cover their young son's ears. That young boy was my grandfather, who had the same stubborn temper as his father. You will meet him shortly, dear Reader.

My maternal grandfather immigrated to America from Ireland when he was in his twenties. He was a talented cook and became the head chef at his cousin's restaurant. It was there he met his wife; she was a hostess who had also recently immigrated to America from Ireland. It turned out they had lived less than two miles apart from one another their entire childhood. They were married and had a daughter, my mother, within the first year of knowing one another. I never met my maternal grandparents; they tragically died in a car accident back in Ireland when Mother was in college.

My life as a boy was quite common for the most part, but it was influenced by the divergent cultures of my elders. I grew up an only child to loving—but passionate—parents. My mother, Sierra, stayed at home with me when I was young, but became a librarian when I was old enough to be left alone after school. She clearly acquired the love of cooking from her father, and Irish cuisine was frequently on the menu. We lived comfortably, but make no mistake, hard work was fervently instilled in me early on. My grandfather was a farmer who retired at age ninety-two—and my father, David, was a doctor. I spent a notable amount of time on the farm, where corn, strawberries, and cotton were grown. I could drive a combine by the time I was ten and knew the process and business of farming by the time I was a teenager. I helped my grandfather every summer during my schooling years. He lived a couple hours away, which was a prohibitive distance during the school year until I could drive myself. As soon as I turned sixteen, I worked on the farm every week.

Farming was deeply instilled in Father. We had an expansive orchard with apple, peach, and cherry trees he tended, by hand for the most part, every day after working at the hospital. The orchard was an immense source of both pride and relaxation. It was Father's refuge. The quality of the fruit Father expected was a driving force in his care of the trees. He was methodical—dare I say surgical—in his approach. The orchard contributed to his personal identity and cast its importance among our family. Mother and I helped at harvest time, but there was no mistaking this was Father's orchard.

The fact that Father chose to be a doctor made for paralyzing tension throughout my childhood as Grandfather was always bitter that his only child—and a son no less—did not take up the family business. Father, in turn, was bitter he had become a nationally known doctor and never so much as got a single word of encouragement nor praise from Grandfather. This was compounded by Grandfather being unfairly critical of the orchard. If there was so much as a single rotten fruit either on the ground or on a tree, Grandfather would raise a scene as though the Heavens themselves had been compromised. Mind you, finding such fruit was a near impossibility, so the commentary was summarily dismissed through a confident silence every time.

There were several years I can remember the two not speaking at all. Mother would handle all the conversation at family gatherings and Father would make himself busy either in his workshop or in the orchard when Grandfather visited us. Mother and Grandfather were quite close; he loved her like a daughter, and he was every bit the father she longed for after losing her own. Family meals, though, were events that commingled opposing polarities between Father and Grandfather, and as such, were a fascinating ballet of conversation. Uncomfortable, extended silences were normal and conversation attempts were tragic pirouettes. Mother would discuss both the farm and the hospital to bridge an impossible gap between father and son. This remained true until Grandfather became sick and did something strange: he asked for help.

Grandfather had just turned ninety and was told by his doctor that he had the beginning signs of dementia. He had lost my grandmother forty-five years prior to cancer—diagnosed two days before it claimed her life. It was from that point on that this prideful farmer made it a regular practice to go to the doctor. Ironically, it was this same tragic event that gave Father a fervent conviction to become a member of the medical community. Father lost his mother at age sixteen. He was old enough to understand the severity of cancer, and just young enough to be shaken violently to his core by his mother's death. He put himself on a path to help others not suffer the same end. He was the most widely known oncologist in the South and saved scores of people from death with unique treatment plans. He became intimately involved with the family of the patient, something he believed to his core assisted in the healing and recovery processes accompanying a cancer fight. I learned as I got older precisely how right he was, for patients of all kinds.

With the farm in the balance, Father became much more involved with Grandfather's care. His dementia progressed so slowly that it only impacted Grandfather's near-term memory. He'd forget what he ate for breakfast, and sometimes he'd forget if he had turned on the irrigation system. Unlike many who have dementia, his personality remained intact, his speech never suffered, and his health remained extraordinarily good for a man in his nineties. The degenerative disease seemingly erased decades of angst, and what one would expect of a loving relationship between father and son blossomed.

Father became intimately involved with every phase of Grandfather's medical care. They had a cadence: whenever Grandfather had a doctor's appointment, they would go to dinner together. On these nights, Mother and I would cook together and have a quiet evening between the two of us. One such night, Mother and I were doing just that: preparing dinner for the two of us. I remember it so clearly. I was cutting an onion and my mother was washing a head of lettuce in the sink. As I wiped an onion-fueled tear from my eye, I heard what sounded like my mother's voice say, "*Hello, Olaf.*"

"Mother—did you need something?" I responded.

"No, my dear, crying boy. I didn't say anything," she said, smiling.

"But—you just said 'Hello'…"

"No Sweetheart, I didn't. Is that onion making you hear things?"

Perplexed, I finished cutting up the onion and convinced myself I was hearing things. That night we had jointly prepared shepherd's pie and salad. We both loved shepherd's pie and Father didn't, so this night was our chance to make the dish without Father's disappointed sighs.

"*I'm glad you can hear me now. I knew you would. We spoke so often when you were a baby,*" the voice returned, again sounding like Mother, but slightly different.

"Who are you?" I responded quizzically, and Mother quickly turned to face me.

"Olaf—is something wrong? What's going on?!" she exclaimed, glaring at me with a combination of anger, fear, and concern.

"Mother," I said, "please don't be upset. I'm hearing a voice and I'm trying to figure out what's happening."

"Do you need to go to the doctor?" she said nervously.

"Don't worry, Olaf—you're not going crazy. I am part of your Mother," the voice returned.

"No, Mother, I feel fine. I think perhaps I was hearing things. Let's eat! I'm starving!" I said, trying to dismiss what had become an unintendedly inflammatory situation.

Mother nervously nodded, and we brought the food to the table. After a couple minutes, she gently said, "Olaf, do you think you heard the voice of God, or an Angel, or maybe a ghost?" Mother had a very open belief system. She was accepting of even the most obscure notions. I think I caught her off guard in the beginning of the conversation, and she had started to slowly rationalize what I potentially heard.

"No, Mother, I don't think it was any of those things. The voice indicated something different," I said, wanting desperately not to continue with this conversation. "Let's just eat. We made such a delicious dinner we never get to have anymore!"

She persisted, "My dear boy, you heard something. Let's talk about this. I promise you I will not get upset. Tell me what you heard." She was still agitated at this point.

The voice then said something surreal, something I will never forget.

"Tell her you rolled in her belly so much she would call you 'My Amazing Little Acrobat.'"

So, nervously shaking, I said, "Mother, um, when you were pregnant with me, did you call me your 'Amazing Little Acrobat'?"

A warm smile on her face formed, and a tear slowly streamed down her cheek. All signs of anger or frustration had disappeared. She chuckled a bit, wiping the tear away and said, "Yes, my dear Olaf. I did."

She got up from her seat and came over to where I was sitting. Bending down she hugged me so tightly I couldn't breathe. She happily chuckled, and said, "Okay. Now tell me how you knew that. Father doesn't even know. I used to say that when you woke me up from a nap toward the end of my pregnancy. Your father would work so late sometimes that, even then, it was you and me—My Amazing Little Acrobat."

She got up, wiped the tears from her eyes and returned to her seat. Before doing anything else, she said, "I promise you, no more tears, no more fear, and absolutely no anger or judgment. Nothing evil would say such a thing. I want to understand. Please, will you tell me what you heard?"

The amazing thing about Mother was, though she could be quick to judge a situation, she would seamlessly reduce it to something she would seek to understand. Knowing this, I formed the words to begin explaining the events of the previous half hour, but I did not get them out before the voice returned.

"You have a talent for hearing a voice few outside of themselves hear. Because of that, Olaf, you will help many people. The first is your mother," the voice spoke matter-of-factly, but with unexpected emotion.

"Mother," I asked, "would you mind if I spoke with this voice for a moment?"

"Not at all, Olaf. But please promise me we will talk about this," she responded.

I was taken aback after hearing what the voice had just said. I wasn't sure how to discuss such a thing, so I avoided the topic as best I could. I began, "Can you tell me why you are communicating with me?" I asked, not really sure where to look, though I tended to look at Mother's belly.

The voice responded, "*It is simple, Olaf: you are willing to listen.*"

"Okay, but how am I to respond to the things I hear?" I asked, with Mother looking on with intense curiosity.

"*That is up to you, Olaf.*"

I sat pensively for a couple seconds, trying desperately to understand what in the world I should do next. Do I talk to Mother? Do I talk to her body? Do I consider this whole thing to be nuts and pretend like it never happened? Nothing felt intuitively right to me. This was uncharted territory in so many ways. I was fourteen years old, days away from my fifteenth birthday. For some reason, that night I became much more aware of things around me. I heard the breeze as it hit our window screens. It was August, and the fireflies were starting to appear outside as it was twilight. I saw these amazing creatures in greater quantities than I had before and saw their patterns as they danced through the twilight. I smelled the fruit trees with the mix of sweet and arboreal smells they emitted as the fruit grew. The essence of the blossoms was still there in spirit with the fruit they became. All of this hit me at the same time the voice—the *vox corporis*—made itself heard. In one fell swoop, my life changed radically.

I was filled with a new sense of being. My new awareness made me feel vibrantly alive and at the same time at peace with my ability to hear the *vox corporis*. A confidence grew inside me. I changed my tone with the *vox corporis*, how I spoke to it in particular. Thusly, I began, "If this is up to me, can I trust I will get responses about the person in question if I ask?"

Mother's face was flush with confusion and a bit of concern. She warily asked, "Olaf, are you okay?"

"Yes, Mother, I truly am. I think I'm starting to understand this. I promise I will tell you everything."

The voice then returned, also with a different tone. It was softer, but with conviction. *"Yes, Olaf. That which I am, solely speaks truth. At the same time, as I am part of your Mother, I feel, I love, I laugh. This is something important you must know and know to the core of you."*

"I think I understand," I said. "Will you please clarify what you said about Mother? What do I need to know?"

"Your mother has cancer. She must address this, or her life will be compromised. There is still time, but it is quickly running out."

Tears welled up in my eyes. In that instant, I was reduced to a maturity level more in line with my (almost) fifteen years. I was scared. At my age, mortality of a parent was unthinkable. I knew the horrors of cancer from all Father had told me. The sum of all the above showed clearly in my expression. Seeing this, Mother panicked.

"Olaf! What's wrong? What have you heard?" she emphatically said, her expression intense.

The voice broke in, almost as intensely as Mother. *"Olaf, you must address this with a maturity beyond your years. Tread carefully."*

I wiped the tears from my eyes, took several deep breaths and found strength within me. I'm sure my eyes were red, and I certainly didn't exude the strength I felt, but I took Mother's hands in mine and looked her square in the eye. She was taken aback by this, and her expression changed from a person in a panic to one with scared curiosity.

I began, "Mother, it seems the voice I was hearing is a part of you. I believe it is your body. It... um, she told me she cannot say anything untrue. I must ask you, Mother, are you feeling alright?" My eyes did not leave hers, and my hands gripped a little tighter.

"For the most part, Olaf, yes. It's just that..." she answered, stopping herself as though she didn't want to upset me.

"Mother, I was just told something about your health that is a concern," I said, "please tell me what you're feeling."

"I've been losing weight and have been so tired lately. I just chalked it up to getting older, though," she responded.

The voice returned, "*Olaf, speak carefully.*"

I took another deep breath. "Mother, you should talk to Father."

Her expression dropped, as though a profound recognition was being revealed for the first time, something she had considered at some point but dismissed.

My hands tightened further. I continued, "Mother, I can promise you if this is not ignored, all will be okay. I can also tell you I am completely committed to doing for you what I can, even if it seems strange coming from your son."

It was here I heard something I still remember today, and how I felt when I heard it.

Mother's *vox corporis* returned; her voice laced with Mother's innate ability to impart lessons. She said, "*Olaf, you have just spoken your first truth for the benefit of another, but it is not at all strange. Please promise me you will use your ability without judging it.*"

I was shocked by this, and ashamed, I responded, "I am so sorry. Please understand this is new to me, and still quite strange."

"This is natural, Olaf. But you must know this is a gift, one you must cherish, one you must honor. It is now your responsibility to continue refining this gift. You'll have that chance quite soon as your Father is close."

I had a loving relationship with Father, but he was *intense*. Not mean, per se, but *intense*. His life—especially the way it played out after my grandmother passed—was a fight. He fought through college and medical school. He fought for respect as a physician among colleagues. He fought to create a wonderful life for Mother and I. Father's intensity was a means to an end, something he had relied on to become a brilliant doctor.

Despite Father's intensity, he relaxed when he worked in the orchard. Given the time of night he was returning, this was not to be the case. Nervously, I prepared myself for a potentially gut-wrenching experience. As I did so, however, Mother interjected.

"Olaf," she began, "I need to ask you a couple things." Her expression was soft, but the intensity in her eyes could have sliced me clean in two. "Are you scared, my son?"

"No, Mother," I responded. "Why do you ask?"

"I am concerned for you. People who speak truths that are difficult to swallow for the recipient often endure difficult lives."

The voice interjected here. *"Olaf, you..."*

I cut it off with a response that silenced both Mother and the voice—and created a perverse sense of both curiosity and contemplation on the face of Father, who had just entered the room. Emphatically, I said, "You are right to be concerned Mother, as you and Father have raised me to know right from wrong. I now understand this to be my responsibility, one I cannot—and *will not*—ignore."

Father shot a look at me of both shock and anger, his intense nature propelling him toward correcting me. Before he could say anything, Mother ran over and hugged me, tears streaming down her face. "I am so proud of the person you are, Olaf. Please, promise to talk to me about this, because I feel there will be times ahead that will not be kind to you if you truly succumb to this gift of yours."

Father's look turned solely to confusion. "I clearly have missed something here. Are you both alright?"

Here, a second voice joined the conversation, sounding quite a bit like Father's, but a bit lower in timbre. *"Hello, Olaf!"* it said, a tad more enthusiastically than when Mother's bodily voice first said *"Hello."* *"It is so wonderful you can hear me now! I must tell you something so your father understands all is okay. Tell him that he used to sing you to sleep when you were a baby."*

Father angrily began, "Olaf, I…"

I interrupted him, for the first time I could remember doing so. "Father, I'm sorry, but I must ask you something."

A bit aghast, he responded *"Okay?"*

"When I was a baby, did you sing me to sleep?"

Mother began to smile and said, "David, did you?!"

Father smiled genuinely and said, "Why yes, Olaf, I did. How did you know that? You were just a baby."

Mother could hardly contain herself. "What did you sing to him? Why did I never hear you?" Her eyes got big, and her smile widened as she put her arms around his neck.

Father grinned, "I never wanted to wake you, my love. It was always so late at night. I'd begin rocking you, Olaf, and the rhythm of the chair always reminded me of the blues. Grandpa played blues music all the time when I was a kid, and it stuck with me. When I held you for the first time in the hospital and looked into your baby blue eyes, this song popped into my head and it also stuck with me. So, when it was crazy late at night, I'd calm you down both by rocking and attempting to sing that song to you. How in God's name did you know that?!"

Mother was emphatically bouncing up and down in an excited display of both love and excitement. "Sing it to me, David! Please!" she said, smiling so large it looked like it hurt. Her arms were still around his neck, and she was practically tackling him in the process.

"Aw Si," he said, "You don't want to hear that."

"Yes, David, I do. SING!" Mother seemed to be falling in love with Father all over again after learning this simple detail about him.

He retorted, "Sierra, really, I…"

"DAVID—SING! NOW!" Mother was seemingly losing her mind at the prospect of Father singing.

Her *vox corporis* then broke in, "*You see what you can do, Olaf?*"

It was then that Father's *vox corporis* got into the conversation. "*Yep, see, Olaf? You can do great things with this gift of yours.*"

I could not believe what I had just heard. They could communicate with each other! I said, "You mean, you two *understand* each other?"

Nearly simultaneously, both of my parents looked at me and very intriguingly said, "What? Who?"

"Father," I began, "I discovered I have a gift today."

"What kind of gift?" he responded, his intensity pointed as he prepared to dissect my answer.

"I can hear conversations others cannot." I became nervous after saying this, and I think my concern was all over my face. Father, after all, was a profoundly intellectual man. He had derived several paths of cancer treatment which did not involve drugs. In many cases, this helped people treat the disease without getting sick with chemo and live well beyond others with cancer being treated with conventional means. He had done so after pouring over the human body in layers of detail that superseded that of his peers and colleagues. So, to hear I could speak to a person's *body* hit him like Copernicus stating the Earth was not the center of the universe to a legion of folks declaring it heresy.

He began, "Olaf, what conversations are these?" His brow furrowed, his mind spinning to places of medical theory that would rather clearly put me in the care of a psychologist and padded rooms. Trust me, dear Reader, he may have been the first, but was definitely not the last to feel such a thing. I digress....

Here, Mother said something astounding. "David, Olaf told me I should speak with you about my health."

Father's expression dropped to abject fear and concern. "What's wrong, Si? Tell me!"

She smiled and said, "I think our son saved my life."

Father shot a look of confusion my way. "Olaf, what did you say?"

I addressed Father in a similar way I did with Mother. I walked over to him and looked into his eyes. His body's voice interrupted *me* this time. "*He is going to listen, Olaf. Don't let him interrupt you.*"

I smiled and began saying what earlier in the day would have seemed like pure insanity. "Father, I've heard from a voice of honesty that Mother is sick. I believe you can help her."

"Olaf—this is in—" I cut off Father before he could finish the word.

"Father, listen to me. Mother needs your help. If she is not sick, you may finish that sentence. If she is, though, you must admit that perhaps what I say is plausible. Bear in mind what I asked you about singing to me."

Mother couldn't stand herself at this point. "You never sang for us, David." She smiled cutely and put her arms around both of us. "I think you should consider what Olaf is saying. He's said things tonight he could never have known, lest it be from a very unique source."

He relaxed a bit but was still clearly bothered by what he had heard. "Sierra, what did he say to you?"

She smiled and said, "Did you ever hear me call Olaf 'My Amazing Little Acrobat', David?"

His face was awash in thought. After a moment, he said, "No, I don't remember you ever saying that."

She hugged him and said, "I did when it was late in my pregnancy and he'd wake me from a nap by 'flipping' around. It was always while you were away at the hospital. No one knew but me, and Olaf reminded me of that during dinner tonight."

He hugged her tightly and seemingly allowed all of this to set in. His son was hearing some voice, and his wife was potentially sick. "Si, are you okay? Tell me what's going on."

"David," she smiled, "you never sang for us."

I did not see Father cry until many years later, but there were tiny droplets in the corners of his eyes. "*My sweet baby boy, you're my pride n' joy,*" He sung with a fairly pleasant singing voice, raspy and in tune. "*Rest those baby blues and drift into the best dream you can,*" he sang.

Mother looked deep into Father's eyes and said, "Sing *me* to sleep tonight, David!" Tears streamed down her face. I can only imagine they represented the totality of the emotional spectrum.

They embraced for a long time, in which I heard nothing. When they separated, Mother's *vox corporis* said, "*You really saved your Mother tonight, Olaf.*"

****

The next morning, the diagnosis was confirmed: Mother had early stage Lymphoma. Father immediately took control of her care, something completely forbidden at the hospital. He would have it no other way and practically signed his life away in agreements in order to do so. I would have hated to be the person standing in the middle of that argument. Remember the intensity I mentioned Father possessed? This was the first time patient care would be dictated by a family member at the hospital, and I had no doubt, at some point, Father would likely threaten to leave the hospital were it not to go as he instructed.

The next night during dinner, he accepted what he had learned the previous night. "Olaf," he said, "would you please tell me what you heard last night?"

I took a minute to form my thoughts, and in doing so, his *vox corporis* spoke to me.

"*Your father is comfortable with you telling the truth, Olaf. Please do not be afraid.*"

I smiled and said, "Thank you. I appreciate that," as calmly but politely as I could.

When I said that, Father furrowed his brow curiously. "Who did you just speak to, Olaf? I have a feeling you were not responding to me," he said, as Mother carefully measured his response.

I began, "Well Father, last night I became aware that I could hear a voice I did not know existed, and I feel you likely are the same. I've learned the human body itself has a voice I can hear, and what I learned last night is that the voice can portray many of the same characteristics of the person, but it can say only truthful things."

He responded, "So then, were you responding to such a voice a moment ago?" His voice was riddled with both intense curiosity and an analytical angst.

"Yes, Father, I was. In fact, it was your body who was speaking to me."

His eyes flashed with excitement upon hearing this, much like a kid on Christmas morning. Mother approvingly smiled at the reaction, which she was still carefully measuring.

"Really?! What did it, um, I, um he, say?" His face in this moment was anything but what I had remembered up to this point. His eyes were wide and seemed to be brighter than I remembered. He smiled widely, in a way that consumed his entire face. The omnipresent intensity in his expression had faded completely away. It was as though I had summarily deepened his curiosity about, well… *life* simply by revealing that his *vox corporis* had spoken.

"He told me you were comfortable with me telling you the truth… to not be afraid," I said, "and because I know he is bound to speak truthfully to me, I was comfortable in doing so."

"Is he speaking to you now, Olaf?" Father was on the edge of his seat, his fingers intertwined as though in prayer.

"*You see, Olaf? Your ability will bridge many gaps and help so many people,*" Father's *vox corporis* said.

"*You saved your mother's life, dear boy. You've awakened a new passion in your father. Do you see just how special you are, and how profound this gift really is?"* Mother's *vox corporis* said kindly, but in a matter-of-fact way.

Looking at Father, I said, "In fact, Father, yes. Both you and Mother's bodies just spoke." I continued to both *vox corpora*, "Thank you to both of you for such kind words. I'm truly not sure what this means for me."

"Olaf," Mother began, "I think this is a wonderful gift, but I must be honest and say I am a bit scared for you. I'm not sure how other people are going to react to this talent of yours."

"I agree with your mother, son, but I see an opportunity for you that no other physician possesses. You can converse with the body. I would imagine you could save thousands of people, simply because you can ask precisely what is wrong if someone is sick and diagnosis is difficult or impossible," Father said, his voice possessing the intensity with which I was all-too familiar.

"I'm not sure, Father," I said, "I think this is a skill that could definitely help people like Mother, but I'm not entirely sure how. Until I'm older, no one is going to take me seriously."

Both of my parents nodded in agreement and we returned to what otherwise was a normal, quiet dinner. Well, "normal" maybe isn't quite the way to describe this. Though it was caught in time, Mother was still a new cancer patient. I had declared a strange ability to my parents and myself as well. This was not something I accepted easily, if I'm being completely honest. So, that night ended as most of my others had, albeit with a couple large changes that were our new "normal."

As part of this normal, Grandfather took a different stance. He was made aware of my ability two days later at dinner after a doctor's appointment. While he felt my ability was remarkable, he also felt this was his cue that I needed to learn how to fight. Mind you, I was not taught exclusively how to defend myself. I was taught how to end an altercation. I had not known this prior, but my grandfather was a well-known boxer in the Army. His *vox corporis* was particularly interesting in that regard, saying, "*Your grandfather got himself into a horrible jam against Johnny Malloy. Something in him found a strength not present in the prior eight rounds, and he caught Johnny in the same spot on his jaw with a right and a left. Johnny was knocked out and left with a shattered jaw. From that point on, he was known as 'Iron Hands Waniglia'.*"

The weekend that followed began a yearlong period in which I learned to fight. This culminated in an amateur fight in some boxing gym a couple towns over. Ironically, I was paired with Johnny Malloy III, the grandson of the man my grandfather had knocked out in the Army. Our bout made its way through Grandfather's Army buddies, and a good number of them showed up for the fight. Mother and Father were there as well, with Mother vocally opposing the bout all the way to the first-round bell. Johnny was about three inches taller than me and had been boxing for about a year longer at this gym. All in all, the fight did not last long. I took an overhand right to the side of the head that soundly stunned me. I panicked and hit Johnny with a quick left hook on the jaw and followed it with an immediate canon of a right hook on the chin as his momentum drifted to the right. He was knocked out with a mid-grade concussion, and I earned the nickname "Iron Hands Junior."

I continued to use boxing to exercise until I was well into my later years. Heck, I still have a heavy bag in the garage and beat on it from time to time. Regardless, I have a lifetime record of 2-0. The second fight is not a story for now, though.

I was well aware that my ability would not be something I shared with anyone at school for fear what little credibility I had would be drawn and quartered. As such, I did not speak of this to any of my friends until I had graduated. Rather, I honed my ability to hear—to understand—the *vox corporis* in the chaos of high school. The hardest part about this, though, was I often carried on two conversations at once. I'd hear a classmate's *vox corporis* say, "*Hello, Olaf,*" even if I were having a conversation with that classmate. It was my first introduction into this complication of my ability, and it was where I was forced to figure out how to handle it. In the beginning, it was intensely trying as I couldn't figure out which voice, *vox corporis* or otherwise, had originated a statement or question. There were times the frustration was so consuming, I left conversations well before they had concluded. It wasn't until I found by accident that clapping seemed to keep the *vox corporis* at bay that I was able to resolve this. I got plenty of strange looks when I used the clap trick, dear Reader, but at least I finished conversations!

There were still other times where, again, I would hear the *vox corporis* of someone I did not know, and I would always say hello to that person in response. What came next were a few curious looks and others who were taken aback by my greeting in the typical teenage way and walked away with an air of incredulousness. Still others, who perhaps didn't get much attention, would smile shyly and say "Hello" back. It broke my heart one day when the *vox corporis* of one such girl, Rebecca Redd, said, "*Olaf, you are the first person to speak to Rebecca in over a month. Thank you, so very much.*" I talked to Rebecca every day from that point forward, even if it was a simple, "Hello." I learned, after several months, that she had an awful home life with no father and an alcoholic and often-absent mother. She supported herself financially— from getting clothing, to paying rent and utility bills, to simply eating every day. She unfortunately got an awful stigma because she wasn't wearing the latest and greatest fashions, and she was very shy as well. In addition, she was a person who worked seven days a week *and* did school work six of those seven. In the end, Rebecca was a tired, shy, hungry child who had no one to talk to. I hate to say this, dear Reader, but I've lost count over the years of how many voices I've heard that have told me eerily similar stories. Incidentally, Rebecca and I are still friends, all these years later. She is such a sweet woman—so kind— and her children are wonderful people. I smile every time I see them, as I see their profoundly strong mother in their eyes. It takes me back to my shy friend who was introduced to me via her *vox corporis*.

The range of things I heard from my classmates' bodies taught me so much about the *vox corporis*, things I have continually observed to this day. There are varying gradations of the many colors of humanity. I must say it was painfully hard for me to walk away from the conversations I heard from my classmates' bodies—or to let them walk away for that matter—without saying *something*. I heard conversations about abuse, conversations that shook me violently, and truthfully made me look at my parents differently. I heard conversations about deep depression that were causing the person to harm themselves and hide it from everyone in their lives. I heard still other conversations that were explicitly sexual. Needless to say, I knew who was experienced and who wasn't. I became skilled at expressing no alarm when I heard any of the above. Bear in mind, dear Reader, not every conversation with the *vox corporis* was negative or controversial, but they reflected truths of the life of the person they are a part of.

The teenage life is not an easy one given the myriad of social, educational, and personal identities that are being established through what I consider to be varying kinds of warfare. The worst of those battles, mind you, is without a doubt that with the self. There are those that win this battle outright and become healthy adults bearing lessons learned. There are others who win but are badly damaged in the process and become adults with a few emotional issues. There are then others who lose, and of those who do, few survive to adulthood. The whole of humanity does not fit into these tight little categories, and I do not pretend to assert such a thing. I do assert, however, that many *do*.

My childhood (including adolescence) was profound in some ways, challenging in others, and curious in yet others. In short, it truly was a comedy in an Ancient Greek sense. There were many amusing things that happened, and I learned about fundamental "inner workings" of life. We will be looking at this intently through several examples in the coming pages. I do not look poorly on any of the experiences of my childhood, and though the challenges were indeed transformational at times, the core of that time was incredible. I saved Mother's life. I earned honest respect from Father that never waned. I learned the intricacies of farming and had a close relationship with my grandfather. I learned to see the world through a special lens, one that has helped me to see through the human experience to layers of warmth and meaning even during the darkest moments.

It is in that sense I say the following: this thing we do on Earth is fascinating. It is special. It is steeped in meaning that few realize without something nudging them, usually forcefully, to that truth. Some mistakenly accept this truth as negative, that life is a punishment of some kind. Though it may feel like it at times, the truth is quite contrary. I will prove this to you, dear Reader.

Nol Glassburé, Gentleman Extraordinaire

Nol is short for Nolan, but to see and hear my dear friend, "Nolan" simply did not fit. Nol, to this day, is a good two-hundred pounds overweight, but is the lightest man I have ever seen on his feet. Nol constantly smiles, and when doing so it is nothing short of contagious. Nol is also the funniest man I have ever met. His sense of humor at times is crass, but his overall take on life and all of her contents is boisterous. Nol literally can make me laugh even if he talks about the most mundane thing possible. I was reduced to tears recently when he launched into a diatribe about coffee temperature of all things. Mind you, he's no spring chicken currently, but this has been a complaint of his for about fifty years or so.

When he leaves the house, Nol always wears a hat. His favorite has been a Fedora his grandfather gave him when he started driving. "A man needs a stylish lid when he rides, Nol," he said when presenting his grandson with what would become a major part of his personal style. I was there when he got it, and I have truly never seen a person so overcome with both awe and happiness than in that moment. Nol was ridiculously particular about his headwear. He also had a Derby he wore on "special occasions" and a Straw Boater Hat he wore to the dock. Nol is an avid fisherman and has made his living doing charters for folks in addition to tutoring special needs children in a school that he founded. Nol is retired now, but remains an active member of the board for those special needs kids he once tutored, and he still fishes regularly. Oh, and though the hats have changed through the years, he still wears one every time he leaves the house or goes fishing, without fail.

One other fact: Nol was the first person other than Mother, Father, and Grandfather to whom I admitted that I heard his *vox corporis* speak. That story, dear reader, begins the summer after we had graduated high school. In fact, the day this happened was the day after our graduation ceremony. I was preparing for an uncertain career as a consultant in Father's hospital amid pursuing my collegiate studies in medicine and Nol was preparing to go to college to study education. We both had decided to go to the University of South Carolina so we remained close to family. There were a couple of graduation parties on the horizon, and we decided to go out and get a few things for the events. It was hot and humid that day, so we thought, after the running around, we would head to the dock and do some swimming off his family's boat.

Nol and I decided to grab some brunch at Leila's Diner (best hash in the South without question).

"Can you believe we are done with high school, Nol? I can't begin to believe it," I said.

"Yes, I can Olaf. Damn school was a lifetime. I'm relieved," Nol replied.

"I get it, but looking back, it just seemed to go so fast. I cannot believe we're going to college in a few weeks."

Nol, sipping his coffee, shot me a look one might construe as judgment. Still holding his cup by his lip, he said, "Did you hit your head or something? Are you concussed and thus without the sense of a damn fly? We *survived*, Olaf. How could you think our time in Hell went quickly?" he quipped, returning to his coffee in relief, shaking his head in disapproval.

Mind you, Nol did not have a rough time in school, but he did deal with his fair share of teasing due to his weight early on in elementary school. It was for this reason that Nol took up football as a young boy and primarily played nose tackle. He was a four-year starter in high school and was recruited by several schools in the South for college. He was the meanest person on the field by a large margin and made anyone who targeted his weight understand that he did not approve of it off the field. He took a tremendous amount of pride when he sacked an opposing quarterback. After getting up, he'd rub his belly as though he had just consumed a large meal. This caught on, and whenever a sack was recorded, the whole of the crowd cheering for our school rubbed their bellies.

Off the field, Nol was popular in school, but kept his home life as private as he could. His little brother, Rick, was born with Down syndrome. As much as Nol was a dignitary in school and on the football field, his brother was his best friend, someone that Nol fiercely defended at all times, and ultimately the person who showed Nol what his true calling was with special needs kids. Because Rick knew he was different, he rarely went out in public. He only saw a single one of his brother's games: his final game in high school. Nol set a state record with six sacks in a single half (he ended the game with eleven total). Every time, he'd point at Rick, rub his belly and do a dance that looked like the Hawaiian Hula. Rick did the same dance. After the game, a reporter for the local newspaper interviewed Nol. The reporter asked, "Nol, what in the heck got into you tonight?"

Nol smiled and said, "The whole thing was for my kid brother, someone who displayed more courage and more strength than I ever could simply for coming to the game."

The reporter looked over at Rick and said, "That retarded kid is your brother?"

Nol, his hands still taped, punched the reporter square in the side of the head, concussing him and knocking him to the ground. As he walked away, Nol said, "He's my brother. He has Down syndrome. The only damn retarded thing here is your ass on the ground."

Nol walked over to a police officer standing nearby and asked, "I just punched a man. Am I being arrested?"

Sargent McNally smiled and said, "Kid, I didn't see anything. I'd have done the same to the son of a bitch. Hell of a game! Can't wait to see you on Sundays."

Nol walked over to Rick, hugged him and walked with his family back to their car. Nol's mother, Eleanor, looked up at her son and had tears in her eyes. She said not a single word, hugged him tightly, and got into the car. Nol's father, Carolas, nodded at Nol, a fiercely proud and approving look on his face. Nol walked over to Rick and said, "I will never be able to thank you enough for coming tonight, Rick. It meant the world to me you were here and saw me play."

Rick smiled, giggled a little bit, and started doing the (sort of) Hula. Nol obliged and joined him, and so did every person who was close enough to see what had taken place. It was truly something special to see a conservative Southern community display itself as it did that night.

When Nol got back to the field house, the entire team, coaches included, started rubbing their bellies and doing the Hula. Nol won that game with one of his sacks that resulted in a safety. The team won by two points. Not one person said anything about Rick, and I have to believe that was at least in part due to what Nol had done to that reporter.

So you see, dear Reader, amid my rambling, you can clearly discern Nol's schooling career was anything but hard. He was an above-average student and was liked by all; not simply due to his football acumen, but because of the person he was. For some reason, though, Nol didn't see it that way.

For all of his personality and athletic talent, Nol was absurdly critical of himself. Part of this was due to his size. He towered over our classmates. He always had. He was taller and stronger than some of our teachers by the time we hit junior high. When we finished our eighth-grade year, Nol had grown to be 6'2" of his 6'6" frame. One of our teachers, who was maybe 4'1" in the heels, asked Nol for a hug. Nol obliged, bent down, and embraced her. Thing is, that killed his back so he stood upright, still hugging the tiny teacher. She laughed and asked that he put her down. He did. He dropped her, and she sprained both ankles having fallen about two *feet* to the ground. Her footwear did little to assist with a good landing, unfortunately. Regardless, this did little for his inward criticality.

He was 14 years old. Nol's self-criticism continued through high school and was amplified by a single empty-headed girl. His one and only girlfriend, Mitsy Brock, busted that boy's heart into a billion pieces the day after we had finished our junior year of high school. She had been with Nol for the full school year solely to get close to the team quarterback in the run-up to our senior year, and she wasn't terribly shy about saying so post-fact. It was also unfortunate for that quarterback. Nol hit that kid so hard during fall practices at the start of the senior season that he was knocked unconscious. He did this four times across six practices before the coach disallowed Nol from being on the field when said quarterback was. This wasn't the coach's decision, mind you. He loved watching Nol "do his thing." He received threats from the quarterback's parents *and* Mitsy Brock's parents that forced him to keep Nol on the sidelines. It was never about the quarterback's health. Rather, it was entirely about social status.

Despite many apologies from the quarterback, and threats from Mitsy herself, Nol remained steadfast in his hurt and anger when our senior year began, but not for long. He began calling the quarterback "Tackle Dummy" in practices and the hallways, and outright laughing at Mitsy, who he easily intimidated. Mitsy's pathetic plan became known to the rest of our class that *adored* Nol. As a result, the pair became a target for our classmates' scorn. The storybook quarterback-debutante euphoria never materialized to the chagrin of both Misty and the quarterback, and their parents. Nol got all of our classmates' attention, and that certainly helped his high school experience.

"Nol, aside from Mitsy, you didn't have a single hard day in school, and in no way was it Hell for you," I said, reaching for my coffee cup.

"*The man with the he-titties is a fool, Olaf,*" Nol's *vox corporis* said. Upon hearing this, I started laughing uncontrollably.

"What the hell got into you, son?" Nol annoyingly responded.

"I'm sorry. I just, um, heard something," I said, immediately regretting my choice of words.

"You *heard* something? What the hell was it? Did ol' Helen here pass gas again?" Nol responded, referring to our waitress who rarely controlled her flatulence in public.

"No, Nol. It was something else," I responded, desperately looking for a means of escape.

"*He'll believe you, Olaf. Just be honest,*" Nol's *vox corporis* said, in stark contrast to the comment that started this mess. Mind you, dear Reader, I had heard Nol's *vox corporis* many times before. I was usually very good at containing my response to his commentary as it often was tear-inducing hilarity.

"Nol, I have to tell you something," I began, my heart racing and my mind searching for the right words.

"Olaf, whatever it is, tell me. I can see this is hard for you," Nol responded, seeing my struggle.

"Okay. Well, it goes like this. I— I—" I found myself unable to get the words out.

"What is it Olaf? Jesus man, you're scaring me. Just tell me!" Nol interrupted, clearly looking concerned.

"I'm sorry. The only people who know this are family, and it wasn't all that pleasant telling them, either. The only reason I did was to save Mother's life," I said, finding some strength.

"This saved your Mother's life?" Nol's eyes widened.

I took a deep breath and found enough confidence to continue. "It did. What I have discovered is that I can hear a voice we all have, a voice that solely speaks truth, and in the same way reflects our personalities. What I just heard a second go was something that you would say, but instead your body said it," I explained, bracing myself for Nol to call me an idiot and walk away.

"What the hell did it say that was so funny?" Nol asked, sitting back in his seat.

"It said, 'The man with the he-titties is a fool.'"

Nol smiled widely and started giggling. "Yep, that's funny, and I am a fool," he said.

"*I told you, Olaf,*" Nol's *vox corporis* said, not missing a beat.

"How did this save your Mother's life, though? I don't get that part," Nol said, leaning closer.

"Mother's body told me about her lymphoma in the very early stages. Had she not gotten treatment when she did, her chances of survival based on that type of lymphoma would have been quite small," I said.

"Seriously? What else have you heard?" Nol asked.

"Well, I got enough encouragement from Father's inner voice that I told him about it, and he believed me. And I can tell you an awful lot about our classmates," I said, as I became more comfortable with the subject.

"I have to know, what did you hear in school? I can only imagine what came out of those sick minds," Nol said, adjusting his hat and sipping sweet tea he had just ordered to replace the coffee. The day was sticky and heating up fast.

"Well on the one hand, there's Rebecca Redd, whose story broke my heart. I couldn't keep from being her friend because I knew her truth and it was awful," I began, though remembering the beginnings of what I had heard from Rebecca's *vox corporis* stirred intense emotion.

"I don't think I know. What happened with her, Olaf?" Nol asked, genuinely looking concerned.

"Nol, she basically was on her own from the time she was ten. She cooked for herself, bought her own clothes, paid rent, got all of her own school supplies, AND took care of her drunk mother. Dammit, Nol, how the hell are some people allowed to be parents?" I said angrily.

"She was on her own? My God, Olaf, I never knew that! Hell, I could have never survived such a thing. Next time I see her, we gonna hug this out. I won't say nothin'—I promise. I'll just grab 'er, and hug it out. Cannot believe she went through that," Nol said, shaking his head.

I continued, "Then there was Joe Wecki, 'sumbitch gave over a dozen girls crabs and threatened all of 'em to keep quiet."

"Yeah. Wecki is an ass, Olaf. He told me things too, but not the crabs thing. Did you ever hear the voices of the girls he did it to?" Nol asked.

"Yes I did, and it ranged from pure anger to shock, and all pervaded a sense of fear, betrayal, and guilt. The guilt and fear ranged from person to person, but it was definitely there. I never said a word to any of them, but I made sure those I knew stayed away from him."

"Like Rebecca?" Nol asked.

"Yes, she was one for sure I made sure stayed away," I replied.

"How come you two were never a thing? You seemed so close through school."

"Honestly, Nol," I said, "that never crossed my mind. We were such good friends. Dating I guess seemed wrong."

"I get it, Olaf. I think you were smitten anyway," Nol responded, referring to Annie Glaush, the daughter of Dr. Franklin Glaush who you, dear Reader, will meet in the next chapter. Annie's father and my father were colleagues.

"Smitten, Nol? Come on, I don't have an ice cube's chance on King Street in July with her!" I replied.

"If I could hear *your* inner voice, I think I might know the truth, Olaf. Hell, I can practically see it on your face." Nol sat back in his seat, adjusted his hat smugly, and sipped his tea.

"Y'all cain't see *shit*, my friend. Truth is truth, and dammit if she ain't three leagues away from anywhere I am," I replied, and in so doing likely confirmed what Nol was saying. The honest truth was this: Annie was the most beautiful, kindest soul I had ever met. But, her father hated me from the beginning.

"I can see shit all right, Olaf. Look at ya! A giant talkin' shit nugget! Dammit! Where the hell is Guinness when y'all need 'em? Helen! You ever seen a giant talkin' shit nugget before?" Nol asked as our waitress walked by.

"Sho nuff, Nol. I'm talkin' to you ain't I?" Helen winked at us and continued walking.

"You done been *served*, boy!" I proudly exclaimed.

"*The boy with the he-titties has been shamed, Olaf?*" Nol's *vox corporis* returned.

"Dammit, Olaf," Nol lowered and shook his head.

"Your voice spoke again, Nol," I said, regaining some composure.

"Really? I can't wait to hear this now," Nol replied, leaning in.

"It said, 'The boy with the he-titties has been *shamed*.'"

"Well, that is truth, and the he-titty thing is still funny," Nol chuckled. "Thank you for telling me what you did, Olaf. It couldn't have been easy."

"No, Nol, it wasn't. But I'm glad you know," I said. "Let's go to the dock. This heat is getting bad."

With that, we paid our bill and headed to the dock. We swam off the boat all afternoon. With my admission to him now complete, many more conversations were had about the notion of the *vox corporis*. Nol, as it turned out, did *not* keep his word and did tell someone about my ability, and truly helped me out in doing so. That story, dear Reader, is a bit in the future though, so y'all have to wait a bit for it.

Bear in mind—I am writing this memoir of mine as close to in sequence as I possibly can, within reason. I can promise you, dear Reader, this is not the last time you'll hear about Nol. For now, let's meet Dr. Glaush.

Dr. Franklin Glaush &
Family Insanity

Dr. Franklin Philippe Glaush earned his doctorate in medicine and became a nationally respected surgeon. He married Helene Noe, a debutante who competed and won several regional titles. They met when she was competing in Dallas and Dr. Glaush was there for a convention early in his career. They discovered they had grown up less than a mile from each other, but had gone to different schools as kids. They married in a beautiful ceremony on her family's plantation and had two children, a son and a daughter—Gill and Annie. Dr. Glaush and Father became colleagues as young doctors, and actually made decisions on their careers in tandem. Mother and I did not meet the Glaush family until I was in a junior in high school. That, dear Reader is where Dr. Glaush began to dislike me, because I knocked out his nephew.

Yes, my intrepid Reader, Dr. Glaush's nephew was none other than Johnny Malloy III, the boy who I knocked out in my first boxing experience. Helene's sister, Mary Anne, married Johnny Malloy II and their only child was, yes, Johnny Malloy III. So, the tension felt the first few times I met the family was thick; there were silly snide comments here or there, like *"Boxers are empty-headed buffoons."* Still others were condescending, like *"He got lucky—two more seconds and Johnny would have put you in the hospital."* Then others were downright cruel, like *"We do not associate with people like you. I'm not sure why you're here."* Mother kept close watch over me and gave me a commanding look when such things were said; she knew I would react tactlessly, and in so doing, would have made things worse.

The sole reason I didn't mind these very infrequent gatherings was quite simple—I had an irrepressible crush on Annie Glaush. She was gorgeous and extremely athletic; she was an incredible tennis player, and had been riding horses since she was but a toddler. She had her mother's debutante looks and her father's competitiveness. Amid it all, though, was her kindness. She did not participate in the harassment that her family did. If anything, she was the only person who said more than "Hello" to Mother and me.

The cadence at the Glaush residence went something like this: we would arrive, Dr. and Mrs. Glaush would welcome us to their home, whisk Father swiftly away, and basically leave Mother and me standing in the foyer. The first time it happened, Mother and I were shocked. Each time after—we gave each other a knowing glance and made our way to the back yard, where we would be joined by Annie, who would bring sweet tea and snacks to our little assembly. The three of us would talk for hours on end. We'd be called in for dinner and our trio would be separated; dinners were semi-formal and conversation was kept to a minimum. The only person who would say goodbye to Mother and I was Annie. Father was painfully unaware of this *and* the tension until some years later, despite the fact that we offered him insights after each visit.

It was July after my high school graduation, and we had gotten together for a barbeque at the Glaush's house. It so happened that the Malloys were also invited to the occasion, I think mostly to make things more uncomfortable. They succeeded.

When Mother, Father, and I arrived on this occasion, we had no sooner entered the Glaush residence than Johnny Malloy II met us, looked right at me and said, "Well looky there—*Shit Hands Waniglia has just graced us with his presence.* You here to show us what a coward looks like?"

Father, shocked into a knee-jerk response, looked at Johnny and said, "Um, as I remember it, my son knocked your son out. In fact, I recall a colleague of ours treating him for about a month afterwards given the concussion and broken jaw that Olaf gave him. Does your boy have a lisp, Johnny?"

"Father," I said, "please—we're here for a barbecue. Can we just…"

I was interrupted by Johnny, who said, "Are you calling my son weak, Waniglia?"

Mother, horrified by all of this, grabbed Father and I and took us outside. "We are not here to fight, you two. We were invited for a visit. David—that was an awful thing to say. Let's go back in and try to make this right."

"But Si, no one has the right to speak to our son that way," he responded, obviously still upset.

"I agree, David, but that does not give us the right to be crass in response," Mother said sternly.

Father took a nice, deep breath and said, "I see your point, Sierra. I'll try to fix this."

We went back inside to find Dr. Glaush, obviously upset. "David what the hell did your son do?" he asked, looking squarely at me.

Mother put her hand on Father's chest, stopping him before he could speak. "Dr. Glaush, Olaf did nothing to provoke Mr. Malloy. We had taken a step into the house when the insults began," Mother said.

"Mrs. Waniglia," Dr. Glaush began, "your son obviously made Johnny upset," he said, putting his hands on his hips and furrowing his brow.

Father, incensed at this assertion snapped, "Franklin, we had just walked in when Malloy tore into Olaf. He said not one word," his face was red, and his hands began shaking.

"David, Johnny would not do such a thing. I've known him for fifteen years and never before has he treated anyone unfairly," Dr. Glaush responded, smugly turning away.

"Franklin, what are you saying about my son?" Father asked, his eyes widening.

"Your son, David, is a bully and a coward—and I have no time for him," Dr. Glaush said flatly.

Father's *vox corporis* interjected before the next exchange, saying, "*Olaf, your father is getting extremely upset. Can you do anything?*"

Heeding this advice, I said, "Dr. Glaush, if there was anything I did to make you feel this way, I apologize. I did not mean to be disrespectful."

Mother was visibly upset. She smiled at me when I said what I did, but apparently that slight bit of solace was not good enough for Dr. Glaush.

"Olaf, you have never shown yourself to be anything but foul," Dr. Glaush pronounced.

Hearing the commotion, Annie appeared and was appalled at what she was hearing. "Daddy, you have no right to say these things—you and Mom have never said a single word to Olaf aside from an insult here or there at dinner. How could you characterize someone so negatively if you don't know them?" she asked, shocking everyone present.

"Annie, you have no…" Dr. Glaush began.

"I have no right, Daddy? I am the only member of this family that entertained the Waniglias when they have been here. I can tell you Olaf is a wonderful person and not at all as you have labeled him," Annie said, her voice ringing with anger.

"Is this right, Sierra? How could I have missed this?" Father said, his voice apologetic.

"Yes, David—Olaf, Annie, and I have had many wonderful afternoons together after you, Franklin, and Helene disappear to wherever it is you go. We basically get you back at dinner. I've honestly never said anything beyond 'Hello' to them, which is rather shocking given how many times we have had occasions like this," Mother said, her voice calm.

"Franklin—why is this?" Father asked, his brow furrowing and his attention turning to his colleague.

"David-I-I-I'm so sorry. I had no idea-I guess-I don't—I... I'm so *embarrassed*," Dr. Glaush stammered, rubbing his head as he searched for words. He continued, "Sierra, please—join us inside. Olaf—you too. I apparently have been quite unfair to you. Annie—thank you, sweetheart."

The lot of us made our way into the Glaush residence where an impressive array of food had been prepared and strategically placed in their palatial kitchen and dining area. Annie came up to me as I perused the appetizers.

"All these times you've been here—have you ever seen this part of the house?" she asked, her tone apologetic.

"No—I've not seen this part before. It's gorgeous. I've never seen anything quite like this," I said as I looked at shrimp cocktail that were the size of lobsters. "Where in God's oceans exist shrimp this large?"

"Well," she said sheepishly, "I actually caught those the last time we went out on the boat. Daddy has taken us shrimping as long as I can remember. I took up free diving last summer and actually saw these little guys in the trap. I was so happy that I almost came up too quickly," she said proudly.

"You guys go shrimping? Where in the heck do you go to catch lobsters like these?!" I said, pointing at the behemoth crustaceans before us.

"Yep—we go shrimping just off the islands, and we do deep sea fishing too. I caught part of dinner yesterday afternoon," she said, motioning to what looked to me like large sea bass on the center island of the kitchen.

"That's easily one of the largest fish I've ever seen caught in the waters by home—did you have help wrestling that monster in?" I asked, amazed at what I was hearing.

"Actually Olaf," Dr. Glaush started, "Annie is the best fisherwoman I've ever seen. She caught those shrimp after studying the waters off the islands for a week or so—and that bass she fought for over an hour. She slept the entire way back to the marina," he said, grinning widely.

"Daddy—*please*..." Annie turned away, shyly embarrassed.

"Truthfully Annie, the biggest thing I ever caught was about four inches long, and I tossed it back," I said. "I can't imagine getting anything on a line that I actually had to *fight*."

Perhaps on cue, Johnny Malloy III appeared in the kitchen. "*Fight?* Hell Olaf—that's the one thing you know not a damn thing about," he said smugly, leaning up against the island where the bass was.

"Johnny, *please*," Annie said, "that is in the past—can we just have a nice afternoon?"

Johnny shrugged her off and walked outside.

Annie, clearly agitated by this most recent verbal assailing grabbed my hand and led me down a long hallway. "I need some air—join me?"

"I'm not sure I have a choice, to be honest," I said, feeling my shoulder being pulled out of its socket.

She led me out a side door to a bench by a huge oak tree. I hadn't seen this courtyard before.

"I cannot believe the things that were said to you today, Olaf. I am so sorry my family is being like this," she said, her voice a stark distance from the intensity that brought us to the bench.

"It's not a big deal, Annie," I said. "It doesn't bother me as much as you think."

"That's not the point, Olaf. You've not done a thing to anyone, and yet you're a villain," she said.

"Annie, I broke Johnny's jaw and knocked him out. I can't say I did nothing," I responded, noticing we were still holding hands.

I think she noticed the same thing at the same time, and shockingly, *didn't move*. It must have shown on my face I was surprised, and she added her other hand to our joined hands, smiling wryly.

"Is this *okay*, Olaf?" she said, smiling devilishly.

"Um…" I swallowed, at a loss for words.

"What did it feel like to do that to Johnny?" she asked, leaning in.

Now, dear Reader, I could have embellished the life out of this moment, but I didn't. It's apparently just not my thing.

"It was surreal, Annie," I said. "I knew I hurt him, badly, and that set strangely with me. On the one hand, I was happy I won and the fight was over—but on the other, I knew I put this kid in the hospital."

"That's understandable, honestly," she said. "Still—what did it *feel* like?" Her eyes widened and met mine.

"It was panic and rage, all mixed into one. In a sense, I just let my hands go like I was taught and he made the mistake of not protecting himself. My left caught him on the chin, and my hard right that followed connected with his jaw when his mouth was open. I watched his head bounce off the canvas and was immediately pulled away by the ref. Before that exchange, he caught me making essentially the same mistake, not protecting myself," I said, recounting the fight from a couple years ago.

"You saw his head *bounce*?" she said, her combined grip on my hand tightening.

"Yeah, that's what caused the concussion I think," I responded.

That last detail seemed to settle the matter in her head, and we sat there on that bench for a while. Her hands never left mine, which, to this day I do not understand—it was hot, and South Carolina humid. However, that big oak tree gave us amazing shade through the late afternoon heat. We had been sitting there until the sun started to sink to the West, and we heard Dr. Glaush behind us. Mind you, Annie did not flinch when we did.

"Kids, it's time for dinner—will you please wash up?" he said, I think then noticing his daughter holding my hand. He rather hastily disappeared back into the house.

"Thanks for sitting with me, Olaf—I needed that," she said, smiling.

"It was my pleasure, Annie—such a relaxing afternoon! That oak is something else," I said.

We got up, stretched, and she turned toward me and hugged me. The shock running through me was something unlike anything I had ever felt; I was elated and confused in a tornado of emotion. The embrace lasted what seemed like a long time, but in actuality may have been around twenty seconds. We separated, she grabbed my hand, and led me back into the house. It was here I heard Annie's *vox corporis* for the first time.

"*Hello, Olaf,*" her beautiful voice said. "*Annie needs you in her life, and she knows that now.*"

Words formed in my head, and I almost spoke. I caught myself short of what would have been a devastatingly awkward situation, smiled widely, and squeezed her hand. This caused her to look back at me with a quizzical look on her face. When she saw my smile, she smiled shyly and turned away.

It was here, dear Reader, that my infatuation with Annie Glaush changed. I became painfully aware that my feelings for this woman ran deeper than a simple crush—and I needed her in my life too. This recognition was new to me, and is a moment I still look back on and smile. I would have taken that moment and relived it over and over if I could.

Annie led me into the house, down the long hallway into the kitchen. It was here both sets of parents were waiting for us. As we entered the room, I saw Mother smiling, Father with a look of approval, and Annie's parents with looks of disgust that were unmistakable. Annie's brother Gill, who had been talking with Mother, looked at us, but didn't display any emotion.

"Annie, what are you doing?" Helene Glaush asked callously. For all her debutante upbringing, dear Reader, Mrs. Glaush had no filter whatsoever. She spoke her mind wherever and whenever she pleased.

"I'm holding Olaf's hand, Mom. Is there a problem?" Annie replied.

"Annie, do not be disrespectful to your mother," Dr. Glaush said.

"I am eighteen years old, at this point, I do not need your approval if I choose to hold someone's hand," Annie said matter-of-factly.

"But Annie, Olaf is not to your *status*," Mrs. Glaush responded.

"Excuse me, Helene?" Mother intervened. "Olaf is not to her *status?*"

"Yes, I'd like to understand this as well," Father said angrily. "Last I checked, Franklin and I have worked together for almost twenty-five years and are among the most well respected doctors in the South. I'm not sure how my son isn't to your *status*."

"David, I think Helene…" Dr. Glaush began.

"Your son is an empty-headed coward, David," Mrs. Glaush said flatly, interrupting her husband.

Everyone in the kitchen looked at her disappointedly, most of all, her daughter. Oddly though, it was Gill who spoke first. Honestly, I think this may have been the first time I had heard him say anything—he always stood quietly next to his father and did not speak.

"Mother," Gill said, "I think what we were told was incorrect. I spoke to Nol Glassburé yesterday and heard a vastly different story than what we were told. He offered me proof I found to be credible."

"What are you talking about, Gill?" Annie asked.

"Well, right after the boxing nonsense, we were talking to Johnny, and he said that Olaf was a mere farm hand—uneducated. He did not attend Annie's school, so I figured that Sierra had led him down such a path. I've heard nothing different from my friends at the club, so…" Mrs. Glaush said smugly.

"Helene, I've known you almost as long as I've known Franklin—how could you mistake my wife and son like this?" Father said, obviously upset.

"David, I trust my friends," Mrs. Glaush said callously.

"Helene!" Dr. Glaush said, shocked at what he was hearing.

"Well, Helene, Olaf finished high school as valedictorian," Mother said. "We gave him the choice of private education, but he chose public schools for the social aspect. He attended the highest ranked public school in South Carolina. From what we saw, students from his school fared quite well in college, including Ivy League schools. He had offers from so many colleges—Ivy League, private, and public. He is anything but empty headed, and I truly don't see how he is a coward."

"Olaf got offers from Ivy League schools?" Mrs. Glaush asked, her tone curious and much softer than before.

"Yes, Mrs. Glaush—I did. I visited several of them, but in the end the best school for me is closer to home. I intend to work with Father at the hospital and continue to help my grandfather as well," I said confidently.

"Olaf—Ivy League?" Annie asked, astonished.

"Yes—just not my thing I guess," I said. "I have no doubt I would get a stellar education, but I think the kind of work I want to do introduces other factors that are more important than the status of an Ivy League education."

"What is more important than status, Olaf?" Mrs. Glaush asked, horrified.

"The ability to relate to others, Mrs. Glaush. What I found is being book smart trumped being 'people smart' at said institutions and that is counter-intuitive to what I intend to practice," I said.

"Where does farming fit into that plan, Olaf?" Dr. Glaush said arrogantly.

"It *fits* in that Olaf has helped run my dad's business since he was fourteen, Franklin. You're looking at an eighteen-year-old boy who runs a multi-million-dollar farm. He organizes contracts, determines yields, and in general, has helped three other family farms by my dad's and several other businesses as well. Say what you will, but he is the hardest-working, most selfless, brightest kid I could ever be lucky enough to have," Father said, choking up a bit. "I did not raise a coward—and my dad made damn sure of that. The thing that bothers me so much is that I've told you two about this for years. How could you possibly feel this way?"

"Jesus, David—I had no idea," Dr. Glaush said.

"You run a multi-million-dollar business, Olaf?" Mrs. Glaush asked sheepishly.

"Well, yes Mrs. Glaush. Last quarter we posted a net profit that puts us on pace to exceed $3.25 million this year—so long as this weather remains as we expect. It's a blessing as it allows us to have exemplary care for my grandfather all the time," I said.

"How did you do that and still have time for school work?" Annie asked.

"I studied as I could and found unique ways to reinforce what I was being taught as I worked in the fields. I used the crops themselves as memory cues for almost every subject. The business side was a real-world lesson that helped me with my economics work and everything else just, well... worked," I said, trying to figure a way to explain this; in truth, I just went with what I had to do and it all came out as I had hoped.

"You see, Mother?" Gill said. "Nol told me about this and I was floored. He took me down to the farm and I saw it for myself—and the crops their farm grows, do you know they're in every grocery store and most markets in South Carolina? The cotton they grow is sold all over the world. The strawberries we have today are theirs."

"Yeah, those strawberries came out nice this year, and they're 100% organic. I'm pretty proud of that—you can taste the difference in pies especially," I said, recounting the experiment done among the Glassburé clan. I made two different pies, with identical ingredients and crusts, but one had organic and one had non-organic strawberries. Nol *knows* his pies—and Rick was especially passionate about the difference. Damn, that kid was special!

"Olaf—you *bake*?" Annie asked, astonished.

"Annie, you've not lived until you've had his strawberry pie," Mother said, smiling.

"Clearly," Dr. Glaush said, "we have been misinformed about you. I want to hear more—especially about this pie of yours. I'm quite fond of strawberry pie."

Years of implied truth and judgment on said truth were removed. My accomplishments, though not a huge deal to me, became the basis of a new-found respect from Dr. and Mrs. Glaush—and apparently Gill, too.

We made our way outside to find the Malloys sitting at the table. The outdoor setup was similar to previous dinners. Everything was bathed in light as the entire backyard had a pattern of lights that were enhanced by torches placed around the property. The table itself was on part of a large deck; Dr. Glaush was grilling on a higher level of the deck, adjacent to the table.

Two other families were also at the table—the Toths and the Poes. Both were friends of Mrs. Glaush primarily. The Poes claimed some kind of lineage via a distant second cousin (or something) to Edgar Allen, and the Toth family had come from generations of oil money. I had met Mr. Toth a couple years ago in one of my farming meetings and had worked with him on a couple projects for his companies. He offered a kind and accepting nod as we approached the table. The Malloys, though—were a different story altogether; all three glared at me with apparent hatred, so much so that Mrs. Glaush addressed it.

"Mary Ann—is everything okay?" Mrs. Glaush asked quizzically.

"I suppose, Helene—but why are *they* here? Didn't we agree…?" Mrs. Malloy responded. I was surprised to see Mrs. Malloy, dear Reader. She, like her sister, had no restraint. It was odd she wasn't with her husband when we arrived.

"*They* are here because they were invited, Mary Ann. Let's not be rude," Mrs. Glaush ironically responded, cutting off her sister.

"Olaf—would you sit close enough to me that we can talk? I have a couple things I'd like to discuss with you," Mr. Toth said.

"Wait—Hollister? You know Olaf?" Mrs. Glaush asked.

"Yes Helene. Olaf and I have done business together, and I have an opportunity that I'd like to discuss with him. After the last conversation we had, our profit increased 200% in a single *quarter*," Mr. Toth said.

"No business at the table, gentlemen. It's dinner time," Dr. Glaush said, persisting the pattern of dinners at their house—though it was barbecue, it was mostly formal and thus conversation was kept at a minimum.

Dinner happened as it had in the past; the food was delicious, conversation was sparse, and focused solely on the food. It was after the meal had completed that things got interesting.

We all finished our meals and people began milling around the backyard and inside the house. I was still at the table, chatting with Mr. Toth about his opportunity. It was another angle on a project he and I had worked on previously, and I had identified a couple risks he and his team had missed.

"You see, Olaf—this is why we needed your input. Thank you again, so much!" Mr. Toth grinned mightily.

"It's my pleasure, Mr. Toth. I'd love to…" I had started to speak, but could not finish my sentence on account of an arm that had found its way around my neck. I was being choked, and panic began to set in as my ability to breathe stopped.

"MY GOD MAN, STOP!" Mr. Toth exclaimed.

"Johnny – stop at once!" Mrs. Glaush said, astonished at what she was seeing.

I saw everyone who had been at the table run—the Poes, the Toths, Gill, Helene, and Mrs. Malloy. I then caught Father out of the corner of my eye running toward me from the house. Not wanting him to become involved, I stopped struggling to free myself and instead felt all over the table for anything I could find. My hands furiously searched the area around me, as I felt myself starting to lose consciousness. In my right hand, I found a salad fork; my left found a steak knife. I knew my assailant's legs were behind me—so with all I had, I thrust both pieces of silverware down and behind me, praying that the pointy ends were facing the right way.

The fork found its way into my assailant's thigh; the knife penetrated just above his left knee. Despite the shout I heard from my assailant and a jerk that indicated he was in pain, his grip did not release. Thus, I tightened my grip on both items, and *twisted*.

I continued this until I could feel the ligaments starting to pop in my assailant's knee. I believe that he began to go into shock; his grip released and he fell backwards.

I coughed tremendously to regain my breath. As I was doing so, I heard Mrs. Glaush scream in horror. I heard Dr. Glaush yelling as well. As I regained my senses, I saw Johnny Malloy III choking Annie.

"Johnny! Let her go and fight *me*. Show me who the coward is between us," I said, my voice shaky.

"Gladly," Johnny said and let Annie go; she was immediately attended to by both Father and Dr. Glaush.

I stood up and looked down to see Johnny Malloy II laying on the ground, writhing in pain. In a quick, panicked motion, he thrust the knife from his left leg at me, catching the front of my left shin. I recoiled in pain, then stepped into the most vicious kick I had ever mustered. I broke his elbow joint; the knife went flying. I started to see a picture of what was at play here: the Malloys wanted retribution. As such, I knelt down next to Mr. Malloy and said the following:

"You and your boy made a mistake, Johnny. This ends badly for both of you," I said, feeling a rage unlike anything I had ever felt before.

"Olaf?" Mother looked at me, concerned.

"This ends here, Mother. It's one thing to hurt me—it's another to involve someone I care about out of pure spite."

We made our way further down the lawn, where Johnny ran at me. Mind you, dear Reader, I was taught how to finish a fight. I was taught how to box—and I was also taught how to *fight*.

I stepped to the side of Johnny's rush and threw an elbow into his solar plexus. He gasped in pain, regained himself, and walked toward me again. He stepped into a punch which I deflected and countered with a left into his surgically repaired jaw. He cried out in pain as blood began pouring out of the side of his mouth.

"You apologize to Annie and all the folks here, then this ends now. You don't, and you're going to get hurt, Johnny," I said coldly, still feeling this rage running through me.

"No, you piece of shit. I'm done playing around," Johnny said, walking away and apparently shaking off the pain. Adrenaline began to take over. He set himself, turned, and again began running at me. I stood still, assessing his movement. As he got closer, I saw him lean forward and clench his fists. I stood still, my hands at my sides. As he got closer still, he drew his right hand back.

When he was about two steps away, I took one step forward and aimed at his liver with my uninjured right leg. I connected with my foot, he fell, and I lunged into his damaged jaw with two punches— then reset and lunged into a couple punches to his ribs while he was on the ground. I again shattered his jaw—much worse than I had in the ring, and I broke three ribs in his chest. His bottom jaw had dislocated, blood flowing from both sides of his mouth. I broke both of my hands in the process.

"I *told* you, Johnny. I gave y'all a chance. Next time, *take it*," I said, walking over the sobbing, gurgling lump of humanity that laid before me. His father still laid on the ground, his wife next to him.

"How could you do this to them, Olaf?" Mrs. Malloy said to me, tears streaming down her face.

"Mrs. Malloy, with all due respect, your husband tried to kill me this evening. Your son injured his cousin out of pure spite. Both had choices they could have made differently. Both now have reminders of those choices. How you make this right with your niece and sister is probably something you should start thinking about," I said, confidently.

I hadn't noticed the gash on my shin; the bottom half of my leg was covered in blood. Both hands were bloody, too.

My parents ran to me—the Glaushs too. Dr. Glaush spoke first.

"I cannot believe what just happened, but I think you saved my daughter's life. I can promise you that you will never see the Malloys again. What they did here, tonight, was despicable. Those officers will handle things from here," he said, disgusted.

I looked to the side to see two uniformed police officers. Both nodded at me and approached the broken Malloy men.

"Olaf, you are bleeding. We need to attend to this. Franklin, will you assist, please?" Father said, obviously shaken.

"You're two and oh, champ," Annie said, smiling. She had a noticeable bruise around her neck, but beamed with pride at what she had witnessed.

"I should say so, dear boy! My God I've never seen anyone finish a fight like that. I guess I can take solace in being on your *good* side," Mr. Toth said. "Once the docs attend to you, could we maybe finish that conversation?"

"You have ten minutes, Mr. Toth. Then he's mine," Annie said, garnering looks from everyone present.

"Well, I guess there we have it then. I'll talk quickly, Olaf— the lady here has spoken," Mr. Toth smiled and returned to his seat at the table.

The cut on my leg needed stitches, which Dr. Glaush did in their kitchen. Father found towels that he cut into strips and began carefully wrapping my hands; he did one layer, then a layer of ice, and then another layer of towels. As he was doing this, one of the officers came inside.

"Son, I need to know if you are pressing charges on Johnny Malloy II," the officer said.

"Yes, he is and I don't give a damn if that wasn't what you were going to say, Olaf," Mrs. Glaush said emphatically.

"Yes sir, I am pressing charges. One cannot attempt to take the life of another without consequence," I said, wincing as a stitch went into my shin.

"Olaf, I am so sorry—this should have never happened," Dr. Glaush said, shaking his head.

"Dr. Glaush—*I'm* sorry. The Malloys had it out for me. I am the reason for this," I said, conciliatorily.

"No, dear boy. This is not for you to apologize. We brought them here, it is therefore our apology to you that is necessary," Mrs. Glaush said. "I just need you to know—you have our blessing to spend whatever time you wish with our daughter." She grinned and kissed me on the cheek.

"I agree, Mr. Waniglia. It is our apology that carries weight here. You were assaulted, and you handled an insane situation better than I believe I could have," Dr. Glaush said.

"My son—maybe we use our legs instead of our fists next time? You're going to need casts on these hands," Father said, still noticeably shaken from the events of the evening.

"David, I'll handle this. I think we may need to be creative here so he doesn't develop arthritis prematurely and full range of motion can be restored. I'll handle everything—I promise you," Dr. Glaush said.

My stitches complete, my hands wrapped, I made my way outside and had my conversation with Mr. Toth. It happened that Mr. Poe joined us, and based on what he heard, asked that I help him with an issue his foundation had. The conversation was also overseen by all of the Glaush family members, who asked random questions here or there. With each one, Mr. Toth would look at them, furrow his brow, shake his head, and return to the conversation. Each time he did, it made Mother giggle, and that too would elicit a furrowed brow and a head shake. She was seated about as close to me as she could possibly get on my right. Father was on my left, drinking copious amounts of scotch.

When all was said and done, I "shook" hands with both Mr. Toth and Mr. Poe, and stood to make my way back to the house to find Annie. I had no sooner moved my chair when I felt her left hand wrap around my waist and pull me backwards. I looked back and she smiled warmly.

"Come on—we need to talk," she said as she pulled me close. I wrapped my right arm around her shoulder, and we headed back to that gigantic oak tree.

The sun had set and a very bizarre late July, nighttime chill had begun to set in as we sat on that bench. I had no sooner begun to shiver than I heard footsteps behind us, and a big, soft blanket enveloped us. Dr. Glaush went about essentially tucking us in.

"Now Olaf—I need you at the hospital tomorrow morning at 9:00 sharp, okay? Before you leave, I'm going to re-wrap those hands for the nighttime. I think we may need to wheel your dad out on a dolly tonight so I know he can't do it."

"Thanks Dr. Glaush," I said.

Annie leaned in close, and her arms wrapped around me. We sat there for a few minutes under that giant oak tree, just letting the events of the night wither away into nothingness. The fireflies danced in the near distance, and the breeze wove through the tree branches giving life to the leaves. It was a clear night, and the moon was full. I could feel Annie's heartbeat slow as she relaxed; with every breath, we seemed to get closer. Despite my injuries, the only thing I felt was her heartbeat.

"I knew you worked on your grandfather's farm Olaf, but I had no idea you ran the business or that you worked with other businesses. And—I had no idea you were valedictorian. Why didn't I know these things? What *else* should I know?" Annie said, not moving from her snuggle.

"Well, in the end, our conversations focused on what is truly important, what is relevant. It's not important that I was valedictorian. It's not important to anyone but my family that I run the family business. The guys I help in business—I do so because I can't find a reason not to, and they need help," I said, doing all I could to reflect truth about these things without being arrogant. I continued, "In terms of what else you should know.... there is a lot about me you do not know, and that's just because we've only spoken about impersonal things for the most part. Heck—I had no idea you fished and had the command of the sea that you do. I suspect there is a bunch I don't know about you, either."

"Can we change that?" she asked, still unmoving.

"I'm sure we could, but aren't you going away to college?" I asked.

"Well, the truth is I never made up my mind on what school to attend and decided to take a little break. I'm not at all sure what I want to study, but I have a feeling that may be changing. The conversation today in the kitchen gave me a whole different thought on college."

As I came down from the insanity of the night—the verbal situations, the physical situations, the successful business conversations—the present moment, all of a sudden, became amplified. The earlier time on this bench had sort of felt like an escape for Annie. She was upset and removed herself from the situation, finding solace under the giant oak tree. The fact her *vox corporis* had spoken meant something, but I really wasn't sure what.

This situation was different from the first, for obvious reasons. As I sat there, I became overtly confused by the appearance of Annie's *vox corporis* after our first encounter on the bench. My previous experiences with the *vox corporis* suggested the person needed to tell me their truth the first time I saw them, and it wasn't necessarily something emotionally weighty. I hadn't had the occasion where someone I knew for literally *years* had a delayed *vox corporis* communication, and I wasn't sure why this was the case with Annie. I knew that my feelings for this girl hadn't changed, but this was that same beautiful soul wrapped in an exquisite physicality I had swooned over for a good six years. My confusion here was as much steeped in hope as it was unbelievable to me given my feelings for her. No part of me wanted to screw this moment up, so I measured my words carefully.

"I didn't realize college was a tricky subject for you, but I understand. It's a big decision," I said, giving myself a separate avenue to talk about while I sorted out the bigger situation in my mind.

"*Olaf,*" Annie's *vox corporis* said, "*she needs to hear something different from you.*"

This put me into a conundrum; I couldn't respond to this, and at the same time I needed clarity. So, before she could answer my last verbal volley, I pulled her tighter to me and simply said, "Annie, I love being here with you."

Her grip around me tightened, and she took a deep breath.

"Finally," she said as she exhaled.

"Finally?" I asked, my curiosity peaking.

Her grip loosened, and she turned toward me. In the moonlight, I saw her smile. Her hands found their way to my cheeks. She leaned in and kissed me—romantically, but softly.

"I kind of kidnapped you," Annie said, her face still close to mine. She kissed me again, and said, "I wasn't sure you wanted to be here with me."

"What in the world would give you that thought?" I said, shocked.

"Well, in all this time we have known each other, there have been no handshakes, no hugs, no kisses on the cheek, no nothing. We had never touched before today," she said, her hands now on my shoulders.

I put my arms around her torso, and squeezed, carefully protecting my wrapped hands. She leaned in closer and matched the intensity of my embrace.

"Okay," I said as I began to let go, "can we talk about this?" I asked. As soon as I let go, she returned to her original spot, her arms wrapped around me and her body so close that I could again feel her heartbeat.

"What would you like to talk about?" she asked after taking a deep, contented breath in.

"Well truthfully, I never in a million years thought we would be, well... *here*," I said, praying I wasn't making a mistake in doing so.

"The last couple times you've left, I've missed you," she said, moving tighter to my side.

"I've missed you too," I said, squeezing *her* tighter.

The conversation stopped there, and we sat on that bench for at least an hour. I never let my grip on her go, and she held tightly to me as well. I felt an immense closeness to Annie; her heartbeat was comforting in a way I hadn't felt. It made me feel loved and protected at the same time. Its rhythmic pulse seemed to take control over my own heart, my mind, and all the rest of me too.

There came a point where I heard footsteps behind us, and soon Mother appeared.

"Well…" Mother said, her voice soft, "I've hoped I would see this for a few years now. You've both been very hurt today. Are you feeling okay?"

"Yes, Mrs. Waniglia—I feel absolutely fine," Annie said. "You've hoped for this?"

"Yes, Annie—I have. All of those times we sat out, laughing hysterically—I saw something between the two of you that was more than just friendship. There is a comfort between the two of you I have always seen. It makes me so happy that you've found each other—though getting here should not have taken you getting so hurt."

"You have a wonderful son, Mrs. Waniglia. I hope you mean that," Annie said, a tinge of concern in her voice.

"Sweetheart, I have not been more sincere since the last time I told my husband I loved him," Mother said smiling. "Olaf, as much as I would love for this moment to not end for you two, we have to get your Father home. I have to prepare the house for what will be a very interesting morning tomorrow."

"I understand, Mother," I said and started to let go.

"Just five more minutes?" Annie said, her grip tightening around me.

"Of course, Sweetheart. I'll come back once Dr. Waniglia is in the car," Mother said and returned to the house.

We sat there for a good minute or so, before I upped the courage to speak. "Annie—I will never forget this, for so many reasons. Our time under this amazing oak, well.... There's Heaven, and then there's this. Please, please promise me this won't be the last time."

"*You* promise *me*. You may have put two grown men in the hospital today, but I will find you and beat you senselessly if this is the last time you hold me," she said, tightening her grip even more.

"I promise, Annie," I said, struggling to breathe.

She released, switched her posture, and kissed me. I switched my position as well and made it clear that *I* was kissing *her*.

"*Well then*, Mr. Waniglia. I see I have just uncovered something else about you I'd like to learn more about," Annie said with a smile.

That night, I found it desperately hard to sleep. I'll be honest and say it was mostly due to the fact that I was in a massive amount of pain. My mind wandered, though, through the events of the day. I thought through the mindless judgment I had witnessed, and tried to make sense of it. Yes, I personally was worth a sizable amount of money. Yes, I had turned down the most notable of the Ivy League schools and did so without second guessing it. Yes, I was valedictorian of my high school class and it beat several of the area's public schools in terms of graduation rate and college attendance. No—none of the facts had been disclosed because I didn't see a reason to—and simply because I worked on Grandfather's farm, I was mindless in the eyes of the Glaushs. The Malloys—well, that was not quite the conundrum, but it highlighted something in my mind I had never given credence to before: I needed to be able to fight. I knew this almost assuredly would not be my last fight given my ability. Lastly, there was Annie

Glaush, the girl I had fawned over for literally *years* of my life. She was so close I *felt* that girl's heart beating. My crush had turned into something I couldn't call love, but I was falling in that direction about as fast as a Texas-sized anvil falls from the sky.

Theodore "Joe" Overton & the Nice Folks at Haybrook

The summer took a different turn after the night with the Malloys at the Glaush residence. Annie and I began seeing one another nearly every day. As a result, she and Nol became great friends. One of their favorite pastimes was making fun of me in tandem, especially when it came to fishing. The two of them were quite skilled when it came to catching fish, and I absolutely was not. I had something of a pass as my hands healed—but they still found a way to exploit my lack of knowledge on the subject at almost every turn. I knew some of the fish in the sea, but certainly not all. I knew what many fish tasted like, but in no way could I identify them. My, did they have a field day with that!

This three-way friendship continued throughout college. I was still able to see Annie every day as I lived at home to continue my work at the farm. College itself changed for me; I found many of the things I heard in the hospital were not those I needed to become a medical doctor, and that was surprising. Instead, the language from the myriad of *vox corpora* I heard relayed afflictions in a way I could understand with the cursory medical knowledge I had acquired in college. I addressed this with Father, and he thought perhaps completing my studies in medicine, but not going on to graduate studies, would suffice. Regardless, I had both Father and Dr. Glaush as resources for anything I did not understand and this was more than sufficient when I began working at the hospital.

I initially added a minor in psychology to my collegiate studies, but increased it to a second major after working in the hospital and seeing a direct correlation between that discipline and what I was doing for patients. I did not pursue graduate studies in psychology either; I was pleasantly surprised to find that I got the knowledge I needed to be successful through my undergraduate studies alone.

Though Nol was content to remain single throughout college—given the time commitments he had with the football team, time spent with Rick at home, and his abject attention to collegiate studies—he met the lady who would challenge this conviction. Sadie Easton formally met Nol after one of his football games during our last year in college. She was a journalism major who worked for the school newspaper and had become quite smitten with my friend after watching a couple other interviews he did with her colleagues. Sadie interviewed Nol after a particularly dominant game in which he recorded a school record number of tackles for loss. She hinted at her attraction both in what she said and her mannerisms throughout the interview.

Nol didn't pick up on Ms. Easton's interest and that frustrated Sadie, so she confronted him as he was leaving the field house. My dear Reader, this was a southern lady who would not take 'no' for an answer.

"Nolan! I need to have a word with you," Sadie demanded.

"Why hello, Ms. Easton—did you need something else for your article?" Nol asked naively.

"I don't need anything for the article, but I do need you to take me to dinner tonight," she said flatly.

"Excuse me? Dinner?" Nol said, confused about what was taking place.

"We're going out to dinner tonight. Pick me up at 6:00, right here," Sadie said and walked away.

"Where we goin' tonight?" Nol asked, still confused.

"That's up to y'all, Darlin'. Don't be late," she said in the distance.

Nol stood for a second and let what just happened soak in. He was gun-shy when it came to relationships, because of that idiot of a girlfriend he had in high school, Mitsy Brock. Sadly, this cast doubt into Nol's mind when it came to *all* women, and his guard was up for sure with Sadie.

Regardless, he picked her up as he was instructed, and they went out to his favorite seafood restaurant. The conversation was tepid in the beginning. She talked and he listened for a good hour or so. This changed when she talked about fishing with her dad. Nol's eyes lit up and his silence broke. They sat in that restaurant for hours swapping fishing stories, laughing mightily together. Their chemistry became undeniable. Physically, though, they made an *odd* pair; Nol was tall and, well… plump, but diesel-train powerful. Sadie was notably short, and maybe 100 pounds soaking wet in a full ball gown. I fully believe they fell in the kind of love that never ends, but regardless, Nol had to address the elephant in the room.

"Sadie, you ain't just trying to get to Colton are ya?" Nol asked, referring to Colton James, the team's dashing starting quarterback. The memory of the Mitsy Brock debacle fueled intense speculation in his mind.

"You're an idiot, Nolan," Sadie said. "Last I recall, I instructed *you* to take me to dinner tonight, did I not?" Sadie said, annoyed.

"I'm sorry—it's just that…"

"Shut up and kiss me, Nolan," Sadie said, effectively ending Nol's worry and cementing a relationship so steeped in love that this tiny, hell bent woman commandeered my behemoth of a friend, even though he was resolute on not allowing such a thing.

So you remember, dear Reader, when I said Nol and Annie had a field day with me on fishing trips? Well, things got much worse once Nol had Sadie's help to make fun of my fishing IQ. Holy hell!

The three of them would tee-off on me as though their brains were tied together. Nol would start an insult, Sadie would continue it, and Annie would finish it. The cadence herein was impressive, but it was entirely different when Dr. Glaush took us all fishing on *his* boat. In that case, he would start something that felt like an insult—playfully but not hurtfully—Sadie would follow with assists from Annie, and Nol would finish while everybody laughed. I tried to get my fishing acumen up to snuff, but that part of my brain was seemingly broken. I literally brought farm business with me; I would review while the lot of them caught dinner. I had one single point of power: I always supplied dessert. If things got too close to being over the line, I would threaten to feed whatever I had made to the dog and force them all to watch. That usually shut the lot of them up, and I'd get a nice smooch from Annie as consolation.

She taught me how to free dive, and I took a liking to that. I had taught Annie quite a lot about the farm over the previous years, and she began helping me on the business side in earnest during my last year of college. Because my grandfather had retired several years prior, I hired a family I was introduced to by a friend to assist with farming operations. They had emigrated from Mexico and had an immense knowledge of farming—but had nothing to their name. The Rodriguez clan—father José, mother Maria, sons Carlos and Julio—were such hard workers! We bridged our combined knowledge and added a couple more crops, soybeans and wheat, to the mix after I bought a little bit more land. The Rodriguez folks tended to both the new crops and those I couldn't due to time constraints. Maria helped my grandfather every day, and the boys very graciously helped anywhere they were needed—especially when it came to equipment. Both were skilled mechanics and Carlos had an engineering mind that was positively remarkable. Annie eventually made inroads with new companies I had never considered while further cementing existing relationships. She had made such an impression on my grandfather, at 102 years old, that he never forgot her name though he met her on the doorstep of his 100th birthday *and* had dementia.

I surprised the Rodriguez clan one night after two successful planting rotations. They had been staying in Grandfather's house, but things were cramped, especially for the boys. I secretly bought some land just behind the crops they tended, equidistant to the barn but from the opposite side of Grandfather's house. I engaged the help of Mr. Toth's building company, and we built them a sizable eight-bedroom house so they could house their family from Mexico when they came to visit and still have a spare room should the need arise. I made absolutely sure the kitchen was the most spacious, incredible room in the house. Dear Heaven, you have not experienced food until you've had Maria's cooking. Grandfather happily survived on homemade enchiladas until he passed away peacefully, but unexpectedly, one afternoon on his porch swing.

It was Maria who found him on that very swing where she spent afternoons with my grandfather, talking about just about anything one can imagine. I can only guess what those conversations were like, but I imagine they had become quite close based on what I found when I went to the farm that afternoon.

José met me as I got out of my car. "Señor Olaf, something happened," he said, his voice shaking.

"What happened, José? Are you okay? The boys? Are they okay?" I asked, imagining the worst.

"It's your gran-papa, Señor Olaf," he said and wrapped his arm around me. He guided me up to the porch, where Maria was sobbing, her head down. She was heartbroken—that was obvious.

I knelt down in front of her. "Maria—can you tell me what's wrong?" I asked, my sadness rising.

"Señor Olaf, I… I…" Maria began.

José sat next to her, wrapping his arms around her. His sadness was very obvious too.

"He died on this swing today. I had so much to tell him," Maria said, tears streaming down her face. "He loved you so much, Señor Olaf. You have no idea. He was so proud."

I felt tears falling down my cheeks, and my sniffles started in earnest. "Where is he now, Maria?" I asked, smiling through my sniffles.

"He is inside, on his bed," José said.

I made my way inside to find Carlos and Julio sitting in Grandfather's bedroom, praying. Grandfather was on his bed, his arms folded across his chest. Both boys were extremely emotional.

"He was so kind to us," Julio said, his voice choked.

"I'm so sorry Señor Olaf," Carlos said.

"He loved the work you both have done," I said. "He told me all the time about the things he watched you do with the equipment and the way you worked."

It wasn't long before Annie, her parents, and my parents arrived. I heard each of them talk to Maria before they made their way inside. Annie came into the house first and ran over to me crying hysterically. I hugged her until she settled herself down enough to speak. "He was amazing, Olaf. Amazing," she said, her face red and very teary.

"He loved you, Annie," I said, trying to keep what little composure I had.

Both sets of parents entered the house, with Dr. Glaush keeping his arm around Father's shoulders. Everyone was emotional, especially Father.

"I cannot believe he's gone," Father said, his voice broken.

"I know how bad this hurts David. I am so sorry for your loss," Dr. Glaush said. "Olaf—you doing okay, son?"

It was here an odd thing happened. Mrs. Glaush approached me and gave me a huge hug. It was the first time she had ever embraced me.

"I'm so sorry Olaf. Annie has been telling me about your grandfather. He was such an amazing man. This is a sad, sad day," she said, still hugging me.

Mother smiled when she saw this, but it was obvious she was heartbroken. Grandfather had been a father to her for so many years. The loss of her dad had created a void my grandfather joyfully filled. She went back outside and sat with Maria. The two of them rocked in that swing and cried.

My Lord, that was such a sorrowful day for all of us, the Rodriquez family included. So much of what I am as a person came from Grandfather. I learned how to be successful in business because of him. I learned how to be respectful of all people, even if they were not giving me the same treatment. I learned how to protect myself, and why it was important to have such a skill. I guess, to put a bow on this, my grandfather played a large role in teaching me how to be a man. Mind you, Father did as well, but in a complimentary, non-physical way.

The funeral was attended by an incredible number of people; there was standing room only in the church. It seemed Grandfather had touched the lives of almost every person in South Carolina, some from Florida, a bunch from Europe, a couple villages in Mexico, and almost every major city west of the Mississippi. We hadn't heard who was to deliver his eulogy, but he had laid this out in a rather specific script provided to the funeral home after his death by his lawyer. Mind you—no one knew he even had a lawyer.

When the time arrived for his eulogy, an old man in an Army uniform stood up and made his way to the podium. No one knew who this was, nor how he knew my grandfather.

"Iron Hands was an amazing son of a bitch, and I am proud to have been his friend for the better part of eighty years. My name is John Malloy. Chris and I served in the Army together."

All of our jaws simultaneously dropped. None of us knew John Sr. was still alive as he hadn't been seen in at least a decade.

"Chris and I have spoken nearly every day since we returned stateside. I was there when his boy, David, was born. I was there when he lost his bride to cancer. I was there when his boy got married to Sierra. I was there when their son Olaf was born. He was there for every event for me, too. We have watched this beautiful family grow. We, together, have been so proud. My boy and my grandson made horrible mistakes, but it was Chris who helped me to help them—and it was him who showed true compassion. He helped me stay strong after I lost my wife a couple years ago.

He had no idea what his grandson was capable of—and was so proud of his son and the lives he has saved. There were so many that found their way into his life in his later years. Were he sitting here today, he would have me mention Maria Rodriguez's cooking and would claim it kept him alive for an extra couple of years. I guarantee you that.

Chris was an amazing man. For those of you in the family, you have no idea what's coming next. I've lost my friend, and y'all have lost an amazing person. He's home with the love of his life now, though, and he's waited too damn long for that, again probably on account of Mrs. Rodriguez's cooking."

Mr. Malloy returned to his seat, and all of us looked at one another, wondering what in the world he was talking about. The rest of the ceremony was nice, and after he was laid to rest next to my grandmother, we returned to the farmhouse where we had set up a massive tent for a reception. We heard so many stories about my grandfather none of us knew, Father included.

It was two days later when we—my parents and I, Annie and her parents, and the Rodriguez family—met at the phantom lawyer's office in regard to Grandfather's estate.

"We are here to settle the estate of Christopher David Waniglia. I must inform each of you this is but a first step in the fulfillment of Christopher's wishes. Each of you will receive an envelope, or envelopes, and based on the contents therein, you will then discover Christopher's wishes for your portion of the estate," the lawyer, Mr. Lating, said.

He passed out an envelope to each member of the Rodriguez family and gave one extra to both José and Maria. Dr. and Mrs. Glaush each got an envelope, and Annie got two. Mother got two envelopes, Father got four, and I got six.

When all of the envelopes had been distributed, Mr. Lating said, "Christopher was specific. These envelopes should not be opened here. He did, *ahem*, not like law offices. That said, please ensure your envelopes are opened within three days—some of this is very time sensitive, and specific meetings have been set up with a starting point based on our time right now. I will see some of you soon. For those I do not see again, I am sorry for your loss and wish you the best."

After he said this, Mr. Lating got up and left the room through a door behind him. We all looked at each other, shrugged, and left the office.

For those with multiple envelopes, they were numbered based on the order they were to be opened. Grandfather was mighty strategic in how he did things, and ultimately the whole process was heartwarming. It was hard to lose him, but what he did in death was nothing short of amazing.

I apologize if what follows is hard to understand, dear Reader. I'm going to cover each of the envelope "paths," but because several happened simultaneously, this is not sequential in any sense other than in terms of an individual's envelope order.

The first to open their envelopes were the Rodriguez boys. Both were directed to a local investment broker, who informed them of two things:

1) They both had been given $1 million dollars, of which $800,000 was to remain under the careful watch of said investment broker until they were each thirty years old.
2) They had both been enrolled at a very well-known academy of engineering. $200,000 had been put in escrow for academic expenses, and their housing had been paid for in advance.

Both boys cried so hard in this investment broker's office, he called an ambulance.

The second envelopes to be opened were those of Maria and José Rodriguez. Maria was instructed to take José with her to a specified address, and was to ask for a "Mrs. B." She did so, and they were ushered into a conference room. A couple minutes later, Mrs. B. found her way into the room, giving each a warm hug, and in Spanish informed them that my grandfather had arranged for both her and José's remaining living relatives to come to the United States. This included her sister Carla, her brother-in-law Jorge, her nephew Manny, his brother Manuel and his father Luis. Their green card process had started two years prior, with a full path to citizenship for *all of them* initiated and due to complete well prior to their green cards expiring. By the time the initial green cards were available, the second part of their gift "should be ready." In addition, Grandfather had contacted a publisher who had, on Grandfather's word alone, crafted a book deal for Maria to share her favorite recipes.

This was so much, they thought: what was this "second part?"

They left Mrs. B.'s office and started the journey home, excitedly talking during the drive about having their family together in America. Luis, José's father, was ill and had been receiving horrible medical care in his village in Mexico. This change would mean the boys would have the chance to learn about their family from their grandfather, something that had occupied José's mind quite a bit over the past year, knowing his father was sick.

When they got home, Maria decided to open her second envelope. In it, she and José were directed to the same investment broker to which the boys had been pointed. They were informed by said investment broker they had been given $2 million dollars, $1.4 million of which was to remain under management for at least two years. She fainted, he found he couldn't breathe, and again the rattled investment broker called an ambulance.

This latest experience prompted José to open his first envelope when he got home. He was instructed to return to Mr. Lating's office in two days at 12:00 PM. He made his way to the meeting, where Mr. Lating informed him he had become the official, titled owner of 25% of Grandfather's farmhouse and 100% title holder of the barn. It was after this news Mr. Lating said he had something he was instructed to read. He handed José a handkerchief and began reading.

He began, "José, you and your family have been such a blessing as long as I've known you. Thank you so much for spending the time with me you did. I have contracted with Hollister Toth, the same person who built your current house, to make some amendments to your home, the farmhouse, and barn. One last thing, my friend. I have instructed the porch swing remain untouched amid all the construction. Please promise me you will take my place on that swing with Maria. God bless you, José." Mr. Lating then produced a set of architecture plans, and said, "This should commence within the next two weeks, and should complete before your family arrives. Please don't open the plans—just give them to Olaf Waniglia."

"Who owns 25% of a house?" José asked, wiping a tear with the handkerchief.

"This will make sense in the coming days, José. I promise," Mr. Lating responded. "Please make sure you open your second envelope when you get home. You have another meeting, and you don't want to miss it."

Perplexed, José shook Mr. Lating's hand and left the office. He returned home and opened his second envelope. Inside it, he found an address and the instruction he was to meet a "Mr. Williamson" the next day at 1:00 PM.

José travelled to an imposingly tall office building, and made his way inside to find a nicely appointed office. He was led to Mr. Williamson's office where he was informed he had been transferred the deed for fifty acres of land to support a new contract, with an option for an additional 100 acres "if the second deal hits."

"What contract are you talking about, Mr. Williamson?" José asked, confused.

Mr. Williamson was about to respond when his phone rang. There was a series of succinct responses including, "Yes," "I see," "Okay," "Understood," and then finally, "I'll let him know. Thank you."

José, still confused, didn't pay any attention to the conversation. He was startled when Mr. Williamson started speaking to him again.

"Mr. Rodriguez, the second deal has hit. You now have the additional 100 acres. Congratulations, and good luck, sir," Mr. Williamson said.

"Thank you, but I have no idea what you are talking about, Mr. Williamson," José responded.

"After Annie Glaush opens her second envelope, this will become clear," Mr. Williamson said, winking. "Trust me when I say this, Mr. Rodriguez, Chris Waniglia loved you and your family."

José shook Mr. Williamson's hand, thanked him, and immediately thought about what he needed to do to farm all that new land. *Thank God in Heaven Manuel, Jorge, and Manny are on their way here,* he thought. Thing is, my grandfather had carefully thought through all of this and in due time, the entire puzzle would come together.

Speaking of Annie—she opened her first envelope and was instructed to meet Mr. Lating in his offices at 10:00 AM on the following day. She went to his office, signed something notarized, and was given a subsequent envelope that read "Your dad should open this after he talks to Theodore 'Joe' Overton and the nice folks at Haybrook."

"What happens if *I* open this before Daddy talks to this 'Joe' person?" Annie asked sarcastically.

"Well, in truth, the contents would make no sense to you," Mr. Lating said, looking sternly at Annie over his reading glasses.

Annie took the envelope and ventured home, gave her father this new envelope and asked him if he had opened his envelope yet.

"Yep, and it's the strangest thing. There was a single note: 'Go see Theodore 'Joe' Overton and the nice folks at Haybrook after David has opened his first envelope and Olaf has opened his first three envelopes. Coordinate with David and Olaf. Joe's expecting the three of you.' I have no idea what this means, and this new envelope is even stranger to me, but I'll go see this guy. Can you find out where Olaf and his dad stand with their envelopes, Sweetheart?" Dr. Glaush asked, hesitatingly.

Well, for Father's part, his first envelope contained two notes. The first was in concert with Dr. Glaush's and said, "Go see Theodore 'Joe' Overton and the nice folks at Haybrook after Franklin has opened his envelope and Olaf has opened his first three envelopes. Coordinate with Franklin and Olaf. Joe's expecting the three of you." The second note was a bit more personal. It read:

> "David, I don't know if I said this nearly enough, but I am so proud of the man you are. I certainly did not make you this way. You did this all on your own. You are an amazing husband and father, and the work you do in the hospital is nothing short of revolutionary to me. Your mother, God rest her soul, would have been relieved you took the tragedy of her death as you did, though I know it was so painful for you. You helped me more than I ever said after she passed. Though you were suffering tremendously, you cared for me. You saved my life, son.
>
> Last thing: I would never admit this previously, but son, that orchard of yours is *perfect*.
>
> I love you, David.
>
> Dad"

"Dammit, Dad," Father said as he blew his nose and wiped his tears away.

Mother saw this and started crying too. "Aw babe, I hate when you're sad," she said, hugging him tightly.

"I wonder who this 'Joe' guy is. Si, ever hear Dad talk about him?" Father asked.

"No, that name doesn't ring a bell to me. Maybe Olaf knows, or Maria, or even Annie for that matter," Mother said, still hugging Father.

Annie's second envelope had two notes in it. The first had an address on it and indicated she had an appointment with a "Mr. Tate." The second indicated she was to meet with Mr. Lating together with me after I had opened my fourth envelope.

So, that morning, Annie arrived at an office complex and, as instructed, asked for Mr. Tate with the receptionist. The receptionist smiled and said, "Right this way, Ms. Glaush."

Mr. Tate, a tall and rotund man, rose from his chair and in a deep voice said, "Well, hello, Ms. Glaush. It is a pleasure to finally meet you."

"Mr. Tate, I'm so sorry, but I can't place how you might know me," Annie said, confused.

"This is understandable, Ms. Glaush, but I think I can clear this up. Do you recall submitting a bid to the Orange Group?"

The Orange Group was a massive conglomerate responsible for multiple product distribution channels around the world. Annie had found, through a contact she had at a local market, the Orange Group was taking bids to replace their cotton textile channel. Though the cotton grown on the farm had been distributed internationally, it was to specific sources in a couple countries. The Orange Group would increase the farm's distribution by about 3,000%. She talked to my grandfather about it, and he encouraged her to pursue it, saying, "If it hits, we'll figure it out." She created the bid but was nervous about submitting it because she was relatively unknown in the farming world, so she left her name off the document. Grandfather mentioned he would submit it for her. Instead, he filled in *her* name on the bid sheet and called Mr. Tate, saying Annie was the point person for the bid. Nothing had happened on the bid until now, and because it had been a few months without word, she assumed their bid had not been accepted.

"I remember the bid, but it should have come from Chris Waniglia," Annie said, confused.

Mr. Tate handed her the document and said, "Well, darlin', it sure looks like it came from you."

Annie looked at the bid and saw my grandfather had filled in her name. She covered her mouth in abject disbelief, and tears formed in her eyes.

Mr. Tate handed her his handkerchief and said, "Annie, I am the president of the Orange Group. This was the most impressive bid we received, and this is one of our most important channels. I truly look forward to working with you, and I believe you will be an incredible partner to us. Bear in mind, we increased the terms of the bid by an additional 125%. I communicated that to Chris, and he told me you would be able to fulfill the need without any issue. I think the quality alone y'all will provide us makes this an amazing partnership."

He stood and extended his hand. She too stood, extended her hand and they shook. "You can keep that kerchief, darlin'," Mr. Tate said, smiling.

Annie smiled, sniffed, and made her way out of the office, completely unable to speak. She cried the entire car ride back to the farm, where she found José and told him the news.

"Well, the additional land makes a lot of sense now," he said, "but do you know anything about the house? Chris gave me 25% of it. I can't figure that out."

She shrugged, and they chatted about what had been discovered in the envelopes thus far. They both could not believe what the other said. It became clear to them that my grandfather had woven an amazing tapestry of human interaction, and the whole thing wasn't completely visible yet.

Mother opened her first envelope. It simply contained a note from my grandfather. It read:

"Sierra,

There were so many years David and I were at each other's throats, and as much as I couldn't stand being with my son during that time, I never wanted to miss your dinners. Thank you for giving my son all you have. He needed you to show him what it felt like to be loved. Thank you for allowing me to know what it's like to have a daughter. In God's eyes, you are mine, kid. Thank you for giving me a grandson who changed my life. Olaf would have never done for me what he did unless you trusted me all those years ago. When it all comes right down to it, you took in an old farmer who had given up, and gave him reason after reason to start caring again.

I will miss that smile of yours greatly.

I love you Sierra,

Dad"

Both Mother and Father stood sobbing, hugging each other after they read her note together.

"What does your second envelope contain, Si?" Father asked between sniffing.

"I don't know, let's look," she responded as she dabbed at her eyes.

She opened her second envelope to find instructions to go to the same investment broker the others had, with Father. It was there the investment broker passionately told them every other person who had received news from him had required an ambulance. Father confidently said he was a doctor, and there was nothing to fear. The investment broker took a deep, nervous breath and told them my grandfather had left them $5 million dollars, $4.5 million of which was to remain with the investment broker for at least two years. Mother fainted, Father became unable to speak, and the investment broker swore like a sailor and called an ambulance.

Father's second envelope contained a key, and a note with an address and instruction to take his remaining envelopes with him when he went to the address. So, he and Mother went to the address indicated and found they were at a large bank. He imagined the key was for a safe deposit box, so they asked to be let into that area, found the number on the key, and opened the door. Inside, they found a note and a number of letters, photos, and jewelry. The note read:

> "David, these are your Mom's things. It hurt too bad to keep them at the house, so they have been here for quite a few years. I think you'll enjoy looking through the pictures, and the jewelry will have another purpose. Hold onto it, and Olaf will fill in that blank. Now, open envelope #3."

He did as instructed and found a note and another key. The note read:

> "Same place, different box. Dad"

So, they found the next box and inside found yet another note and a host of documentation with some old photos. The note read:

> "David, these are my documents for all the property, and my old records and photos from the military. Please make sure the property documents get back to Mr. Lating once you review them. It's important to me you understand them so my plan works the way I want it to. Please take the military

stuff when you go to Haybrook. Now, open your last envelope."

Again, he did what he was instructed and opened the last envelope. Inside, they found an address and a name, "Mrs. Klipkewitcz."

They took the contents of the safe deposit boxes and went to the address indicated on the note. It was a travel agency. They went inside and asked for Mrs. Klipkewitcz. From the back of the room, they saw a person wave and loudly say, "THAT'S ME! COME ON BACK, BABIES!"

Though they were apprehensive after witnessing this display, they went back to find the source of the voice. Mrs. Klipkewitcz was a large woman, adorned with an absurd amount of both jewelry and makeup.

"Hi, I'm David Waniglia. I think my dad may have made arrangements with you?" Father said nervously.

"Baby, I knew it when I saw you," Mrs. Klipkewitcz said. "Your daddy told me about your beautiful bride's smile. Christopher was such a lovely man. We had lunch every month for at least twenty years."

"Wait, you knew my dad?" Father asked, his curiosity piquing.

"I sure did, David. I am the daughter of your Momma's best friend. I knew your daddy as 'Uncle Chris' and your momma as 'Aunt Madelyn.' I think you may have seen me when I was younger a couple times," Mrs. Klipkewitcz said, smiling.

"I really don't remember. I'm so sorry," Father said, shaking his head.

"Baby, it's not worth your concern. You were always busy on the farm. I doubt you were half conscious when I was around," she said. "But, the reason you're here is more than just reminiscing. Uncle Chris wanted you to see where your parents met, and what he and Aunt Madelyn saw on their honeymoon, from the location to the restaurants, to the place where he said he fell in love with your momma, and yet another that made her light up like Fourth of July fireworks. Y'all are going to Hawaii in a couple months. Your daddy made all the arrangements, including your hospital for your time away. There are a couple things y'all need to do before you go, though, and that starts with Joe at Haybrook."

"Who is Joe, Mrs. Klipkewitcz?" Mother asked.

"Sweetie, as much as I would love to say, Uncle Chris would be upset if I did," she responded.

So, the three stood, exchanged hugs and made promises to meet for lunch soon to trade stories about my grandfather. "When this whole, complex thing that your Daddy created is done, we'll have a bunch more to talk about," Mrs. Klipkewitcz said.

That leaves me with my envelopes, my dear Reader. All the others were open at this point, except the one Dr. Glaush got via Annie.

My first envelope contained a note to meet with Mr. Lating. So, it was to his office I travelled, and he produced a manila folder with a bunch of documents in it.

"Olaf, the business of the farm has been given to you, along with deeds for most of the land. I know you've been running it for a few years now, but this gives you legal signing authority for all the contracts, and also puts you in control of specified assets of the property. In addition, you have been given 75% of the farmhouse for a period of four years. After the specified period, your ownership drops to 5% and the remainder transfers to Carlos and Julio Rodriguez in equal shares as it is to become their residence when they are adults. Your ownership is purely a stopgap measure in the event something unforeseen happens with their citizenship process," Mr. Lating said.

"Citizenship process?" I asked.

"Yes, José can fill in that detail for you. For now, though, let's finish this business transfer as you should open your second envelope and get going because you have an appointment specified in your third envelope. I will see you again after envelope five," Mr. Lating said flatly.

I hadn't brought the envelopes with me, so I ran home and opened the second envelope. It contained a key and a note with an address on it, and the instruction to bring my third envelope with me. I did as it instructed and went to the address on the note. It was the same bank my parents had visited. I was led back to the safe deposit boxes, located and opened a specified box. Inside was a note and a small black velvet bag. The note read:

> "Olaf, these are your great, great grandmother's diamonds. They came from Africa when her husband travelled there, and I believe are much more valuable than anything you can buy in the stores today. I had always intended to give them to your grandmother, but she passed away so young I never had the chance. I had forgotten about them until I started looking though the safe deposit boxes. Take them to the specified location indicated in your third envelope, and after that meeting, go with your dad and Dr. Glaush to Haybrook and talk to Joe."

My third envelope had an address not far from the bank with an appointment time that gave me about an hour to have lunch and get there in time for the meeting.

The building was tall, but had no windows. I approached a marble-filled reception area to find two heavily-armed gentlemen flanking the receptionist with fierce expressions on their faces. I told the woman who I was and that I had an appointment. She nodded, made a quick phone call, and motioned for me to go toward an entrance gate.

I went through metal detectors and was led by a separate security guard to a set of elevators.

"Go up to the 20th floor and ask for Mr. Marks at the window," he said sternly.

I did as I was told and approached a tiny window in what looked like concrete walls several feet thick. I asked for Mr. Marks, and was directed through a door and down a long hallway to the left. A single door was located on my right. I knocked, and an older voice said, "Come in, Mr. Waniglia."

At a large desk sat a tiny, older gentleman who stood up slowly and extended his hand. "My name is Ted Marks, Mr. Waniglia. I served in the Army with your Grandfather," the man said.

"It's a pleasure to meet you, sir. Can you tell me what this building is? I've never seen such a thing before," I said as I sat down.

"We deal in extraordinarily expensive things here, and we don't take chances," Mr. Marks responded.

"Why in the world am I here, sir?" I asked, perplexed beyond belief.

"Well, I am to have a conversation with you your grandfather wished to have. It's about Annie," Mr. Marks said and produced a plaster hand.

"Annie?" I asked, completely confused.

"Son, your grandfather saw a love between you that is the kind reserved for angels in Heaven. It's pure, it's honest, and it's true.

While it is completely your call here, your grandfather craftily got this mold of her left hand, and sneakily found out what she wanted in an engagement ring," Mr. Marks said.

I nodded. I had absolutely been thinking about proposing. Annie and I had been together for almost six years. We never had anything more than a mild disagreement, laughed constantly, and were itching to take the next step. Thing is: I had not disclosed my ability to hear *vox corpora*, and that had to be done before a proposal. Regardless, I intended to propose, but had not the first clue about the ring. Luckily, my grandfather had figured this out for me.

"You brought the diamonds in the safe deposit box, right son?" Mr. Marks asked.

I pulled the velvet pouch out of my pocket and handed it to Mr. Marks. He pulled out a loupe and examined each one.

"It was very important to your grandfather that you have the chance to use these stones. It works out perfectly because you can build both bands very nicely and still have a couple nice-sized diamonds left. He drew this. I guess it came out of several conversations with Arnie," Mr. Marks said as he handed me a drawing of two rings.

It touched me deeply that Grandfather had done this. I had to take a minute to really absorb all of this, and it struck me that I still had three envelopes to open.

"Mr. Marks, can we change topics for a minute? This is really hitting me in a powerful way," I said, my voice shaking.

There was a chair next to me, and the fragile Mr. Marks got up, moved it next to me, and sat down.

"Son, we can talk about any damn thing you like. Chris was a dear friend of mine, and what he did for all of you is really… what is the word… surreal. I'm sure it hits you in the heart pretty damn hard," Mr. Marks said, his arm around my shoulders.

"I still cannot believe he's gone, Mr. Marks."

"Neither can I, son. Chris saved my life despite being shot when we were in the war. He was the toughest son of a bitch I ever knew. Christ could that man fight! I hear you ain't so bad yourself, kid. You put two men in the hospital for a month with your bare fists. He and I talked about that a lot," Mr. Marks said, his grip on my shoulder tighter.

"He saved your life? I never knew he was shot in the war," I said, surprised.

"He never would have said a word of this to anyone. The only way I knew he was shot was because I was there. I saw the bullet wound and the blood coming out of his chest. Otherwise, he didn't say a word to anyone because it didn't matter to him. He did what he thought he should do, and that didn't mean he shared it with anyone," Mr. Marks said.

"I understand. I'm built the same way," I said, appreciating there was a reason I was as I was.

"Yeah, I know. You took the farm and blew that thing into orbit, Olaf. Your grandfather could not believe what you did to his little farm. And bringing in the Rodriguez people—genius, son. They did more for him than you'll ever know," Mr. Marks said emotionally.

"I appreciate you saying that, Mr. Marks. I truly do."

"It's my pleasure kid. Tell me about this girl of yours. She sounds like a keeper."

Our conversation turned to Annie, her ring and a constant cadence of, "You should marry that girl, son." In the end, we did design a ring set, I picked the diamonds to be used in it, then took the remaining diamonds and created necklaces for Mother, Mrs. Glaush, and Maria Rodriguez. I thought the three of them for sure would appreciate sharing in what my grandfather had given me. Mr. Marks told me the ring would take about two weeks to make, and he would be in touch when it was ready. The last thing he said, though, was in regard to Haybrook, the mystery place that had been confusing Father and Dr. Glaush. "Call your Pop and Dr. Glaush, son. They're expecting you to take a little ride with them."

Perplexed, I agreed, thanked Mr. Marks for everything, and set about making my way out of the fortress.

I went home, talked to Father, and we called Dr. Glaush. We decided to "see Theodore 'Joe' Overton and the nice folks at Haybrook" that night after an early dinner to see what this was all about.

****

It took us maybe an hour and a half to arrive at Haybrook, which turned out to be a retirement community outside of town. It was an impressive campus, with a wooded backdrop and a stream through the middle. We found a main office and asked for Mr. Overton. He was paged and soon appeared pushing a wheelchair carrying none other than John Malloy, Sr. Once again, our collective jaws dropped when we saw him.

"What's a-matter boys? Grow some balls and let's go drink. Joe! To the tavern please!" Mr. Malloy was something else.

Mr. Overton led us down a path parallel to a little stream with wildflowers growing on the banks. As we did, I had to settle a curiosity of mine.

"Mr. Overton, how did you get the nickname 'Joe'?" I asked.

"Actually, Master Waniglia, Mr. Malloy felt it inconvenient to say 'Theodore' due to the fact it was not monosyllabic," Mr. Overton said in a refined British accent.

"Joe! Quit using big words. You know I hate that," Mr. Malloy said from his chariot.

"As you wish, Mr. Malloy," Mr. Overton said with a tinge of arrogance.

We arrived at the tavern, which was nicely appointed with hard wood practically everywhere and leather chairs throughout. The lighting was dim, with candles on all the tables and scattered along the bar. We sat at a small table, and Mr. Overton excused himself to retrieve drinks.

"I assume whiskey is fine?" Mr. Malloy said flatly.

I was freshly twenty-one, so I could drink, though whiskey wasn't my favorite beverage by any means, nor Father or Dr. Glaush, but we went along with what Mr. Malloy wanted.

Soon, Mr. Overton returned with a tray full of whiskey-filled glasses, distributed them and sat next to Mr. Malloy. He too had a glass.

"Gentlemen, I can assure you'll warm up to the taste by about the third round," Mr. Overton said.

"Kid, you saw Marksy today, right?" Mr. Malloy asked me.

"Yes, Mr. Malloy, I did. That's quite a place!" I responded.

"Okay. Is there anything you need to ask him?" Mr. Malloy said, motioning to Dr. Glaush.

I became flush with nervousness; I'm sure my face was red. As I searched for the words to say, Dr. Glaush's *vox corporis* spoke to me. It wasn't the first time, but it still surprised me tremendously.

"Olaf, he cares for you and respects you. Relax—he has been hoping to hear the words you are about to say for about a year now. Oh—and he knows you can hear me," his *vox corporis* said.

"Yep—he does, Olaf," Father's *vox corporis* said. *"You gave it away at the hospital six months ago. Your father explained this very loosely so Dr. Glaush didn't overreact,"* Father's *vox corporis* said.

I could not believe what I was hearing; I was floored. Father saw this, and asked, "Olaf, who is 'Marksy?' Where did you go today?"

I regained my composure, digested what I had heard, drank the rest of my whiskey, and took a deep breath. Before I could say anything, Mr. Malloy looked at Mr. Overton, barked, "Joe, empty glass," and nodded in my direction. Mr. Overton nodded, took my glass, and returned with a full glass quickly.

"Father, 'Marksy' is Mr. Marks. He served in the Army with Grandfather. You would not have believed this place I went to. Lots of scary guys with guns and walls made of concrete several feet thick," I said and sipped my fresh whiskey. "Mr. Malloy, what kind of whiskey is this? I kind of like it."

"It's Irish whiskey, kid. That's all you need to know," Mr. Malloy said. "Marksy—that son of a bitch—I miss him. Joe, we gotta go see Marksy soon."

"Of course, Mr. Malloy. I will coordinate," Joe responded dutifully.

"Olaf, what was it you wanted to ask me?" Dr. Glaush said suggestively.

I gathered my thoughts and said, "Dr. Glaush, I love your daughter and would like to ask for your blessing to ask for her hand in marriage."

"Son, I would welcome you doing so, and I know Helene would as well," Dr. Glaush said, smiling.

"That's what Chris thought you'd say, Doc. Before any of this happens, the house needs to be fixed," Mr. Malloy said.

"The house?" Father asked curiously.

"The family, Doc," Mr. Malloy said coarsely. "My son and my grandson did a terrible thing. What Johnny did to Annie was wrong. What Junior did to you, kid, was wrong. What you did to both of them was not. I want to be clear about that. You needed to do what you did. But, the truth is, the house needs to be fixed."

Mr. Malloy took a sip of whiskey and continued, "Junior and Johnny know what they did was wrong, and I can promise you they are sorry. I may be old, but I beat the shit out of both of 'em for that crap."

"I can assure you, gentlemen, Mr. Malloy is telling you the truth. Both men stayed an extra week in the hospital and earned an extra year of therapy as a result," Mr. Overton said.

"Here's the thing though. Johnny is a month away from getting a college degree in the joint. Junior is getting certified as a mechanic. They both are going to be in prison for a while yet, and they should be, but I think they honestly are being rehabilitated," Mr. Malloy said.

"What is Johnny studying?" I asked curiously.

"Law, kid. He wants to go to law school when he gets out," Mr. Malloy said.

"How is Mary Ann doing, Mr. Malloy? We haven't seen nor heard from her in years," Dr. Glaush said.

"That is one important part of the house that needs to be fixed, Doc. She's embarrassed, she's alone, and she misses her sister terribly. I talk to her almost every day, and she still cries. She misses her husband, she misses her son, and she needs her sister," Mr. Malloy said seriously.

"Helene misses her too, Mr. Malloy. What can we do?" Dr. Glaush said.

"Well, this is part of why you're here. Chris and I talked about this a lot. He wanted to be sure this was said, and he knew he wouldn't be around to say it," Mr. Malloy said sadly. "He and I agreed all of you—your wives, all your kids, everybody—need to go to the prison and see the boys. We need to get Mary Ann out of this funk she's in. Once that's done and the lot of you are whole again, the house will be fixed and this marriage can move forward."

"I don't want to say anything out of turn here, gentlemen, but Christopher was indeed quite serious about addressing this. It was a part of every conversation he and Mr. Malloy had for the past couple years," Mr. Overton said.

"I feel awful for Mary Ann," Dr. Glaush said. "I had no idea she was alone."

"I do too," I said. "This is definitely something we need to do."

"Now kid, there's one other thing we need to talk about before you leave. It's this ability of yours," Mr. Malloy said stoutly.

I was horrified. My grandfather had told a secret I held so tightly. I learned from Dr. Glaush's *vox corporis* that *he* knew about it. Now Mr. Malloy knew?

"Olaf, please don't be apprehensive. I've seen what this can do for patients at the hospital. You saved a man just last week. There was no medical way possible to diagnose the man, *but you did*. A son would have lost his father had you not intervened when you did," Dr. Glaush said.

"Yes, Olaf. Mr. Douglass, that tall guy with the handlebar moustache. Remember?" Father asked.

"Of course," I said, "You guys were able to treat him? I didn't see him in the hospital on Friday and assumed the worst."

"He went home, Olaf. That heart defect you uncovered was easy to treat once we knew about it. He was treated, observed for a day, and sent home," Dr. Glaush said.

"He wasn't the only one, though, Olaf. To date you've saved 162 people for whom we thought there was no hope. Franklin and I keep track. I am so proud of you, son. I told you this would do amazing things for so many people," Father said, smiling.

"I, um… I… I don't know what to say," I said nervously. "Mr. Malloy, why did my grandfather discuss this with you?"

"Kid, your Pop wanted you to understand that you need to spend more time helping people with your ability and less time at the farm. Those were his exact words to me," Mr. Malloy said.

"Indeed, Master Waniglia. Your grandfather was also insistent you continue to refine your self-defense skills. He was nervous for your safety," Mr. Overton said. "In terms of the farm, your subsequent envelopes will further clarify what is expected of you. You are not giving up your present responsibilities by any means, but balance is essential as you look at your time."

"You helped Grandfather with the envelopes, Mr. Overton?" I asked, astonished.

"Yes, Master Waniglia, I did. As I understand it, he had help from several people depending on the topic or who the gift was for. I worked with Mr. Lating on your grandfather's behalf once I understood his wishes. Mr. Malloy accompanied me to every meeting to ensure what I said was as he understood it as well," Mr. Overton said as Mr. Malloy nodded in approval.

"I'm still struggling with y'all knowing about my ability," I said as I rubbed my forehead.

"Olaf, there are many people who know. Most of the nursing staff, though they remain outside of the room as you communicate, have heard you and are so appreciative of what you can do. It helps them do their jobs in a way that truly helps their patients. Several have asked if they can be in the room with you," Dr. Glaush said.

"This is true, son. I'm not sure about the other doctors, because we are mostly secluded where we are, but the nurses do know," Father said comfortingly.

"It's not normal, kid, but it's incredible. You can't ignore this," Mr. Malloy said before finishing his glass of whiskey. "Let's get back to business, gents. Do I have your word you will go see the boys, and get back in touch with Mary Ann?"

"Absolutely, Mr. Malloy. I will ensure we see Mary Ann soon. For my and my family's part, I absolutely commit to going to see the boys as well," Dr. Glaush said.

"I'm willing to go as well, Mr. Malloy," I said, though I had many concerns about doing so, and I was sure Annie would as well.

"Sierra and I will also do as you ask, Mr. Malloy," Father said after he finished his whiskey.

"Thank you. Doc, did you bring the envelope your daughter gave you?" Mr. Malloy asked Dr. Glaush.

"Yes, I did," he said and produced the envelope.

"Open it now, please, so I can explain it," Mr. Malloy said sternly.

Dr. Glaush did, and found an official check inside for $1,500,000 made out to him and Mrs. Glaush. "What is this for?" he asked, astonished.

"It's for the wedding and the travel to get there. It certainly won't cost that much, but Chris was specific in what he hoped for the occasion. Because you are responsible for the expenses of the ceremony as father of the bride to be, Chris wanted to cover it because of his wishes. Joe, do you have the envelope?" Mr. Malloy asked.

Mr. Overton nodded and produced an envelope. "These are Christopher's wishes. The travel arrangements have been specified through Mrs. Klipkewitcz, though no dates have been established for obvious reasons. Dr. Glaush, I'd ask you open this in private with your wife to review," Mr. Overton said.

"Mrs. Klip-who?" Dr. Glaush asked.

"I'll fill in that gap, Franklin," Father said calmly.

"Okay then. You have your marching orders, right boys?" Mr. Malloy asked as he looked at each of us.

We all nodded, then he said, "Good, one more round, we shoot the shit, and then I go to bed. Joe, empty glasses!"

Mr. Overton nodded and returned to the bar. While we waited, Mr. Malloy asked me about the diamonds.

"They are amazing, Mr. Malloy. There were enough for both Annie's rings as well as three pieces of jewelry I designed as gifts," I responded.

"Diamonds, Olaf? I cannot figure out where Dad's money, or these things I keep hearing about, came from. Dad gave away an astonishing amount of money to people," Father said.

"Well, the diamonds were my great-great grandmother's that Grandpa had forgotten about. The money I know nothing about," I said, having not gotten to that detail yet.

"Well, the money was because of you, kid. You'll learn soon enough, so the rest of you shut the hell up about it," Mr. Malloy said angrily. "Kid, make sure you open your fourth envelope when you go home. Envelopes four, five, and six are all very different, but you should try to get all of this done within the next day or so if you can."

Mr. Overton soon returned with our whiskey, and we talked about all kinds of things as we sipped our way through our glasses. Mr. Marks was a big topic, which eventually led us to talking about the relationship he, my grandfather, and Mr. Malloy had in the Army. Father never knew my grandfather had been shot; this absolutely shocked him. We eventually made plans to go see the Malloys in prison, and Dr. Glaush talked about picking Mary Ann up and taking her to dinner with Mrs. Glaush. When our glasses were empty, Mr. Malloy was visibly exhausted.

"Sir, I believe the night has come to an end. Would you like to return to your suite?" Mr. Overton said kindly.

"Yes, Joe, I'm tired. Boys, thank you for the time. Please be safe going home," Mr. Malloy said with heavy eyes.

We all stood and took turns shaking hands with both Mr. Malloy and Mr. Overton, saying our goodbyes. The car ride back was mostly silent as we had so much on our minds. When we got home, I opened my fourth envelope. In it was a handwritten note:

"Take Nolan to the Easton Marina and ask for Mr. Harris."

It was late, so I figured I would do this in the morning, assuming Nol was free. I then opened my fifth envelope. It contained a note to set up an appointment with Mr. Lating with Annie after I propose, and I was not to open my sixth envelope until after that meeting. It was late, my buzz was substantial, and given the events of the day, I decided to crash.

****

The next day, Nol and I went to the Easton Marina and asked for Mr. Harris. A short man in stature with very weathered skin, Mr. Harris wore a warm, inviting smile.

"Doug Harris. What can I do you gentlemen fer?" he asked with a deep Southern drawl.

"My grandfather, Chris Waniglia, passed away recently and gave me instruction to come here with Nol and ask for you," I said.

"I'm so sorry, son. Yer grandpop was somethin' else. One sec—I have to grab somethin' and then we takin' a lil' walk," Mr. Harris said.

He reappeared a short time later with a box and an envelope. "Come on, fellers. Follow me," he said with a smile.

We walked a complicated maze through several docks and finally arrived at a good size boat. Here, Mr. Harris handed Nol the envelope and box. "Envelope first, son," he said.

Nol opened the envelope which had a note, which read:

"Nolan, you've been such a wonderful friend both to me and my family for quite a few years now. I know you are almost assuredly going into the NFL, and I want to be sure you have a reason to come home when you do. So, I bought you this boat and had it completely outfitted with the latest and greatest fishing tools. I left the naming rights to you, and

Doug Harris will take care of it for you. Lastly, you are paid up in this marina for the next 20 years.

All the best,

Chris"

"Wow—this is incredible!" Nol exclaimed, a huge smile on his face.

"Y'all have to open this guy up 'fer you get a-board, my friend," Mr. Harris said, handing the box to Nol.

Inside, Nol found a hat, a note and an official check for $100,000. The note read:

"All good captains have hats, my friend. -Chris"

Nol pulled out a captain's hat from the box and looked at the check. "I cannot believe your granddad did this for me, Olaf. It's absolutely incredible," he said as he looked the boat over.

"She's a beaut, son. I helped Chris pick 'er out fer ya. Let's hop aboard and I'll show y'all around. Then, since I have a couple minutes, I'll show y'all how to get to open water and where I normally fish," Mr. Harris said.

We all boarded the boat, which was a massive upgrade over his family's boat—and a step up from even Dr. Glaush's boat. The fishing technology was amazing for the time, with activity sensors onboard for deep sea fishing. There were "pole stands" all over the place to have multiple lines in at once, and seating for twelve people comfortably on the deck. I think Nol and I had our mouths wide open in awe, which only continued when Mr. Harris instructed Nol to start the boat.

The engines sounded like a fine sports car when they started. The purr was unlike anything I had heard in a boat. Mr. Harris stood by Nol and showed him where the familiar controls were. He then coached Nol as we made our way from the dock, through a narrow channel's twists and turns. Dolphins joined us in the channel as we made our way through. When we hit the ocean, they all jumped with us as we sped up. The boat accelerated so evenly, and handled even bigger swells with ease. We went out maybe a mile and a half when Mr. Harris told Nol to slow down and turn on the motion sensors.

"Looky at all dem feesh don 'ere, Nol. Plenty 'a good eatn' I tell 'ya. This place hasn't disappointed in years—y'all always can catch somethin' tasty," Mr. Harris said enthusiastically.

We stayed there for a minute and Nol just took it all in. "Thank you so much, Chris! I love this so much!" he yelled from the captain's chair.

"I promise y'all, he be grinnin'," Mr. Harris said, smiling.

At this point, I only knew about a few of the gifts Grandfather had given people. I could not believe the monetary amounts he dispersed, or the things he had left me. I truly wondered what may lie in the sixth envelope, and certainly what it was Mr. Lating had with both Annie and I. That, though, was to wait until a couple things happened: a visit to jail, and a wedding proposal, followed by me telling Annie about my ability. I was prepared for none of the above.

Fixing the House & Building a New One

Though it took some sizable convincing for Mother, Annie, and Mrs. Glaush to agree to go see the Malloy men in prison, some sweet talking and concessions here and there got them on board to join the caravan and fulfill Grandfather's and Mr. Malloy's wishes. I had trepidations about going, but we coordinated a night to both see the boys and take Mrs. Malloy to dinner not far from the prison. We also ensured that we would be able to visit the Malloys in jail, which turned out to be a bit more difficult than anticipated because the younger Malloy man was involved in an altercation with another inmate, which pushed our visit back a few days.

When the day eventually came, we gathered at the Glaush residence, did a final encouraging pow-wow for all our nerves, and headed toward the jail which was about two hours away. We were all able to go in the same vehicle, as Mother had a giant SUV that fit us comfortably. The entire drive there, Annie held my hand and shook every so often. I felt horrible for her; I'm sure facing the man who strangled her was not on her list of life's priorities. The rest of the car was quiet too, in an eerie way. It was as though we were travelling to our executions or something equally horrific, and we all were in some way aware of it.

We arrived at the prison and checked in with the deputy. He took us to a meeting room and brought us all water to drink. I made sure that I was front and center; I wanted to drive the conversation. Annie sat directly behind me, and each set of parents flanked her on either side. There was a table in the middle of the room with two chairs that were chained to the floor on the opposite side of the table. John Jr. was the first one to be led in, and was chained at both the hands and ankles. He was seated and chained to the same fixtures on the floor to which the chair was connected. He nervously looked at us, but said nothing.

Johnny was then led in by two extra officers due to the aforementioned altercation. He too was chained at the hands and ankles, but had an additional chain connected to a loop around his neck. If he moved any part of himself more than minimally, he was choked by this loop. He was seated and chained to the floor. He looked at us vacantly, then looked down, and said nothing.

"I told you to stay away from Santiago, didn't I? Look where it got you," John growled, looking at Johnny.

Johnny said nothing and continued to glare at the floor.

"How are you, John?" I asked nervously.

He looked at me for a second, shook his head, and asked, "Why?"

"Do you know why we are here?" I asked, a little bit more confidently.

"I literally have no idea why you'd ask to see us, least of all, you," John said callously.

"Was my grandfather ever here?" I asked, concerned perhaps we had been sent here without any possibility of doing as we were asked.

"Yeah, he was here," John barked, "but why the hell would *you* come here?"

"We came here to talk, John. I need *you* to know I have forgiven you," I said, surprised I could say what I had.

Everyone in the room looked at me. I felt Annie's head press against my back. I had said something I told myself, but never really believed, but it was true. I had learned in one of my psych courses what negativity does to the subconscious over time and actively sought to put the events of that night behind me. I'd done quite a bit to accomplish this. Meditation was the primary activity, though it was in its infancy back then. Thing is, I never before said aloud I had forgiven John or Johnny. The truth I felt as I said it was real, and I trusted it.

"You forgive me? That's interesting because who says I forgive you?" John snapped back.

"Well, John, if you haven't forgiven me, that is not something I can affect. Forgiveness comes from within as one accepts it," I said as I recalled what a colleague told me on the subject, and realized how right it really was.

Johnny looked up at me, a horrible scowl on his face.

"I know I hurt both of you, and I'm sorry," I said, trying to be as sincere as I could.

"You put us in the hospital for over a month, Olaf. Why the hell would we forgive you?!" John yelled.

"You tried to kill him, John. You have no room to say a single word here," Mother said calmly.

"And you, Johnny, you tried to kill your cousin. For what?" Dr. Glaush asked aggressively.

Johnny continued looking down, unmoving. John sank in his chair, the weight of the situation taking a toll. He sat for a few seconds, gathered himself, and looked me square in the eyes.

"What would forgiveness do for me? Why would I give you that satisfaction?" he asked with a softer voice.

"John, your forgiveness does nothing for me. You forgive to no longer allow something or someone to continue causing you pain. You can never truly heal from that night until you forgive *yourself*. I come second here, but it's not my call, when or even if, you forgive me," I said, looking right back at him as I spoke.

When I said that, an enormous weight lifted from the room.

"Wow, son. I never looked at it that way, but you're right," Father said.

"Yep, I agree. I did not look at this as something *I* had to do, but you're right, Olaf. I think we all had this wrong," Dr. Glaush said introspectively.

Johnny looked up at me, still saying nothing. He then looked at his dad and said, "You were right about Santiago, Dad. Thing is, he never would have left me alone unless I hurt him, so I did."

"But that was an idiot move. You had a job lined up after the joint that is gone now, and your sentence increased," John said angrily.

"I know," Johnny said and cast his eyes down again.

"Johnny, I forgive you too," Annie said softly from behind my back.

Johnny again looked up, his expression decidedly different.

"Annie, I– I'm– I'm so, so sorry," he said, a single tear falling down his right cheek. "I should have never done what I did. You had no part in it."

"No, Johnny you shouldn't have. Let me be very clear about something here for both of you. Forgiveness is one thing, but trust is something completely different. Just because you are forgiven does not mean trust is restored," Mrs. Glaush said confidently.

"I understand, Helene," John said calmly. "Just please don't hold this against Mary Ann."

"We're taking her to dinner after this, John," Dr. Glaush said.

"I'm so glad to hear that. She misses you so much, Helene," John said, choking up.

"I understand you are almost done with your law degree, Johnny. Do you know what kind of law you would like to practice?" I asked.

He looked at me for a second, assessing what he should say. Eventually, he took a breath and said, "I'm hoping to become a criminal defense attorney, but I'm not sure what this sentence does to my chances."

"I think that's incredible, Johnny," I said genuinely.

"You're getting a law degree?" Annie asked, coming out from behind me.

"Yeah, but it's just undergraduate. I have to go to law school to be able to practice. I am in a program that was going to give me a paid internship I could do while I went to law school, but I think I screwed that up," Johnny said calmly, his eyes still red.

"Still, it's wonderful you've accomplished what you have," Annie said.

"Olaf, I'm truly sorry for what I did to you. I really—God above—I really hope you meant what you said. I think about it almost every day," John said, his eyes heavy with emotion.

I reached across the table and John reached out his shackled hands as far as he could. I grabbed them both, looked him in the eye, and said, "I meant it, John. You have to forgive yourself and let this go now."

John's *vox corporis* then spoke. *"Hello Olaf. Thank you for saying that—he needed to hear it again to believe it."*

I smiled, squeezed his hands a little tighter, and said, "If you need to talk this through beyond tonight, I am absolutely game."

"I would like that—in fact I think I need that," John said and cracked a small smile.

"Olaf, would you do that for me too?" Johnny asked sheepishly.

"Of course, Johnny. I think since we were all in this from the start, we can all come out of it together too," I said as I released my grip on John's hands.

As the tension in the room loosened, the other people present began to participate in the conversation. Both Dr. and Mrs. Glaush forgave Johnny sincerely, and my parents forgave John with truth in their voices.

The visit concluded with a feeling that wounds sown with years of emotion and angst had started to finally heal. To Mrs. Glaush's point, forgiveness and trust were two different things, but that night, both began to head in the direction Grandfather and Mr. Malloy had hoped. The house repairs had begun, and that was the most important first step.

We headed to Salters, a seafood restaurant not far from the jail to meet Mrs. Malloy. We were seated and all ordered drinks. We were all on our second round by the time Mrs. Malloy arrived. She walked in, took a look at us, and turned around to leave. Mrs. Glaush saw this and ran over to her, grabbing her in a wicked embrace, of which I think only sisters are capable.

The two cried and said unintelligible things to one another, using a form of communication, again only sisters are capable of understanding.

They eventually walked over to where we were seated, each with an arm around the other. Instead of walking to her seat, though, Mrs. Malloy walked over to me, wound up, and smacked the back of my head fairly hard.

"Mary Ann! What are you doing?" Mrs. Glaush asked, shocked at what she had just seen.

I turned around, and she quickly wound up and smacked me across the face. Father began to get up from his chair, but I held up my hand to keep him where he was. She again wound up and fired, but I caught her wrist before she struck me. With her opposing hand, she again swung, and I caught that wrist too before it could strike.

"How could you do that to my boys, you *monster*?!" Mrs. Malloy screamed as the rest of the restaurant watched.

I stood, still holding her wrists. I looked squarely at her and said, "Mrs. Malloy, your husband tried to kill me. I did what I had to do to defend myself. I gave your son a chance to avoid violence, and he did not take it. I am sorry for hurting them as I did, but neither man acted as they should have that night, and they were punished for it based on their choices. Your boys are now able to let this go. Are you?"

With this, tears started pouring out of her eyes. I released her wrists and hugged her gently; she reluctantly embraced me as well, and when she sensed I was being genuine, she too hugged me tightly. We stood there for a couple seconds as she gathered herself. Annie handed me a napkin I then passed to Mrs. Malloy, and she dabbed at her swollen, red eyes.

"I'm sorry Olaf, it's just so hard for me. All of it," Mrs. Malloy said sadly.

"I can only imagine, Mrs. Malloy. That's why we are all here tonight," I said.

Mrs. Glaush got up from her seat, her eyes also noticeably damp. She quickly walked over to her sister and the two hugged and cried together with more sister babble, from which none of us could infer meaning.

Eventually, they both sat down, and we had a pleasantly uneventful dinner. Well, aside from my throbbing head; I wore a horrible headache due to the smacks I received. The sole positive was that it garnered quite a few conciliatory, "Aw, babe," moments from Annie, and made me *almost* completely unconcerned with the discomfort.

When the night came to an end, we all hugged Mrs. Malloy. She again apologized to me, and I made it clear to her all was forgiven. As we finished saying our goodbyes, it became obvious that the deep division between the Malloys and the Glaushs was no more. For our part, we forgave the events of that awful night, and I believe the Malloy men had as well. I think, as a result, we did exactly as Grandfather and Mr. Malloy wanted. The house was fixed.

Knowing this, my brain immediately turned to my next item: telling Annie about my ability. My anxiety was akin to a heart attack, dear Reader. I had decided to take her to one of our favorite places: a little inlet jutting off the Intracoastal Waterway where we saw all kinds of marine wildlife. We saw dolphins there all the time. There was an occasional manatee, a host of turtles and fish, and birds galore. It was a lovely place to relax and watch nature happen. I figured, if nothing else, I would be able to ease into the conversation and quickly change topics if necessary.

I told Annie I would pick her up from the farm around four o'clock or so. I was home, tending the orchard with Mother, and she could see I was very nervous.

"Sweetheart, what's bothering you? You're so quiet this morning," she said as she inspected an apple tree.

"Well, Mother, I'm going to finally tell Annie about my ability, and the thought is holding me hostage," I said, looking at the cherries.

"You haven't told her yet?! My goodness, Olaf, you've been together for quite a few years now!" she exclaimed.

"Honestly, this has never come into my mind, Mother. I haven't consciously kept it from her, but realize this is something of a key detail she needs to know. I made a ring for her, Mother. I'm going to propose, but not before she knows about my ability," I said, moving to my next tree.

"Aw, Olaf, you two are so good together!" Mother said as she came over to me. "I think this will go fine as long as her voice—what do you call it now?"

"*Vox corporis.*"

"That's right—that Latin thing. You and your father—I swear! You have to take simple things and make them elegant. Regardless, as long as her *vox corporis* helps like it did for me, your father, Grandfather, and Nol, all should be okay," she said, moving from me to the next apple tree.

"That's the thing, Mother. The *vox corporis* is a fickle thing. I've heard Annie's quite a few times, but it's been at very random times. I'm not sure if 'she' will talk in this instance," I said, moving over to my big addition in the orchard: grapes. Father and I had planted thirty grapevines as an experiment the week prior.

"I don't think you have anything to worry about, silly thing. Just be you and even if you don't hear it, all will be fine. You have handled far more difficult situations recently," she said confidently.

"I'm not so sure, Mother. I am nervous this may cast me in a bad light with her," I said.

"If it does, Olaf, she is not the person I think she is, and you wouldn't need her anyway."

"Easy for you to say, Mother. It's not that simple. I'm not sure what I would do if the conversation went south. She's deeply involved with the farm now, and beyond my feelings, that would be abject hell to handle," I said, the realization of this truly making me second guess saying anything at all.

"Olaf, Sweetheart, relax. You're taking your brain to a fatalistic place, and you need to stop. Annie is in love with you. That is clear to me. In my experience, love conquers all, and this will be no different," she said reassuringly.

"I so hope you're right, Mother," I said nervously.

We finished our audit of the orchard and went in to cook lunch. Even as an adult, Mother and I cooked together for at least one meal per week. Our record, though, was when we cooked every meal together for a string of six weeks. It was so nice to spend all that time in the kitchen with Mother, and we happily forced Father to eat shepherd's pie twice. Yes, dear Reader, he disappointingly sighed and we laughed mightily both times.

The afternoon seemed to fly by, much to my chagrin. Four o'clock rolled around, and I picked up Annie, who skipped out to the car.

"Where we goin' today, babe?" she asked excitedly and leaned in for a kiss.

"The inlet. We haven't been in a few weeks," I said nervously.

"What's wrong, weirdo?" she asked playfully.

"Nothing, Sweetheart, just been a busy day so far. I desperately need *you* time," I said, re-thinking my plan due to pure nervousness.

The inlet was about forty-five minutes away. During the car ride, we talked about the farm, the Rodriguez clan and the impending additions, and the things we knew about what my grandfather had done for everyone. We did not know the extent of the changes to the farm property, nor the monetary amounts given to certain people.

When we finally arrived at the inlet, we walked our normal path out to a little hill that overlooked everything. We sat and saw a familiar pod of dolphins swim by, seemingly chatting the whole way. I watched a sea turtle surface and quickly head back down into the water. An osprey surveyed the water in search of dinner, but headed out along the Intracoastal Waterway to continue the search. The whole time I tried desperately to clear my mind and prepare myself for the conversation I knew was long overdue.

"Babe, I need to talk to you about something," I said nervously.

"I knew there was something. What's wrong?" she asked gently.

"There's something– something about me that–" I began.

"*She knows, Olaf, and it's not a big deal. I promise you,*" her *vox corporis* said.

I had no idea what to say. I knew that the *vox corporis* solely spoke truth, but I found this incredibly hard to believe.

"Something about you? What, weirdo?"

"I can–"

"You can–?"

"I–"

"You?"

"I'm sorry Annie, this is so hard for me," I said, rubbing my forehead.

In typical Annie fashion, she sat in front of me, put her hands on my cheeks, pulled me close, and kissed me passionately, holding me gently. She did this whenever she felt I needed it; the last time was at Grandfather's funeral.

She looked me dead in the eyes and said, "I know, weirdo. Nol told me this would be hard for you, so I've been patient. Now spill it, what have you heard my body tell you?"

Tears formed at the corners of my eyes. I was speechless and awestruck and, at the same time angry as anything at Nol.

"Nol told y'all? What the hell is that?" I asked, shocked. "This has been a major secret of mine that seems to be well known. Why aren't y'all upset at me for not telling you?"

"It's easy, babe. I love you. And the way I see it, this voice of mine has paved the way for the best sex any woman has ever experienced, *ever*. There is no way you know to do what you do, when you do, how you do every single time without some kind of inside information," she said seductively. "Besides, my dad told me what you have been doing at the hospital, and it is incredible. He told me the other day that you saved a guy who was unconscious and dying? How in the world?"

"I'm stuck on the Nol thing. Tell me about that, and I'll tell you a bunch," I said with my best bribe voice.

"You must promise to answer every question if I tell you this. He told me if I ever told anyone, lest you, that he would feed me to a shark. I kinda think he might," she said nervously.

"Promise."

"Okay, goes like this. Remember about six months ago, when we were with Sadie and Nol on his family's boat? It was the time that Nol mistakenly ripped Sadie's bikini top off when he threw her in the ocean. Remember?" she asked, her eyes smiling.

"Yes, I definitely remember that. Nol was so worried he royally upset her," I said, recounting the day.

"Yep, and he asked you to find out 'your way' how he should fix it," she said. "I was just about to jump in the water when I heard him say that. It bugged me because I thought maybe you were an assassin, or skilled in the art of torture or something, so I made him tell me."

"How did you 'make' him tell you?" I asked curiously. "Last I checked he had a good foot plus on you and maybe three-hundred pounds."

"Well–"

"Annie–?"

"I promised to tell him a secret want of hers that would be valuable for him to know," she said alluringly.

"A secret want?" I asked, completely confused.

"Think bedroom."

"Okay?"

"That girl has specific things she likes to do and others that she had wanted to, um. . have done that Nol wasn't picking up on. He knew something was amiss there, and after I filled in the blank, both participants, dare I say, became quite *satisfied.*"

"So you bribed him then?" I asked playfully.

"Pretty much, yeah. Now, spill it," she said, leaning in.

"No, not quite yet, babe. We're not done with Nol yet. I can't possibly begin to believe that was the entirety of the conversation. *You* spill."

Annie took a huge breath and said, "Well, I asked him what it meant. He told me I was hearing things. I told him I wasn't. He said I was. I told him I knew things about his girlfriend. He asked me what things. I told him you tell me, I tell you. He said no. I said these things are mighty valuable. He said he couldn't, that he made a promise. I said I didn't care and needed to know if you weren't an assassin, then what? He said he'd tell me, but if I told anyone he'd feed me to a shark. I told him okay. He told me it was painfully hard for you to tell him about this, and only your family knew. I told him to carry on. He told me you had an ability. I asked him, 'what ability?' He reiterated I would be fed to sharks if I told anyone. I promised I wouldn't. He made me promise this wouldn't make me end our relationship. I said I make no promises if you were in fact skilled in torture or the black arts. He said you weren't. I said okay, spill. He told me you can hear a voice that comes from a person's body, only tells the truth, and it reflects the personality of the person. I thought about this for a second, realized you had to have used said ability between the sheets among other things, made my peace with you not telling me, and proceeded to tell him what I knew about Sadie."

Annie took a breath, looked at me squarely, and said, "Okay, I told you, now spill it."

"What is it y'all want to know? I think you have the bases covered from what Nol told you," I said.

"Let's start with the guy who was unconscious," she said intently.

"Well, I can communicate with a body as long as it is alive. It takes patience at times, but I haven't yet encountered a living person with whose body I cannot communicate."

"So, does that mean you can start a conversation at any time then?" she asked, her curiosity apparent.

"Usually, yes," I said, fearing I knew the next question that was coming.

"Okay, have a conversation with my body then, and tell me what it says," she said, her smile growing.

"Annie, I really don't–"

"Just do this, Olaf. You know that she won't let up until we talk—and frankly I've been waiting for this for quite some time," Annie's *vox corporis* said.

"Okay, and you are right. What would you like to talk about?" I asked awkwardly, as Annie's expression changed to interest.

"Annie really wants to be with you every day. She misses you terribly when you are apart and there is a reason for that," she said.

"I truly feel the same, and I promise it will be addressed soon," I said, gaining some confidence, but being careful not to say something I would regret. Annie's expression drew more intense.

"I need you to know I appreciate you listening to me when there is physical intimacy. Because the physical aspects of those moments have been as profound as they have been, my connection with your essence is equally as profound. There is a connection between me and your essence that will continue to grow deeply, and will be amplified when we are together more. Love is so much more than what is felt physically, and when it grows as deeply as I know yours will, I promise you will see new shades of life as you did when you first heard your Mother's essence speak," she said calmly, but directly.

I paused for a second, then asked, "You know what happened when I first heard Mother's *vox corporis speak* all those years ago?"

"*Yes Olaf, I do. The reason for that, though, is not something that I am going to tell you today,*" she said. "*Now, as to what to say when pressed what this conversation is about, please understand I have shared with you something to be understood nonverbally. I've done so because it was time. However, it is not something to be discussed verbally with Annie. It will be felt and developed as you age. Do you agree to this?*" she asked with an intensity harking back to when Mother's *vox corporis* scolded me.

"I will honor that request, yes. Is there anything else you would like to talk about right now?" I asked, fully committing in my mind what had just been asked of me.

"*Just one more thing, Olaf. I simply want to say I knew this day would come, and I'm so glad that it has. I'll talk to you again soon,*" she said kindly.

I looked up at Annie, whose stare was fixed and intense. "Okay, babe. We talked. What would you like me to tell you?" I asked, grabbing her hand.

"I would like to know all of it. What did she say?" Annie asked intently.

"Well, as is the case with many of these conversations, I can only tell you certain things at the request of the *vox corporis*. That is what I call the voice. It's Latin for 'the voice of the body,'" I said.

"Can you explain that to me? Why can't I hear everything," she asked, her intensity unwavering.

"Well, because what they tell me is never false, oftentimes I am asked to keep certain details 'nonverbal.' This is never the case with someone who is sick, but for those who trust me enough to communicate freely, there are topics I am asked to keep to myself. In this case, the reason for that is simply because of our relationship," I said reassuringly.

"What was the item you said about your Mother?"

"That shocked me, Annie. I've witnessed two *vox corpora* speaking, which is absolutely unreal to me, but your *vox corporis* actually knew about the first time I heard one—Mother's. I was not yet fifteen when that happened!" I said excitedly.

"What can you tell me about what she said?" Annie said, a tad defeated.

"She was so glad that we finally talked, Annie. She said some amazing things I honestly will never forget. I've heard her speak literally for years, babe. I never felt I was able to respond to her, and somehow she knew that," I said.

"When did you first hear her, babe?"

"I heard her after the first time we sat under the oak tree the day of the fight," I said, a chill going down my spine.

"Really? Do you remember what she said?" Annie said, leaning closer to me.

"I'll never, ever forget it. She said, 'Annie needs you in her life, Olaf, and she knows that now.'"

"She does speak truth, babe," Annie said, smiled, leaned in, and kissed me. "Has she told you things when we've made love? I have to believe that she has."

"Yes, Annie, she has. There were specific times, I think for specific reasons, but I'm speculating there."

"Speculate away, my prince! I've never, ever, felt anything like it. The pleasure is so intense I still feel it hours later, all through my body, and babe, it keeps getting *better*. This isn't just the case sexually. Just being close to you makes me feel– loved. I'm not sure how else to describe it. Do you feel it too?"

"Of course I do, my love," I said, as I laid her down and kissed her.

"We are not ending the night without– you–" Annie breathed passionately.

"No, love, we aren't," I whispered.

We laid there for a while, not saying much. I held her next to me, her head on my shoulder and her right arm extended across my chest. I held her close, but she held me closer. We simply but truly experienced that moment—the gentle water sounds of the inlet, moving water in the Intracoastal, bird wings caressing the air, waves in the distance. In the exact same way, I felt Annie's heartbeat and her soft breaths as a gentle warm breeze glided over us. It was as though the things that her *vox corporis* told me about our connection somehow were manifesting. I recognized this, smiled, and submitted to it.

****

The things Annie's *vox corporis* told me were profound in so many ways. The fact she knew the circumstances of my physical changes when I first heard a *vox corporis* confounded me. The fact that our intimacy had created what it had with our "essences," as she had called it, was another topic altogether. After that day, I no longer heard Annie's *vox corporis* when we were intimate. Instead, I *felt* her and the result was more profound than I can, or will even attempt to, express. Mind you, this extended beyond "the sheets" as Annie puts it. Whenever we were together, there was a closeness that produced a calm, a warmth that, in the same way, created a light depression when we were apart.

About a week later, I got a call from Mr. Marks. My jewelry was ready, and he gave me a time to return to his office later that day. I thought I was better prepared this time for the scary men with guns, but to my chagrin, they scared me worse this time. Mr. Marks was his normal cheery self and had me inspect each piece with his guidance.

Annie's rings were stunning—and the necklaces I made for Mother, Mrs. Glaush, and Maria Rodriguez were gorgeous. I thanked him and set upon forming my proposal plan.

I was consumed by thoughts of this proposal. Where I was stuck, though, was whether I took her somewhere private or involved others. I decided to stop by the hospital and show both Father and Dr. Glaush Mr. Marks' creations.

"Holy crap, that's a *ring!*" Dr. Glaush exclaimed. "Annie is going to love that and the band to match is positively gorgeous!"

"You were so kind to make something for Maria, your Mother, and Helene, Olaf. That means a lot to me. I'm sure your grandfather would be very proud," Father said.

We chatted about the proposal and settled on a plan. I picked Annie up and we traveled to the marina where we met Nol and Sadie. Both sets of parents were there, but were hiding in the cabin below deck. I framed the whole thing as a fishing trip, and as soon as we were out to sea, the parents would emerge, and I would propose.

This is precisely what happened. As soon as the parents were on the deck, I got down on one knee, and said, "Annie, I have loved you for as long as I remember knowing you. You are my everything. So, would you please be my everything forever?" I produced her ring, then asked, "Annie, will you marry me?"

Her eyes got wide and teary; she nodded furiously and said, "Of course I will, babe!"

I put the ring on her finger, and she hugged me tightly. Mother and Sadie both dabbed at tears and the men in attendance nodded in approval. Annie looked in awe at her ring, which blinded anyone unfortunate enough to look directly at it when the sun was reflecting off it. The center stone was near flawless and cut in such a way that refracted light like a laser beam in every direction. I kept the matching band a secret, which drove her insane.

"In due time, love. You need to have something to look forward to," I said.

"I *have* something to look forward to already—being your wife. Show me the ring!" she demanded.

"In time, love," I said slyly and kissed her cheek.

I had brought the mothers' gifts as well, and handed them to both Mrs. Glaush and Mother. I had given Maria her necklace earlier that day. They were each slightly different, but similar enough to keep the meaning of the day. They were wrapped, which seemed to confound both women.

"Who wrapped these things, Olaf? It's like a damn fortress," Mrs. Glaush said angrily.

"A guy in a fortress, Mrs. Glaush," I responded.

"Son, no more Mrs. Glaush. Sierra, I hope you're okay with this. Olaf, I am 'Mom' to you from this moment forward. Clear?"

"Of course, Helene!" Mother said.

Eventually, Nol produced his pocket knife and the containers were cut open. Both women could not believe their eyes, and Father was perhaps the most surprised.

"Dad had all of this in a safe deposit box *and forgot about it?*" he asked, astonished.

"That's what his note said, yeah. I was able to make both of Annie's rings and the necklaces with the contents of that safe deposit box," I said.

"Yeah, the ring I'm not allowed to see," Annie said sarcastically.

"In time, love. I promise, it's worth the wait," I said calmly.

With that, the fishermen and fisherwomen began the task of catching dinner whilst bashing my knowledge of the topic, as was the pattern. The lot of us went back to the Glaushs' to have a cookout. They had decorated the house with "Happy Engagement" fodder with Gill, of all people, doing much of the decorating. He was first to greet me when we arrived at the house.

"Congratulations, Olaf! I am so happy for you! Annie, I need to see this ring, Dad told me—" Gill said before Annie held out her hand. "– HOLY GOD LOOK AT THAT ROCK!" he exclaimed.

We had a wonderful evening. Dinner was delicious and the conversations were light, but energized. We talked about the wedding, which was, to our surprise, already essentially planned. Our fathers talked about what they had learned both from their envelopes and Mr. Malloy. We were both astounded by what Grandfather had done for us. The lot of us started talking about timing. Sadie was going to be Annie's maid of honor and Nol was going to be my best man, but he had to report to New York in a couple weeks for training camp. Because of this, we didn't plan to go to Hawaii until after his season ended.

Our night ended and the crowd dispersed. Annie and I retired to the bench under the huge oak tree—where our romantic relationship started. She brought a blanket and wrapped it around us before doing her normal pretzel-like arm-leg wrap thing that essentially bound us together in several places.

"So, fiancé, here we are," she said gently.

"Are you happy about this, love?" I asked. "We're still relatively young."

"I would have married you at eighteen, weirdo. Yours are the only arms meant to hold me," she said. "I knew that a long time ago."

We sat there under that tree having taken a leap toward our future. I found such comfort in just having her close to me. Her heartbeat and breath took every bit of stress I had and wiped it away. When the time came for me to return home, I attempted to unwind myself from the pretzel, but was stopped as Annie tightened her grip.

"Not yet, you," she said, got up and led me to the guest house she had been living in. She said nothing, lit a bevy of candles, undressed, and took me by hand into the bedroom.

We said nothing; we made love, but it was different than in the past. It was something more than sex. It was a communion of two souls. Our lives were slowly merging together in a way I couldn't verbalize, but could definitely feel. If this was the definition of a "soulmate," I had found mine.

Christopher Waniglia's Final Act

Talk of the envelopes the night of the engagement dinner reminded me—I needed to make an appointment with Mr. Lating and Annie. I did so, and he indicated that we needed daylight and a couple hours to spend. Apparently, Father also needed to be available, "if necessary." I found the requirement to be strange, but I nevertheless assembled the group with the needed requirements.

On the day of the appointment, I picked up Annie, and we headed to Mr. Lating's office. He promptly said, "Come with me," and we followed him out to his car. "We have a short drive ahead of us. I've chilled champagne and have two glasses back there if you'd be so inclined to have some bubbly," he said, much more relaxed than I had ever heard him.

"Don't mind if I do! Babe—bubbly!" Annie said, happily.

I poured us both a glass, and in so doing, lost where we were. I had been keeping track of our location to try and figure out where in the world we were going. When I looked up again, I had absolutely no idea where we were. We drove east—that I knew as it was passed midday and the sun was behind us. I didn't recognize where we were though.

We got to a stop light, and Mr. Lating handed us each a blindfold. "I'm sorry—Chris' orders. Please put these on until we get out of the car. It won't be too much further now," he said apologetically. With blindfolds on, we continued for several blocks and twisty roads. Finally, the car stopped and Mr. Lating said, "We're here! One second and I'll get you out."

When Annie's door opened, I could hear the familiar sounds of the Intracoastal Waterway. When I was let out, I confirmed that with the smell in the air.

"Okay you two—before you take your blindfolds off, I need to explain something. Christopher did quite a bit of looking and research before he settled here. Annie, you are a big reason for the location based on the conversations you had with him. In fact, you presently own this..." Mr. Lating said, then paused. "Now, take your blindfolds off."

I was correct, in that we were right by the Intracoastal Waterway. Before me was an impressively sizable home under construction, sitting at an odd angle. Father soon emerged, and exclaimed, "Welcome home, kids!"

We all went inside and Father giddily showed us around. The house was in the midst of being finished inside. The floors were still just plywood and the walls, in most cases, were studs. The kitchen was immense and the appliances were set in the middle of the room, waiting to be installed.

"Olaf, you have no idea how hard it's been for me to keep this secret. Annie sweetheart, your dad agonized too—he helped me with this. Your grandfather had a very specific goal for this house, and it took both Franklin and I to win over Mr. Toth's builders to fulfill it. Here's the thing, you have a two-acre plot that is mostly pointed northeast due to the lay of the land and the Intracoastal. Dad needed you to have a house that caught the easterly breeze off the ocean, and that was a crazy fight with the builder he knew would have to be fought. So, your house is angled kinda funky, but you got a wickedly creative deck because of it," Father said excitedly. He was right; the deck off the back was a nonstandard shape that gave us an amazing view of the Intracoastal Waterway, and at the same time, we could see waves crashing down on a beach maybe a half mile or so away.

Mr. Lating then said, "Yes, Christopher was very specific that this house was to have a chef's kitchen, a master suite with a fireplace, and at least four bedrooms. In addition, it was to have an office capable of holding a desk for each of you and plenty of storage was essential. Lastly, with the easterly facing, the exterior has been triple reinforced and has very specific protections for hurricanes around the whole of the structure. Annie, do you recall the document I had you sign?"

"Yes. You essentially had me sign it, but wouldn't let me read it. I remember that," she said nervously.

"Trust me when I say this, my dear—your father reviewed it prior to your signing. He never would have had you do such a thing blindly," he said reassuringly.

"This is true, Annie. He reviewed it and ensured you weren't signing anything you'd regret," Father said.

"That document made you the owner of the land and allowed building to begin. What we'll need to do is transition the deed to both of your names. This is on tap in addition to a couple other things later today. So, as much as I hate to say it, we have to head back to the office in order to have enough time for the next item. You will have time to come back here for sunset—promise," Mr. Lating said.

"Your house sits high enough to the east, and both high and away enough to the west, that you can see sunrises *and* sunsets. I came out and have verified both, per your grandfather's request," Father said, smiling.

Annie and I were positively stunned; while this wasn't the inlet we had frequented for a couple years, it was our own piece of earth in a location that was almost identical to it. We would be able to sit out on that eclectic deck of ours and watch a myriad of sea creatures and other activity on the Intracoastal. Our children would know this place as home. None of this had really sunk in yet; we just looked at each other with semi-vacant stares, attempting to comprehend what we had just seen.

We got back into Mr. Lating's car and very promptly, Annie said, "Babe—bubbly!"

I smiled and obliged.

Mr. Lating looked back at us, smiling. "So, what do you two think?" he asked, a twinkle in his eyes.

"I'm stunned, Mr. Lating. This doesn't feel real yet," I said.

"Me too. I haven't processed this yet," Annie said after a sip of champagne.

"Well, I promise you both this is real! If you're ready, we have three more stops to make," Mr. Lating said happily.

"Three more? I thought we just had to go back to your office," I said, confused.

"Well, that's one of the three. Sit back, have some bubbly and enjoy the ride. This time, maybe you can get a sense of how to get to your house. It's super simple once you get out to the main drag. I'll give you a map as soon as we get back to my office," Mr. Lating said.

He was right; I knew where we were when we got out onto the main road. In fact, we weren't far from our inlet at all, and maybe twenty-five minutes each way to either the farm or toward our parents' houses. And no more than thirty-five minutes to the hospital. Location-wise, this couldn't have been any better. It was apparent Grandfather had indeed done some serious research before buying this land.

We drove to the farm next, speaking of, and found Mr. Toth standing in a spot by the barn.

"Okay kids—stop one of three. Let's go talk to Mr. Toth," Mr. Lating said.

We approached Mr. Toth, who wore a bright smile and a look indicating he was eager to reveal his part of this. He extended his hand to me and kissed Annie on the cheek.

"Been a busy day thus far for you two, but I must say it's just getting started," he said. "Where we are standing is to be the site of your new office. It will have enough space for both of you to work comfortably, but there will also be conference space and additional work areas should the need arise. Then, if you look over here toward the barn, you should see an outline of what the new barn, completely designed in concept by Chris, will be. Your need for equipment space has increased three-fold, so this new barn will accommodate that need. Lastly—your grandfather's house. Olaf, I mentioned this to you when this project started. The one detail, left untouched per Chris' wishes, is that porch swing. Shall we take a look inside?" Mr. Toth rattled off.

"We're going to have an office?" Annie asked emotionally. "I've been working on the Rodriguez's kitchen table. I haven't been able to go back into the house since Chris...."

"I can't go back in either, babe," I said sadly.

"While I completely understand how you both feel, please come with me," Mr. Toth said.

He led us up to Grandfather's house. I had spent years of my life, cumulatively speaking, in that house. When he died, the house changed. Even though it was filled with memories, it became an entity that no longer felt comfortable. I felt a heavy sadness grow with each step toward the door.

"Now, I know you both have a ton of history here, and the good parts I think are still here. The rest is now transitioning to a duplex so the boys will have their own living space," Mr. Toth said calmly.

He opened the door, and the house we knew was gone. The only thing that remained was his kitchen table in the near corner. Annie and I saw this, and we both absolutely lost it.

"It's amazing, Mr. Toth, but I just can't...." I said, sniffing.

"It's okay son. I completely understand. Just know, when you can, that table where you sat for all those years, and Annie, where you and Chris talked so often, will be right here. This is too important an artifact and space to lose. So, when you're ready, come back. I promise both of you—one day you'll sit there with your kids and talk about their great-grandfather," Mr. Toth said kindly.

"Okay, enough tears, enough sadness. This is a happy day! Let's go kids!" Mr. Lating said cheerily.

"This is true—sorry to have given you a downer, you two. Trust me, this place is becoming what the two of you have built it to be. You will see that soon," Mr. Toth said. "Oh, by the way, how 'bout that house of yours? Like it so far?"

"I've dreamed about that house for years, but you took that dream and made it better. Thank you so much, Mr. Toth," Annie said as she dabbed at her eyes.

We again piled into Mr. Lating's car, and before Annie could say it, I filled her glass and chugged the rest of the champagne from the bottle.

"You may have needed more of that after our next stop, Olaf. I get it, though," Mr. Lating said. We headed toward town and about twenty minutes later, arrived at an office. "Okay kids. This next guy is a little high strung—be forewarned," Mr. Lating said.

We went inside and were introduced to a man named Mr. Bace, pronounced "Bahchay". He was a small Italian guy and very well dressed. The look on his face was panic; that was unmistakable. Oddly, a pair of EMTs sat in the back corner of the room.

"You were *that* proactive, Thomas? Come on," Mr. Lating said condescendingly.

"Joe—after what I been through… *Damnit*," Mr. Bace said angrily. "You two—sit."

Annie and I looked at each other curiously. I said hello to the EMTs, and we sat down.

"Every damn person who sat in those chairs went in an ambulance after I told 'em what I told 'em. I ain't takin' chances *no more*. We are here to talk about your financial inheritance from Christopher Waniglia. You are his grandson and you are his fiancé—right?" Mr. Bace said emphatically.

"Yes sir, that is correct. I must ask—what in the world caused people to need emergency care?" I asked, profoundly confused.

Mr. Bace looked at Mr. Lating and asked, "He doesn't know anything?"

"No—that was Chris' request, Thomas. It'll be okay—I promise," Mr. Lating said.

Mr. Bace looked at the EMTs, looked back at us, looked at the EMTs, put his head in his hands, started mumbling something that sounded like emphatic Italian, looked back at the EMTs, and said, "Your bus is runnin', right?"

"Yes, sir. We are ready per your request," one of the EMTs said.

"I ain't comfortable with you's being all the way over there. Get closer," Mr. Bace said. Both rolled their eyes and moved behind us. "If they faint or somethin', you can catch 'em?" Mr. Bace said nervously.

"Yes, sir. I have to say though, if we get a real emergency, we're going to have to leave. You understand that, right?" the EMT behind me said.

"Real emergency? REAL EMERGENCY?! How is this not an emergency?!" Mr. Bace yelled, and then bellowed an extended diatribe in Italian.

"Thomas, why don't you just tell the kids what you have to tell them and be done with it? This is getting a tad ridiculous, don't you think?" Mr. Lating asked.

"Joe—your mouth needs to stop. *Dammit*," Mr. Bace said.

The lot of us giggled at this most recent response. Truthfully, the whole display was entertaining.

Mr. Bace took a deep breath, then a sip of water. He began, "As I was saying, we are here to talk about your financial inheritance from Christopher Waniglia. Son—Olaf—you have run the farm for quite a few years, right?"

"Yes sir, that is correct," I said.

"And in that time, you only took $100 a month as payment?" Mr. Bace said coarsely.

"I wouldn't say every month, no. I just took gas money and a little bit of spending money before my time in the hospital. I wanted the money to remain for Grandfather's care and the costs of the farm," I said.

"Babe, you've paid me much more than that. Why did you take so little?" Annie asked.

"You earned it, love, and you had many more expenses than I did. I made sure everyone at the farm got what they needed, and a little bit more to keep life enjoyable," I said.

"Well kid, apparently your grandfather disagreed with you," Mr. Bace said condescendingly.

"What are you talking about sir? I talked to my grandfather about this all the time," I said sternly.

"He felt you were worth much more than you were being paid. He knew you wouldn't take it, so he took everything you should have been making and invested it with me. This started about six years ago," Mr. Bace said.

"But—his medical care. Father and I ensured he had the highest standard of care in that time frame. That wasn't cheap," I said. This very much concerned me.

"Kid, I know. Honestly though, it was a drop in the ocean compared to the farm's income, less cost. You arranged care that averaged $150,000 per year until you brought in the Rodriguez family. At that point, the cost dropped to $95,000 due to Maria's influence," Mr. Bace said.

"Okay, but then I built the Rodriguez's home. I paid for that out of the farm's assets. It was $575,000," I said, getting very confused.

"Kid, I know. That still is a drop in the bucket. You know this. You've run the books for years now," Mr. Bace said emphatically.

"Yes, I did, and I never saw huge outflows of cash that would have come to you. So how did y'all get the money?" I asked angrily.

"Easy kid. I know I'm the one that needs these bozos if you get angry," Mr. Bace said, motioning to the EMTs. "Do you recall your Grandfather asking you to account for 'equipment money', and at other times, 'Thomas money'?"

I thought about it and remembered many instances of that request. "Yes, I remember that, but I don't remember there being a pattern to it. It was just an as-needed item," I said.

"Well, your grandfather knew you'd figure out what he was doing if he did it in a normal pattern. It worked out to be quarterly," Mr. Bace said.

"But—I know the equipment was worked on, and the 'Thomas money' was for crop dusting," I said, trying to recall those conversations.

"Well kid, he duped you kinda bad. The equipment cost was never more than $200. Each crop dust was $75. Chris had deals with everybody," Mr. Bace said as he cracked a smile.

I thought some more and remembered many conversations about both topics. There were plane issues that my grandfather helped with, and the equipment guy always needed a little extra for a variety of reasons.

"But—I remember so many conversations where I could justify the expense based on what he said," I said as this ruse became a tad obvious.

"Looks like he got 'ya babe," Annie said, smiling.

"Kid—you have no idea the conversations Chris and I had when we talked about the money. We laughed so hard we cried. He felt awful that he was being dishonest, but he needed you to get the money you deserved, and he positively knew you wouldn't take," Mr. Bace said.

"This is true, Olaf. Your grandfather and I talked about this as well. He felt bad, but also felt it was unethical for the farm to be making what it was on account of what you had done if you weren't being paid. It never set right with him that you did not take an appropriate salary. I mean—my God, Olaf—the original Toth deal was worth $4 million all by itself, with monthly income of an additional $300,000. You did that by yourself, and the net cost to the farm was *nothing*. The whole of that deal was free money. *Free*, Olaf. There are at least ten other deals where the cost to income ratio was less than one to *fifty-thousand*. You were brilliant, positively brilliant, throughout and should have been taking a salary. Thomas—Hollister Toth was also a source of money to you, correct?" Mr. Lating said.

"Whoa—wait a second. The Toth deal didn't make an additional $300,000 a month," I said nervously.

"Yes, kid, it did. I've thus far received sixty-two payments from him of $300,000 apiece. I've also received quarterly payments from Chris ranging from $17,000 to $30,000 for the past five years. With an average annual rate of return at 16.5%, what would that give you approximately?" Mr. Bace asked.

"Um, I think that would be over $20 million dollars, easily," I said.

"You're close, kid. It was $37,675,612," Mr. Bace said.

I sat back in my chair, astonished. All of this had happened without me knowing it.

"Gentlemen, what else don't I know about the business I've run for the past five years?" I asked, concern obvious in my voice.

"Chris knew this would hit you hard, Olaf. Please read this," Mr. Lating said, handing me an envelope.

I opened it and the note read:

"My Dear Olaf,

Please don't be upset. I hated keeping this from you, but if we go back to when you worked summers with me, you would only take $20 a day. Those days, you worked sixteen hour days and cooked me both lunch and dinner. When you got older, I _forced_ you to take $100 a month for gas money, and if you remember, you fought me on that detail for months.

Olaf, you took a farm that was barely breaking even and turned it into a fortified business making on average $16 million a year in net profit. I had never seen a million dollars in my life, and you, my dear grandchild, gave me that chance. The care you arranged for me was exemplary. The things you did on my behalf went so far beyond what I needed.

The secrets are no more. I've instructed both Thomas and Joe to inform you as to the actual state of income and the business. Again, I am sorry I kept this from you, but there was no other way for me to get you what you deserve.

Love,

Grandfather"

I closed the letter and tried my best to process what it said.

"So, effectively, the costs I thought were present for equipment and crop dusting were mostly bunk and there was an extra stream of income I was not aware of. Is there anything else?" I asked, exasperated.

Annie grabbed my hand. "Babe—you okay?" she asked.

"I really don't know, love. This is big, and I cannot believe I was duped like this," I said.

"Well, if it makes you feel any better, there were many more people involved in the cover-up because we all knew you'd never take what you deserved," she said.

"Wait—you were a part of this?" I asked, absolutely shocked.

"In truth, pretty much everyone you know was. Nol, Sadie, your parents, my parents, me, the Toths…" Annie said casually.

"It's true, Olaf. Some of this got pretty extravagant," Mr. Lating said.

"Why did all of you do this? I'm confused, and honestly, pretty upset about it," I said.

"That's why, babe. What would you have said to any of us if we asked you to pay yourself, say $200, one month? Or—let's take it up a notch and say I asked you to pay yourself what you pay me. What would you say to that, prior to knowing this?" Annie asked. "You would have gotten upset. That is a plain fact every last one of us knew—and we positively love you for it. My mom hasn't a clue why you're this way, but she respects you."

"Kid, you have no idea the guilt your grandfather had when he came here. It was awful. That's why he enlisted the help. Honestly, I loved meeting everyone and heard some stories about you I still can't believe. The Toth deal—that's one. You were sixteen years old. There are three others that the brightest people I know couldn't come up with, and you did before you were twenty. The respect I, and everyone involved, have for you is monumental," Mr. Bace said.

"It's true, Olaf. I could not wait to meet you because I too am in awe of your skill in business," Mr. Lating said kindly.

"See, babe—we did this for you because we love you. We respect you. And, we know you're so damn stubborn you never take what is rightfully yours," Annie said.

"Okay, okay—I get it. But, what about the taxes? My God, I never reported any of the Toth dollars to the accountant. And—anything else that was taken out of the business and invested. That never would have been reported either," I said nervously.

"That is covered, Olaf. Hollister worked with your grandfather, and then Annie when she was in the picture, to ensure everything was reported to the accountant. Thomas worked with him too, so there are no issues there either. There are no loose ends. I have all the records back at the office to give you," Mr. Lating said reassuringly.

"Okay, so can I tell you the news that has these gentlemen here?" Mr. Bace asked, motioning to the EMTs.

I nodded, still in a form of shock. Mr. Bace produced several glasses and poured something brown into all of them. He passed them out, and Annie promptly handed hers to me.

Mr. Bace then winced and said, "Gentlemen! Please be ready! Olaf, Annie, I am pleased to tell you that you have inherited $12,345,678.90. It is expected that 60% of this balance remain with me for a period of at least five years—and the remaining 40% be transferred to a combination of personal joint investment accounts and joint banking accounts within 48 hours. The amount was specified by Chris himself, and when he did, he laughed so hard he cried."

Annie looked at me, tears in her eyes. "Babe—thank you so, so much. This is all because of you," she said emotionally.

I attempted to gather myself, but was stuck. Mr. Bace saw this and yelled, "He's crashing! I told you morons! That one—right there! He's fainting!" He then downed his drink in a single gulp and put his head in his hands.

The EMT behind me moved to my side and looked at me. "Sir, are you feeling okay?" he asked, his brow furrowed.

I looked at him, looked back at Annie, then grabbed my first drink and drank it down.

I looked at Mr. Bace, then Mr. Lating, picked up my second glass, and extended it. "Cheers, gentlemen," I said, exhausted.

Mr. Lating smiled and extended his glass as well. Mr. Bace poured a little more into his glass and extended it.

"So, basically you're telling me that I need to find a home for approximately $5 million dollars in two days?" I asked.

"Give or take, yes," Mr. Bace said.

"And the Toth money—it now will flow into the farm's account moving forward, right?" I asked.

"In part, Olaf. Half will go to the farm's investment account, and the other to your joint investment account. This too has been specified by your grandfather," Mr. Lating said.

"So, I'm getting a house that is paid for, my wedding in Hawaii is paid for, and all this money is mine essentially for nothing?" I asked.

"No, babe. You earned every last part of it. You're getting five years of a CEO's salary all at once," Annie said. "That's how Chris explained it to me. He also said that you're still underpaid by the nation's standard," Annie said.

"Yes, Olaf—this is true. Because of that, there will be an automatic draft on a quarterly basis for your salary. You can specify the destination of those funds," Mr. Lating said.

"How much is this draft?" I asked, curious beyond belief.

"It will be two and a half percent of net profit. That amount is bound by the terms of the company charter for the farm your grandfather established four years ago," Mr. Lating said.

I sat and thought about that for a moment. "Are my establishments for the rest of the staff still intact?" I asked.

"Of course, Olaf. As chief executive and owner of the business, your direction remains for those who work for the farm. Your compensation, if you care to look at it this way, is dictated by a third party to protect the business. It is thus out of your hands and instead in the hands of a controller," Mr. Lating said. "I am that controller."

"Sir, if you are okay, we are going to need to leave," the EMT by me said.

"I think we are good here. Thank you, gentlemen," Mr. Bace said.

"You understand that you will be billed for our time, right?" the EMT said coldly.

"Worth every penny—send me the bill," Mr. Bace said.

"If we're all done here, we need to head back to my firm. Everybody ready?" Mr. Lating said.

"What alcohol was that, Mr. Bace? Very tasty," I said.

"I'll send you a case, kid. I have the address," he said.

We all shook hands and left Mr. Bace's office. We piled back into Mr. Lating's car and headed across town.

"How are the both of you feeling? This has been quite a day," Mr. Lating said. "Thankfully, the bulk of what I have for you is rather anemic."

"I knew part of this and I'm at a loss for words. I can't imagine how you feel, babe," Annie said.

"I am numb—positively numb," I said. "I still cannot believe the effort that went into me not knowing about these money flows. The fact I never caught it is unacceptable to me."

"It shouldn't be, Olaf. It was known to all you'd never take what you had rightfully earned, so a collective effort made sure you got it one way or another," Mr. Lating said kindly. "Nothing about that should be unacceptable to you."

"I agree babe—completely," Annie said and smiled at me.

"Where in the holy hell are we putting $5 million dollars, love?" I asked, defeated.

"Hollister Toth made a recommendation that he asked I pass on to you. By the way, Olaf, do you know how much that man adores you? He is easily one of the most influential people in this part of the country, and you have him wrapped around your pinky. Anyway, his recommendation was to keep a predominant amount of the funds with Thomas. No more than $250,000 should be in liquid assets—and of that sum, no more than $100,000 should be in checking. The additional $150,000 solely would allow you to be in the preferred banking program if it were in savings. The gross amount is the most that is insurable too," Mr. Lating said.

"Makes sense, I suppose," I said.

When we finally got back to Mr. Lating's office, we signed a few documents related to the house and a couple others that simply acknowledged our part of the inheritance. He then gave me quite a few folders that documented all the money flows I hadn't been aware of, and also showed me the company charter document that had been updated to include the directive for my income. Lastly, he told us about all the other things that my grandfather had done for everyone.

"Now, there's just one more thing that we need to cover, relative to you, the farm, and your work with the hospital. Your grandfather was specific in his request that you limit your time at the farm. I don't have anything for you to sign, but he knew you saving lives was more important than being at the farm. Please, limit what you do there as much as you can. Annie is running both sales and some operations. The Rodriguez clan is doing the farming. As long as things remain status quo, your time at the farm should be limited. Agree?" Mr. Lating asked.

"For the most part, yes. I think I will keep essentially the same split I have now as long as I can. It's working nicely," I said.

"Babe, seriously. You're working hundred-hour weeks," Annie said sternly. "You can't keep up this pace and get the house ready with me."

"That was your grandfather's concern, Olaf. You are about to get married. You have a new house you'll be moving into. I'm positive you'll want to see Nolan play a few games up in New York. None of these things, including a new marriage, can survive the schedule that you presently have," Mr. Lating said gently.

"I'll say this to both of you then, in the spirit of Grandfather's request, I will try. As soon as the rest of the Rodriguez family is here, that should help. As soon as the new equipment is in, that should help. But, the boys are going to school, and that is a concern. I will positively do what I can to scale back but if things start to suffer at the farm, I will inject my time there. Does that work?" I asked, understanding their concern.

"It works, but listen to me, Olaf Waniglia—I am going to make rules that you must follow. I know you too well, babe. There will be a set of checks and balances, and if it is tested, there will be consequences. Got me?" Annie said authoritatively.

"Hollister told me that you were a strong lady, Annie. You think you can bring his schedule back to the healthy range?" Mr. Lating said enthusiastically.

"Oh Mr. Lating—I know I can," Annie said smugly.

"Really now? You know you can? Mr. Lating, I believe I am being railroaded," I said, smiling.

"Olaf—two things. First, from now on, I am Joe. Mr. Lating is too formal, and I am going to see you frequently enough we should be on a first name basis. Second, if you are being railroaded, it's best not to be in the caboose. Understand what I'm saying?" Joe said.

Annie shot a look at me that put two laser holes through my head.

"Yes, Joe—crystal clear."

"Okay you two, we are done here. I stole the bottle from Thomas—go back to the house, drink, and watch the sunset. Oh, and Olaf, open your last envelope when you can," Joe said.

He then produced the bottle, which turned out to be scotch. I smiled and said, "Looks like I enjoy what Father drinks. This is interesting indeed."

We stood and shook hands. Annie and I headed back to our house, which turned out to be in a gated community, but the gate itself was a good mile and a half from the house.

"I didn't realize this—did you?" I asked Annie.

"No, but I like the security even if it's kind of far from the house," she said.

We made our way past the gate and back to the house. It was an impressive structure; we went through it again, just the two of us, and saw things we had missed earlier. Annie realized many of the details in the design of the house were things she had talked to my grandfather about. The location, the features of the kitchen, the way the rooms were oriented were all things they had talked about at one point or another. The master was pointed toward the East and the rest of the bedrooms were up and away from it, but access to them was quick.

"Perfect for babies, you. Simply perfect," she said happily.

"So, on that topic, how many and when are you hoping for the first?" I asked cautiously.

"Two, in a couple years. I want to live a bit and make sure you are my one before we procreate. Lord knows that we could procreate now, but then I'd have to say I have a 'baby-daddy' to men at the bar because you've tired of me and left me broken hearted and alone," she said half-seriously.

"I'll be long dead before you have such conversations," I said seriously.

"You never know, Mr. Waniglia. I may be the one making you dead. That's part of this review period, you see. Now, if you don't kiss me—right now—you might fail this…."

I picked that woman up and laid a kiss on her that ended her sentence.

"Go ahead and say that, love. What was it about this thing I was failing?" I asked seductively.

"I don't recall saying such a thing, babe. I'm honestly not sure what would give you an occasion to suggest such a thing," she said innocently.

We sat out on our deck and watched the sunset, letting the day set with our star. Our life was slowly starting to take shape despite the blitzkrieg we had endured over the past several days.

The entirety of what Grandfather had done for us—for everyone—was starting to sink in. I'll tell you, dear Reader—it was a lot to absorb. Peace had been made with the Malloys. I was engaged. The Rodriguez family was going to be whole again for the first time in *years*. Annie landed the deal of the century and was given credit for doing so. Nol got the boat of his dreams. Everyone got a windfall of cash. Father and I were introduced to parts of Grandfather's past. The farm was getting a sizable makeover. We had a house on the Intracoastal. Annie and I were getting married in Hawaii. Life for all of us had changed for the better, all because of the incredible Christopher Waniglia.

When I got back to my parents' house, I opened my final letter. It read:

"My Dear Olaf,

So, by now you know everything. You know about the farm, the Rodriguez family, Mr. Marks, Mr. Malloy, Mr. Toth, Mr. Lating, Mr. Bace, your new house, the diamonds, and all that money. I have to tell you, my grandson—it was a hell of a lot of fun to do what I did.

Knowing that you will be where I picked in Hawaii makes me smile as I write this. There are more surprises in store for that trip, and I sincerely promise they are the good kind. It is my intention to be there, with my bride who I've missed for most of my life, watching you and Annie wed in the same paradise where we first kissed.

Olaf, Annie loves you. I saw it in her eyes every time we spoke about you. There is a truth to her that is rare, and it is a truth that is very good for you. Cherish her always, because I know the pain of losing your mate and missing her every day until you die—and that is a life I pray to Heaven you never experience.

Understand life is not work. Rather, understand life is life, and it needs to be lived. You were put here to help people, you were put here to guide and assist in business, but Olaf you were put here to *live*. You were put here to be loved and to know what it means to truly love. Do not, for any reason, ignore those facts. The farm will run. You made it so it will. Patients will get better. You're not the sole person treating them. What you will never get back is time, so take it. Love your girl. Watch sunsets. Watch sunrises, and then go back to sleep. Do what you are good at, but know at the end of the day where your heart, and the body that holds it, belong. Never forget that.

Please Olaf—do not miss me. Know that I am finally home. Know that I am always in your heart. Know that you are always, always in mine. You gave me a lifetime of happiness in the last years of my life on this planet. I am eternally grateful to you, and I hope to God you know that.

I love you with all that I am, was, or will ever be.

Grandpa"

Apparently, I'm Crazy

With all of Grandfather's requests fulfilled, changes to our collective world were fast and furious. The farm changes were transformative; the new barn was massive and the new equipment was gorgeous. Construction completed on Grandfather's house, which in and of itself was impressive. If you can picture it, the front quarter remained completely intact. The rest of it, though, became a large duplex which gave Carlos and Julio perfect living space that wasn't too far away from their family. Speaking of, their relatives arrived. I have never in my life seen emotion expressed so fully in one place as I did when they first entered the house. They cried, they laughed, they yelled fragmented sentences in Spanish, and hugged each other at least a dozen times each. They had a party that night, and the food —holy God the food—was incredible. I happily cherished the leftovers for days after the party.

Maria began work on her cookbook, which was tremendous fun because Annie and I got to be her test subjects. See, Maria never wrote down recipes; she just made food by instinct. She would essentially make a dish, Jose would record what she thought the amount of each ingredient was, and then we would eat it. There were sometimes she made the same dish five, six, seven times just because something wasn't *right* to her. Annie and I were happy to assist with the eating part, and I couldn't tell you how dish A differed from dish B. Everything Maria made had layers upon layers of flavor and determining recipes or her preparation steps was not at all easy for her. I gained an easy five pounds per test, and it was completely worth it!

Our house construction was completed, and we began transitioning our stuff into the new domicile. We bought a ridiculous amount of furniture and useless accoutrement—end tables, couches, chairs, decorative tables, decorative chairs, questionable rack things, massive dog beds, more tables, more chairs, a couple more couches, something I couldn't identify if I tried—and still had radical swaths of space that were awkwardly open. I started living there as it cut my driving distance in half to the farm and hospital. We decided to wait until we were married for Annie to move in, but she fell asleep there more times than I could count on all fingers, toes, and limbs multiplied by three and ended up staying. I'll put it to you this way, dear Reader: she had every one of her dresser drawers full, most of the closet and a good three quarters of the master bathroom occupied by the third time she "fell asleep" at the house.

Nol ended up buying a place up in New York for cash with the money my grandfather gave him, and we collectively moved Sadie up there with him. It was an unexpectedly teary event as Sadie and Annie had gotten extremely close, spending time planning the little bit of the wedding that was left to plan. So, to get the two-way tears to stop falling, I said we would come up for every one of Nol's home games. This didn't placate them, unfortunately, so the tears continued falling. I piled everyone into the car and went to the stadium. I bought tickets for every home game, went to a hotel not far from Nol's house, and booked rooms for all of those dates, found a restaurant not far away (as the sobbing hadn't completely stopped) and got the two ladies good n' numb with strawberry daiquiris. Nol and I looked at each other helplessly throughout, and ended up carrying our respective mates back into his house at the end of the day.

The tears again fell when Annie and I prepared to leave the next day, and emotion was further stirred by mild hangovers in the ladies. So, Nol held Sadie back, and I quickly ushered Annie to our running car when we absolutely had to leave to catch our flight home. It was a little bit like pulling a sugar-deprived child from the steps of a candy store; the pouting that ensued was professional-grade. The fit that accompanied said pouting matched the analogy to a T. I got her to come around by promising she could stay in the house when we got home, and I'd make her favorite dinner. This at least halved the pouting.

The wedding plans were finally complete after our trip to New York! We intended to head to Hawaii the next February and marry on Grandfather's birthday—the 16th. We had everything in place and the waiting game was underway.

I did better, I think, in terms of my schedule. I reduced my schedule to being about sixty hours a week, which was nearly half of where I had been most of the time. I was spending about twenty hours at the farm and the rest at the hospital. I continued to refine my skills with the *vox corporis* and had amazing success working with patients who were unconscious. I got to a point where I was given a rotation and the official title of "Patient Care Consultant", and was put on the hospital payroll. Despite this, there was a sizable quotient of the hospital staff who had no idea who I was.

This came to an unfortunate head one day approximately a month away from our wedding. Father and Dr. Glaush had to go to a conference and took their nursing staff with them to attend a partner training session for nursing staff. I did not go as there were two patients that still needed help. Both were unconscious, both were declining, and though I was making headway, I was nowhere near the point I needed to be for them to be treated. Father had brought in a pair of younger doctors to cover for Dr. Glaush and himself, and informed them that I would remain there addressing patients. He did not explain my role and this became problematic.

The first patient was a lady in her mid-forties who was discovered unconscious in her apartment. Her name was Lucy. There were no drugs nor alcohol in her system and her primary organs were working fine. There was no reason for this woman to be unconscious, and her *vox corporis* was communicating strangely; she only said one phrase: "*Blue oranges.*"

The second patient was a man in his late sixties who was injured in a construction accident. No one saw what happened, but his unconscious body was found lying in a wheelbarrow full of concrete.

Again, there was no obvious reason for him to be unconscious. His name was Charlie.

The replacement doctors—Dr. Small and Dr. Lubbot—did not understand my role, and did not like me being around the patients. Thing was, both Charlie and Lucy were dying, and I'd be damned not to do what I needed to do to get them diagnosed and treated. I would wait patiently for a nurse or one of the doctors to finish what they were doing and leave the room, pull up a chair, and attempt a conversation. By day three of this, Dr. Small had become particularly abrasive with me, repeatedly questioning what I was doing. His tone became increasingly accusatory, and I told him that if he had concerns, he should contact Father. This was met with scoffing, but seemed to diffuse the concern.

I had made some sizable progress with Charlie. His *vox corporis* had finally begun to give me some information.

"*Olaf, Charlie has an issue in his head,*" he said.

"Really now? Can you tell me about his issue a bit more specifically?" I asked.

"*It's a mass, but it isn't cancerous. It's putting pressure on his brain stem. If it isn't addressed, he will not survive much longer,*" he said with a touch of sadness.

"Why are you sa—" I began, but was cut short on account of being injected with a powerful sedative.

Before I fell unconscious, I heard two things. The first was Charlie's *vox corporis* saying, "*You tried. Thank y—*"

The second was Dr. Small saying, "This man has psych—"

I tried to say that I didn't have anything, but instead, I drooled and fell unconscious.

****

I opened my eyes and found my wrists and ankles bound. I was not in normal clothes. Everything was fuzzy and sounds were amplified, but it was as if I was under water. Every so often, I saw an extremely bright light and disturbing faces. Their eyes were enormous, they had no noses, and their mouths had sharpened fangs. I couldn't move at all, not move a single muscle. My brain was not able to process anything, and though I wanted to rationalize what I was seeing and hearing, I couldn't. All of my normal human faculties had seemingly left. I had no idea where I was, why I was there, or what was happening to me.

My ability was doing disturbing things too. I kept hearing insane conversations that I could not understand in any way, but I couldn't react to them either. It was literally as though I was the victim in a horror film, but I could not scream, I could not defend myself, I could not cry, I could not feel. I could hear *vox corpora* as I had for many years, but I didn't care what I was told no matter how disturbing it was.

"The Devil ate your brain for breakfast."

"I am going to melt your insides and drink them."

"You are dead and this is hell. The Devil took you."

"Clown."

"Usted es mierda de murciélago hombre blanco loco."

"Clowns."

"Bubbly insides taste so good."

"The Devil has your heart. You have no hope."

"You're here to kill me. I know you're here to kill me. So do it already—DO IT NOW!"

"Clown. Clown clown clown CLOWN! Clown clown clown clown clown clown… CLOWN!"

"Speak to me! Now! I demand you speak to me now! DEVIL CLOWN!"

"The Devil hates clowns. You are a clown."

"She hates you. She doesn't forgive you. She despises you. Your mother hates clowns."

"I need you to die. Slowly, and painfully. I need you to die. I need your blood on my hands."

"The Devil is waiting. Don't keep him waiting, clown."

I heard insane, disturbing laughter throughout. It wasn't happy laughter. It was evil. I also heard random vocalizations: hums, screams, and howls held out the way vocalists do to warm up. Every so often, I'd see the bright light and the scary faces. Eventually, everything went black, and all sound stopped. I still could not move.

****

I opened my eyes and found myself somewhere else. The bounds were gone, but I was hooked up to IVs and still couldn't move. My vision was hazy and my hearing was still heavily affected. I heard sound as though I were under water. Every so often, I would see the bright light and a blob where the scary face had been, and I would feel intensely painful burns all over my body. Again, all at once, everything went black and all sound stopped.

****

I opened my eyes and saw alternating solid colors—red, then yellow, then black, then white, then red, then yellow, then black. No sound happened at all during this experience. The colors stopped—everything went black.

****

I opened my eyes and could see I was in the same hospital room Charlie had been in—there was a painting in the room that I recognized. My vision had improved, but it still sounded like I was underwater.

Dr. Glaush appeared, said something I couldn't understand and quickly left. Father soon appeared and again said something I couldn't make out. It was as though their voices produced sounds like blue whales, not the high-pitched ones that killer whales make.

Both men disappeared, everything went black, and all sound stopped.

****

I opened my eyes and was on my deck, a strange feeling on my right hand. I turned and saw a massive dog licking my hand. I then heard Trudy, one of Father's nurses yell, "Dr. Waniglia! He's conscious!"

I attempted to lift my hand to pet the dog, but I couldn't. He then put his head under my hand and sat perfectly still, almost as though he understood what my intention was. It was amazing to experience such love and compassion from a dog, especially because I had never seen it before.

Father and Annie then appeared to my left, actively staying away from the dog, who had taken a defensive stance on my right side and was growling fiercely.

"Olaf—can you hear me?" Father asked cautiously.

"I can, Father. whose dog is this?" I asked weakly.

"He's your dog. He's been protecting you, Olaf. He's been by your side every day for the past three months," Father said.

"Three months? What are you talking about? What happened?" I asked.

"Dr. Small had you committed, Olaf. He had you *committed*," Annie said angrily.

The dog growled.

"What about the wedding? Weren't we supposed to go in February?" I asked.

"Olaf, babe, it's almost May. We'll go when you can," Annie said sadly.

"The dog?" I asked.

"Well…that's why you aren't in the hospital anymore," Father said. "He was a service dog in training who somehow found you in your hospital room and would not leave your side. Olaf, he has been with you, dutifully watching over you, the entire time. We've had to reassure him that we weren't hurting you every time we treated you. He damn near killed three nurses and gave several people near heart attacks."

"Can you tell me what's happened for the past few months? I saw and heard such strange things," I said. My dog moved under my arm, close to my head.

"Well, that asshole Small lost his license to practice medicine. Joe Lating sued the shit out of him. He was insane in the trial," Annie said agitatedly. "He's currently serving twenty-five years in jail without the possibility of parole. With any luck, he's been beaten a few times by now."

"Trial? I've been out that long?" I asked.

"Lating fast tracked the criminal trial after the medical board's review, which itself happened really quickly. Regardless though, you've been revived at least three times in the past three months, Olaf. You'd start to improve, then your body would shut down. You're so lucky to be alive. I have no idea how you survived the first day given what we've seen since then. Your body was attacked so harshly it should have completely shut down. Small gave you a massive dose of sedative, then the folks at the crazy ward added a double dose of their own cocktail, per Small. Your heart stopped several times in the hospital," Father said as tears formed in his eyes. Annie began sobbing.

"Franklin was the one who saved you first. I got the other three times," he said. "Your Mom has been here every day for the entire time—she's been sleeping with Annie at night. She's the only one who can be near you without saying a word to the dog. You've been under twenty-four-hour surveillance. We turned your living room into a hospital room. The dog and a nurse have been with you constantly. There was one time you stopped breathing and the dog went nuts; he practically tore my arm off dragging me into your room. That's why he's still here. He saved your life, Olaf."

"Damn dog. I love him for saving you, but hate him for not letting me be close to you," Annie said angrily. "I've missed you so much, babe. You have no idea how hard this has been."

It turned out every time I opened my eyes, a month or so had passed. I was in the psych ward for six weeks, despite the fact that Dr. Small admitted to Father and the police what he had done, and the district attorney had threatened to shut the place down if I weren't released.

"The best we could do was to station one of our nurses there to care for you until you were released. Then, we took you into our care and about a week in, this pup found you and never left," Father said. "You scared us so bad, Olaf. So, so bad."

"I can't move, Father—is this permanent?" I asked nervously.

"Well, this is sort of uncharted territory, Olaf. No one, to our knowledge, at the hospital has ever survived with the combination of things you had in your system," he responded. "I checked with several specialists at other hospitals and none of them could offer me any insights as to what to expect. This is going to be a step at a time recovery."

It wasn't too long after that Mother appeared.

"Olaf, baby—can you hear me?" she asked.

"Yes, Mother, I can. I'm so sorry I scared you like this," I said weakly.

"Sweetheart, no. That animal Small did this. Annie and I are hoping for frequent beatings to occur to that man. Has she told you about our time together?" she asked.

"I told him, Mrs. Waniglia. If I had just a minute alone with that man, I swear," Annie said angrily.

"Annie Louise, what have I said about this 'Mrs. Waniglia' nonsense? Sierra, Si, or Mom. Those are your choices young lady," Mother said playfully.

"Sorry—old habit I guess. Olaf, *Mom* has been amazing to me. Aside from being the only one who thought you'd actually wake up, she has made my life so much more tolerable over the past few months. She sleeps with me in our room. I was crying myself to sleep every night," Annie said.

"Yeah, and I've been on an inflatable mattress this whole time. My back loves this—so much," Father said wryly.

"I have to ask, did Charlie survive, Father? I had a breakthrough the day of the incident with him," I said hopefully.

"Son, I'm sorry, but both he and Lucy died about a week after you were in the psych ward. Lating tried to argue their deaths as part of Small's sentence, but the judge wouldn't buy it. One of the nurses who was there heard your breakthrough. What was the cause, Son? Charlie's family disallowed an autopsy," Father asked.

I was pretty upset when I heard this. That was why Charlie's *vox corporis* was sad—he knew what was happening to me. Tears formed that were promptly licked off my face. The dog then put his massive head on my chest—almost as though he was listening to my heartbeat.

"He has done that frequently, Olaf. I don't know what kind of a soul he is, but this is the work of an angel," Mother said.

"Charlie had a non-cancerous mass that was pushing on his brain stem. It was causing so much pressure that his brain was no longer able to control his bodily functions. I was still struggling with Lucy, but she had more time than Charlie did," I said, frustrated. "I cannot believe he is dead. It would have been routine."

"Aren't they always, Olaf? They all seem to have such simple things that, if they go undetected, will end up killing them," Father said.

"Has anyone named the dog?" I asked curiously.

"We started calling him 'Doc' because he's been caring for you," Mother responded.

"No one at the hospital claimed him? This is a little strange to me," I said.

"Olaf, they *tried*. The training staff attempted many times to remove him, but he would not move from your side the second he arrived by your bed at the hospital. He would go outside, then sprint back to your room. He ate there, he slept there, and he watched over you every single second. It's remarkable really—truly remarkable," Father said.

"Well then, what say you, Doc?" I asked, looking at the pup.

His large, expressive eyes looked at me, and he offered a very soft "woof."

Trudy then appeared and asked, "Everybody, a 'Nol' and 'Sadie' are here. Are they permitted back here?"

Annie ran into the house and soon returned with Nol and Sadie. "Yes, they are absolutely permitted back here!" she said enthusiastically.

"Damn son, you done scared us but good," Nol said. "Seems you have a guardian angel in the form of a very protective dog!"

Doc woofed in approval.

"Olaf, how are you feeling?" Sadie asked shyly.

"Well, aside from the fact that I can't move, I'm good I guess," I said.

"The hell you cain't. Son, y'all gonna move, and y'all gonna move now. Show me. I ain't leavin' till y'all do it," Nol said like a drill sergeant.

I tried to lift my right arm, but couldn't. I then attempted to wiggle my toes, which I was partially successful in doing.

"There, bully. Moved the pigs. That suffice?" I asked sarcastically.

"Works for me, Son. Y'all gotta get betta so's y'all can come fishin' with us. Found a killa spot about a mile out," Nol said.

"You and I both know that I'm worthless to y'all fishin'," I responded tiredly.

"But babe, it's not the same without you. It's just not the same," Annie said sadly.

"It's true, Olaf—we go, but it doesn't feel right," Sadie said. "By the way, look what I got!" she said happily and showed me her left ring finger, which had a beautiful engagement ring on it.

"Congratulations you two! Son, I'm damn proud 'a y'all!" I said excitedly. "When y'all gettin' hitched?"

"Well…. what if we all got married on the same day when we go to the islands? We've sorta been talking about it, but didn't finalize anything because we wanted your opinion on it," Annie said coyly.

"Works for me," I said to two elated women, who bounced and hugged and said unintelligible things to one another to the amazement of all present.

"They hoped you'd say that. Hear me when I say this—it's been the Annie and Sadie show, Son," Nol said happily.

"We'd have to do this soon, wouldn't we? Nol you have to report soon don't you?" I asked, thinking about Nol's football responsibilities.

"We have a little time since I'm not a rookie anymore I just have to report with the rest of the veterans closer to camp. I'd guess as long as we go by mid-July I should be okay. Plus—coach is a sucker for weddings, so I'm sure I'll get a pass if need be."

It turned out that Nol's coach was more than a sucker for weddings. He was a sucker to his superstar nose tackle who had set a rookie record for sacks in a season, passes defended, tackles and—get this—interceptions. Nol mentioned my situation as part of a conversation about our weddings with said coach, and the next day, the lead trainer and the trainer's staff arrived at my door and started an intensive six-week rehabilitation program. They were impressed with my knowledge of fighting, and used that throughout. The head trainer, Chad, used boxing as their primary platform to get me mobile again. Mind you, dear Reader, when they arrived, I could not move anything but my toes. So, the first step they focused on was me making a fist. The next, holding up my hands as though I was blocking a punch in the boxing ring. Next, light jabs from each hand. It took almost two weeks to get there.

Then, they started working on my legs. They first got me to move my feet, then bend my knees and move them from side to side. That took a full week to accomplish. Next, the process of getting me to stand began. That took another week and took the whole training staff. As soon as I could stand, they walked me into the garage, where my boxing coach was—holding sets of wraps and gloves next to a brand new heavy bag and speed bag stand.

"Y'all are mine now, kid. Thanks gents for getting my boy here to this point. Iron Hands, I'm kicking your ass from here on out," Coach George said to me gruffly.

"Can we watch, coach?" Chad asked.

"Absolutely, boys. I always like breaking people with an audience," Coach said.

Break me, he did. The last week the staff were in town, coach alternated heavy bag and speed bag work in *fifteen-minute intervals*. Annie, Nol, Sadie, and both my and Annie's parents watched every session. Doc sat in front of Mother and seemed to have a proud look on his face. None of them had seen how I trained for the past several years. At my best, before the nut house, I needed at least two people holding the heavy bag still. When Coach was done with me, it took four—and I hurt every one of 'em, especially with my overhands and my crosses. Nol, at one point, looked at the lot of 'em and asked Coach if he could have a turn by himself.

"I wouldn't, 64. You have a season coming up. Iron Hands is back, and he's stronger than I've felt him in the past," Coach said proudly, but cautiously. 64 was Nol's number from junior high through the pros; it represented Rick's birthday of June 4th.

"How bad could it be?" Nol asked arrogantly and walked behind the back of the bag.

"One-two, one-two, four, four, four, four kid. Don't hold back and don't disappoint me," Coach whispered intensely. I nodded, cracked my neck to the side, got in my stance, and fired. My first two jabs made Nol step back, and my crosses knocked him down.

"Coach P is gonna love this, Nol," Chad said, laughing.

"Son, you got cannons for hands. No wonder them Malloy boys were hospitalized for a month. Damn!" Nol said as he picked himself up. "I think you may have sprained my wrists."

"Let me take a look, Nol. We'll tape you up if so," Chad said, still laughing.

"Well kid, I'd say that you're back. How do you feel?" Coach asked, nicer than I had ever heard him before. "You scared us—bad. All the guys back in the gym keep asking how you are."

"Physically, I feel strong, and that's thanks to Chad and his amazing team and of course you, Coach. I still have awful dreams though, almost like I'm back in the same state I was before. Some parts of my memory are gone. I can't really remember high school or college. And, I have this very weird feeling in my head. It's not a headache, but I feel *something*," I said, as honestly as I could.

"It may take a while for those drugs to completely leave your body, Olaf. Don't forget, to date, no one on record has ever survived the amount of sedatives you had in your system at once. We may need to really monitor this and get you some additional treatment," Dr. Glaush said.

"This is true, Olaf. It's wonderful you are back physically, but we don't know how long it may take for your *brain* to recover," Father said.

"Well, I always knew you were nuts anyway, babe. I still love you, though," Annie said sarcastically.

"Huh, imagine that. I'm crazy and Annie Glaush still loves me," I said as I took my gloves off.

"Yep, and I'm gonna marry your crazy ass as soon as I possibly can," she said, smiling.

That said, I chased her and hugged her as long as I could. I was so sweaty that my arms and legs were dripping; so a very displeased Annie felt my response to the allegations.

"I'm... crazy?" I asked as she pushed and wiggled, and trying her best to get away.

"Babe, seriously! I have to shower again now. Let me go!" she said amid her struggles.

"Um, apparently I'm crazy, y'all. I'm not sure I can do that," I said with the best smart-ass voice I could.

Eventually, I let her go, and she slapped my chest good; Doc did not like that. He chased her back into the house, and we all chuckled as we heard her screams and subsequent chorus of "Stop! Damn dog STOP! Olaf! Call Doc! Stop! Damn dog!"

Eventually, I whistled and Doc came bounding back to the garage, his tongue out, and his eyes wide. He loved every second of that, we all could tell. I gave him a pat and went in to find the battered, and now overtly sweat-covered, Annie.

"Olaf Waniglia! I was cuteiful and now look at me. Look what you've done!" Annie said in a near-stomping fit.

"Cuteiful?" I asked, chuckling.

"That impossibly hard place that merges cute and beautiful. I was there. I was THERE, Olaf," Annie said madly.

"You still are, my love," I said, smiling mightily and doing my best not to laugh.

Annie huffed and marched into the bathroom fully engaged in her fit.

I went back to the garage and thanked Chad and his staff, promising Coach I'd be back to the gym the next week. I got such good care from those folks. I was incredibly fortunate to have friends like I did, and connections that were willing to go the extra mile on my behalf.

Soon after, our talk of Hawaii resumed. We called Mrs. Klipkewitcz, and she was able to get all of our plans moved to the second week in July. So, preparations began for our trip to paradise.

Paradise and the Wondrous Musings of a Saint

Collective planning ensued amongst all the folks who were headed to Hawaii. Father and Dr. Glaush arranged for their absence. Annie and I made sure that the farm and all related business items were either resolved or able to be in a holding pattern until we returned. Nol and Sadie got a house sitter for their new place in South Carolina. Acquiring this humble abode had been in the works since before my time in the psych ward, and they finally were able to close during my rehab. Nol wanted to be as close to his boat as he could, and the house they bought was less than a block away. He didn't see the need for a house sitter, but Sadie was insistent; she'd never gone away from home without one, and that included the ten years or so she lived in an apartment. No, dear Reader, she had no pets. To the best of my knowledge, she had a cactus that would have been the sole living thing in her possession that needed to be "watched." Both Sadie and Nol's parents were going to be a part of this procession to Hawaii.

Nol's brother, Rick, and Annie's brother, Gill, were both unable to travel for differing reasons. Rick's health had been challenging over the previous month, and the decision was made for him to stay with Nol's aunt. The poor guy would get better, and almost immediately feel awful again. As for Gill, well a year and a half prior, he had planned to climb some mountain with a buddy of his. Seeing his sister get hitched apparently wasn't as exciting as going up and down a massive rock. Rick was promised a wealth of pictures; Gill was asked to find other plans for Thanksgiving.

Annie and I registered our time away with our neighborhood folks and made sure the security company knew we would be away too. Per my grandfather, a sophisticated security system would be installed in the house once all construction was complete, and we were required to inform them of changes to our routine. Apparently, it tracked our movements and activity relative to the time, and any changes to this routine—within a certain tolerance—triggered a response from the security company. Doc was making the flight with us as he was going to be the ring bearer for both ceremonies. Someone—I can't recall who—mentioned that he was going to be the flower girl too; both he and I dismissed said suggestion rather succinctly. My boy was no flower girl. I can tell you that, dear Reader, all 120 pounds of his muscular self mildly fit as the bearer of rings for no other reason than to make it near impossible for the rings to be taken. To suggest that he too would dispense flower petals was patently wrong on so many levels.

So, with all our ducks in a row, we departed South Carolina for Hawaii. I worried mightily for Doc as he rode in a crate with the rest of the cargo. He did not like being confined, or being away from me, in the least. After the insane trip across the country, and one connecting flight to the islands, he was a groggy mess by the time we got him back after landing in Hawaii. It apparently took three guys to put his crate onto a motorized cart. Once that task was accomplished, they said that the cart had died about a quarter of the way to us, in the baggage area. So, the same three guys got a manual cart and pushed Doc the rest of the way. They were half-dead themselves by the time they reached us. Doc looked at us from the crate, slowly laid his head back down, and covered his eyes with one of his massive paws. It took a decent amount of coaxing, and a new rawhide, to get him into the car; and even then, he collapsed with the rawhide under his polar bear-like paws and fell asleep in the back seat almost immediately. He barely fit in the car; I had to maneuver both paws out of the way in order to close the doors.

Hawaii is such a beautiful place. There is no other way to describe it; it is simply beautiful. The humidity we left back in South Carolina was nowhere to be found, and the temperature was about as perfect as perfect gets—mid-seventies and sunshine at every turn. The volcanoes off in the distance, and the subsequent lava parks, were a bit of a departure from what we have on the East coast, and demonstrated an aspect of our planet that you have to see to appreciate.

I think the greatest possible example of total appreciation, was shown to me by my amazing buddy, Doc. When we got to the set of villas we were staying in, I opened the sliding glass door to the deck that overlooked a gorgeous inlet from the Pacific. Doc marched himself, and his rawhide, right out there, sat down, put his nose to the air, and closed his big brown eyes. I think, for him, that was a defining moment of *amazingness* in his short life—and I'll never, ever forget it. Annie saw him do it too and went out there to give him a big hug. He thanked her with a single lick on the cheek, then went back to his appreciation of the Pacific air. He was so much in the zone that he didn't flinch when a dolphin approached and greeted him vocally. He offered little more than a tiny, barely audible "*woof*", and otherwise changed nothing about his physicality.

Technically speaking, this was the night before my wedding; so Annie just visited as Doc and I settled in. Nol and I were sharing a villa that night. The parents each got their own, and Sadie and Annie were staying together for the evening. This being as it was, I was quite thankful to be the farthest away from the ladies' villa. I imagined a lengthy amount of giggling, possible screaming, and likely hours of dancing—Nol concurred. As a group, we coordinated locations for the night after we had the "rehearsal dinner," which in no way actually followed a rehearsal. Our minister, who was arranged for us, believed in an "organic" ceremony, and thus rehearsals were disallowed.

So, the lot of us planned on having dinner together, then the men would head west and the ladies would head east. We also reserved the right to head to other islands while the ladies had to remain on the Big Island. In retrospect, that may have been sexist, but Dr. Glaush knew of a place on Maui that he insisted we go to for a "plan". He was being particularly cagey around Mrs. Glaush and Annie, so it was obvious something was up. We all had dinner and said our goodbyes for the night.

"I cannot wait to be your bride, babe," Annie said, hugging me tightly.

"I still can't even believe we're engaged, my love. I still feel like that kid who wanted so desperately to be with you for all those years," I replied, remembering my teenage crush.

"I have loved you much longer than you realize, Olaf Waniglia, and I get to do that for the rest of our lives," she said, holding me tighter.

"I'll very kindly let you, my love." I, in turn, squeezed her tighter.

"Be good tonight, you. I mean it, no Hawaiian maidens. They are going to be all over you," she said, looking up at me sternly.

"Understood, no Hawaiian maidens. Me thinks your dad may kill me should I indulge, so I doubt you have anything to worry about," I said sarcastically.

"So, you're thinking about these maidens then? Must I brand you prior to your departure?" she threatened, grabbing my arms.

I slipped from her grip, embraced her, and lifted her off the ground. "You are the only maiden that I'd care to be with this evening, my love," I said, holding her tightly.

"You better mean that, you," she said, looking me square in the eye.

"I think you know that I do," I said and kissed her passionately.

"Just like that tomorrow, and the next day, and all the other ones too," she said completely out of breath.

"Of course, my love," I whispered, smiling.

With our goodbyes complete, we headed our way and the ladies headed theirs. Our plan was to meet at 1:00 the next afternoon, on the beach, where our minister was to join us together in our dual ceremony. It turned out that Dr. Glaush had arranged a flight with a buddy of his, so we had a schedule both going and coming that night. We were going to this same buddy's place on Maui, which purportedly was a mini resort close to a bevy of bars and other debaucheries. This was the aforementioned "plan."

Before we did, Nol, Dr. Glaush, Father, and I drove to a bar close to the airport and kicked off our festivities. The name of the place struck us rather funny—"Leis and Happy Endings"—but the exterior of the building didn't match. There was an old airplane out front with what looked like a real skeleton dressed in aviator glasses and a Hawaiian shirt inside the cockpit.

"That ain't yer guy is it Doc G?" Nol asked Dr. Glaush.

"No—the shirt isn't right—it's closed," he responded with a chuckle. "Let's prime the pump, boys. Tonight is a celebration, and I'm intending to have a headache in the morning."

We all chuckled and went inside. A topless hostess met us, kissed us all on the cheek, and put leis around our necks. The lot of us looked at each other, shrugged, and made our way to the bar.

A topless bartender wearing a pilot's hat greeted us, kissed us all on the cheek, and made us some drink that none of us could identify. We did not order these drinks, dear Reader. Looking back, we should have been much more suspect given this detail. We were all half-drunk from that single drink—including Nol, who could drink nearly a bottle of whisky in a single sitting and not read as intoxicated if given a breathalyzer test. We did an experiment one time, with an officer buddy of ours, and were astonished and terrified at the result. Two thirds of a liter of 100 proof vodka produced a 0.02 result in the breathalyzer.

So, we began our way out of the bar, heavily buzzed, and received another several leis as we made our way to the door from other topless women. The topless hostess stopped us at the door, gave us all hugs, and said we couldn't leave without our happy endings. Father grabbed me and Nol and ran out the door. Dr. Glaush attached himself to the back of my shirt and was towed out with the lot of us. We laughed mighty hard as we made our way to the car.

"A pro football star, two nationally known surgeons, and one of the most brilliant business minds in recent history enter a bar..." Father started.

"...Topless broads feed them some kind of liquor," Dr. Glaush continued.

"…And now none of them know where their balls are!" Nol concluded enthusiastically.

We all laughed and limped our way to the airport to find Dr. Glaush's buddy, Rupert Allendia. To the best of our knowledge, we were looking for a guy with an open Hawaiian shirt. We had no idea what else we were in for.

As we made our way into the airport, we immediately saw a shirtless man with slicked-back hair holding a sign that read: "Franklin and Yucky Wedding People." He was standing just prior to the security gates. We approached this man, he looked each of us from top to bottom, and said simply, "Shame," then motioned for us to follow him.

We were led to a private part of the airport where a security guard scanned us cursorily for weaponry. The man lazily motioned us through a door and out to a tarmac where a large private plane sat waiting—its pilot standing by the door. His arms outstretched overhead with his hands expressively bent at the wrist outward, Rupert Allendia presented himself wearing unbelievably short shorts, the expected open Hawaiian shirt, and a pilot's hat cocked to the side.

"This way to the party, sweeties. Franklin, by the nectar of the Gods, man, you will be mine by the end of the evening," Rupert said, as I suppose only Rupert could.

"Um, Franklin… anything you'd like to tell us?" Father said, looking sternly at Dr. Glaush.

"I don't lean that way, David, and you know it, but Rupert likes to think he can change that. Once you meet him, and get past this flamboyant exterior, he is such a good man. Right now, this is all show for you three. Have fun, he is a really, really good friend," Dr. Glaush said genuinely.

"I'll take your word for it," Father said nervously.

We boarded the plane, which was outfitted about as elegantly as anything I had ever seen. The seating was the finest grain leather I had ever felt. There were marble accents everywhere and a 100% quartz bar. I'd never seen, nor imagined, such a thing ever in my life.

"Make yourselves comfortable, you delicious specimens. We'll be in Maui in two twists of a fabulous peacock," Rupert gushed.

Dr. Glaush knew the layout of the plane and poured us each a glass of scotch. He handed one to the gentleman who held the sign in the airport and asked, "It's Michael, right?"

"Yes, and thank you, Doctor," he replied.

We soon landed in Maui and were led to a waiting limousine. We drove maybe twenty minutes to, what I imagined was, the nearby coastline and entered an ornately decorated gate. We stopped in a horseshoe-shaped driveway in front of a sprawling estate that went about as far as one's eyes could see.

We had just started to plod our way inside when Rupert stopped us rather suddenly.

"All who enter my house must be cleansed. Drink this and earn entrance into a night you shall never, ever forget," Rupert said seriously.

What it was we drank, I have no idea, dear Reader. It was clear, but did not taste like any alcohol I was familiar with. It was smooth, whatever it was. Rupert smiled acceptingly as we finished our drinks and led us toward the back of the house.

"The tour starts for you three now," Rupert said, motioning to everyone, but me. "For you, dear Olaf, there is someone who must speak to you. Michael will take you to him."

Nol patted me on the back and wished me luck. Michael then wrapped an arm around my back, led me down a corridor, and through a door leading to the outside. We got into a golf cart and rode a short distance to what looked like a handmade arch on the edge of the beach, leading toward a pathway.

"This is where I leave you. Please go inside. You'll know you have arrived when you get there," Michael said cryptically.

"Um…okay," I said hesitantly and headed through the opening. I walked along a path lit by torches. Tropical flowers lined the way along with a forest of palm trees behind them. I heard all kinds of animal noises as I walked and could tell that the ocean was close by.

Maybe a quarter mile down the path, I heard a faint voice say, "I'm over here, Olaf. Not too much further now."

I walked maybe another fifteen feet or so, and came to another arch surrounded by several torches. The beach was visible at this distance; I could see moonlit waves as they rolled in. Off to my right was a man seated in a chair wearing what looked like traditional Hawaiian clothing. He was a heavy-set man with long, greying hair.

Around his neck was a necklace with a symbol I hadn't seen before. His eyes looked to be shut.

"Hello, Olaf. It is an absolute pleasure to finally meet you," he said in a scratchy voice. "My name is Akamu. Please join me."

"How did you know that I was coming?" I asked curiously.

"You and I are connected to the same thing, my friend. You can hear what I can see, but they are one in the same. You use your gift wisely, to help. I do as well, but it is you I must help now," Akamu said genuinely.

"How did you know...?" I began.

"You too will know in due time. Those of us blessed with this gift are one, and if one of us has been hurt, it is the responsibility of the whole to heal that one. Please Olaf, close your eyes and allow the majesty and the power of the ocean to give you a different kind of sight," he said before I could finish my question.

I closed my eyes and to my amazement, I saw Akamu standing before me, his eyes open and clear. Everything I looked at glowed with a beautiful light. I felt the ocean coursing through my head; it was a strange feeling, but it was comforting as much as it was strange.

"Where am I, Akamu?" I asked, astounded.

"You are essentially on the same beach, but you are seeing that which allows you to hear the people's inner voices—their truths. All that is glowing reflects the foundation of this truth. This is how I see—and it's how I began your healing process back in South Carolina," he said. "As soon as you were close to the Atlantic, the power of the ocean amplified my ability to see the truth of your experience. I saw firsthand the damage that was present. I was able to begin the healing process, but it is here that I will finish it."

"You... you healed me?" I asked, trying to comprehend what I was being told.

"Yes, dear boy, I did. In time, you will be able to do this as well. But, until I rid you completely of the toxins that found their way into your head, you will be stuck. We cannot have this anymore, my friend. Please, come closer to me," Akamu said and outstretched his arms.

I took a step toward him, but my feet left the ground. I started to panic.

"Relax, Olaf. You are moving to the place you seek. Allow yourself to move there," he said comfortingly.

I continued rising with each step. I finally got to a place that was above the tops of the trees, where moonlight was unobstructed. Almost as soon as I was in full view of the moon, I felt the ocean in my mind become much more active—in a sense, much more violent. The trees below me were extremely agitated; their movement matched what I felt in my head.

"Submit to it, Olaf. Feel the incredible power and allow it to erase the evil that was done. Allow it to make you whole. Submit, Olaf! Feel the power—ALLOW YOURSELF TO BE HEALED!" Akamu's voice rose in intensity with each word. With that intensity, the activity in my head reached a complete fever pitch. Within a heartbeat, I found myself back on the beach—a smiling Akamu before me.

"Welcome back, my friend. How do you feel?" Akamu asked kindly.

I was astounded! The ocean was peaceful and the trees were calm. There was no physical remnant of what I had just experienced, and this made no rational sense to me. I realized, though, that the symptoms I still had from the nut-house nonsense were gone. I could remember what I hadn't been able to—memories, both good and bad, of high school and college had returned. The odd feeling I had in my head was gone. I felt *normal* again.

"This is incredible, Akamu—I feel right again! Thank you so much!" I said, excited.

"I was merely the conduit, Olaf—you healed *yourself*," he said nicely. "I'd imagine your dreams won't be what they have been either."

"You could see them?" I asked, positively amazed.

"I saw your truths just as you hear truths. The part of your brain responsible for dreaming was damaged. I couldn't see what you were dreaming per se, but it couldn't have been anything good. I observed that the part of your brain instilling fear was like nothing I've ever witnessed. I can only imagine what you were seeing at night, Olaf," he said with an intriguing honesty.

"Yeah… they have been pretty awful of late," I said. "I have a question for you, though. Where the heck was I?"

"I'll simply say this, it's the foundation of everything that is. Starting today, and for the rest of your life, you will create your definition of what that is. I suspect you will treat people in that space, but your way. Marrying the beautiful Annie will further this process in earnest. Love that is present, if true, forces you to evolve. You will see some amazing changes in your ability soon, *because* of the person you are," he said, almost as though he were teaching a class.

"You are a saint, Akamu. Thank you so much for what you have done and for what you have taught me. Will I ever see you again?" I asked hopefully.

"I am no saint, my dear boy. I've merely done what I felt was right. And, I'm not dead yet, so no sainthood for me," he said smiling. "Yes, you will see me again quite soon. For now, though, I am going to rest. Please go join the party and enjoy yourself."

I hugged him. I was completely overcome with emotion. I also realized that his eyes were still closed.

"Akamu, are you blind?" I asked as I collected myself.

"Yes, my friend. I've been blind for most of my life, but it's completely irrelevant unless I decide to drive," he said, chuckling. "In terms of your healing, I solely have done for you what you do for others. Never underestimate *your* ability to heal," he said kindly. "I'll see you soon."

"I look forward to it, my friend," I said. "Thank you so much, and have a wonderful evening."

"Always, dear boy. Always," he said and sat back in his chair.

I headed back through the large arch and down the pathway. The flowers moved gently in the breeze, and the trees seemed more vibrant than I had remembered. When I could finally see the sky again, I was astounded to see the stars They were so bright; I wondered if perhaps they had been there all along and the damage in my head somehow made it so I couldn't see or appreciate them.

I got back to the house to find everybody on the back patio.

"Welcome back, delicious. What can I do to talk you out of this marriage thing? Or, better yet, how drunk do you need to get before I can take full advantage of you?" Rupert said bluntly.

"No disrespect sir, but nothing is going to make me stop loving Annie, and my tolerance is pretty high," I responded.

"Well, it was worth a try. Lord knows I try every time I see Franklin," he said kindly. "Who was at the end of that path?"

"Wait… you didn't know?" I asked, confused.

"Nope. We simply got a note that when you arrived, you were to go down that path. Oddly, those torches and the archway were not there this morning," Rupert said.

"And…um, I'm guessing that no one outside of this group knew I was going to be here, right?" I asked, allowing the whole experience to sink in.

"Nope, the tickets were private for the flight, and in general, no one knows you're here but us. I figured that you arranged a meeting or something," Rupert said, with some concern in his voice.

"I didn't," I said, smiling widely.

"Explain your happiness, please. I'm not nearly drunk enough to handle this," Rupert said exasperatedly.

"Suffice to say, it was a mighty interesting, mighty special time. I'll tell y'all about it someday," I said, still smiling.

"Olaf, you didn't just make a mistake, did you? With a girl?" Father asked nervously.

"Dear God no, Father. No, I'll tell you guys what happened when I know for sure you won't commit me. I know how that goes, and I would prefer not to repeat the experience," I said sarcastically.

"How 'bout high level, son?" Nol asked. "I'm kinda worried about you now."

"I'm sorry Nol. Don't mean to scare y'all. High level, I just talked to a saint. It was amazing. Now, who's pouring me a drink? My ass ain't single for much longer. In the words of my father-in-Law to be, 'I want a headache in the morning.' Somebody pour me somethin' tasty," I said, my smile still cemented in place.

"A *saint*, son? What the hell?" Nol asked.

"Let's drink, my boy. We get hitched tomorrow—gotta celebrate our freedom while we got it! And, I promise you I will spill all the details of tonight when we get back to the villa. Deal?" I asked, trying to get Nol to relax.

"You promise?" he asked intensely. "I am worried, son."

"Nothing to worry about. Promise." That said, we all returned to a much less serious state. Drinks were poured, laughs were had, and the conversation was light. Eventually, cigars found their way into ours hands, speech got good n' slurry, and it finally began to feel like a night that our respective mates would not approve of.

I asked how Rupert knew Dr. Glaush and was shocked to hear the response.

"Well Olaf, my brother, Steven, was Rupert's partner. They had been together for the last fifteen years of his life," Dr. Glaush said.

"My dear Steven, God rest his beautiful soul," Rupert said. "He was an amazing person."

"I didn't know you had a brother, Dr. Glaush," I said.

"He was one of Annie's favorite people when she was young. And Helene—God—I think half the reason she married me was to be close to Steven. He was so kind, so accepting. His death hurt her badly, and truthfully, I don't think she really ever recovered," he said sadly.

"He got AIDS from a blood transfusion—a goddamned blood transfusion. His body simply could not fight anymore once that horrible disease weakened him so," Rupert explained sadly. "There are many pictures inside, and I owe you a tour. Come Olaf! Let us go wander!"

Rupert led me inside his palatial house and showed me around. I'm not kidding you, dear Reader, when I say that this place was a small city in and of itself. It took us nearly thirty-five minutes to get from end to end. All throughout were pictures of Rupert and Steven together. They seemed so happy—so complete. It was obvious they were deeply in love—the same kind of love Annie's *vox corporis* had told me about.

"Steven was cut from a very unique cloth, Olaf. I've not met anyone, ever, who was as kind, as loving, as he was. Losing him was tragic, but I still feel lucky to have had him as long as I did. He continues to inspire me today. This house was built from the inspiration he gave me," Rupert said, looking around.

"If I may ask, what do you do for a living?" I asked, praying that I wasn't making a mistake in doing so.

"I was an architect. I designed buildings. My creations are all over the world," he said proudly. "Steven inspired my creativity and fed my drive. When he passed, I didn't have it in me anymore."

"I am so sorry to hear that, but how in the world do you keep your lifestyle if you're retired?"

"Well, truthfully, I was a big investor back when I was working. I bought nearly everything I have today besides clothes and food from investment assets alone. So, truly, I am retired now, but I still do some consulting from time to time," he said. "And believe me when I say this, it would be very hard for me to spend all of the money I have. I tried at one point when I was very depressed, but decided it was silly and started focusing on the community here instead. I think that is what Steven would have wanted honestly, and it gives me a tremendous amount of happiness to make a difference."

"That's very understandable. Steven sounds wonderful," I said.

"Oh Olaf, he was. He truly, truly was. Now then, I must talk to you about Miss Annie. You understand she is very important to me, right?" he asked enthusiastically.

"Yes, I completely understand. She is very important to me too!"

"I expect you to bring her here to see me—got it?"

"I would be happy to, Rupert. Absolutely. Are you coming to the wedding tomorrow?"

"I wouldn't miss it! I can't wait, but I think I will be a blubbery mess. Do you know who's marrying you?"

"Honestly, no. Per our travel agent, who set this whole thing up, he doesn't believe in rehearsals, so I haven't had the pleasure of meeting him yet," I said, scratching my head.

"Interesting… I am now vastly intrigued for the ceremony. Are you at all nervous?" he asked, his flamboyant nature returning.

"Truthfully, no… I've loved Annie for as long as I can remember. I can't wait to make her and I a family tomorrow."

"I could not be happier for you! Now, your glass is empty, neither of us has a cigar, and our time is becoming an issue. Come, let us rectify this immediately!"

So, Rupert and I made our way back to the group and enjoyed a final round of drinks and one more cigar each. Then, we had another drink, and another cigar, and then another drink, some very elegant snacks, and then another drink.

We woke up the next morning and all of us were on the back deck. It was 9:00.

Father and Dr. Glaush were a little panicked that their wives were going to kill them. In an attempt to resolve that, Rupert called the villas and spoke to Mrs. Glaush. He then talked to Mother. He promised them both that we had behaved and promised we would be there shortly.

Michael made us all a wonderful breakfast of corned beef hash and eggs and, we headed to the airport. All of us had headaches—mission accomplished. Arriving back at the villas, Nol and I headed to our place. Doc hadn't been out and hadn't been fed, so I feared the condition of the place upon our return—it was likely he had eaten a couch or something. We went in to find him completely passed out on a bed, his rawhide close by. He barely moved when we went in, and it took a few minutes for him to begrudgingly go outside.

"So, since we weren't here last night, what was this 'saint' thing Olaf?" Nol asked.

"I'll tell you what I know—some of this is kind of a guess. The guy I met was named Akamu, and he had a similar ability to mine, but much stronger. Instead of hearing a person's truth, he can see it. The thing is… he's *blind*. What he did was unbelievable. He basically healed the damage in my head that Small and the psych ward caused. It was unreal," I said.

"He healed you? How in the world did he do that?" Nol asked, his confusion obvious.

"He did. You know how I had some problems with my memory, and I that weird feeling in my head? And those awful dreams I was having?"

"Yeah, I remember."

"He could see that the part of my brain responsible for dreaming was damaged, and he fixed it—along with whatever else he did. Then, the odd feeling was gone, and now my memory is back to what it was. I don't recall dreaming last night, but I didn't have a nightmare," I said, my excitement evident.

"This is incredible, son. I'm happy for you!" Nol said and gave me a hug.

"Here's the weird thing though…he said that he started the healing process as soon as I was on the deck back home. Somehow, he used the ocean to connect to me. I dunno—last night was the last part of the healing process, and it was an intense experience," I said, shaking my head.

"Okay, now that is downright strange. No matter what, I am so glad you are better—however he did it. You scared all of us so bad. I mean seriously, son. You get how bad that was right, just seeing you lay in that bed? Dammit—I tried everything to get you to wake up. I begged you, son. I begged you to go fishin' with us. I begged you to just say something or move something. I begged you to cook me pie. You just laid there. There was no life in y'all until you went out on that deck. Annie cried every day because she knew in her heart you were gone. Your dad lost it at least once a week. Sadie and I cried when we got home after every visit. I lost it when I went to the dock, and I lost it fishin'. You are my best friend, Olaf. Don't you dare do anything like that to me again," he said, tears streaming down his face. I'll tell you, dear Reader, there is nothing that breaks one's heart like seeing a dear friend cry, especially when that friend's job is hitting people as hard as he possibly can

"Nol, I don't know what to say. I truly don't. Here's the thing though—I'm here. I'm not on that bed anymore. My head isn't a mess anymore. When we go back to South Carolina, we are going fishin', all of us, and I promise I'll make you a pie. So please know how sorry I am that this was as hard as it was. You are the best friend I could ever hope for. Thank you for never giving up on me," I said, my own tears had started to fall.

Doc looked up at both of us, and seeing our compromised state, took turns leaning up against our legs. To say that dog knew how to care is a complete understatement—and he wasn't yet a year old. To the best of my knowledge, he was born ten months prior. So technically, he was a 120-pound puppy.

"Now listen—we gotta get it together. We gotta be on the beach in about an hour. Let's get ready, get Doc ready, have a drink, and go get married. Deal?" I asked hopefully.

"Deal. Let's do this thing," Nol said, every bit the pro football player he was.

We cleaned ourselves up and got changed into our wedding garb. Mind you, this was not typical black-tie dress. We decided the girls would wear sun dresses and we would wear nice shorts and dress shirts. Doc was outfitted with a bowtie and a harness that would hold the rings. We then headed to the bar in the center of the villas, offered a final toast to one another being single, and headed down to the beach.

We were directed to an area that was outfitted with a couple rows of chairs, an altar, and an arch—not unlike the one on the beach where I met Akamu. Hawaiian dancers were milling about, and a band was warming up. One of the Hawaiian dancers walked up to us and put leis around our necks.

"In keeping with Hawaiian culture, please accept these gifts on your special day," she said kindly and walked away.

As we got closer to the time, I started to get nervous. I can't explain why, dear Reader. I was marrying the girl I had loved for as long as I could remember. I had waited so long for this day—for us to officially become a family. My nerves made no sense, and Nol unfortunately was no help as he had the same jitters.

"You scared, son? I'm starting to shake over here, and I ain't even hungry," Nol said nervously.

"Yeah, and I can't put my finger on why. Makes no sense, y'all," I said exasperatedly.

Soon thereafter, our parents arrived, then Rupert, and two older couples. Then, from behind me, I heard a very familiar voice say, "Hello again, my friend." Akamu was being led toward the altar by a smiling assistant. "He has been looking forward to this for months," the assistant whispered to me.

"Are you ready to be married, Olaf? Your grandfather and I loved talking about this day! I cannot wait to be your priest!" Akamu gushed. He was wearing what I had to assumed was a traditional Hawaiian priest's robe and a necklace. He never stopped smiling, beginning from this first conversation until the end of the day.

"Now hold on here... Akamu, you knew my grandfather?" I asked, shocked by this realization.

"You could say that, yes Olaf. My dad served with your grandfather, and all of those fine looking gents seated over there, in the war. I knew him as 'Uncle Chris' and was honored when he asked me to be a part of this. I knew your grandmother too. She would have been so proud of the man you've become," he said, smiling from his heart.

"So, is this how you knew I'd be in Maui yesterday?" I asked, still trying to put the pieces together.

"No, my boy—I knew months ago. We will have more time, I promise. I'll explain," he said comfortingly.

"So, wait, that's your saint, son?" Nol asked with incredulity.

"Olaf Waniglia, what did I tell you about saints?" Akamu playfully scolded.

"Sorry Akamu—to me you will always be a saint, even if you *are* still alive," I said.

"You both should take your places. We are about to begin," Akamu said.

Almost immediately after he said this, the band started to play. However he did it, Akamu was about as tuned into existence as anyone I had ever met, and could see things in the physical world that I missed.

Doc moseyed down the aisle and laid down next to me. Then, Sadie came down the aisle accompanied by her father. He shook Nol's hand, kissed her on the cheek, and sat down. She was positively glowing in her dress, and was so happy that she was bouncing up and down a little bit. I'll never forget how she and Nol were looking at one another.

Next, Annie was accompanied by Dr. Glaush. He shook my hand, gave me a hug, and sat down. I'd never seen a woman so beautiful in all my life. Her eyes sparkled, her smile was genuine, and she looked absolutely stunning in her dress. She had a bright orange flower in the right side of her hair, and was wearing my great-grandmother's jewelry. She bent down and gave Doc a kiss, then looked up at me and said, "You gotta wait for yours," rather seductively.

Akamu stepped forward and raised his hands. "Today, we are given the gift of seeing two beautiful families created. Love has brought us all here. So I ask that you join me, Nol, Sadie, Olaf, and Annie in this celebration of wonderful, powerful, endearing love. I believe this ceremony is not one that should ever have structure. We are here together in love. Let this alone guide our celebration," he said powerfully, but genuinely. "I believe there are a couple of people here who would like to say a few words. Gentlemen?"

One of the older gentlemen stood up and made his way over to us. "My name is Walter Gerheart. I served with Chris Waniglia in the Army. After the war, we all came here and none of us left alone. Chris, Pete, and I came here worn-out veterans of a horrible war and found the women who we would later marry—who then essentially saved our lives. Chris asked me to tell you one thing—no matter how dark your world may become, after today, you will have a partner who will always light the darkness. Bless you all," he said with a notable honesty in his voice. He kissed Annie and Sadie and shook both Nol's and my hand, then sat down.

The second gentleman got up and approached the alter. "My name is Peter Ruglia, and I too served with Chris in the Army. Chris would never want me to say this, but it goes with what he asked me to say. Chris saved several members of our company after he himself had been shot. Every one of us would have died had he not risked his own life to save us. He asked me to say this—never underestimate the power of being selfless for another," he said, the same honesty present in his voice.

Akamu stepped forward again, "Thank you gentlemen. Among the parents of the members of our wedding party, would you like to say anything to our young people? Any wisdom you would like to share before they start their lives together?"

Nol's mother spoke first, "Take time to understand one another—once you do, nothing will ever come between you."

Nol's father agreed, saying, "This is so, so true. Be willing to never stop learning about your partner, and they will never stop surprising you." Nol's mother smiled and kissed him.

Sadie's father spoke next, "Disagreements will happen, but never let them become fights."

Sadie's mother nodded in agreement, "And never, ever go to bed without an honest to goodness kiss goodnight."

Mrs. Glaush added, "This goes for mornings too. I have never let Franklin leave the house if either of us were upset. Going through your day angry is no way to live!"

Dr. Glaush grinned and said, "This is true, and it is probably the single greatest thing you can do for one another. Find ways, every day, to show you love one another."

Mother spoke next. "Really listen to your children. They will amaze you and show you a love you never thought possible."

This made comment made Father smile. "Really listen to your spouse too. *They* will amaze you and show you a love you never thought possible."

Akamu beamed from ear to ear, "Beautiful, wonderful guidance. Thank you all for your words of wisdom. Nol and Sadie, would you like to exchange vows?"

"YES!!!!" Sadie answered enthusiastically.

"That's what I like to hear, child. This is how I prefer to do this. I want you to speak from your heart all of the things you would like to promise. I will give you topics if you get stuck. Are we ready?"

Nol's face dropped; you could see his nerves go through the roof.

"Nolan, there is no fear allowed at my altar. Have no fear. I will help you, but this is your promise to speak," Akamu said gently, but authoritatively. Nol was shocked, but his fear visibly disappeared. "Nolan, do you have your rings?" Akamu asked.

He bent down to get the rings from Doc's harness and got a big kiss on the face in the process. "Thanks Doc, I needed that," he said, chuckling. He wiped his face off and faced Sadie in the altar.

Akamu took the rings and held them up, "These are the everlasting symbols of Nolan and Sadie's love for one another. They are blessed by the love both here and unseen."

He then handed Nol's ring to Sadie and Sadie's ring to Nol. He turned to Nol and asked, "Nol, what are you promising to Sadie today?"

Nol smiled, took her hands and said, "I promise to honor you. I promise to care for you, always. I promise to give you children. I promise to love you forever, Sadie." He then gently slid Sadie's ring onto her finger.

After this, every woman in attendance was swept into a wave of emotion. Eyes were dabbed like synchronized swimmers gliding to one of Mahler's great symphonies. This lasted a good minute or so, dear Reader. I was so impressed, given how nervous he was, to hear something so sweet.

Akamu was also quite impressed. "That was wonderful, Nol! Why in the world were you nervous? Now then, Sadie, would you please tell Nolan what you are promising him today?"

Sadie took a deep breath, took Nol's hands in hers and said, "I'm not sure I can improve upon that. So, my sweet Nol, I promise to honor you. I promise to care for you, always. I promise to give you a child, and *maybe* children. I promise with all my heart, Nolan Glassburé, that I will love you forever." She smiled widely, tears rolling down her face, and put Nol's ring on his finger.

"Such honesty—wonderful, my dear. Simply wonderful. Okay now, Olaf and Annie, it's your turn. Olaf, do you have your rings?"

I bent down to get our rings from Doc's harness and was treated to the same giant kiss Nol was given. I gave Doc a big kiss too and a hug. "Here we go, boy. You ready?"

He replied with a very simple "*woof*". I handed our rings to Akamu, who again held them up and blessed them. He handed my ring to Annie and Annie's ring—she still had never seen— to me. He then turned to me and asked, "Olaf, what are you promising to Annie today?"

I thought for a moment. "I promise to be your 'you'. I promise to honor and support you in all that you do. I promise to care for and protect you with all that I am, always. I promise to give you children. I promise, Annie, to love you forever and at least an eternity after that." I then put Annie's ring on, and her eyes lit up rather noticeably.

She looked at her ring, looked back at me, and whispered, "It's more beautiful than I ever imagined. Thank you so much, babe!" Tears appeared in the corners of her eyes.

"Wonderful, Olaf! Annie, what are you going to promise Olaf?" Akamu exclaimed.

She gathered herself, took my hands and said, "Olaf, I promise to be your 'love.' I promise to honor you, to care for you, and to always believe in you. I promise to give you a family, whatever that ends up meaning. I promise to never, ever take you for granted. I promise to love you, Olaf Waniglia, forever and at least an eternity after *that*." She slid my ring on as Akamu raised his hands.

"We gathered together on this day and have witnessed the power of love, of family, of togetherness. As such, with the authority of the state of Hawaii, it is my absolute pleasure to introduce to you for the very first time, Mr. and Mrs. Nolan Glassburé and Mr. and Mrs. Olaf Waniglia! Gentlemen, kiss your brides!"

We made it official and indeed kissed our brides. The band began playing a wonderfully happy song—I have absolutely no idea what it was, but it was beautiful and happy. Our parents got up and surrounded us. Akamu hugged each of us, thanking us for the opportunity to be a part of our momentous day.

The two older gentlemen who spoke at the start of the ceremony then approached us.

"Please follow us to the reception. It's just a short walk this way," Peter instructed. We had no idea a reception had been planned, so this was sure to be interesting.

Thus, the whole lot of us, Akamu and his assistant included, proceeded away from the ocean on a small path that eventually arrived at a small bridge over a bubbling brook. We stopped here and Walter said, "Everyone—this is an important place. If you look closely at the outside of the railing, you will see the initials 'CW + MD'. It was on this bridge that Christopher Waniglia fell deeply in love with Madelyn Dolby. They kissed here for the first time. It was Chris' wish that each couple stop on this bridge and kiss before they pass."

So—starting with Walter and his wife, and Peter and his wife— we each stopped, kissed on the bridge, and crossed. Father found the experience to be emotionally trying; he put his hands on the carved initials and cried. The wounds of his parents' deaths were still so fresh. Mother stayed with him the whole time, shedding a few tears of her own. When he eventually crossed, Peter gave Father a hug and said, "David, I am so, so sorry. Your dad knew this would be tough, but he sincerely hoped you would see how special it is and that it would help you heal. The echoes of your mom are everywhere here. You'll see what I mean shortly."

We eventually came upon a large, outdoor pavilion with extremely ornate lights everywhere on the property. No two were alike, but there were similarities throughout. Some were hanging in the pavilion, others were hanging in trees, and they all seemed to form a pattern.

"All the lights you see here were designed by Madelyn Waniglia—but back then, she was Madelyn Dolby. She had fallen for Chris, and the lights are the pattern she said their love travelled. They met at a party here, and everywhere you see a light outside was where they walked together that night," Peter said.

"The people who live here signed an agreement to preserve the lights as long as possible when Madelyn died. She was loved dearly by many people here," Walter said.

"I was one of them. She was my best friend and such a beautiful person. David, my God, would she have been proud of you," Walter's wife Eleanor said, giving Father a hug.

The entire area was so vibrant—so alive. In the pavilion, a huge feast had been prepared. The band set up and played music that drew what felt like the whole community to our celebration. There was easily enough food for twice the number of people there, and none of us minded the additional celebrants. I think I easily received two hundred hugs that night, and Doc was probably fed about thirty times what he should have been. He crashed not far from a fire pit and snored for a good couple of hours.

I had a chance to talk to Akamu before he left with his assistant.

"So, my non-saint saint. Can we please talk about our conversation earlier—specifically how you knew that I was going to be where I was in Maui and when?" I asked.

"Olaf, my boy, do you recall me saying that there is a foundation to everything?" he asked as though he were again teaching me rather than telling me.

"Yes, I do, but how did that enable you to identify where I would be? I didn't know where we were going, so it couldn't have been through a connection to me," I said, trying to figure out the best way to explain my confusion.

"But, my boy, you are alive, correct?" he asked, a knowing, patient smile on his face.

"Yes…"

"Well, then all I had to do was listen, and I knew. Let me remind you… your understanding for all of this shall come with what you observe—just as was the case when you discovered your ability. I'm purposely being evasive. I fully believe this will become clearer much sooner than you think, but I am insistent that it be *you* who interpret this as your own truth. My mentor did that for me, and it shaped my experience immeasurably," he said earnestly.

"So then, you are my mentor?" I asked, thinking I had just stumbled onto something.

"For this conversation I am, my dear boy," he said, smiling. "Olaf, I am tired. I wish to thank you from the bottom of my heart for allowing me to be a part of your wedding. It truly meant the world to me."

"You are so, so welcome, Akamu. Will I see you again?" I asked hopefully.

"This is not the last time we will speak, no, Olaf. Thank you again for a magical day," he said and hugged me. "Goodnight, my friend. Until the next time."

"Goodnight, my saint," I responded, smiling.

"Olaf Waniglia…" he scolded as he was led away.

"Sorry Akamu. I couldn't resist," I laughed.

I returned to the party, which was starting to wind down. Annie walked over to me and gave me a huge hug.

"Hi husband," she said, a huge smile on her face. "My dad has something he wants to talk to you about."

We walked over to where he and Mrs. Glaush were standing. He smiled as we approached.

"Hello, Olaf. You're married to my daughter now, so some of the formalities have to leave. Just as your mom has insisted that Annie call her anything but 'Mrs. Waniglia', and my bride has insisted that you call her 'Mom,' I am asking that the formality for me go away too. I don't care what you choose, but 'Dr. Glaush' no longer applies. Understand?" he asked, his voice comforting, but commanding like only a surgeon can.

"Of course...what would you prefer?" I asked, my mind spinning.

"Well, I'm fine with either 'Dad' or 'Franklin'."

"I can do that, but I may slip up from time to time," I said nervously. My parents were close by and joined us in the conversation.

"Annie, the same rule applies to me. Mo more 'Dr. Waniglia,' okay?" Father asked.

"'Dad' okay?" Annie responded, smiling shyly. "I already am in the habit of calling your wife 'Mom' now... kind of makes sense."

"Works for me, kid! I am so happy this day finally came for you two," Father responded.

"This has been quite a night! I had no idea about all our history here. These lights are gorgeous. How could I not have known about them before? Why in the world did Dad never tell me about this?" Father asked, emotion of the day weaving a tapestry of confusion in his mind.

"In a sense, this has to be a bit overwhelming, David. You doing okay?" Dr. Glaush asked kindly.

"It has definitely been hard at times, but I'm so glad I'm learning more about my mom's history. I had no idea she was such a fixture here, nor that she and Dad met here. I don't remember them ever talking about it," Father responded with introspection obvious in his voice.

"Well, given everything we have been shown since Grandpa passed, I'd say all of this was intended to fill in gaps that none of us knew existed. Did you ever have a chance to talk to Peter, Father? He filled in even more for me, and it's quite a story. They intended to stay here, but Grandpa got a call from his mom about his dad. They apparently had the farm first, and great-grandpa got sick. So, Grandpa made the decision to go home and help with the farm until his great-grandpa was better. What had intended to be just a couple months turned into decades and Grandpa taking ownership of the farm once his dad passed away. They came back here for a festival when Grandma's parents—yes, both of them—became ill. She ended up staying here for several months, and the only thing that kept her mind straight was thinking about Grandpa. That's when she made the lights and hung them up. I guess she walked that path a couple times a day. After her parents' funerals, she came back to South Carolina. A couple years later, Father was born, and they intended to come here for another festival when he was young. They never got back though. Life on the farm took over, and when *she* got sick, Grandpa intended to bring her here, but she passed too suddenly. He never could bring himself to return, even though his closest friends for the most part were here. I spent hours talking to Grandpa about Grandma, and he never once mentioned any of this," I said.

"I did too—we talked about her all the time," Annie said. "I knew that Hawaii was in the picture somehow, but never like this."

"It's just so special," Mother said. "Dad led us all on these adventures and showed us parts of his life that were so meaningful to him, and now they can be meaningful for all of us as well. I think in some way, that's what he truly wanted."

"I only met him a couple times, but the affect he's had on me is really incredible," Mrs. Glaush said. "I am so very grateful to be a part of all this."

"I am too, Mom, but I still miss him so much," Annie said sadly. "He was so good to all of us."

"I thank him every time we go out on the boat," Nol said as he and Sadie joined the group. "The first fish I ever caught on that boat, I threw back. I told him, 'Thanks to Chris you swim another day, pal.'"

"Yeah and to date that is the only fish I have ever seen Nol throw back," Sadie said, laughing.

"Well everybody, it's been one heck of a wonderful day. What say we head back to the villas, have one final drink with the wedding party and go our separate ways?" Dr. Glaush asked. "I brought a very special beverage for the men, and a derivative for the ladies. Plan? The guys at the lounge have it."

"Deal! I'm ready for a break," Nol said. "The past couple days have been spectacular, but very tiring."

"It is a plan then! Let's head back," Dr. Glaush said.

The whole lot of us headed back over the bridge, to the beach, and across to the villas. We met at the lounge where Nol and I had toasted earlier in the day. Dr. Glaush brought all of us drinks; the ladies got whiskey sours and the men had plain Irish whiskey.

"I figured this is likely what Chris drank with everybody," Dr. Glaush said. "So, one last tribute to honor him after this amazing day seemed appropriate. Therefore, everyone, let's lift our glasses and toast. To wonderful marriages for Nol and Sadie, Olaf and Annie."

We ended the night together with very nice, calm conversation. The Pacific was gently rolling in and out as high tide had come earlier and was gradually moving back down the beach. The moonlight was bright and the breeze was whimsical. By the time our glasses were empty, we were ready to head back to the villas.

Annie and I had a wonderful, emotional, passionate night. Our married life had begun in paradise, though for me, simply being next to her rivaled the beauty of Hawaii.

Merging Old and New

We—Annie, Sadie, Nol, and I—stayed in Hawaii for a full week after the ceremony. We saw each of the islands, which I'll tell you, dear Reader, is no easy feat inside of a week. In our case, it was only possible because we had an aide that showed us around—and he had his own plane. Rupert was simply extraordinary; he flew us to each island and showed us all his favorite places. The culture differed so mightily between each island I likely could write a chapter about each one. But, dear Reader, there are too many other things to tell you about, and I'm fairly sure I'd bore you to death on the topic. I truly don't want that to happen.

With our trip all over Hawaii complete, we returned to South Carolina and settled into daily life. Annie finished moving in what little was left to move; I think it may have been a sweater and maybe a tube of lip balm, if memory serves. I decided to go back to school and complete my necessary education to be an independent therapist. To my surprise, it wasn't much; I literally had to do a single semester part-time and take a certification exam. I did not become a doctor, as it really didn't make sense for me to do so. Even though I devoted a large portion of my time to the hospital diagnosing people, the farm and Annie were too important to me to have the inflexibility of a doctor's schedule—especially young doctors.

So, once I had my necessary certifications in place, I decided to open my own office and spend at least a day or two there. I found a building about ten minutes from the hospital for sale. I had Mr. Toth and his architect take a look at it, and we decided on a few changes to the layout—a couple walls were removed, a sound-proof, double-reinforced door was installed, and the whole place seemed to be transformed. It took about a month for those changes to complete, and in that time, I made it known to an increasing pool of doctors I did work for that I was opening my office as a secondary option for people they felt would benefit from my service, but who did not necessarily need to be in the hospital. I only saw people by appointment. In the beginning, my case load was light and my schedule remained simple.

Things got more interesting as more doctors heard about what I was doing for patients, especially when it involved going to a new hospital. It was a particularly stressful situation when I first started consulting for these new doctors. I'll tell you about two different groups as really every single new doctor fit into one of two buckets.

The first bucket had doctors who were receptive to hearing just about anything I told them, no matter how crazy it was. One case I remember, in particular, was when I first did work for a doctor named Dr. Smithson. He had a colleague in Father's hospital who referred me to him for a patient who was unconscious and nothing they checked showed what the problem was.

So, I met Dr. Smithson, and he showed me to where the patient was.

"Thank you, Doctor," I said. "Sometimes the conversation starts quickly and other times it takes a couple sessions. I'll let you know what I learn."

"Conversations Olaf? I don't understand," Dr. Smithson said, confused.

"I'm sorry about that. I thought that Dr. Klark told you what I do. I am able to get information from the body itself through conversation. That's how I can understand an unconscious patient's issues without them telling me verbally," I said, unaware of the kind of reaction I would get.

"Oh… okay. Can I watch?" Dr. Smithson asked with abject acceptance.

"You certainly can," I said, smiling.

It turned out that his patient had a host of things wrong. Her heart had a defect that caused it to poorly oxygenate her blood, and her brain had essentially gone into a protective state because of this. Her organs were slowly beginning to shut down as a result of this protective state. As I spoke to her *vox corporis*, Dr. Smithson sat and watched, astonished at what he was seeing and hearing.

"Olaf, thank you so much for talking to me. Susan is not ready for her life to end, and you have given me hope that all is going to be okay for her fetus too," the patient's *vox corporis* said.

"Her fetus?! She is pregnant?!" I asked, astounded.

"Yes, she is four weeks pregnant. Her brain's self-protective state is as serious as it is because of the life in her womb," she said.

"Why in the world would this not be showing up in tests?" I asked, extremely confused.

"There isn't enough blood flow for the baby's signature to be detectable," she said succinctly, almost condescendingly.

"I understand. Doctor, do you have any questions before I leave you to get this woman the treatment that she needs?" I asked, turning my attention to Dr. Smithson.

"Um, honestly I'm dumbfounded here. If we get a little bit down the road, and need you again, can I call you?" Dr. Smithson said, scratching his head.

"Of course, Doctor," I said. I then turned my attention back to Susan's *vox corporis* and asked, "Thank you so much for the conversation. Is there anything else you need me to know?"

"Olaf, you will see Susan again. When you do, please don't discredit what you hear," she said *"Thank you for saving her—she would not have lasted much longer without your help."*

Dr. Smithson and I stood and left Susan's room and went into the hallway.

"So, in the course of maybe twenty minutes, you learned this woman has a massive heart defect that is affecting the rest of her organs in protection of a fetus we cannot detect. Absolutely unreal. Thank you for your help, Olaf—I cannot say that enough," Dr. Smithson said.

So you see, dear Reader, there was a group of doctors that believed what I told them no matter how insane it sounded. For Dr. Smithson, the fact Susan was pregnant, and that it hadn't been detectable despite the fetus being four weeks old, would have spelled a sloppy end for me in the eyes of the second group of doctors.

That group, unfortunately, apologized to me...a lot. The thing is, it's a bucket containing only three doctors.

The first actually was a referral from Dr. Smithson. His colleague, Dr. Lau, had a patient who had been sedated because he came into the hospital, collapsed, then some time later, woke up, punched a nurse, and strangled a doctor. His vital signs kept degrading, and ultimately that was where I was called in.

"Dr. Smithson explained what I do, correct Dr. Lau?" I asked, hoping that I would be lucky and work with another doctor like Dr. Smithson.

"Yes, he did, but I am having a very hard time believing it," he responded. "If you can help this man, that's all that matters. Please see what you can do."

So, with that, I proceeded to the patient and began a conversation with his *vox corporis*.

"*Sean is bi-polar, Olaf. Unfortunately, when he is not medicated, he panics and resorts to being violent as a defense mechanism. When he is medicated, he's fine without any issues,*" he said.

"How long has he been off his medication?" I asked.

"*The last time he took it was about three weeks ago. He's unfortunately giving up because he doesn't feel that he fits into this world in any way,*" he said.

"I understand. Does he have a therapist he's working with? Or a family that we can contact?" I asked.

"*His therapist unfortunately won't see him anymore because Sean has been unable to pay. His therapist is named Dr. Vire. He has a family he has never met. He was placed in an orphanage shortly after birth. His birth parents are alive, but he has never met them. He was never adopted, so he has no one in his life,*" he said.

"Okay. Let me see what I can do for you. I'll do my best," I said cautiously.

"*I know you will, Olaf. Thank you. Remember the ice tonight,*" he said.

"Ice?" I asked, very confused and did not get a response. This concerned me.

With that, I left the room and found Dr. Lau.

"Sean is bi-polar, Dr. Lau. He has not been medicated for about three weeks. He has a therapist named Dr. Vire that has stopped seeing him due to non-payment. He was given up for adoption as a baby, but was never adopted. He has no immediate family to contact," I said.

"How in the world could you know that? It's impossible," he said angrily, waited a second, and smacked me hard enough to make my face bruise and swell. "Get the hell out of here."

"Two things. One—you ever so much as hint to me that you are going to be physical again, and I will have you in one of these beds for several days with a single punch. Two—check what I told you. I will not help you again under any circumstance. Good day, Doctor," I said angrily.

So, I left, amazed. Annie had a fit that night when she saw the lump on my face.

"That jackass *hit* you? You told him what was wrong and he *hit* you?" she asked furiously. "I cannot believe some people!"

"Well, I should have expected it. The guy's *vox corporis* told me to 'remember the ice' before our conversation ended," I said.

The next day, I got two phone calls. The first was from Dr. Smithson apologizing profusely for the referral. The second was Dr. Lau's assistant asking me to come back to the hospital. I remember distinctly telling her "no" several times before she convinced me to come back. I honestly don't recall how she did such a thing, but I suppose that to be irrelevant.

So, I very reluctantly returned to Dr. Lau's office and found him with another person in his office. I did not sit down; rather, I stood in the doorway. I'm positive my expression was anything but pleasant.

"Olaf, please hear me out. You have every reason to leave, but I need your help," Dr. Lau said nervously.

"I'm not sure why I'm here then, Doctor. You understood what I said yesterday before I left, correct?" I snapped.

"I'm sorry I hit you. I had no right to do so. Please, will you sit down?" he asked, even more timidly than before.

"I'll stand, thank you. What was it that you needed?" I asked callously.

The man sitting opposite Dr. Lau then spoke. "Olaf, my name is Hank Vire. I was treating the patient that you diagnosed yesterday. There are a couple things you learned that I never did. Would you be willing to discuss them with me?"

"Of course, Doctor. What would you like to know?" I asked, moving into the office.

"Lau mentioned that Sean was orphaned and was never adopted. Is this what you have understood?" Dr. Vire asked me.

"That is what I was told, yes. I also learned that both of his parents are living, but he has never met them," I responded.

"Well, we were able to find Sean in the state's files. You are correct about the orphanage. Sean never told me this. His file with his parents' names is sealed. We still do not know who they are or where they live. Regardless, I have secured state funding to treat Sean based on these facts. You have absolutely no idea how profound this is for his care. I want to thank you from the bottom of my heart for your help here," Dr. Vire said.

"It is my pleasure, Doctor. Gentlemen, is there anything else?" I asked, still not at all happy to be in Dr. Lau's office despite the apology.

"Will you work with me again, Olaf?" Dr. Lau asked, almost pleading.

"Maybe. Good day, gentlemen," I answered and left his office.

As I passed Sean's room, his *vox corporis* spoke to me, saying, "*You've given a life hope, Olaf. Thank you.*"

"You are more than welcome," I said, smiling.

The second example I will offer has echoes of the past. Enjoy, dear Reader.

I was referred to a Dr. Torino at a surgery center about two miles from the hospital. He and his team had done a routine, outpatient appendectomy and the patient had not woken up as they expected. So, I went to the surgery center, thinking the referrer in this case, Dr. Lau, would have paved a clear path for me. Why did I think such a thing, dear Reader?

I introduced myself and Dr. Torino escorted me to where the patient was.

"She endured no complications that we are aware of, Mr. Waniglia. Can you please see what you can find out?" Dr. Torino asked politely.

"Sure—I'll see what I can learn," I responded. So, I proceeded to start a conversation with the girl's *vox corporis*.

"*Hello Olaf,*" she said. "*This is fairly straightforward. They would have seen this had they simply scanned her in any number of ways. There is still a clamp on Jill's large intestine. She's basically in shock right now.*"

"What?! I will get the team on this immediately!" I exclaimed.

"*You won't unless you turn around RIGHT NOW!*" she said with urgency.

I turned around to see Dr. Torino with a syringe about three inches from me—two of his associates, one on each side, joined him.

I lifted my leg and stopped Dr. Torino. The associate on his right lunged at me, and I punched him square in the jaw, making him fall down unconscious. The other associate attempted to do the same, at the same time, but just bumped into Dr. Torino, who I still kept away with my left leg.

"If y'all want to lose your licenses, your homes and your freedom, continue what you're doing. This girl has a clamp you failed to remove and is in shock. Don't believe me?" I grabbed a nearby ultrasound machine and moved the wand over her large intestine. There, on the monitor was the clamp her *vox corporis* had mentioned. "Had you not been incompetent, we would not be having this conversation. Do not expect to ever see me here again. Good day, gentlemen," I said. I then kicked Dr. Torino away from me and stepped on the idiot.

I had a very hard time coming to terms with what happened. I could not even talk about it. It shook me terribly—to the point where I intermittently was shaking. Doc would not leave my side for any reason. Annie called Nol and the four of us went out on his boat. I brought a bottle of whiskey and was about a third of the way through it when Sadie sat down next to me.

"What happened today, Olaf? We're awfully worried about you right now," she said kindly.

"It almost happened again," I slurred.

"What almost happened again?" she asked with obvious concern in her voice.

"A doctor…" I started and began shaking again.

Annie sat down on my other side and hugged me tightly. "Babe—please. What happened?" she asked sadly.

"He had a needle," I said.

"What the holy hell?!" Nol exclaimed. "Some fool tried to inject you again?"

"Yes," I said and finished the whisky in my glass.

"Aw son, tell me you hurt the son of a bitch. You gotta tell your dad and Doc G. They have to know," Nol said emphatically.

"He had two guys. I knocked one of them out. The other missed. I kicked the guy with the syringe. They left a clamp in a poor teenage girl after a routine appendectomy. It was her *vox corporis* who told me to turn around. If she hadn't...." I said and started shaking again.

"As soon as we are home, we're calling Joe, babe. This is insane," Annie said, holding me tighter.

"Yes—get Lating involved. He will fix this," Nol said.

Fix it, he did, dear Reader. Joe went to the surgical center the next day and met with the center's board of trustees, Dr. Torino, and his team. He said, in no uncertain terms, that we would be pressing charges given the events of the day before. He brought with him Dr. Small's trial details and apparently looked squarely at Dr. Torino as he said that he would not hesitate to go after their licenses.

The chairman of the board indicated that it would not be necessary to go after their licenses because Dr. Torino and his staff were terminated, effective immediately and all were already going before the medical board for malpractice. He encouraged us to press charges regardless, but warned that we were not first in line. Apparently, the girl's family was suing the surgery center because she had to be transferred to a hospital and was in critical condition. It was the fourth lawsuit for Dr. Torino and his team.

The chairman then asked Joe if I would be willing to remain connected to the girl to ensure she had the best possible care. He added that the compensation for this would be equal to that which would have been paid to Dr. Torino and his team for the month. Joe nodded, they shook on it, and it was over.

I oversaw the girl's care, which took several weeks. Eventually, she was transferred to Dr. Glaush's team, and from there, we got her back on her feet. Incidentally, I got yet another call from Dr. Lau's assistant in which she said, "Dr. Lau wishes to pass on his sincere apology for the situation with Dr. Torino."

I replied, "Dr. Lau will kindly not request nor offer my assistance to anyone going forward. Thank you for your time."

There is one final individual from this group of doctors that literally shaped the manner in which I agree to assist patients. You see, dear Reader, after the situation with Dr. Torino, Joe wrote up a contract every doctor I did work for signed, then filed. That contract was amended after the time I met Dr. Stephens, a doctor who was not referred to me, but rather one who heard about me from a colleague.

I reluctantly took the referral and had Dr. Stephens review and sign my agreement. He then told me about a patient of his whose health was declining for no reason whatsoever.

"His complete health record does not explain at all what we are seeing, Olaf. Would you mind taking a look and seeing what you can?" he asked politely.

"Are you aware of my methodology, Doctor?" I asked.

"I am not, but you came highly recommended to me," he responded.

"From whom, Doctor?" I asked.

"I'd rather not say. Would you please just take a look at my patient?" he responded impatiently.

"I would much prefer you tell me who referred me to you. Please, Doctor—what does this hurt?" I asked, not understanding what the secrecy was for.

"Please, would you just look at the patient?"

"You read the terms of my agreement, yes?" I asked, my own patience tested.

"I did. Would you please just go to the patient?" he responded, anger escalating.

"Yep, show me the way," I said callously.

He took me to a patient who was lucid with no apparent issues whatsoever. I no more than began to form a question I my mind before I found myself in handcuffs.

"This man has no right to be here," Dr. Stephens said emphatically.

"Wow, you are a bigger fool than I took you for. Who just got you to throw away your career?" I asked as I was led away.

"Bill Torino sends his love, asshole," he responded.

"You just lost a hell of a lot more than the satisfaction you feel right now. Officer, there is a signed agreement in my coat pocket and a voice recorder in the other. Would you please get them before this goes further?" I asked.

"At the station," he responded callously. I was indeed arrested, booked, and was sitting in a jail cell when Joe and the chief of police came and got me.

"The officer was doing his job, Mr. Waniglia. I'm very sorry for this. All charges are dropped," the chief said.

"Um, sir, ours are just beginning. Olaf, I'll take you home," Joe said with a tone that threatened everyone in the room.

You cannot possibly imagine, dear Reader, the teasing that ensued among the following people: Annie, Nol, Sadie, my in-laws, my parents, and my lawyer. It was as though this insane, disgusting, ridiculous situation I was cast in, was part of a situation comedy show. I hated to be the person who was sour about the whole thing, but I was the damn victim in this and it straight made me angry. I could not separate my anger or disappointment and enjoy the fun the group was having with this.

Regardless, the aforementioned group had a blast calling me "convict" to a point that absolutely made my blood boil. I cannot possibly explain why this happened, but I can tell you the result. I went through three speed bags, two light bags, and six sets of gloves at home. The boys at the gym would not spar with me anymore. I broke two speed bags, three light bags, and one heavy bag in the gym. I paid for all of them out of complete guilt.

Yes, dear Reader, I was angry. I was so angry I didn't care how many people were impacted when we sued Stephens, and by extension, Torino. I took everything Torino had, liquidated it, and gave it to the orphanage that Sean grew up in. I sued Stephens and ultimately agreed to a deal that I myself wrote. Joe was reluctant to submit it for consideration, but as I said, I was angry and did not take "no" for an answer. Stephens agreed to leave his medical practice and give 100% of the proceeds from the sale to an escrow fund for those who could not pay for medical care.

As a result, Torino and his family lost their house. Stephens too. I remember both of their families being in the courtroom when everything settled. Torino's son came up to me and asked me, "Why did you do this, mister?"

I looked at him, and in the nicest way possible, said, "Ask your father. If he tells you the truth, you'll understand."

The lot of the folks in my life learned to not call me "convict." Annie got the silent treatment from me for a good few hours. This was one of the times I subsequently broke a speed bag at home. On another occasion, I jumped off Nol's boat, swam to shore, and walked home when Nol made the comment. I left both my parents' house and Joe's office when they said it, and my in-laws were hushed by their daughter when they tried to make light of it. No one at the farm said a word about it.... ever.

I was angry. I discovered that when I was angry, people kept their distance. Perhaps this was due to my fists. Perhaps it was due to what I said, or how I said it. Regardless of the reason, everyone in my life learned quickly what *not* to do when I was angry. The only one who did not endure my anger was Doc.

I eventually got out of my funk, but no one involved moved forward without addressing their relationship with me first. Doctors in area hospitals no longer questioned me when I asked a first-time doctor to sign my agreement. I never, ever agreed to do an appointment for a new doctor unless the referring physician was known and was also under agreement. My wife, Nol, and Sadie all apologized in their own ways and we talked through it all. My in-laws took their cues from Annie and spoke carefully on the subject. My parents and I talked it out as we always had when difficult situations presented themselves. The difference here was apparent; the old Olaf was never angry and let basically anything at all roll cleanly off his back. The new Olaf—the one who should have died, and ultimately the one who was arrested—had a line. If that line was crossed, he had no soul; he just had blind anger.

These two individuals had merged. Call it what you will, dear Reader; in my mind, it was cause and effect. Old merged with new; simple as that.

The Amazing Fanny McNutter

As time passed and the number of doctors who requested my help stabilized, I found the amount of appointments I was getting on my own to be something I had trouble balancing. As such, the notion of an assistant cropped up and the search began for the perfect person.

I had thought a family member may be best for such a thing, but Annie was busy with the farm, and both Mother and Mrs. Glaush had more to do than I could ever imagine. Sadie crossed my mind too, but she was doing freelance journalism and split her time with Nol between New York and South Carolina. Gill was also a thought, but that man's social calendar was fuller than the ocean has water. If I remember correctly, he had two years planned when I spoke to him about the position. So—the family/friend possibilities were disappointing to say the least.

I then turned my attention to people I knew in the medical industry, but there wasn't a single clerical person I felt comfortable asking. Simply put, I didn't want to hurt any of the professional relationships I had built over the previous couple years. I then employed the help of those I knew well—Mr. Toth, Joe, and the Rodriguez's in particular. Here, I started to get a few possibilities. Looking back, this was some of the most fun I've had talking to people—ever.

The first candidate suggested to me was Mr. Toth's wife's second cousin, Gertrude. She was 89 years young and had retired twenty-five years prior. I brought her into the office for an interview.

"Hi Gertrude," I said, "Can you tell me a little bit about yourself?"

"What?" she replied loudly.

"Sorry—I asked if you could tell me a little bit about yourself," I asked a bit louder.

"Oh—well, I retired after forty years of being a secretary for the energy company. I like to knit and do my crosswords," she said frailly.

"Are you able to work at least four days a week on a part-time basis?" I asked, my voice still raised in volume.

"Oh gosh no! I have pinochle on Tuesdays, and I get my hair done on Thursdays, and I have tea with the ladies on Mondays, Tuesdays, Wednesdays, and Fridays. We take a break on Thursdays and that's when I see Gwendolyn at the hair parlor," she said, sounding a tad offended at the question.

"Thank you so much for your time, Gertrude. That is all for today," I said.

"What?" she asked.

"Thank you for coming in," I said a bit louder.

"What? Quit whispering you fool," she said angrily.

"THANK YOU FOR YOUR TIME!" I said much louder.

"Oh—I'm sorry. Why am I here again?" she asked innocently.

I called Mrs. Toth and she agreed to pick Gertrude up. While we waited, I made her a cup of tea. Doc laid next to me and apparently made her nervous as he slept.

"What is that behemoth?" she asked as she sipped her tea.

"That's my dog, Doc. He won't hurt you," I replied at a volume I thought would suffice.

"It's going to hurt me?! What kind of animal are you?" she exclaimed.

Doc looked up at her, woofed, and laid back down.

"HE'S NOT GOING TO HURT YOU," I replied loudly.

Just as that exchange ended, Mrs. Toth appeared in the doorway.

"How did it go, Olaf?" she asked.

"Well, there are some hearing challenges, and I think she's afraid of Doc," I replied.

"Yeah, I figured. Sorry about this, Olaf," Mrs. Toth replied kindly. "Gertrude, are you ready to go home?" she asked loudly.

"Yes I am. I think that elephant may eat me," Gertrude replied.

Mrs. Toth and I laughed, Doc looked up from his nap briefly, and the interview was over.

The next person to interview was someone that Maria Rodriguez knew from one of her outreach groups at church. This person—Sofia—spoke not one word of English *at all*—not "Please," not "Thank you," not "Hello." Our interview was the most awkward conversation I have ever had. I tried to meet her half way based on the Spanish I knew, and I *think* she did too, but she knew absolutely no English. In the end, she sat next to Doc and pet him a bunch before she left. When doing so, there still was not a single word of English—not one—spoken though many words were part of the conversation. Maria and I spoke after my time with Sofia, and we laughed hardtop tears when I told her what happened.

Joe told me that his neighbor, Steven Garfield, might be a good fit and set up a time for us to meet the next day. Steven was a part-time personal shopper for high-end customers at one of the department stores in Charleston. His hours were based on appointment, and because the work I had would only be part-time, both Joe and I figured this may work out well.

So, Steven came in for an interview dressed about as fashionably as anyone I think I had ever seen. He wasn't wearing a traditional suit, but his shirt, pants, and tie all looked to be made from exotic fabrics. He carried himself extremely well, very properly.

"Hi Steven. Can you tell me a little bit about yourself?" I asked.

"Well, I specialize in making people look their absolute best. *That* is my talent," he said.

"Joe indicated that you work part-time. Is that correct?" I asked.

"My work never stops. Never," he said emotionally.

"Um, okay—I understand this. But in terms of your schedule, you have some parts of your day that are available, correct? I'm in need of a part-time assistant," I said, trying to respect his sensitivity.

"What kind of assistant is this? I do see that some help is needed in your wardrobe, but I am doubting this is the type of assistant of which you speak," he said arrogantly.

"I am a therapist. I work here part of the time, at a few hospitals some of the time, and at my family's farm the other part. I need someone to help me with the case load here."

"I feel perhaps that you have overlooked a couple key details here, sir," he said cagily.

"What details am I missing? I'd be interested in your opinion," I said genuinely.

"For starters, farms are nasty places no one in their right mind belongs in. Secondly, you would do much better with pleated pants as opposed to plain front. The contour of your body dictates this. And your shirt, my goodness man—did you get it at a thrift store? What kind of therapist dresses like a homeless man?"

"Well, I make several million dollars a year with the farm, and work with people I care deeply for, so I disagree with your first point. Your second perhaps warrants some investigation. Your third point, however, makes no sense as I purchased this shirt at the very store in which you work."

"Um, the farm makes you *millions?*" he asked with astonishment in his voice.

"Yes, it does. Now then, do you have the time necessary for what I have outlined?" I asked, beginning to lose patience.

"I might—I don't know," he said with the same bravado as before.

"If you don't have the time, it's really unnecessary to continue talking. Thank you for your time," I said, my patience completely gone.

"But—what if I did?"

"Well, you should have said so the first time I asked you. Have a wonderful day, and best of luck at the store. Perhaps I will see you there some day."

With that, he got up, looked squarely at me, and said, "You are the worst dressed millionaire I have ever seen, and that is just sad."

"Steven, I could literally buy the entire franchise you do such precious, important work for and burn every last stitch of clothing for fun. The sad part here is, I was looking to offer you an opportunity and instead you've embarrassed yourself. I appreciate your time today. Take care," I said, glaring right back at him.

"You'd never…"

"Get out, Steven."

In a flurry of fabulous, he left the office. Doc and I looked at each other in absolute disgust.

I called Joe the next day and told him about the interview. He laughed and said, "Yeah, I guess I figured it might go down like that."

"Really, Joe?" I asked.

"In hindsight, it's a little funny, isn't it, Pleat Boy?" he said, chuckling.

"One may suppose. Thank you, counselor," I responded.

So, I did three interviews, and I had not one viable candidate. I thought about putting an ad in the paper, but really didn't want to do that. So, I went about my days and figured, after a little break, I'd resume my search.

Two weeks later, I had received an unreal number of requests for appointments and started to panic. Annie helped as much as she could, but I saw my need for an assistant was becoming more urgent as time went.

One night, there was a knock on the office door at the farm as Annie and I were closing up.

"Are you expecting anyone, love?" I asked.

"No, I would never schedule anything this late."

So, I opened the door and was greeted by a rotund woman with a gorgeous smile.

"Hello child. I understand you are in need of some help in the form of an assistant. Is this so?" she asked.

"Yes—in fact it is. Would you come in?" I replied.

"Thank you kindly. I'd love to meet your bride. I've heard so much about her," she said.

I went back in my mind, wondering if someone had indicated they were sending someone to the farm to interview. I quickly squashed that as I always interviewed at my office. I then suspected that Joe had something to do with this.

"Oh my goodness—child you are beautiful. Give Fanny a hug," she said to Annie.

Annie looked at me with obvious confusion, stood up, and hugged her.

"How do you know me?" Annie asked.

"Akamu sends his love to both of you beautiful children. Honey Boy, he told me of your struggles of late, and I couldn't bear to let you suffer any further. My name is Fanny McNutter. I would be honored if you would consider me to be your assistant," she said kindly.

"Akamu sent you? Were you in Hawaii?" I asked, confused.

"No Honey Boy—I was in Charleston with my husband Gerard," she said. "I've known Akamu for years. He is such a dear man. He told me how hard it's been keeping things straight for 'ya, and I can fix that."

"Really? Do you have a background as an assistant?" Annie asked.

"Well Honey Girl, I can't honestly say I do, but I just sent my youngest of six off to college. I managed six wonderful boys—seven if you include my husband—through all the schooling, all the sports, and all of their personal lives. I'd say I am prepared for anything Honey Boy may need," she said, smiling.

"Well, I need someone to help me with scheduling, primarily. I think at this point it's part-time, but if the need grows, I may need you full-time. Is that possible?" I asked.

"Honey Boy, anything you need. If there's one thing I know, it's that I can help you out of this difficulty you find yourself in. You just take some time and think this over, okay?" she asked kindly.

"I'm not sure there is anything to think about. If you can, let's start tomorrow morning. I'll pay you $2,000 a month to start—sound okay?" I asked, hoping that I'd truly found the person I needed.

"Honey Boy, I have a different idea. How 'bout you pay me what you feel I deserve and you agree to help me and my wonderful husband with that ability of yours? I promise you we'd ask for no more than one appointment each, each month," she said softly.

"Of course, Fanny! I'd be absolutely happy to! Just one thing—I always have my dog at the office. Is that going to bother you?" I asked, nervous that somehow I just killed the deal.

"The amazing Doc? I cannot wait to meet the beautiful creature who saved your life," she said, smiling.

"Are you a saint?" Annie asked.

Fanny laughed a little bit, smiled, and hugged her. "No, child—I am no saint. I'm just happy I can help you two," she said, and hugged Annie tightly.

"We've been so busy—this is going to help us so much," Annie said with a strained voice.

"I know, child. I know. Fanny will make this all better for 'ya," she said, hugging Annie tighter.

So, dear Reader, I had found my assistant through a common link to a man I think may have saved the sanctity of my existence. Akamu did more for me than I could have ever imagined. With this latest instance of help, he ended up doing for me what Akamu told me about in Hawaii—my capacity to heal.

Fanny came to work the next day and completely changed the way my schedule was being managed. She not only maintained the schedule for my office appointments, she kept track of my hospital time, and also inserted farm time in the schedule too. The best thing she did, though, was make absolutely sure I was home by 6:30 every night at the very latest. More often, Annie and I were eating by that time, as I'd be home by 5:30 and would get cooking pretty much immediately.

When I first met Fanny's husband, Gerard, I felt like I had known him my entire life. He was such a kind, warm-hearted man. He had some definite health challenges though, and this was what Fanny had hoped I would be able to help with. So many other supposed "specialists" had tried and failed to fix him. In short, he had horrible back pain, and at times it got to a point that affected his legs, and he could not walk.

So, at our first appointment, I walked through my approach.

"I'm hoping Fanny told you about what I do, Gerard. Did she?" I asked.

"Yes, Mr. Waniglia, she did. You just tell me what I need to do, okay?" he responded kindly.

"Well first thing, I am not 'Mr. Waniglia' to you. It's Olaf from here on out, okay?" I said, mimicking Akamu when he insisted I not call him a saint.

"Of course—this I can do," he said with a big smile.

"Otherwise, just relax. You will hear me talking, but just relax, and I'll let you know when the session is done. Any questions?" I asked.

"Just one, Olaf. What happens if you can't communicate with my body?" he asked with some nervousness in his voice.

"Then we will try again another day, Gerard. I will say, though, the only times I have a problem there is when the individual has been unconscious for a long time. Even then, I have had success. I truly don't think this will be a problem," I said smiling.

"*Hello Olaf—you are correct!*" Gerard's *vox corporis* said as if on cue.

"Well then, there we go! Hello! Gerard, we are already communicating. Please relax," I said.

"*Gerard's spine has been degenerating for the past several years. This is the cause of his pain and causes him to have issues walking,*" Gerard's *vox corporis* said directly. "*However, you are going to stop this.*"

I paused for a couple seconds, thinking perhaps I heard him wrong.

"I understand the issue for sure, but could you repeat that second item please? I want to be sure that I heard you correctly," I said with some nervous curiosity.

"*I believe you understood me, Olaf. You are going to heal Gerard's spine. This will not happen today, but it will happen,*" he said with his voice ringing of honesty.

"In the meantime, what is it I can do to alleviate his pain?" I asked intently.

"*Make contact with him physically and trust in your ability,*" he said comfortingly.

I grasped Gerard's hand, closed my eyes, and was astounded at what happened. The overall feel of the environment was like it was when Akamu healed me; everything around us glowed and the air had shimmering ripples of brightness in it, almost like cresting waves. I looked down at Gerard and could see the parts of his spine that were badly degenerated. As soon as I saw this, I felt a profound sadness and said, "I'm so sorry." It was as though I could see the degeneration stop and the damaged areas reversed slightly. They were by no means resolved, but they looked much better than before.

Almost as quickly as this happened, I found that Gerard was shaking me. Apparently, this took so much out of me that I passed out.

"Olaf—you in there?" he asked nervously.

"I'm sorry about that, Gerard—that was unexpected," I said sleepily.

"What in God's amazing world are you sorry about? You took away almost all my pain, Olaf. I felt you do it. It was as though you touched each place on my back that hurt and healed them. I have no idea what just happened, but I haven't felt like this in years," he said excitedly.

"I'm so glad, Gerard—I truly am. Thing is, you're not completely healed. Your *vox corporis*—I'm sorry that's what I call your body's voice—indicated the healing process would not be complete today. I think I need to find out exactly what in the world just happened to make sure I do what you need me to do," I said, still very tired.

"Whatever you need to do is fine with me, Olaf. I feel normal for the first time in forever. Mind if I go tell my bride?" he asked excitedly.

"Of course, Gerard. I'm gonna sit here a minute," I said and slouched in my chair. Doc stood up and rested his head on my lap. As soon as he did, it became obvious that what had just happened was remarkable.

The area where I did my appointments was down a long hallway, behind a closed door. Before the appointment, Gerard had a very difficult time just getting to the appointment room. After the appointment, I heard him practically run down the hallway to where Fanny was. Shortly thereafter, they both returned.

"Olaf Wanigla!" Fanny said excitedly. "I knew you could do it—I just knew it! You gave me my Gerard back. The boys are going to be so excited! Thank you so much! I cannot say this enough!"

"It's just a start, Fanny. Gerard, you still need to be careful, okay? Let's meet again in a couple weeks. Fanny—can you see what my schedule holds over the next few days? I think I may have to go see Akamu in Hawaii," I said, still tired.

"Honey Boy, he's at your house with Annie. He knew this was going to be an important day for you," she said kindly.

"He's where?" I asked, astonished.

"He's at your house, Olaf. Gerard was your last appointment for the day—you go home now. I'll close up here. You have a 10:00 consultation in the morning at Mercy. Then you're here for two appointments, and then you have farm time. I left your itinerary by your keys," she said smiling.

"You are amazing, Fanny. I cannot thank you enough," I said as I tried to sit up.

"Uh, Honey Boy, you are the amazing one here," she said.

"I second that! Thank you, Olaf. This is remarkable!" Gerard said, smiling. "May I pet your dog?"

Doc walked over to him and sat down. He was absolutely willing to accept affection from just about anyone.

As my strength returned to me, I made my way out of the office with Doc and headed home. I couldn't wait to talk to Akamu—and could not believe that he was in South Carolina! I spent the entire car ride home trying to figure out the questions I needed to ask, and found this to be a nearly impossible task because I was still hung up on the fact he was in town.

When I got home, Doc bounded inside and ran to find my friend. Annie intercepted me a few steps in.

"Look what the cat drug in. Hi babe. Looks like you had the day that Akamu said you'd have. Did you know he was coming?" Annie asked.

"Nope. I found out about a half hour ago he was here, and I'm astonished," I said. "Where might the saint be at the moment?" I asked tiredly.

"He's on the deck. I think Doc may have assaulted him," she said.

So, I made my way to the deck to find Doc sitting patiently next to Akamu. Both were facing the setting sun, kindred spirits enjoying the moment.

"I didn't know you were going to be in town, my friend," I said as I approached him.

"Well, you shouldn't have known, Olaf. If you had, it may have colored your experience, and we can't have this. I knew today would be big for you and knew you would have questions. So—ask away," he said, smiling.

"First, what in the world happened?" I asked, still trying to process the session with Gerard.

"Well, he was willing to accept your help in the deepest parts of his experience, Olaf. The truth of this is something that few will possess," Akamu said. "There will be people like this who you will, in fact, heal. There will be others who you simply will consult and they will find other paths of healing. There are still others who will not accept your or anyone else's help for a whole myriad of reasons. Regardless of the outcome, trust in your ability to remain honest with both yourself and those who you see. There will be times that surprise you the longer you do this," he said, every bit the teacher.

"Can you explain this a little bit? I know I can't essentially go around curing everyone I see, but what makes it such that I can't?" I asked, very confused.

"Well, take a person in the hospital as an example. Their expectation, and thus the truth of their existence, is a doctor will resolve their issue. Your role in those cases is simply to help the doctors to know what they need to do to treat the individual," he said. "There will be other cases, like the one you had today, where an individual had no luck in the care of doctors but believes both they *can* be healed and *you* can heal them. This all comes down to the individual, telling you what their truth is. The voice you hear will give you this truth."

"So, this is what I did with you then?" I asked, beginning to understand.

"Yes, my friend. Though in your case, it was different because of your ability and because I had in part treated you, ironically, from this very deck," he responded.

"Okay—I think I understand this. But, his *vox corporis* told me it would take time to heal him. Why is that?" I asked.

"Well, you are just getting your feet wet and your ability is not yet fully formed. The way in which you navigate the healing space will differ from the way I do. How you ultimately choose to do this will be unique to you. Once you fully understand what is possible for the benefit of others, *and* you understand how *you* heal, it will not take as much energy out of you, and usually a single session will heal the people you treat. Don't stress about this. It will come in time," he said, smiling proudly.

"Would I be able to heal your vision?" I asked.

"No, Olaf—you wouldn't. I have fully accepted my blindness in my experience. I would need to feel as though my blindness were something which needs to be resolved, and I don't. I still 'see' plenty—I do not miss my vision," he said. "Trust me when I say this—I am not the only person you will meet like this. Some will choose the path they are on as their experience of truth."

"Okay, then essentially this is not my choice? It's the choice of the individual?" I asked in response.

"In part, Olaf—yes. The other part *is* your responsibility, but I believe you understand this," he said.

"I think I understand," I said hesitatingly.

"Olaf, you heard your subject indicate you were going to heal him, correct?" Akamu asked.

"Yes, that is correct," I responded.

"Okay, and you did something to initiate the healing process, yes?"

"Yes, I did, but I'm not sure what it was I did to help. I just said I was sorry when I saw the problems in his body," I said, recounting the session.

"So in this instance, your discovery and your subsequent consolation began the healing process. Next time, take a minute to observe what's around you before you do anything. Everything you need is right there," he said intensely.

"I will, Akamu—thank you. Now tell me a couple things. First, how do you know Fanny? Second, how did you know I needed an assistant? Third, how did you send her to me?" I asked, leaning in to him. By this time, Annie had joined our conversation with appetizers and drinks.

"Well, Fanny was a tiny girl when I first met her. Her father passed away suddenly when she was extremely young—I think three— and her mother did not handle it well at all. Back then, I volunteered at some of the area schools. She and I met when Fanny was in kindergarten. It was soon after her mother passed away very tragically. After I discovered she had no family at all, I petitioned the state and I adopted her. There you go—she is my daughter. Second, you told me you needed an assistant. You likely don't remember this, but that's what happened. Third, I called her. Good?" he responded sarcastically.

"Yes, good. I had no idea you had a daughter, Akamu," I said, feeling a little embarrassed.

"My friend, we never talked about it. There are many things about me you do not know," he said chuckling slightly.

"Well, how long are you here?" I asked.

"Long enough for you to hear the high-level stuff, but by no means long enough for you to hear everything," he said with a big smile.

So, that night I learned he had lost his sight as a teenager due to a degenerative disorder, and his mother had been the one to help him understand that such a thing was only as powerful as one allows it to be. I learned he had been widowed after twenty-seven years of marriage. He used his wife as another example of someone who had accepted the reality of their situation. She had a major stroke, and thus did not wish to be healed.

"I miss her every day physically, but spiritually we have not once been apart," he said stoutly.

I learned his ability began as a boy, pretty much as mine had. Further, he had discovered there were others with complimentary abilities who he could communicate with when he was in his 40's— people who he felt I would be hearing from at some point. He told me he had met both of my grandparents when he was a teenager, and that Annie's smile rivaled my grandmother's in intensity. Lastly, he told me his ability to see into my future had stopped as he had taught me all he was intended to, which meant I would hear from him much more frequently. Further, he expected us to come to the islands with some frequency.

This last point elicited a resounding, "Okay!" from Annie, who was actively trying to figure out the context of the conversation as it happened.

"Now then, my friend," Akamu said smiling, "I've heard of the legend of your cooking, but have not yet had the pleasure of enjoying it. Would you mind cooking for me tonight, and then taking me back to my daughter's house? I need to get there early enough to beat Gerard at Poker again a few dozen times."

Our night ended with the three of us eating grilled prime rib with my special au jus, homemade mashed potatoes, and corn. As I understand it, Akamu beat Gerard in Poker in all but two hands—and Fanny won those two. Poor Gerard!

The next time I saw Mr. McNutter in my office, Akamu's tutelage truly paid off.

"*He still believes very deeply in your capacity to heal him, Olaf,*" Gerard's *vox corporis* said, "*and believes firmly this will be so. Please move forward holding this truth in your heart.*"

"I will. I'm going to do this a little bit differently today," I said as I relaxed and grasped Gerard's hand.

As it had happened before, the environment changed; most things had a glow and the bright streams of light that appeared randomly in the air returned. Before I looked down at Gerard, I watched the bright, gliding lines of light around me. I watched what was happening in the room, paying attention to the subtle changes all around me. In the end, I focused my attention on those dancing lines of light.

They seemed to be moving in concert with one another; they never touched but their paths were complimentary, just like the waves of the ocean. At one point, I reached out and touched one, and the whole area around me lit up. There was no sound when I did so, but the feeling was unlike anything I had ever experienced; I felt an energized warmth, but I was not shocked. I'm sorry, dear Reader— I'm not sure how else to describe this.

I had the thought these streams of light could help Gerard heal. It was just a thought. I then looked back at Gerard and several streams of light were moving into the damaged parts of Gerard's spine. Slowly but surely, the damage was removed. When it was, I said, "Thank you," and again the room lit up. I slowly released Gerard's hand.

When I opened my eyes, tears were streaming down his face and the environment around me was back to normal.

"Olaf, you did it. I cannot possibly explain to you what I just felt, but I heard you say, 'Thank you', and as soon as you did, I could feel this incredible rush all around me. When it stopped, I had no pain and my back felt absolutely amazing," he said as he wiped his face.

"Gerard, you were as much a part of this as I was. Thank you, so very much, for allowing me to assist," I said smiling.

I had just helped to completely heal a person. That feeling was positively surreal.

Richard Glassburé, Statesman

The next time I saw Nol, it was in New York as he had a home game that weekend. The four of us had a cadence around these weekends. Annie and I would arrive early enough to have breakfast with Nol and Sadie on Saturday morning as Nol then usually had meetings around midday, but was free again for dinner. We'd then go to the game on Sunday and have dinner prior to heading home.

This particular weekend was about a month after I had my last session with Gerard, and I reported what happened to their amazement. This conversation spread across almost all of our time there that weekend, but the highlight for me was Nol's game. He played absolutely amazingly that day. He was in his fourth season and to this point had a remarkable career. New York had given him an extended contract based on the beast he was on the field. It's still crazy to me just how mean my friend would get on the field, as he was such a sweet person off of it. The depth of that man's care was profound.

Nol became one of the highest paid players of his time; with part of his earnings, he went to school in the off season and became fully certified to teach special needs people, extending his undergraduate studies. With another part of his earning, he established the Richard Carolas Glassburé Fund which, to this day, continues to provide funding to hundreds of thousands of special needs people for education and occupational therapy around the world. With still another part of his earnings, he started the first Richard Carolas Glassburé School, which became the premier educational facility for people with special needs—currently boasting locations in five countries.

Rick was so impressed a school was named after him. He became a fixture in the first school as an example to the students what was possible for someone with special needs. Though Rick still lived with his parents, he was independent because of all the work that Nol had done with him through the years. He had an in-law's suite in their house with his own private entrance, a full kitchen, and the ability to do laundry. He made dinner for his parents at least twice a week, and always ate with them on weekends. He worked at the school; he helped develop the curriculum. He got to work and back home on his own every day.

Rick's determination to be "normal" was something that touched everyone around him. For the students, he represented a person who did not allow what he was born with to dictate his life. *He* dictated his life, and all who witnessed it realized just how special he was. This was why Rick was such a big part of the team who built the curriculum for the school; he was a functional person with Down Syndrome, and thus was the template from which most of the school's education system was built.

Nol was incredibly proud of his little brother, and remained involved with just about every angle of the school even when he was in New York. It was clear to all Nol had found what he felt was his calling, and this was two-fold: first to help Rick find his place in the world, and second to do the exact same for others with similar challenges. The interesting thing about this was that no matter how intensely Nol tried to influence Rick, the opposite happened. In the last conversations they had, Nol was talking to Rick about his time at the school. Nol was in New York, and was nearly complete with his fifth season, though the playoffs were about to begin. One of the administrators at the school called Nol, concerned that Rick was overdoing his work and it was really getting to him physically. As such, Nol called Rick to discuss the situation.

"Little bro, I need you to be taking care of yourself. I'm worried about you," Nol said.

"But Nol, I'm fine. You should be worried about your sacks. Down this year," Rick responded.

"I know, I'm getting double-teamed a bunch this season," Nol said with some dejection.

"Well, I am too but I'm not stopping. What's your excuse?" Rick said playfully.

"Hey now, little bro. I'm just worried about you."

"I worry about you every week, Nolan. I love you and don't want you to get hurt. I'm doing fine. Please just make sure you stay safe," Rick said more seriously.

"I always do. You just need to promise me you are doing the same thing, Rick. Too much work is not good for you."

"It's not for me, Nolan. It's for the students. It's important."

"I don't understand, little bro—what do you mean?"

"My work is for other people. No such thing as too much."

"Oh, I got 'ya now Rick. I understand, but you just need to be sure you're getting enough rest. There are people at the school who will help you with the work. You don't have to do it all yourself," Nol said.

"No Nolan. I help *other people* with the work. Not the other way around."

"Okay, I trust 'ya. Just please make sure you are getting enough rest, okay little bro?" Nol asked.

"I *am*, Nolan. You make sure you stay safe, okay? I love you," Rick responded impatiently.

Almost exactly two weeks later, Rick was found unconscious in the school's office and could not be awoken. He was breathing, but unresponsive. I got four calls at the farm that day—from Nol, Father, Fanny, and Akamu.

"Olaf—please," Nol said frantically, "try to find out what is going on with Rick. I can't leave, and it's killing me. Let me know what happens."

"Olaf, Rick Glassburé is here and is unconscious. Can you please get here as soon as you can to help diagnose?" Father asked.

"Olaf, I heard from your Daddy. Your appointments are all moved. Good luck," Fanny said softly.

"Olaf, remember what I have taught you. This is not going to be easy," Akamu said sadly.

So, I got myself together and headed to the hospital. I was going over and over and over in my mind what I felt I was going to need to do, but nothing prepared me for this.

Rick was unconscious when I arrived, and his heart rate was weak and very erratic.

"Hello, my friend," I began. "Can we please have a conversation?"

"*Hello Olaf,*" Rick's *vox corporis* responded. I was floored when I heard it; his voice was Rick's without any sign of the speech impediment Rick had.

"Can you tell me what's wrong? Is this stress?" I asked.

"*No, Olaf. It's Rick's heart. It is very weak,*" he said.

"Is there any possibility I can help?" I asked, getting a bit emotional.

"No, Olaf. Not this time. Rick knew exactly what he was doing. What he wanted to accomplish, he did. He is at peace," he said kindly. "Your ability to communicate with me is very much appreciated. Please know this."

I became overwhelmed with emotion after this statement. "I understand. Is there anything you need for me to do at this point?" I asked as I choked back tears.

"Rick simply wants all to know he lived a wonderful life, and achieved more than he could have ever imagined. He wants his mom, dad, and brother to know he loves them and appreciates every sacrifice made on his behalf. He wants the students he worked with to know that life is what you make of it. In fact, this was what he last wrote before his heart took the turn that it has," he said calmly, but firmly.

"So, what you are saying is he is not going to survive?" I asked gently.

"No, Olaf. He will not open his eyes again, nor speak a word from his lips. You should contact his parents," he said solemnly.

Richard Carolas Glassburé passed away tragically from congenital heart disease at age twenty-four, two days after I had this conversation. He passed during the playoffs of Nol's fifth season. Nol, seemingly in tribute to his brother, set a playoff sack record. New York won the championship that year in large part to the dominance on defense the team possessed.

Nol did not return for a sixth season. During his press conference announcing his retirement, he openly cried as he spoke about Rick.

"My career, and everything I have done to this point, was because of Rick. It's time for me to honor what my brother taught me and do right by people who have a voice but rarely use it," he said to the press.

Nol finished a storied career and literally the next day put his house on the market in New York, then went to work at the school. He contributed the proceeds from the house's sale to the school's fund and immediately formed a team to find the location for the next school. His intention was to break ground in thirty days or less on that project. Rick hadn't been buried for even fifteen days when he did.

As soon as the gears were turning on the new school, Nol called me and asked that I meet him at the marina. I did, and we headed out to sea.   We got to a place where the water was calm and Nol shut the engines off. He produced two glasses, some ice cubes, and whiskey and motioned for me to sit in the cabin with him.

"Okay, everything happened so fast," Nol began. "Can we talk about your session with Rick in the hospital?"

"Of course, Nol. What would you like to know?"

"Well—first, how come you couldn't heal him like you did Gerard?" Nol asked with a look that pierced my soul though his words were spoken calmly.

"He didn't want that, Nol. I made the suggestion, but it was denied," I said, feeling a bit of fear all of a sudden.

"So, you're saying that Rick wanted to die?" he asked intensely.

"No, Nol. He lived and accomplished what he wanted to accomplish. It's not that he wanted to die at all. He simply had lived the life he intended to live, and it ended when he wanted it to end. Please don't misunderstand—your brother did not commit suicide, nor wanted to die. He had a heart condition that ultimately ended his life. There is nothing in this awful situation you should see as an intent to die," I responded with the same intensity.

"So, this was what Rick wanted? Why would he not want you to heal him?" Nol asked, his voice wringing with sadness.

"For the same reason Akamu won't allow me to heal his blindness, Nol. Rick's condition was part of what he accepted as his truth. The thing that was so hard for me—and I'm sure much harder for you—was this fact. His experience was completed by the truth of his heart condition. I honestly believe he lived longer than he otherwise would have to complete his work. Did you find what he was working on? His *vox corporis* specifically called this out in our conversation," I said.

"Yes, we found it, and it is nothing short of unbelievable. It meant so much to all of us—and most of all to the students. It was revolutionary. It's basically a roadmap for personal success as a special needs person," he said as he wiped his eyes.

"Nol, he loved you so much," I said, a tear falling down my cheek.

"I know he did, Olaf. Losing him has just killed me though. I just don't know how to do this without him," he said sadly.

"Well my friend, this would be completely counter to what he wanted for you. Look at what you've accomplished since he passed. The students in the first academy are entering the world as graduates. The second location has started construction in New York—which I absolutely think was the most brilliant thing you could have done. You ended an amazing football career, and you're healthy. You have a beautiful, supportive wife who will do anything for you. You have friends who will be there for you no matter what. You got me, son. Anything you need, ask."

"I want you to talk to my vox whatever. What do you need me to do?"

"Close your eyes and relax. Is there something you want to know?" I asked, astounded at the request.

"Just see what you can find out," he said and closed his eyes.

"My friend, can we have a conversation please?" I asked.

"*Hello again Olaf! Thank you for saying what you have,*" Nol's *vox corporis* said.

"Is there anything you can tell me in line with Nol's concerns?" I asked.

"*Well, interesting you asked. Nol's greatest fear is that Rick didn't know Nol loved him. That, by far is keeping him from moving forward. Thing is, this is an unfounded fear as the one thing Rick knew, with certainty, was how much his brother loved him. Ask Nol to remember the last conversation they had.*"

"Nol, can you remember your last conversation with Rick?" I asked, hoping that Nol wasn't sleeping.

"Yeah, I remember. What about it?" Nol responded.

"*Ask him to remember all that Rick said, especially the very last thing,*" Nol's *vox corporis* replied.

"Nol, what was the last thing Rick said to you in that conversation?"

He sat silently for a moment, then said, "I think he said that he loved me." Tears immediately started falling from his eyes.

"Nol," I began, "this should tell you exactly what you need to know. Rick loved you so much, and he knew in his heart the feeling was reciprocated. Please, my friend, this is an impossibly hard loss, and it's being made harder because you're not able to recognize this fact. Rick knew you did so much for him, and there was no question in those intentions. Look solely at what you did with the school. You gave him a platform no one else would have. Look further at all you did as kids, as brothers. He was your world, Nol. Please, don't allow yourself to question his feelings for you."

"*I think that did it, Olaf. Thank you so much for your help,*" Nol's *vox corporis* said solemnly.

"But... I just miss him so much. I don't know how to be without him," Nol said sobbing.

"My friend, you said it in your press conference. I have to believe the more disabled people who hear Rick's message, the better. I think it's your time to truly give them their voices," I said reassuringly. "And, let's not forget that amazing girl you married. Pour yourself into your marriage. Your parents need you desperately right now. I think all of you collectively need to figure out how to 'be' without Rick. All of you."

Nol looked and me, got up, and bear hugged me.

After a few seconds, he let go, and looked me in the eyes. "Son, you are the best, most comforting person on this planet. The people in your care are so lucky," he said, wiping his eyes.

"You know son, you can be one of those people. I'm very willing to help you—and for that matter, all of you—through this. I loved Rick, and I think this is exactly what he would want me to do," I said as I wiped a tear from my eye.

That, dear Reader, is exactly what happened. I treated Nol, Sadie, his parents, and several students and faculty members from the school over the next several weeks. Each person brought such profound amounts of sadness to my office. Sadie's poor heart bled all over the place for everyone. Nol's father was so locked in pride that getting him to grieve properly took an unruly amount of time. When he did grieve, we went through a box of tissues and several glasses of scotch. Nol's mother attended the most sessions as her grief was deep and consuming. If I remember correctly, it took me at least six weeks to get her to smile and begin to allow herself to see light again.

The faculty from the school were sad, but from a completely different angle. They had lost the person who gave them such immense clarity into the mind of one with Down Syndrome, and this had translated to a very interesting kind of sadness. The people who I treated had become lost; that's how immensely Rick's passing had impacted them. The students were sad from their own angle; Rick represented the penultimate version of what they aspired to become, and he had *died*. In many cases, this created a fear of death intermixed with their sense of loss. My, those were hard sessions. They took so much out of me emotionally, as the students' mix of confusion, loss, and fear hurt me to hear and were hard to treat as a result. I was successful throughout, but my alcohol consumption and need for hugs from my wife were dramatically increased.

Nol attended three sessions. I believe what we did that day out on the boat began his healing process. In his final session, he seemed to be back to the friend I knew, though his loss was apparent. Rick was a monumental part of his life, and as he had been lost physically it impacted his experience. Nol's grieving process lasted several months; the key there was he allowed himself to grieve.

Richard Carolas Glassburé was an amazing man. His legacy is celebrated still today throughout all the schools that bear his name across the world. To date, millions of students have graduated and celebrated the same kind of success that Rick had late in his short life. To call him a Statesman is appropriate—given his legacy—but it still doesn't do him the kind of justice he deserves. I'm not certain a title exists for someone so special.

Observing the Anonymous

The next couple years were devoted to one thing: living. Annie and I travelled to Hawaii a couple times and spent time with both Akamu and Rupert. Both men seemed to evolve each time we saw them. Akamu celebrated his 79th birthday and looked as though his age was going in reverse. He despised me saying so, and that made it much more fun to say. Annie agreed, and this made him both laugh mightily and pout a little bit. Rupert had started a new non-profit company whose purpose was solely to protect certain parts of the islands. He glowed with pride when he talked about it.

It was all through this time we moved forward in just about every area of our lives. We enjoyed our friendships with Nol and Sadie as we made it a priority to see them as frequently as we could, given all of our schedules. We spent lots of time with our families. My practice grew noticeably larger, and the farm's business increased. The Rodriguez family was positively instrumental; there was absolutely no way we could have accomplished what we did without their contributions across the board.

I started paying much more attention to the people around me—doctors, nurses, and administrative staff at the hospital, the family members or friends of those who came to my practice, people at the boxing gym, and in general, people just out and about. I started to hear a mix of both troubling, and at times, amusing conversations from the myriad of *vox corpora* that I was exposed to. In nearly every case, the voices I was paying attention to were not those of people I knew. I found this to be a very good exercise to continue to hone my ability. In time, I was able to communicate nonverbally with them in a very limited way. I couldn't properly say sentences, but I could communicate both "yes" and "no" responses. I surmised at the time this was simply my own *vox corporis*, but I was shown conclusively this was not the case the next time I spoke with Akamu. He didn't exactly explain to me why I was able to communicate this way, but he told me it was impossible for me to control my own essence consciously.

Prior to nonverbal communication, I made the mistake of beginning verbal conversations with people who did not know who I was, and did not appreciate in any way the things I was telling them. In many cases, these were people who could in no way infer the truths I was saying, nor understand why I was saying what I was. I cannot tell you how many times I was in some way hit, slapped, or punched because of this by those I was observing in public. I must say, this exercise became much easier when I could communicate nonverbally with people.

The people I observed from the hospital were, for the most part, hard to nail down for in-depth conversations, but I learned quite a bit about the culture nonetheless. Many of the nurses cared deeply for the patients they treated, but the same could not be said for a disturbing number of the doctors. This was not, of course, true for all those talented people—but there were enough of them that it made me take note. Almost all the medical staff I observed led such stressful lives that it impacted the kind of relationships they had. Thinking back to when Father was early in his career, we rarely saw him except for maybe a dinner here or a breakfast there. So much of this observation made sense to me given those memories. Nearly all of the administrative staff felt as though they could do better with their choice in careers, and I found this to be surprising. They contributed so much to the way in which the hospital flowed, but with doctors around doing what doctors did, this was not recognized.

The people at my boxing gym were an interesting bunch. I knew a great number of them by name and had cursory conversations with them, but by no means would I call them friends. There I found a myriad of topics from the *vox corpora* that I observed, from athletic aspirations to career and/or life stresses and aspirations to relationship topics both good and bad. Coach was a fun one to listen to; I heard many a diatribe about his strictness in every area of his life. He had basically bullied me back into physical life after the Dr. Small situation, and he also bullied most in his life. He was married to a woman who handed every instance of bullying right back to him. They had a deep love and respect for one another. Coach's son, though, was another story. He was not at all interested in physical exertion. He was not into challenging himself unless it was in an artistic orientation. Father and son had quite a few issues they eventually worked out, but not without some sizable scars on the relationship.

The family members who came into my office fell into two very basic categories: those who became a part of my practice and those who didn't. A vast number of those in the latter category indicated to me they didn't need therapy—but their *vox corporis* strongly disagreed. Fanny was instrumental in this capacity; she would strike up conversations with the people in the waiting room that sometimes went well past the end time of the family member they had accompanied. It was astonishing to see, and better yet, to experience. Quite often, I was pulled into the conversation. The topics I remember ranged from the correct manner of preparing sweet tea or some other southern cuisine, to corruption in Washington, to knitting. Many of the relatives who became patients joined as a result of these conversations, and it was not me who did the selling. Fanny McNutter was in the reason for the growth of my practice. Of those who never became patients, all but one of them were stable people who truly did not need therapy. The one who did was Simon Francis, and you will meet him soon, dear Reader.

One of my favorite observation places was at a coffee shop that was within walking distance to my office. I found I could communicate with just about anyone who was in that building. To my chagrin, that meant all those *vox corpora* could attempt to communicate with me too. This meant I heard quite a few *vox corpora* speaking at the same time when they greeted me. There were quite a few times I had trouble figuring out who was talking. This, dear Reader, was maddening, but such good exercise for me. I found it interesting that once a conversation began with a *vox corporis*, the others stopped talking. It was akin to speaking to the most polite bunch of stock traders ever to commingle on a trading floor, and was a vast departure to what I experienced in high school. That's how I came to see the orientation of it all, anyway.

The coffee shop in the early part of the morning, usually between 6:30 and 7:00, was where I was exposed to some things of a rather tawdry nature. I've never figured this out, dear Reader. I of course heard Annie's *vox corporis* throughout our sex life and surmised that this was because it was a part of our relationship and contributed to our closeness. I understood the *vox corporis* spoke truth, and for the most part, intimacy was not one of those things typically communicated without reason. I of course had conversations touching on the sex lives of the people I saw in my office, but this was always in context. In other words, the first thing I heard from the *vox corporis* one of my patients was not, "Hello Olaf. So and so had quite a romp in the hay last night." What I heard early in that coffee shop, strangely, was akin to this though, and were often about the experiences, both good and bad, the people had the night before.

These conversations came from both men and women of all ages. There was no constraint I observed for such a thing as there was once a sexually-based conversation with a lady who was easily in her 80's—and another that came from a boy who couldn't have been more than fourteen. The topics covered a multitude of subject matter, from lack of sleep to very particular experiences the person had, to an expansion of that person's overall life experience. Almost all the *vox corpora* I heard who communicated items of a sexual nature, also communicated the impact it had on the relationship with the other party or, ahem, *parties*. Most I heard who had been a part of a multi-person experience expressed part exaltation, part concern or shame. The concern itself was often much more softly communicated as compared to the excitement. More often than not, I heard that these people felt less close to those who they had the experience with, despite the excitement that came with the experience itself. Mind you, there were still others who loved every second of the experience and felt nothing less about the other participants involved, aside from a veiled hope the events of the night before would happen again.

Regardless, it became clear to me across many, many early morning conversations of this nature sex was hugely impactful to just about everyone, at every possible turn of their life. This unfortunately was also true for those who had a bad experience. I could not count how many times I heard a *vox corporis* say the person had said, "No" and that statement was not heeded. Rape in any form took something away from a person. It was so sad to me to hear stories of people who had experienced such a thing. It seemed no demographic was safe; male, female, young, old, hetero or homosexual—no one was safe. I recall having a couple repeat conversations of this nature with just two people. One was a heterosexual woman in her late 20's and another was a homosexual man in his mid-20's. I tried several times to start real conversations with both of these people, but neither wanted to talk, understandably. It was so sad to me to hear their stories, and worse to hear the impact on both of them. Every instance of rape took a part of their being away from them, and it seemed to be compounding in impact every time it happened. In this way, it lessened the possibility these individuals would be able to separate themselves from their caustic relationships simply because they had lost so much strength and conviction. I wanted badly to help them, and in time, one of the two found *me*.

In this time of anonymous observations, Annie and I got some very good news: she was pregnant with our first child! We had begun trying to get pregnant and didn't have to wait too long for the proverbial bun to be in the oven, as the saying goes. We waited until the three-month mark to announce the pregnancy to our families. However, Annie told Sadie about a month in—and it was at this point that we found out that they too were expecting. My dear Reader, you cannot begin to understand what this meant. The joint shopping trips they took for all things maternity and baby numbered in the dozens per week. A constant commentary was had by all in terms of nursery design. Rupert and Akamu both communicated their excitement and said they would be in town for the birth. It truly was an amazing time for all of us; we were excited to be parents, our parents were excited to be grandparents, and Gill was excited to be an uncle. I swear—that guy surprised me more often than not. Fanny joined Sadie and Annie on several of the shopping journeys and was happy to report the success or failure of the venture.

About six months after we became pregnant, an interesting thing happened. I had done my ritual of going to the coffee shop early in the morning and listened to a few conversations. I got my customary cup of joe to go and headed toward my office. I had just gotten to the door when I heard someone behind me.

The woman in her late 20's, who I had heard repeat conversations about rape, approached me and said, "I'm sorry sir. I think I might need your help."

I believe my face completely dropped when I heard this. "Please," I said, "come inside."

Fanny smiled as we walked in and said very cheerfully, "Good morning! Who might you be?"

"My name is Debby Francis. I don't have an appointment," she said nervously.

"Fanny, I have time now, don't I?" I asked.

"You have about twenty minutes, Olaf. Sweetheart, can I have you fill out a new patient form really fast?" Fanny asked.

Debby nodded and filled out the paperwork. We then moved back to my treatment office and we both got settled.

"You are a therapist, correct?" she asked nervously.

"Yes, I am Debby. I primarily do work with something I call the *'vox corporis.'* This part of you can truly work to help you." I said as I leaned in.

"I have a friend you treated and she couldn't say enough about the work you do. I've seen you at the coffee shop. I've wanted to talk to you for quite a long time but, I... I'm kind of scared," she said, a tear falling down her cheek.

I handed her a couple tissues. "I know a little bit about you already. I think I know at least part of what you need help with. Can you try to explain to me what is scaring you?" I asked.

"It's my husband. I'm so afraid of him," she said and began to sob.

"Okay. First thing, in here, you are safe. Please know that. Second thing, I am going to help you, but this is going to take much more time than we have today. What I need you to know in your heart, in your mind, implicitly, I will help you," I said.

"I'm going to tell him something so that I can still come here. What should I say?" she asked as she dabbed at her eyes.

"Well, that could be easy. What do you do for a living?" I asked.

"I'm an accountant," she said.

"At Jones or at O'Keefe?" I asked.

"O'Keefe."

"I've known Jim for a long time. Tell your husband this is required for work; I can absolutely back this up with documentation from Jim if need be."

"Thank you—so much," she said and got up to leave.

"Please have Fanny set up at least sixty minutes as soon as possible, Debby. This is not a situation you can take lightly," I said.

"Okay, I will. Thank you, Olaf," she said and walked out of the office.

I had an awful feeling in my gut when she left that I would never see this woman again, and she desperately needed help. I called Jim O'Keefe and let him know about my documentation item. In turn, he thought the whole concept was a great idea and issued an ultimatum to his entire staff to set up sessions with me. He negotiated a heck of a deal for himself, and I smiled when I agreed to it.

He also told me a bit about Debby's husband. Apparently, this guy put off a horrible vibe to all, and she pretty regularly showed up to work with bruises. They had tried to help her, but it got her nowhere. Jim wished me luck, and I gladly accepted it.

A week later, Simon and Debby Francis arrived at the office. I was back in my office, so I did not meet the man in question until after the session was over.

Debby walked in and looked around. "This door—how soundproof is it?" she asked.

"Well, the test we ran with it was my wife screaming in here, with me on the immediate other side, and I could not hear a thing. It locks in two places and is secured with a magnet at the top too," I responded.

"Okay. I'm just so scared right now. I think something very bad is going to happen soon," she said, obviously frightened.

"Trust me, nothing is going to happen to you while you are here. In fact, there is a secret exit from this office should you need to use it," I responded. "Please, get settled there on the couch or chair, whichever you prefer, and relax. Let me see what your *vox corporis* has to say."

"What exactly is this *vox corporis* anyway?" she asked.

"It is a voice we all have that speaks only truth. I have heard your *vox corporis* before. This is painless, though it may be a bit strange. Feel free to ask me questions if they are urgent, but otherwise, please let me finish the conversation before we talk again. That okay as a plan?" I asked.

"Yes, I'll do my best to relax," she replied.

"Please close your eyes. I'll get started."

Debby took a deep breath, wincing as she did so, and closed her eyes. Her *vox corporis* almost immediately spoke.

"*Olaf, you need to do something. Simon's aggression is increasing, and his intentions are not at all good. This man does not love Debby, and in fact, simply looks at her as though she is his property. He has repeatedly raped her over the past several days and has hit her so hard she has bruised ribs. Please get her to safety,*" her *vox corporis* said with urgency.

"I have a plan in place, but needed to hear from you before kicking it into motion. I promise you, from here on out, she is safe," I said. "Debby, with your permission, I am going to have you placed into protective care. I have a car waiting out back. You can safely go now, and at the end of our scheduled time, your husband will be handled."

"Really? What will happen?" she asked nervously.

"Well, I am affiliated with an organization who provides protection for anyone who is abused. Your husband has no means of finding you, and this will remain true through the legal process. You have to understand, if you go this route, you will have a legal representative who will look to terminate your marriage, get proper protective orders in place, and essentially hand your life back to you. Is this something you are willing to do, Debby?" I asked as I leaned in.

"*Olaf, if she doesn't do this, she will be dead soon. Simon is very unstable,*" Debby's *vox corporis* said anxiously.

"Yes, I will do this. Are you sure that Simon can't find me?" Debby asked as she started to cry.

"I promise you—he cannot find you. You will be safe. I've let Jim know what is happening and he has assured me that your job is safe and all details will be worked out in that regard once the process has started," I said, handing her a tissue.

"Okay. Thank you so much for doing this. I think you may have just saved my life," Debby said.

She got up, hugged me tightly, and I escorted her out to the waiting car.

"The police have been notified, correct?" I asked the driver.

"Yes. They are in-route now," she responded.

"Thank you. I'll give you a twenty-minute head start. Debby, best of luck to you. God bless," I said.

Debby nodded and the car sped away.

I returned to my office and called Fanny. We had a special line for situations like this so she knew what was going on. We had a little prepared conversation we used for gauging what was happening in the waiting room. Fanny would pretend to schedule an appointment and the closer to noon she mentioned, the worse things were.

"11:45? Yes, sir this will not be a problem. We're certainly looking forward to seeing you!" she said based on our canned conversation.

"You okay Fanny? I need to stall for about twenty minutes," I said.

"Yes, sir. That absolutely works. You take care now," she responded and hung up.

I could only imagine what she was dealing with, but I knew all too well how tough she was. I called Jim O'Keefe and let him know what had taken place. He thanked me, and asked I keep him in the loop. He also indicated that he had hired a protection company to watch the office until Simon had been apprehended.

"This guy is violent, Olaf. Please be careful," Jim said.

"Is he bigger than me, or resistant to bullets, Jim?" I asked arrogantly.

"No, Olaf, but…" Jim said, "this guy is dangerous. Please don't take this lightly."

"It'll be okay, Jim. I promise."

I waited until the session was due to be over, and emerged from my office, hoping the police detail had arrived.

Simon leapt to his feet and shouted, "Where is my wife?!"

"She has been placed into protective custody," I responded.

"You son of a bitch—how dare you?" he said and started moving toward me.

Fanny produced two large handguns from under her desk and said, "Not so fast, sir. You take one more step and you bleed."

Simon stopped, turned for the door, and said, "You haven't see the last of me."

Outside, we heard a fight and a car speed away. An officer, badly bloodied, limped into the office.

"He got away, Mr. Waniglia. We just put out an APB to bring him into custody. Shouldn't take long—we are on his tail now," he said.

Fanny and I looked at each other, a knowing look between us. We knew until this man was apprehended, none of us were safe. We went to work calling everyone we knew to let them know.

Fanny handed me one of the guns and said, "Olaf, just in case. That man steps two feet onto our property and he's dead. Our house is as much an armory as it is a home. I have a feeling the same is not true at your place."

I smiled and refused the gun. "It'll be okay, Fanny. I promise you."

****

Days passed after the incident with Simon Francis, then weeks. Security details were called off, and business returned to normal. Jim O'Keefe indicated nothing happened at their office, but they had heard from Debby and she was doing well. The police had not captured Simon, and found out that several other warrants had been issued in other states for his arrest, dating back several years. The most eyebrow-raising detail, though, was that he also had *federal warrants* for his arrest for an attempted lynching of a Senator ten years prior. He was the sole person involved who had not been apprehended; it was bewildering to consider this man essentially lived openly with his wife despite having so many outstanding warrants.

It was almost as though he had left town. The lot of us figured with the attention that was placed on a man with a lengthy criminal history, he likely would flee to avoid getting caught. Eventually, Simon Francis was not the focus of anyone's attention and life returned to its normal craziness. My time was spent at hospitals, my office, and the farm. As Annie got deeper into the pregnancy, I carried a much heavier load at the farm so my days were long. Fanny did her best to create a workable schedule, but the lot of it meant that I was working at least six days a week.

This pattern continued for about two months; my time was split pretty evenly between the practice, the hospital, and the farm. Business at the farm continually grew, and it required quite a bit of managing. New ventures with Mr. Toth started that also required an inordinate amount of time to be spent in his office, and ultimately more time away from home. Annie had turned the corner on the last month of her pregnancy, and Sadie had just moved closer to her final month as well. They spent almost every day together.

Sundays were the only day I got to spend time with my wife consistently. More importantly, it was the day I used to run errands. Such was the case one hot Sunday afternoon, and I eventually got everything done and returned home to relax. I got all the groceries put away and sat down next to Annie on our couch in the living room. I was exhausted and fell asleep. For that matter, all of us did, Doc included.

I'm not sure how much time passed, dear Reader. I'll never, ever forget how I woke up, though. I was shot in the right knee. I heard the shot ring out and the pain form all at the same time. It seemed that everything moved in slow motion; I couldn't focus on what was happening with the blinding pain in my knee. My eyes finally focused on the shooter—none other than Simon Francis.

Annie cried hysterically. I moved in front of her as best I could. Doc disappeared; I could not see him anywhere.

"Tell me where my wife is before you die," Simon said coldly.

"I don't know where she is—that is by design," I said, breathing very hard.

"Wrong answer," he said and shot my right knee again.

I bent down in pain and as I did, he shot Annie twice—both in the lower abdomen. She looked at me, shock and panic in her eyes. Blood began to form at the corner of her mouth, and she quickly faded into unconsciousness.

A rage unlike anything I have ever felt consumed me. My life no longer had value; all sense of self-preservation was gone. I was hell bent on torturing this man, then killing him with my hands.

"You take my wife, I take yours. Now, you die," Simon shouted.

As soon as he finished his sentence, Doc assaulted him from the side. Simon was knocked forward into the room where we were and I lunged. I could not stand, but I made it to him and slammed his face into the floor with the full weight of my body behind my forearm.

Doc was biting his side aggressively, when another shot rang out. Simon had shot Doc in the leg, and he fell down. Sensing that Doc was about to be shot again, I moved in front of him, and again, a shot rang out. I was the recipient of a bullet in my side. I cringed in pain, but maintained control. I grabbed the arm with the gun, put my good knee on it and pulled as hard as I could. I dislocated his elbow, but not before he pulled the trigger twice more. Both bullets went into my upper chest.

I felt myself getting weaker. I heard Annie's breath gurgling weakly. I heard Doc whining in pain. Adrenaline filled me, my rage untamed. I flipped Simon over and punched him twice in the face as hard as I could. The second punch dislocated his jaw; it seems I was good at this given my history with jaws.

He grabbed my twice-shot knee and I yelled out in pain.

I felt myself starting to get cold. I was not going to let this man live—I was sure that he had killed my wife, my unborn child, and me. He was not leaving this room alive, and I knew I was losing time to make sure that happened.

I quickly recovered from the shot of pain in my knee and grabbed the gun, which was still hot from the shots that had been fired. I slammed the handle into his broken jaw, then threw it across the room. Simon attempted to punch me, but missed. Instead, he put his fingers into one of the wounds on my chest.

I felt the pain. At the same time, I saw my next target and fired. I punched him as hard as I could in the throat.

Three times.

Then another three.

Then two to his broken jaw.

Then two more to his throat.

His eyes bulged as he struggled to breathe. A strained moan was audible.

I sat back, my eyes cold.

"Now, I watch you die. I hope you enjoy hell, asshole," I said, every bit a monster.

Simon attempted to move toward me, but I punched his now completely disassembled jaw. I cut my hand badly on his teeth. He fell backward and writhed on the floor as he attempted to breathe.

I heard sirens in the background.

After a minute or so Simon's body went limp, a pool of blood forming around his head.

I looked down to see an enormous amount of blood below me. Doc, too, was bleeding—the bullet had to have hit an artery in his leg. He was weak and getting weaker.

I crawled over to where Annie was, and the gravity of the situation fell onto me in ways, dear Reader, that I cannot properly express. My wife—the love of my life—was dead. Our unborn child was dead. My dog, who had saved my life, was suffering and dying. My life was soon to be over. The adrenaline was gone. In its place was sadness and vast amounts of pain.

I cried. I sobbed and sobbed and sobbed. This was worse than the fate my grandfather had suffered. I said I was sorry—I was so, so sorry—over and over and over again. I got weaker. I got colder. I hurt more and more as my body lost more blood. My eyes closed, and my breathing slowed. I slumped forward.

I heard a voice I did not recognize. It said, "I'm so sorry."

I didn't care. I didn't pray, I didn't try and absolve myself of anything. I accepted my death, and also my participation in the death of another. I made peace in chaos.

Everything went black.

The Absolution and Comfort of Darkness

I was still—and was without pain. I was not cold nor hot. I was not standing nor laying. I could not feel myself breathing, nor my heart beating. I did not consider this as good or bad. It just was.

Silence and darkness prevailed. I heard and saw nothing for what felt like weeks on end, but I had no reference for time. I was at peace, but I could not say where I was, nor what was happening. Every so often, I heard very light water sounds, much like a shallow river running over fallen tree branches—or a manatee surfacing and heading back under water. It was gentle and distant—but I saw nothing. Darkness and silence were my norm. These fleeting water sounds were random at best.

At some point, I started to see small flashes of light. There was no sound accompanying these events, and they too seemed to be random in every way. I saw a light slowly, but gradually, form in the distance. It seemed to be very far away, and behaved much like a rising sun in the way it was presenting itself. There was no sound whatsoever.

The distant light started to brighten slowly. Silence persisted its intense grip on me. In the light, a figure became visible far in the distance. Still, there was no sound. The light got a little bit brighter, and the form seemed to move closer to me. I saw new flashes of light. These were similar to the flashes I had seen before, but they appeared in greater numbers, in clusters when they appeared. The distant light grew slightly brighter, and the form continued to move closer to me. It was almost as though this thing was on a conveyor belt, based on how it was moving.

More flashes appeared. They seemed to be growing in intensity. As soon as this group of flashes stopped, the distant light grew brighter. The object coming toward me was an odd shape; light seemed to be coming through the center of it. At once, everything stopped. The light went black and there were no more flashes.

Silence and darkness had returned spontaneously for reasons unknown, and remained this way for another inordinate amount of time that could have been days or weeks. It was quite a while before anything new happened in this place; at some point, the singular flashes returned, but were much less intense than they had been the last time I saw them.

Mind you, dear Reader, I had no idea where I was, whether I was alive or dead, whether I was in Heaven or Hell, or someplace in between, or if this was just what happened when you were dying—or when you had died. I had no sadness, no happiness—no emotion of any kind. I was in some realm ruled by darkness and silence, and I had no thought or feeling. I existed in some form of consciousness, enough to recognize these flashes of light and changes to this place, wherever it happened to be that I was. Though I recognized the things and happenings in my environment, I passed no judgment on them. I was not curious, scared, or intrigued by what was happening; I simply observed.

Darkness and stillness continued holding me hostage, and I really didn't mind. I existed, and I observed; when there was nothing to observe, well, I simply existed in the comfort of darkness. Almost as randomly as it had disappeared, the distant light came back, but this time it was brighter. The form was much closer; I could observe it actually looked to be two things, not one. This time, though, everything stood still. The starkness of this was quite something.

Flashes of light broke the stillness, and the distant light grew dimmer. The form approaching me got closer despite the dimming light.

The water sound I heard previously became audible again, but this time, it seemed to be more intense. The sound was more akin to rapids than a gentle stream. As the sound grew in intensity, the light got brighter. The form, however, did not move. Something odd happened as the intensity of the light and sound increased: I felt as though I was rising. It was a strange sensation as I had no visual or physical reference to base this on. As I rose, the water sound increased.

A light became visible above me, far in the distance. As I rose, it got brighter. The water sound subsided and I heard what sounded like a woman singing far in the distance. She had a beautiful voice, but I could not understand the words she was singing. More flashes of light happened, but they did so below me.

As soon as the last flash of light faded, I found myself in an area light blue in color. There was no visible surface, nor ceiling to speak of. In the distance, I saw what looked like a woman with a dress on. It flowed on all sides and hung below her; she was not standing on anything I could see. The singing was coming from her—it was louder now, but I still couldn't understand the words she was singing.

I felt something approaching me, but I could not tell from what direction.

I began moving toward the woman singing, but I was not controlling my movement. As I moved toward her, her singing became louder. When I finally stopped moving, I was close enough to see fine detail in her dress and face. She was stunningly beautiful. She had long blonde hair and ice blue eyes. Her skin looked to be soft; the beauty of her singing complimented her physical beauty. There was something about her I cannot put into words, an innocence or purity in one way and a profound, emanating love in another. Her dress was ornate with what looked like crystals or diamonds woven throughout it in overlapping wavelike patterns. It flowed on all sides of her, moving gently as she sung.

She looked at me and smiled warmly after she had stopped singing. She moved toward me, her eyes fixed on me with a gentle fierceness. When she was directly in front of me, she again started singing, but did so at a very low volume. I still could not understand her, but it seemed that she was tailoring what she sung for my benefit, based on her expression. Her expression conveyed an honest sadness, almost as though she was comforting me.

When she finished singing this gentle song to me, she raised her arms and embraced me. As soon as her arms enveloped me, I found myself sitting on a rock next to a small river at the edge of a tall waterfall. I could not see where the water terminated. I was wearing a robe similar to the dress the singing woman was wearing. I could not see or feel my body; I just saw this ornate robe. I sat on this rock for what could have been days, watching the water go over the edge of the waterfall. The sound here was gentle and constant; the water bubbled as it approached the edge, and created a wisp of air as it began its descent. At this point, I still was nothing more than an observer. I was not curious, nor amazed, nor anything emotional. I just observed.

I again felt like something or someone was approaching me. It seemed to be coming from behind me. The woman in the ornate dress passed next to me and sat in thin air facing me just across from the edge of the waterfall. She smiled, and motioned me to join her. I still could not feel my body, but I somehow rose and moved next to her. She smiled and looked me squarely in the eye.

"You are not lost, my dear one. Neither are you found. Please, pass no judgment of this and simply be. This is your sole charge until the time comes," she said with a heavy accent that I could not place. "Understand the laws of the physical world do not rule here, but those of the spiritual world do. For now, please close your eyes. When you open them again, you will be with someone familiar to you."

When she finished talking, she gently touched my face. I closed my eyes.

Again, I found myself in the solitude and comfort of darkness, the sound of the gentle stream and waterfall were now gone. The darkness remained for another extended time that felt like several days. I had no desire or reason to open my eyes. Thing is, I'm not terribly sure I had eyes (or eyelids for that matter) as a distant light began to appear again, much as it had previously. Soon thereafter, the random flashes returned. It appeared I had been returned to the original state of being I had experienced in this place.

The difference this time around, though, was the speed of things. The light's brilliance grew much faster than before, and the flashes seemed more intense and dissipated slower, almost like heat lightning on humid days. As the light continued to get brighter, I began to hear what sounded like waves crashing on a beach.

The light accelerated toward me, and I could begin to see what looked like palm trees on a sand beach. I soon found myself on the beach, not far from an active ocean. The waves weren't violent, per se, but they came in numbers I had never seen before.

I sat on the beach facing the waves. The power they were generating was obvious I could feel the thunderous force every time a new wave crested and crashed into the beach. Looking around, the palm trees moved slightly, but I observed no sun or clouds. It was light here, but I wasn't sure how as I didn't see a star in the sky, or some other light source Still, I was nothing more than an observer here. I passed judgment on absolutely nothing.

I again felt something approaching me from behind. Soon, a woman approached and sat next to me. She was wearing a sun dress, and had shoulder-length wavy brown hair. She was dressed for the environment here but her dress was nothing like the singing woman's dress.

"Hello, Olaf. I'm so sorry we are meeting in this way, but I'm so glad we are," she said kindly.

I looked at her; she seemed familiar to me, but I couldn't place how.

"You probably cannot speak, and that's okay. You were involved in a horrific situation. You are here because of the injuries you sustained, but I must tell you, you are not going to remain here for much longer," she said kindly.

I looked at her, but still was simply observing. This last point did not raise any curiosity in me.

The woman continued, "Please know your, actions that night are understandable given the circumstance. You must be able to find peace though. This is of paramount importance."

She put her hand on my back and looked at me with love in her eyes; it was exactly like the singing woman's expression.

"Do you know who I am, Olaf?" she asked.

I shook my head "No".

"Well, let's change that," she said, smiling. "This is a beautiful place, isn't it? Thank you so much for being here with me. It is a place so similar to what I consider to be my home."

"Grandma?" I thought.

"Yes, Olaf. I am indeed your Grandma," she said, smiling.

"I must be dead then," I thought.

"In truth, my grandson, you are not," she said.

As soon as she said this, the beach was gone, the waves were gone and I was again in darkness. There was no sound, no light, nothing. I was again in the pervasive darkness that had ruled my existence at several points of my time in this place. It stayed this way until I again heard my grandmother's voice after what seemed, literally, like days later.

"My sweet Olaf, please remember the laws of the physical world are not applicable here. There is no life or death. There simply is. You are the observer, and it is for you to observe. When it is time, trust me when I say that you will know. Your role as the observer will stop and what comes next will be yours to determine," she said kindly. "For now, the next step is solely to prepare you. I love you, my amazing grandson. Never, ever forget this."

For the first time in this place, I became curious. "What was this next step, and when is it going to happen," I thought.

Almost immediately, a faint light appeared all around me, and I could see that I was suspended with what seemed like an infinite amount of space all around me. I heard the faint water sounds I'd heard when this all began.

But, dear Reader, it was different this time.

The sound quickly and noticeably amplified as though it were above me. In what literally felt like seconds, a wall of water that extended the entire infinitely large expanse above me fell toward me. The speed with which it did this was unbelievable; I barely had time to observe what was happening before I was swallowed by this gargantuan wall of water.

As soon as I was in the belly of this beast, I regained an awful human trait: I panicked.

I looked all around me and couldn't tell what direction was up. I furiously swam, but I had not the first clue which way I was headed. I continued to panic and swim in all directions. I would swim a distance, stop, and try to determine which way was the surface. I did this for hours, then days. Had I been human, I would have died many times over. I eventually got to a point where I was positive this was where my existence stopped; I was going to remain eternally in the middle of this vast expanse of water, desperately trying to find my way out. This was where I was to spend the rest of my existence. This was the end...

Well—no.

I was wrong.

I continued frantically swimming, and for all I knew I hadn't actually moved. It wasn't until I heard my grandmother's voice again about a month later that I began to make at least some sense of this.

"Remember what I told you, my sweet grandchild. You must," her voice echoed in the water.

I stopped swimming. I stopped moving, stopped trying to figure out where the surface was. I stopped panicking. I relaxed my mind, seeking the comfort of the darkness I knew so well. I had forgotten the laws of the physical world did not apply here. When I panicked, my existence degraded. I made this realization and changed directions.

I closed my eyes and thought, "I'm not staying in this water anymore."

As fast as the water had fallen toward me, it fell away. Within a second, the infinitely massive expanse of water was gone.

"I'm safe," I thought.

I opened my eyes and was again in front of the beautiful singing woman. We were suspended in light. The light itself seemed to have weight, almost like clouds appear in the sky. The woman looked at me with the same loving gaze in her eyes my grandmother had. This time, though, she smiled at me in the way a child smiles at their parent; there was a genuineness, yet an innocence I hadn't noticed before.

"Who are you?" I thought.

She smiled more widely, took what looked like a deep breath, and hugged me. We stayed in this embrace much longer than the last; the first time, as soon as she hugged me, I ended up on the rock by the little river. This time, as she released me, she spoke in a way I hadn't heard before; her comforting tone was gone. In its place was a profound sadness. I felt every word as though they forcefully embedded into my heart. She said, "I love you, my dear Olaf—and I'm so, so sorry."

Then, I began falling.

As I fell, I felt pain. Immense, horrible, transformative pain. I writhed as I fell, trying desperately to come to terms with what was happening. I was suffering badly; my body hurt in ways that were very familiar. It was as though I had been shot again, in every location *all at once*. My chest, my side, and my knee all throbbed as though they had fresh bullet holes in them. My hands crippled into ragged fists. I saw no blood, but as I fell, the pain grew more and more intense.

I struggled to come to terms with this. I could not understand what in the world was happening, and there was literally nothing I could do or think that changed what I was experiencing. I thought many thoughts, but it was clear I was no longer in a place ruled solely by all things spiritual. In this place, the physical world played at least some role.

I fell for what had to be hours. My confusion quickly turned into anger. My anger was amplified by complete frustration. Thing is, as the frustration grew, my pain grew. This was a cycle that repeated over, and over again. I was in such pain I could no longer move, nor think. My being was suffering. I had no other state of life. I suffered badly and my intense anger had apparently fueled my demise.

But, I then realized this and stopped writhing. I stopped allowing myself to suffer. I stopped allowing myself to be angry, and I let the frustration dissipate with my descent. I closed my eyes and accepted this state of being. I was still in immense amounts of pain, but it no longer forced a reaction.

As soon as my acceptance was genuine, I heard a tiny voice say, "Daddy, please open your eyes."

Loss and Gain

I heard beeping.

I heard voices—many voices—colliding into a mash of garble.

"Daddy, did you hear me?" the tiny voice said.

I nodded.

I felt a tightening around my chest that I couldn't explain. I had a horrible scratchiness in my throat, and I was extremely sore. I could feel my heart beating in my chest and could feel my breath filling my lungs. I was alive?

"Daddy, please open your eyes. Please?" the tiny voice said sadly.

I mumbled something akin to "Okay" and opened my eyes.

The light was profoundly bright, and I retreated back behind my eyelids and winced.

I heard someone say, "Close the curtains," but I didn't recognize the voice. It was a woman's voice.

"Olaf, the room is darker now. If you can hear me, would you please open your eyes?" she asked.

I cautiously opened my eyes, but I did not move. My vision was very cloudy. I thought I could make out several people in the room as I looked around, and I saw tubes and wires everywhere, and I felt something going down my throat. I was in the hospital.

"I'm going to remove the feeding tube, Olaf. This may make you choke a little bit," the woman said.

I closed my eyes, and indeed the tube made me choke as it was removed. I coughed and felt the tightness around my chest intensify. I again opened my eyes, but looked straight up, unmoving. I was extremely weak; breathing was hard to do.

A familiar sound came from my left side. "Woof," a creature softly spoke.

"Doc?" I asked, my voice scratchy.

"Who else would it be?" Father asked, his voice heavy with emotion.

"Father? Where are you?" I asked. "I can't really see anything," I said.

"One second, Olaf," the woman's voice said.

Soon, a woman strangely familiar to me approached and put drops in my eyes.

"There now. Blink a couple times and look around for me," she said. This was the same woman who had been talking to me.

"Do I know you somehow?" I asked.

"Yes, as a matter of fact you do. You saved my and my baby's life. My name is Susan," she said.

"The lady that Dr. Smithson was treating?" I asked.

"Yep, that's the one. I'm here to return the favor in a way," she said. "But, before we go there, I'm sure you have questions. You should ask what you need to ask."

"For starters, where am I?" I asked.

"You're in the ICU at Mercy. This has been your home for a while now," she said.

"Define 'a while'."

"A year and four months," Father said.

"What the hell?!" I exclaimed.

"You were in a medically induced coma, Olaf. Your body was badly damaged, and you were in shock when you arrived. We lost you several times both travelling to the hospital and again on the operating table. Once you were stable, you did not show signs of waking up, but you were alive. So, you were placed into a coma. Over the past several days, we've been reducing the medicines keeping you in that state," Father said.

"What happened to Annie?" I asked, tears forming in the corners of my eyes.

"Look to your right," Susan said.

I turned my head to the right, and looking square at me was none other than my wife. Her arm was around my chest; this was the pressure I felt.

"I knew you were going to wake up today. Actually, Addie did," Annie said, tears pooling on the pillow she was laying on.

"Who's Addie?" I asked.

"Look to your left," Susan said.

I turned my head to the other side, and there stood a tiny little girl, a worn stuffed pig in her hand. She was a spitting image of Annie, with a tiny bit of her resembling Mother. Her hair was short and strawberry blonde. She smiled a mostly-toothless smile and said, "Dada."

I stretched out my left arm, and Addie grabbed it with her non-pig hand.

"Hi, sweetheart," I said, my eyes wet with tears.

She smiled and showed me her pig. "Shooshoo," she said.

"That good lookin' piggy is named Shooshoo?" I asked, a smile breaking through my tears.

She nodded, smiling. Father lifted her onto the bed and my free hand hugged her. Holding my daughter close for the first time was not something I will ever forget, dear Reader. Doc stayed up by my head, taking in the moment with me.

"You all survived? Annie, I heard you die," I said, looking back at my wife. "I saw Doc's leg and he had lost a ton of blood and was obviously fading. I thought I lost all three of you that horrible day."

"The bullets nicked the sides of both her uterus and stomach and exited into the couch. The pregnancy actually saved her because the bullets were slowed almost immediately upon impact. Addie was not hit, but we had to deliver her to treat Annie," Dr. Glaush said. "Doc was attended to by a colleague of mine from the emergency vet center. They were much better equipped to handle his issues, as they were much more familiar with his anatomy. He was *minutes* away from losing his leg, and because of that, it's been a long recovery for him. Once again though, your guardian was by your side, Olaf."

"He would wait by the garage door every day, babe. I brought him here in the morning and dragged him home at night. Well, that was before Addie could walk. Your daughter can walk him without a problem now. She isn't even up to his chin, but she has complete control. Mind you, he still drags *me*—I don't get it," Annie said disconcertedly.

"Are you okay, love? Are you at all in pain?" I asked intently.

"I'm fine, you. I only have a couple scars, but other than that no pain at all. Question is, how do *you* feel?" she replied. "It's a miracle to me you're talking right now."

"I don't know yet. How should I feel?"

"Well Olaf, that's the big question. Your injuries were extensive. Your right knee no longer existed—literally. Your stomach, large intestine, and both lungs were notably damaged as they took direct, close range bullets, and the amount of blood you lost was immense. Your hands were both broken again and looked like they'd been through a meat grinder. You got a full knee transplant, and surgeries everywhere I just mentioned, *including both hands*. You were in shock, which was no surprise at all given your injuries. This is going to be a tricky road for you to regain mobility and strength," Dr. Glaush said.

"I've been asleep for over a year?" I asked, astounded and upset. "I've missed my daughter's first steps?"

"Yes, you. But listen, I'll take the time you needed if I can have you back again. That's all I want. I just want you back, babe," Annie said, fresh tears hitting the pillow. "We need you."

"Well, I have no plans for an alternative, my love," I said, as my eyes matched Annie's in tear quantity.

"Your rehabilitation is going to be tough, Olaf," Susan said as she handed me a tissue. "That knee of yours is going to take some getting used to. And, honestly, second to that are your *hands*. They were badly damaged. I think you are going to have some challenges ahead, but I promise you I will make you whole. What you did for me and my son... Olaf, I am forever in your debt. He colored you a picture a few months ago. It's right over here."

"Susan, you don't owe me anything, but I will gladly accept your help. I'd love to see your son's picture—would you hand it to me please?" I asked.

Susan smiled and handed me a picture of a robot wearing a bowtie, with the words "Get better Mr. Olaf" along the bottom. I smiled and chuckled a little bit. I was deeply touched by this.

"I have to ask. Did Simon survive?" I asked.

"No, Olaf. He was not able to be resuscitated. He was declared dead when the paramedics arrived at your house," Father said.

"Am I in any legal trouble because of that?" I asked.

"No son. You actually received a federal subsidy for doing their job *for them*. 100% of your care here has been paid for by the government. Besides, everything you did was in self-defense," Father replied.

"I heard sirens at one point. How were they alerted?" I asked.

"The security system. It called 911 and said shots had been fired. Police and ambulances were on their way as soon as the first shot left the gun," Annie said. "Without that thing, you would not be alive babe."

"Are you still living in the house, Annie? I can't imagine going back there was easy," I said.

"We are now, yes. When Addie first arrived, I took turns sleeping at both grandparents' houses. Mr. Toth had a team go in and fix all the damage and make a few changes. The family room has been completely redone. It doesn't look like the same room anymore and that definitely helps," she said.

"I'd imagine the grandparents loved having Addie around!" I said, looking toward Father and Dr. Glaush.

"Well…. I wouldn't trade the time for anything, but the sleep I'm getting now is something I no longer take for granted," Dr. Glaush said.

"I agree, though Mother did not have a single complaint, Olaf. My does she love that little granddaughter of ours!" Father said, smiling.

"Speaking of—where is Mother?" I asked.

"She should be here any minute, Olaf. Our regular rotation begins in approximately two minutes," Father said.

"Regular rotation?" I asked, confused.

"She brings lunch on Tuesdays and Thursdays, I bring lunch on Mondays and Wednesdays, and we go out for lunch on Fridays, then come see you. I think she said today was sandwiches or something," Annie said.

"I hope like anything it's not that crap she got last time. There was mold on the bread for Heaven's sake," Father said.

"Speaking of…" I said. "Guess who I had a chat with?"

"Olaf, what are you talking about?" Dr. Glaush asked.

"Well y'all, I have a few stories to tell 'ya. I have no idea where I just was, but I talked to Grandma briefly on a strange beach among other things."

"My mom?" Father asked and leaned forward.

"Yes, she was wearing a sun dress and had shoulder-length brown hair."

"Yeah, that fits the description. What did she say?"

"Well, she essentially was helping me. She talked to me about the accident, then helped me through some very unique situations," I said, fully recounting everything I had just experienced.

I was then peppered with questions from almost everyone in the room. Dr. Glaush and Father feverishly wrote what I said, saying it was remarkable I could remember what I did. Neither was willing to guess what I had experienced or what it meant.

I was in the middle of talking about my descent into pain when an overly confused, then elated Mother walked into the room.

"Olaf? You're awake? And you're talking?!" she said, her voice escalating in excitement.

"Yes, Mother, I'm awake. So sorry for my extended slumber here," I replied.

"How do you feel, sweetheart? Are you okay?" she said, dropping the food bags she had been carrying onto Father as she made her way over to me. She kissed Addie, pet Doc, and kissed my cheek.

"I'm really not sure yet. I think the true test will be attempting to walk, and I'm not ready to try yet. I feel really weak. I just tried to move my legs, and it was a whole lot of effort to do so."

"Well Olaf, I hate to say it, but this is going to be a process. We're just going to have to try to do a little, then try some more, and so on. It's not going to be fun, but it will get easier as you get stronger," Susan said with some seriousness in her voice.

"You've been through this before, babe. I know you can do it," Annie said kindly.

"True, but I hate to say it Annie—in a sense, this is far worse than before. What Olaf dealt with before was toxins in his body that he was able to work out. This time, he had major surgeries across a large portion of his body, including major organs. This recovery could take a while," Dr. Glaush said.

"Once Susan's done with him, I have a few friends that will be more than willing to help," Nol said, appearing in the room. "Already have 'em waitin'. Now that I hear y'all up son, I'll give 'em a call."

"How did you know to come here today, son?" I asked, shocked at the number of people amassed in my room.

"Nol is here every day at lunchtime, Olaf. Has been since you first arrived," Father said.

"In fact, we all have made a practice of meeting here at lunchtime. Sadie and Jonah should be here shortly as well," Annie said.

"Who's Jonah?" I asked.

"My son, Olaf. Jonah Richard Glassburé. He is nineteen months old now. He and Addie are pals," Nol said.

I became so sad and was at a loss for words after hearing this. I had missed some critical moments in my family's and friends' lives. This really hit me hard, and I didn't know what to say. Doc seemed to sense this and moved closer to me.

"You okay, Olaf?" Dr. Glaush asked.

"I.... I've just missed so much," I said sadly.

"Son, it's a miracle you're alive. Think about this—you'd be missing all of it if you never opened those eyes. You have decades to love your wife, to love your daughter, to go out fishin' with me, to go box with Coach again. Y'all need to be cookin' me some food so quit thinkin' about what you missed, and start lookin' forward to what you haven't. Dammit son, I missed you, but don't think for a second I won't whoop y'all to knock some sense into that dome 'a yours," Nol said emotionally.

Almost as soon as he finished his soliloquy, Sadie walked in with Jonah who immediately toddled over to Addie. He then looked up at me and smiled.

"Hi little guy. How are you?" I asked.

Jonah smiled, and then ran back to Sadie.

"Olaf, you're awake?" Sadie asked, surprised.

"Hi Sadie—yeah, I am. How are you?"

"I'm absolutely fine. I am so happy to hear your voice again. It's been a long time, Olaf," she said kindly.

"I'm shocked y'all have gathered here as often as you have. This means so much to me. I can't say this enough," I said, tears bubbling their way up as I spoke. "I promise each and every one of y'all I will do whatever I need to in order to get my life back. I'm not quite sure where I just was, but my daughter was the one who told me to open my eyes. If nothing else, I owe that little girl a whole lot of love, and I intend to give it to her from somewhere else besides this hospital room."

The conversation shifted at this point; the lot of my family and friends had accepted I was awake. Emotions stirred every so often, and one or more folks would require a tissue or two. Regardless of those instances, we settled into looser conversation as the gathered folks ate lunch. Annie remained glued to my side throughout, making the whole experience easier for me.

I truly thought I had lost everything that day, dear Reader. I had accepted not only losing my wife, unborn child, and dog—I accepted my own death. Opening my eyes was profound. Feeling my wife and daughter was heavenly, and honestly was such an overwhelming experience the weight of it didn't hit me until much later in the day. The crowd began to disperse after lunch. Nol headed back to the Academy, Sadie took Jonah home, Mother took Addie home, and Annie and Doc went off to the farm. Susan told me she was going to give me the next couple hours to relax before we began the rehab marathon.

The shooting itself was something I fixated on for a little while. Had I not killed Simon, I am positive the bullets he shot would not have been the last It hit me strangely that what my grandmother told me rang true, not just in the spiritual realm but also in the logical, physical world. Beyond this, accepting that both Annie and Addie were alive proved to be an incredibly emotional event for me As I laid there alone, the weight of all of it caught up with me and I cried, almost as hard as I did after the shooting. The gratefulness I felt was unlike anything I had ever felt before; my wife, child, and dog were all alive. I had never valued life quite like I did as I processed these feelings and thoughts. I went through about a box and a half of tissues in the process, dear Reader.

I also spent time thinking about the place I had just been. I had hoped to discuss it with Akamu; I figured he most likely would be able to give me perspective to help me make sense of it. I no sooner had that thought, and the phone rang. It took an insurmountable amount of effort to pick up the receiver; I think that phone rang about eight times though I started reaching for it by ring number two. On the other end of the phone was none other than my gifted friend.

"I hear you are again among the conscious in the third dimension. Welcome back, my friend. How are you feeling?" Akamu asked.

"Hi Akamu, I'm doing okay, but am very weak. How in the world did you know to call?" I replied.

"Well, Annie called and told me you had regained consciousness today. I picked up the phone and called as soon as I hung up with her. Why do you ask?"

"I no sooner had a thought about you and you called," I said.

"One must recognize such a thing as more than a coincidence then, no?" Akamu said playfully.

"Indeed, one must," I replied, matching his playfulness.

"What was this thought of yours, Olaf? I'll be happy to talk through anything you need, and honestly I have a couple questions of my own," Akamu said kindly.

"Well Akamu, for starters, I cannot resolve where I was, nor why I can remember every detail given I was in a coma. Any thoughts?" I asked hesitantly.

"In order for me to understand, I think you need to answer *my* questions. Sorry, Olaf. I think we will likely figure this out together," he responded, chuckling slightly.

I proceeded to tell Akamu everything that I could remember: the extended periods of blackness, my observational responsibility, the water sounds and flashes of light, the singing woman and the waterfall, my grandmother and her guidance in the endless ocean, and my descent into pain ending with Addie asking me to open my eyes.

"Olaf, I can't honestly surmise much of your experience. I can guess to a certain extent, but some of this falls outside what I know. The singing woman is one part of this I can't resolve. I'd honestly be drawing at straws to explain it. Your grandmother, though, is consistent with my experience with my wife. You are connected to her, likely by her choice, and I have to believe it meant so much to her to be able to interact with you," Akamu explained.

"Thank you, Akamu. The singing woman was so comforting to me, though in the truest sense, I simply observed. I did not feel until I descended. I have to imagine she was an angel or something similar. She was a steward in that place and I knew she cared for me," I said.

"That may well be the case. The thing that gets me is the environment. I cannot resolve the periods of blackness you had, nor the flashes if they weren't consistent with what you see when you heal others," Akamu postulated. I could almost feel his confusion on the other end of the phone.

"Can we perhaps agree this was a plane of existence that removed enough of my humanity so I could heal the parts of my non-physical being that had been so badly shaken? Is it possible it was a protective state, in a sense?" I asked, this feeling right to me.

"That's absolutely possible, but I'm stuck on the water thing. I'm not sure why you would need to endure something like this simply for perspective," Akamu said seriously. "Olaf, you are the most grounded, connected, person I know."

"Yes, my dear Friend, but I killed a man and truly thought my wife, unborn child, and dog had all been killed as well. I had accepted death—perhaps this experience is what I needed in order to re-enter the conscious world and truly *live* again. I have to admit, there is a part of me that is absolutely changed now. It's almost as though there is a persistent echo of this experience in my mind. It's no different than when a star in the universe explodes—echoes of it remain seemingly forever. This is similar, given it was a trauma on levels of my experience I'm not sure I ever considered before."

"Olaf, I will be there in two days. Not only do I need to see your precious daughter again, but we need to get to the bottom of this.

For now, please rest, and once again be the observer. I think you may hear from your grandmother again, and she may give you a few answers," Akamu said calmly.

My therapy with Susan began that afternoon, and she was spot on with everything she said. My hands were a mess; simply holding silverware was not possible when she first started treating me. That first day was 100% dedicated to my hands, and I'll tell you dear Reader, I learned quickly just how hurt I was. Making a fist was excruciating. By the end of the first day, I could actually hold a tennis ball in both hands without dropping it.

The second day was the start of my knee therapy.

"Olaf, this is not at all going to be pleasant. Can you try to bend that right leg of yours?" Susan asked, nervousness very obvious in her voice.

I did as I was asked, but found I couldn't bend my knee. No matter how much force I applied, it would not bend. Perplexed, I bent forward and interlocked my hands under my knee. Before I proceeded, Susan put her hand gently on my knee, and the message was quite clear.

"This truly may hurt you, Olaf. Please prepare yourself as best as you can. I will be right here, but please proceed carefully. This is not something you need to rush," she said with a notable directness.

"I can't bend my knee with just my leg. Is this normal?" I asked nervously.

"Yes. Essentially, you have a fabricated joint that has been in the same position for quite a long time. Think of it as you would an old bike that hasn't been ridden in many years. You need to help the chain along for the first few rotations before the grease spreads and it moves more freely. Your knee is no different in the mechanical regard. Where it differs, though, is the number of muscle fibers and nerves that will fire for the first time. I know your pain threshold is very high, but this is not something you want to force, Olaf. You will pass out with the level of pain I'm talking about. Let me do the first bend, and you tell me when I need to stop as I do so," she said, her intensity increasing.

I nodded and removed my hands. She then placed one hand under my knee and one on top of it. Slowly, she started to pull.

My knee did not bend.

She pulled a little bit harder, and still, my knee did not bend.

"I don't like this, Olaf. One second," she said and left the room.

A few minutes later, she reappeared with a tall gentleman and Father.

"Olaf, this is Dr. Warren. He did your knee replacement," Susan said.

"Iron Hands… It is an honor to meet you, sir. I was at your fight with Johnny Jr. all those years ago. It was a privilege to put you back together as my respect grew tremendously for you when I heard what you did to save your family. Your sacrifice was positively amazing," Dr. Warren said.

"Thank you, Doctor, but I'm confident you would have done the same thing if faced with the same situation. You were at my fight?" I said, astonished.

"Yes, I was. Back in the day, I trained at that gym. After the fight, I trained for literally years to try and have the same power you generated, but I was never successful," he said, mildly dejected.

"You box, Doctor? Where do you train?" I asked with excited curiosity. I loved talking shop with other people who studied the art of boxing. Yes, dear Reader—it is an art.

"Not anymore, no. I couldn't take continuing to fail."

"Tell you what, you help get me on my feet, and when I finally get back to the gym, you come with me. I'll show you everything I do, and I'm sure the guys at the gym would help you too. Your height would be a true asset once you learn how to channel it. It's simple physics, my friend. You just need to know how to move in concert with your body," I said excitedly. I missed the gym and all of my buddies there, and this was feeding my excitement.

"Okay, that is a deal. Now then, what in the world is going on with this knee of yours?"

"Olaf, please don't minimize this. It might be intensely painful when your knee bends for the first time. I'm going to stay here just in case," Father said, concerned.

"How bad could this be?" I asked flippantly. "For God's sake, I got shot a bunch of times. Equate this to those gunshots at close range."

"Well son, bear in mind that you had a massive amount of adrenaline flowing through you when you were shot. That is not the case here," Father said coarsely.

"Yes, Olaf, this will be painful," Dr. Warren said.

I looked at the collection of people around me and physically dismissed their concern, shaking my head at the lot of them. I put both hands under my knee, and *pulled*...

****

I regained consciousness a short while later. I was covered in vomit. My knee was bent at an oddly intense angle and the pain was barely tolerable. I was surrounded by doctors—Father, Dr. Warren, and Susan were among them.

"That was foolish, Olaf," Father said angrily.

"What happened?" I asked, confused.

"Well… you pulled, your eyes bulged, you puked everywhere, and you passed out. We haven't yet been able to re-bend your knee. It's stuck," Susan said flatly.

"Why are all these other doctors here?" I asked, my embarrassment peaking.

"Well truthfully, they wanted to see this," Father said, shaking his head in disappointment. "Secondarily, we thought perhaps someone would have an idea how to straighten your leg, but so far the giggling hasn't subsided enough to make any headway in that regard."

"That was incredible, Olaf. I can honestly say in all my years of orthopedic surgery, I have never seen a patient force the joint to move on their own, and certainly not to this degree. We often employ a device that ever so gently bends the joint for you. In fact, that was why I was called in to begin with. Dear Lord though… that was *amazing*," Dr. Warren said exasperatedly.

"This is more than a little bit uncomfortable," I said. "Any chance that machine of yours will straighten my leg, Dr. Warren?"

"No, Olaf. It only bends to a ninety-degree angle. You're bent way passed that. We're going to have to figure out how to unstick the joint, and then slowly straighten out your leg. Best I can tell, your joint itself may be questionable. That may be why we can't move your leg," he responded scholarly.

Indeed, dear Reader, my new knee was faulty. Part of this was due to the fact I had remained still, in my coma, for so long after the surgery that put it into my leg. This was not at all a good thing for the new joint. The doctors discovered a notable amount of scar tissue that had essentially woven its way *through* the joint itself. It was akin to vines growing over an old barn door—yes, that door should open—but the vines are keeping it shut. In my case, the scar tissue was holding the joint at about a 102-degree angle like evil little rubber bands. There was no bending that knee without cutting the "vines", so a big name orthopedic surgeon by the name of Dr. DeGitry flew in to assist Dr. Warren.

I had another surgery the day after Dr. DeGitry arrived. Long story short, they cut out all the scar tissue and replaced the faulty knee joint. I was the recipient of a newly-approved joint that prevented the body from interfering with it; the design of the joint itself was closed.

"Well Olaf, this time I think you will be much happier with the result," Dr. Warren said. "But, Dr. DeGitry noticed some additional damage there is no medical fix for. In short, you will be able to walk, but you may need something to steady yourself, especially in the near term. I cannot guarantee you will ever fully regain the stability you have enjoyed to this point in your life."

I was shocked to hear this. I had just turned thirty-one, and I was going to need assistance walking.

"Are we talking a walker or a cane here, Doctor?" I asked callously.

"Probably a walker initially and a cane thereafter. Olaf, you are still young enough this likely isn't a long-term situation. Thing is, the nerve centers on both sides of your knee are damaged. Because of this, your brain isn't going to be able to communicate with your leg. This almost assuredly will cause some stability issues," he said, becoming more animated as he spoke. "The key here is how you heal, and I *promise* you, Susan will make sure you have every chance to get your life back. You just have to be patient, and understand this is something you need to deal with. Your knee was shot to oblivion, Olaf—*hell*—the rest of you was too. It's a damn miracle you're alive and even stand a chance at being upright again."

The weight of this hit me quickly and uncomfortably. Dr. Warren was spot-on correct; it was a true miracle I was alive, and it was terribly elitist of me to look at it as anything else, or expect there not to be something challenging as a result of what I had ultimately survived.

"Thank you, Doctor. I truly appreciate you saying that. I must admit this situation is not something I have completely processed yet, so please forgive me for my reaction. You're right in everything you just said," I responded, introspection heavy in my voice. "I haven't taken a step yet since I woke up. When I do, I believe I will be better prepared. Thank you."

"I have a lot of faith in you, Olaf. Many here do. Your family is strong. Your friends are close. Trust me when I say you are going to be fine, so long as you *allow* yourself to be. This may be challenging, and some days may be harder than others. So long as you realize you've been given a gift to be alive—to hold your precious daughter, to watch glorious sunsets, to grow old with your wife—the bad will never overshadow this gift," he said, placing his hand on my shoulder.

"You're right," I said, sniffing and wiping away a couple tears.

****

The drive to regain a life outside of the hospital kicked into high gear with my new knee in place. Susan, at my urging, pushed me harder than she intended. She frequently asked me, "Who is rehabbing who here?" as I didn't stop a particular movement until I felt it was time to stop said movement. Often, instead of doing something that was to be done for a count of ten, I'd go to one hundred. Something that was to be held for thirty seconds was held for several minutes. If I was to make one pass from my door to the next using the walker, I'd walk to the end of the hall, back passed my room to the other end of the hall, to the prescribed door, then back to my room. Susan knew by the end of our first week she needed to tweak her approach if she was to regain control over my therapy.

Enter the button.

"The button?" you ask, dear Reader.

Yes. Indeed, an evil, devilish button. It had a smiley face sticker on it, and a cord such that it could be placed on an otherwise naïve victim's neck. There it would hang. Its outward innocence masking the cruelty within.

"What did this button do that was so bad?" you ask.

It played a poorly performed instrumental version of "You Are My Sunshine," dear Reader.

I found said evil device next to me when I woke up one morning, with a note that read:

> *When you need help, just press the button, Olaf. No one—*
> *not your family, not any medical staff of any nature—will*
> *assist you unless you do. This includes me.*
>
> *All the best, Susan*

I'll be honest and say this hit me in a way it shouldn't have. I was getting better, but getting out of bed, among other very basic movements, was a challenge, especially if I didn't have a walker close by. As I surveyed the room, my walker was in a far corner, away from the bathroom. I had a bladder that was not at all happy. So, I did what I felt I needed to do.

I crawled. Well—that's perhaps generous. I used my arms to pull myself forward, like a seal. This was successful. As I crawled my way toward my walker, I noticed both Father and Susan standing in the room, smiling.

"I ain't pressin' the damn button, so don't get any hopes up y'all," I said, clumsily pulling myself up on the walker.

"You hungry, Olaf?" Susan asked suggestively.

"Yes, as a matter of fact, I am. Am I no longer getting food unless I press the damn button?" I said, notably out of breath.

"Well, your tray is under a heating lamp in the cafeteria. You have to go get it in order to eat. Oh, unless you press the button," she said, smiling widely.

The cafeteria was a good five-minute ride in a wheelchair from my room.

"Damn you people. I'll get it myself," I said angrily and began moving toward the door.

I made my way to the cafeteria, with both Susan and Father following me. It took me almost a half hour to get there. Indeed, my tray was under a heat lamp, a good twenty feet from any tables. How in the world was I going to carry the thing, given my dependence on my walker? I knew this was strategic on Susan's part, and I wasn't folding.

So, I put the tray on the floor, and scooted it forward with my left foot. I found a table, sat down, retrieved my tray from the floor and ate. I then slept for two hours. I woke up to find Susan, Father, Dr. Glaush, and Annie sitting at the table with me.

"Hi you," Annie said happily. "I hear you're being a bit stubborn."

"Stubborn, my love? What have these people told you to suggest such a thing?"

"Seems that you are refusing help when it's being offered," she said, lowering her brow.

"I guess it figures you would believe that," I said, feeling cornered. "You people think I'm pressing the button? Nope. Ain't gonna happen."

"Your daughter is in your room, babe. Your Mom is there too. Don't you want to see them?" Annie said passive-aggressively.

"Of course I want to see them," I said. "I just need my walker." I looked around as my walker was no longer by my side. "Where have you people put my walker?" I asked, immersed in frustration.

"Well Olaf," Susan said, "if you look over in that far corner of the room, you'll see your walker. It had to be moved so that the cleaning crew could do their job as you slept."

"Dammit! That ain't playin' fair, Susan, and you damn well know that," I said angrily.

"Who said anything about fair, Olaf? I just want you to get better. How you get there is up to you," Susan replied calmly.

"Fine. You wanna play? We play," I said coarsely.

I got up and used both my chair and a chair from the table behind us as makeshift crutches to cross the room and get to my walker. I was mildly out of breath when I reached it. By the time I got to my room, I was covered in sweat and could barely stand. Addie ran over to me as soon as she saw me enter the room.

"Daddy! You walk?" she asked in her tiny voice.

"Olaf sweetheart, you don't look so good. Are you feeling okay?" Mother asked, concern in her voice.

"I just need some water. I'll be okay," I said.

I made my way over to my bed and was asleep before my aft end hit the mattress. I woke up the next day laying perpendicular on the mattress, with my legs hanging over the side of the mattress. It was 8:30 AM. My family, and more importantly for the near term, my walker, were nowhere in sight.

This pattern continued for twenty-eight days, dear Reader. The people involved would change, but the pattern repeated over and over again. I would wake up, crawl to the bathroom, crawl to my walker, go to the cafeteria, eat, nap, go back to my room, and sleep until the next morning. I stopped making progress on my balance, though my naps in the cafeteria became shorter and my trips to and from the cafeteria became less taxing.

Susan would float close to me, but we stopped interacting altogether. She knew I was not reacting well to this change, and I in no way gave her the indication I wanted her help. I entirely stopped speaking to Father, who seemed to think the whole thing was in some way funny. Annie continued her path of passive-aggressiveness in ways that completely set me off. I had no idea what was happening with the farm or practice as I no longer had a phone in my room, starting with day two. I no longer saw Doc or my daughter by day five. Nol quit coming after day seven. Mother was never there, from the beginning, aside from the first day I saw her with Addie and passed out. Coach too. I literally felt as though my life was condemned to be in that hospital, abandoned by my friends, family, and care providers, until I could somehow discharge myself and restart my life somewhere else. I felt alone, I was frustrated, and I did not understand why this happened.

When I woke up on day twenty-nine, I saw someone standing at the end of my bed, but my foggy eyes could not make out who it was.

"Why are you doing this, kid?" a familiar voice asked. "It seems you need your ass to be kicked into next week. Happy to do it. Go take a piss and get back out here."

"Coach?" I asked in a daze.

"Yeah, sunshine. Go drain the pipe and let's go. I ain't got all day. Don' make me come ova 'dere. You do not want dat," Coach replied.

I nodded and pushed my way up to a sitting position. I attempted to stand, but my balance was nowhere close to being good enough, so I went to the floor to crawl.

"No, Iron Hands. You do not crawl. No man crawls. Get the hell up, or I smack you," Coach said angrily.

"I have to pee, and I can't walk without assistance. Hit me if you need to," I replied as I worked my way into the bathroom.

When I was done in the bathroom, I washed my hands and opened the door. I was promptly smacked across the face, hard enough to split my lip.

"I told yer sorry ass you do not crawl. Not while I'm here, Iron Hands. You do, I hit you. Clear?" he said, his face less than an inch from mine.

"I will not get hit without hitting back, Coach. I'm going to do what I need to do here. You come in, I will hit you," I said angrily.

Coach laughed mightily in response. "Yeah kid, ya ain't fast enough. You need help standing. Hit the button."

"No, Coach. I will not do that," I said. I took the necklace with the button off and handed it to him. "If it's so damn important, *you* press it."

"What the hell is your issue, Olaf? Why aren't you taking anyone's help?" Coach asked, his tone changing to concern. I had never heard this before.

"All I can say is, I guess I need to heal my way, alone. None of you are going to understand that," I emotionally responded.

Coach put his hand on my shoulder and looked me in the eye. "Kid, no one is going to look at you any different if you have help healing from a bunch of surgery. Christ Olaf, you were shot a bunch. You *should* need help coming back from that. And, the longer you are in here, the longer you're away from your family. You are losing time with your daughter, kid. You're never getting that back."

"I never refused help. It was taken from me. My crime, Coach, is that I was taking my therapist's instructions and adding to them so I could get home sooner. For this, I was rewarded with a goddamned button and a worse experience, where no one would help me unless I shamed myself. You tell me, why do I need to shame myself to get help? Why should I possibly give a single ounce of goddamned satisfaction to anyone who forces me to do that? I'd rather get back to normal on my own, which I am doing. If that means crawling to take a piss, I'm crawling to take a piss. Clear?"

Coach's eyes widened. He then threw the button on the floor and stomped on it, breaking it into tiny pieces.

"Wait here," he scowled. His tone was much closer to the Coach I knew.

A couple minutes later, I heard a voice in the hallway outside my room yell, "Olaf Waniglia, get out here NOW!"

I grabbed my walker and made my way to the hallway. As I turned the corner, I saw a couple massive men, and Coach was behind them. One of the men was familiar to me, but I didn't know why.

"You're coming with us. Your time here is done. You have what you came here with?" the giant on the right asked.

"Who the hell are you and where are we going?" I asked callously.

"Iron Hands, shut the hell up and answer the man," Coach bellowed.

"Jesus. Yeah, I came here with myself so I have what I came here with," I sarcastically retorted.

"Good enough for me. Where we're going, the walker cannot go," the right giant said. He approached me, put a hand on my shoulder, moved the walker to the side, picked me up and carried me as though I was an infant.

"Does my family know about this?" I asked. "Am I being released?"

"Yes, and sort of," the giant responded with a smile.

"Y'all ain't telling me shit, are 'ya?"

"Nope. Coach scares the hell out of me."

Life, Experienced in Every Spectrum Both Visible and Not

The giant carried me outside and approached a small crowd gathered by a large van. The crowd was made up of people I knew—Annie, Nol, Sadie, Father, Mother, Susan, Coach, Fanny, Gerard, Akamu—and a couple others that I didn't recognize.

"Olaf, you are being taken to a facility to complete your recovery," Father said

"A *facility*? What in the hell did I do to be institutionalized? Can I refuse to go?" I responded, upset at this new prospect of treatment. "Just leave me here. I'll do this on my own."

"Olaf, I misspoke, and I apologize. This is not a facility in the sense you are thinking." Father backpedaled.

"We're coming with you, babe. All of us," Annie said, smiling nervously.

I looked up at the giant and asked, "Sir, can you please put me down? I can't do this anymore."

He smiled and obliged. He continued to steady me after he put me down.

"I need specifics. I will not do this bullshit treatment anymore. Someone tell me where I'm going and what the plan is, or I will discharge myself and figure it out on my own," I said emphatically.

"Olaf, Susan feels horrible about how wrong this has gone. She didn't intend you to feel this way," Susan's *vox corporis* said sadly. This was the first time I'd heard a *vox corporis* since before the shooting.

"We—all you see here, plus Addie, Jonah, and Doc—are flying to Hawaii at Akamu's urging. Rupert is housing us, and a place close to his house is where you are going to do your rehab. The plan is to stay there for two months, but not all of us will be there the whole time. Susan and I will be there for the first two weeks, but the hospital needs us back thereafter. Franklin and Helene will travel there to start the second month, and I will return for the last two weeks," Father said.

I stood silent for a couple moments, contemplating this.

"I don't understand how any of you can afford the time away," I said. "Looking at this group, I see a ton of responsibility that will not endure two months away. None of you should make your lives more difficult on account of my treatment. I'm doing fine on my own."

"That's *why* we are all travelling, Olaf. Specifically, so the responsibilities do not fall any further," Annie said.

"I promise this makes sense, my friend. Can you trust me?" Akamu asked, sadness in his voice.

"I will try. At this point, I don't trust anyone," I said. "I hope to God you all just heard me say that. I do not trust *any* of you. Can I please change out of this gown before I get on an airplane?"

"I *TOLD* YOU PEOPLE. GODDAMMIT!" Coach yelled. "Iron Hands, I swear on my life that things change right now for you. You do not have to trust me. I will prove it to you. You know me as you do, kid, and you damn well know I stand by my word."

Susan started to cry. "Olaf, I'm so sorry. I didn't…."

"We didn't mean... I dunno... We..." Father stammered.

"Can we please just get on with this? I'm standing outside in a hospital gown that I've sweat and bled on and it's open in the back. If that van is how we go, can we please leave?"

Annie ran over to me, hugged me, and squeezed. She was sniffing and breathing as though she were crying. The giant kept his hand on my back as I had no chance of standing on my own.

"Never again, babe. You will never question me, ever again. I'm sorry for what I did too. I should have helped you," she said, sniffing.

I felt a horrible sense of betrayal amid all these people that I positively adored—*including* my wife. The awful thing about this, dear Reader, is that it colored my view of *everything*. I literally had this turbulent undercurrent of anger that washed over me in waves. I could not get passed the fact that the end of my hospital time had been so disgustingly concocted. At minimum, Susan and Father had come up with an approach that apparently Coach had been asked about, dissented, and the plan moved forward anyway. Though I should have limited my feelings to these two people, they extended to the lot of *humanity*. In my mind, the world and all of its inhabitants had turned their backs on me when I needed them the most. In the truest (metaphorical) sense, I was in that massive body of water, and no matter where I swam, I was still in its depths. In this case, the water was my anger, and I was not calming down for anything.

The van stopped at my parents' house, where I rinsed off in the shower and changed. None of this went well. I fell getting into and out of the shower. I hit my head on the exit from the shower, loud enough to prompt Father, Mother, and Annie to come running.

"Olaf, are you okay?!" Mother asked through the door, worried.

"Nope. Be out in a second," I replied, still laying on the floor.

"Let us help you—please," Father said.

"I'll be out in a second," I dismissed.

I got myself upright and sat on the toilet. There, I began to get dressed. Let me tell you, dear Reader, this was a process about as painful as anything I had attempted after the whole leg bending incident in the hospital. Tears flowed down my cheeks as I tried to get my right leg into my boxers, and then into a pair of loose cotton shorts.

Once I was finally dressed, I calmed myself down and stumbled toward the door. When I opened it, I found Father, Mother, Annie, Nol, Sadie, and Susan all standing outside.

"Olaf, you have a nasty lump on your head. Can I take a look?" Father asked, stepping toward me.

"I'm fine, Father. If I could just have a couple Aspirin for the van ride, that'll do," I said. "Could I just have an arm to help me get back outside please?"

Everyone started to move forward, toward me.

I held out my hand with my palm facing them, which stopped the group from moving. "Listen, all. You cannot do this. I appreciate the willingness to help—honestly, I do—but this is overwhelming. Nol, would you please help me get outside?"

He nodded, and we followed the group back to the van.

The plane ride was quiet. Annie sat next to me, and the tension between us was undeniable. There was a time she grabbed my hand, but I didn't grab hers in return. I'm positive she knew I wasn't happy with her, but I'm not sure she knew to what extent. In my mind, she should have known me well enough to understand I was struggling mightily in the hospital. I gave her a pass for the first day, but each day thereafter, the knife cut deeper. Annie could see how badly I hurt, and how frustrated I was, but still stayed the course of this deeply flawed plan. Father fell into this same lot of condemnation in my mind, but it didn't hurt nearly as bad as what Annie had done—though my contempt for him was massive. I could not believe the level to which Annie sank in this plan to make me submissive. In principle, I understood why they did what they did. I didn't like it, but I understood it. Annie's role in the whole thing, though, was to passive-aggressively break me down. It was the same nonsense her mother had done to me when I first met Helene, and I was deeply concerned this side of my wife was something I now needed to contend with. I could handle a lot in life, my dear Reader, but an unsupportive wife who passive-aggressively makes her way through relationship ups-and-downs was *not* one of them.

I fell asleep briefly, and when I woke up, I found her asleep on my shoulder. It was sad to me; I needed to be unconscious for her to get close to me, but that was absolutely the case. I was in such a conflicted place with my wife, and I hated that so much more than contending with my shot-to-hell body.

We landed in Hawaii, and I had a heck of a time getting off the airplane. I waited until everyone else had left, Annie included, and had one of the flight attendants help me to stand up. I used the seats of the plane as crutches, and was sweating by the time I got to the door of the plane. One of the pilots was standing by the door, observing my struggle.

"Sir, can we get you a wheelchair? Or do you have a cane or walker that was stowed?" he asked kindly.

"My walker was left back in South Carolina, sir. I truly would appreciate some assistance. I'll never make it up the ramp into the airport," I said, my breath heavy.

"Take a seat. I will have someone bring a chair for you," he said, smiling.

A couple minutes later, an airport employee arrived with a wheelchair and pushed me up the ramp. Just inside the terminal, I found my group, a mix of worry and frustration on their faces.

"Olaf, I would have helped you," Annie said emotionally.

"I've done the last couple weeks on my own. This was no different. Y'all told me my walker couldn't make the trip, yet I cannot walk without assistance. I'm sorry everyone, but I am not going to rely on a single one of you to help me go from place to place for the next two months. Either we find someplace where I can get something to help me walk, or this trip will be exceptionally short for me," I responded angrily.

"Olaf…" Annie started, but Coach quickly stepped in front of her and whispered something. I didn't hear what he said, but the exchange stopped, and he motioned all of us to start moving.

We made our way through to where Doc was, then on to where Rupert's plane was sitting for the trip to Maui. I had to walk for the last part, which Coach helped me through.

"I promise, kid, we will get you something to do this on your own real soon," he said kindly.

As we approached Rupert's plane, I could see he looked incredibly sad. Annie ran to him and hugged him tightly. The two of them then disappeared into the plane. The rest of us followed. I was the last to make my way up the steps and had to be very creative in doing so. None of the people I was with waited for me, not even Coach. It was Rupert's assistant, Michael, who stood at the top of the stairs, looking at me with condemnation and disgust though my ascent. As I made my way into the plane, I found a seat toward the back of the plane and sat down. I was out of breath, and Doc was the only member of that group who chose to be by me. None of the people who brought me to Hawaii wanted anything to do with me in that moment, and I could only imagine why.

We landed in Maui and it was the same drill; I let everyone go ahead of me, then did my best to get down the stairs and onto the pavement. I must have taken too long; the car left without me, and no one waited for me, not even Doc. I was completely shocked by this, and instantly made my mind up that I wasn't staying there.

So, I used a luggage cart for balance and went into the airport terminal. I made my way to the ticket counter and was in line when I heard running behind me.

"Olaf! Olaf! Wait!!! Please!!!" I heard in the distance, but could not figure out who the hurried voice belonged to.

I had zero intention of giving an ounce of consideration to anyone at this point. I was going home, and I was going to think about how to proceed with every facet of my life. I was very hurt by this last curveball thrown by my family and friends, and in so very many ways, it damned those relationships in profound ways. I could honestly see months, if not years, of isolation from them; and a very likely separation, if not divorce, from Annie. I was running through what my demands were going to be when a man ran up to me.

"Olaf Waniglia, right?" he asked as he tried to catch his breath.

"Why do you ask?" I flatly responded. I did not look at the person.

"I'm Todd from RSI. I'm running late. I was supposed to pick you up."

"No one told me this, and I'm sorry, but I'm damn sick of this whole thing. I'm going back to South Carolina. Go tell whoever you need to, but I'll find a rehab facility back at home."

"Please, sir. We've been working on this treatment for you for quite a while. I think you will be very surprised by the results. This is my fault—I should have been here when you landed. Won't you reconsider?" he pleaded.

"So, you're telling me that you've designed some treatment, and I've never heard of you? Beyond that, no one—not my father, not my wife, no one—told me about this. I'm sorry, sir, but this whole thing is complete crap. I'm going home. As I said, go tell whoever you need to I've refused and to cancel the plan. This is not how I am going to move forward."

I then moved to the counter and asked the ticketing agent for the next flight to Charleston.

"Well, sir, the best I can do is a flight that goes from here to the big island, and from there to L.A., then from there to Charleston. That flight leaves the day after next at 8:00 AM. Do you want to purchase the ticket?" she said kindly.

"Please Olaf," Todd said, "come with me. I promise you that..."

"You cannot promise me shit, Todd. Get the hell away from me and go back to wherever you came from. I am not leaving with you. That's final," I said, glaring at him. I then turned to the ticketing agent and said, "Yes ma'am, I will take the flight. Is there a hotel close by that you can arrange for me, and a car as well?"

"Yes sir. Will that be cash or charge today?" she asked.

I reached for my wallet and as soon as my fingers touched it, the environment changed—very similar to what I experienced when I was healing Gerard, but this time, the ribbons of light around me were stopped.

"What's going on?" I asked. My voice echoed as though I were yelling into a deep canyon.

Several seconds later, I heard a woman's voice say, "Olaf, this is a place where you should stay. You will not be forced to do so, but should you choose to stay, I will guide you to the place you should be. You are not bound by anything but your own choices. Please be kind to those who help you."

As soon as she stopped speaking, the environment around me returned to normal, and I was laying on the ground. Several people were standing around me, all with concerned expressions.

"I'm so sorry, all. Did I hurt anyone?" I said weakly.

"No son, but we're very scared you hit your head. You fell backward so hard," an older gentleman said.

"Would you please help me up?" I asked, as I pushed my torso up.

Two gentlemen extended their hands and pulled me up. I was extremely weak, and they helped me to a nearby chair. I thanked them both and looked around. There was no sign of Todd or any of my family. The older gentlemen sat next down to me.

"Son, looks like you could use a cane. That leg of yours doesn't work terribly well, does it?" he asked, looking down at my leg.

"No, sir. I definitely need something. My right knee was shot and destroyed. I have a fake knee I'm not at all used to yet. I flew here with my family, and they told me when we left home that I couldn't take my walker. I don't know why this was the case, but I definitely need something to steady myself. Do you know where I can get one?" I asked, thinking that this would be a good step forward.

"As a matter of fact, I do, and it's not far from here. It just happens that I'm done working too. If you're comfortable with me driving you there, I'd be happy to do so," he said, a warm smile on his face.

"I'd very much appreciate that, sir. Thank you!"

"I'm gonna call to get us a ride to the parking garage. Stay here," he said and walked away.

The ticketing agent walked over to me and asked, "Sir, did you want to proceed with the transaction? If so, I need you to come with me."

"I'm going to stay for the day and see what happens. I will call you in the morning if my plan to return home resurfaces. Is that okay?"

"Of course, sir. Here is my card. My office number is the second one from the bottom. That will go to my voicemail if I am busy. I am so glad to see you're okay. You fell backward so hard," she said kindly.

"Thank you. I will maybe be in touch," I said.

The older gentleman returned, and a minute or so later, a person driving a mechanized cart arrived.

"Understand you need a lift. Hop a-board, sir!" the driver said.

So, the three of us made our way through the airport and out to the parking garage. I'm almost sure that I saw Todd on a payphone, but I don't believe he saw me.

"Sir, I'd like to address you more formally. My name is Olaf, what is yours?" I asked as we drove away from the airport.

"Stan's the name, son. Pleased to meet 'ya. I called my guy, and he has a great cane for you. We'll be there in a second," he retorted.

We pulled up to a block of stores, and entered one called 'Island Walking Sticks'. Inside, we found a man named Nick who came over to us as soon as we walked in.

"Looks like you need a friend, son. Come over here and meet her," he said, grabbing my arm for support.

We walked over to a counter, where a wooden cane with a tripod for a base sat.

"I think this may just be your answer, friend. Give 'er a go," he said and handed me the cane.

"How do I hold this, sir? On the right? On the left? I'm sorry, in the hospital I had a walker," I said nervously.

"She'll support you where you need 'er to. Looks like that right side is your tough spot—might be most comfortable for you to use it in your left hand to counter-balance your leg. Give that a try, son. Just go slow, and let her guide you," he said. "She will help you if you let her."

What he said struck me, not just because he possessed an uncanny view of canes, but because of what the woman's voice said when I was in the altered state in the airport. I picked up the cane and put it in my left hand. Nick was right; the counter balance was exactly what I needed. I immediately noticed an increase in my stability.

"This is incredible, Nick. Thank you so much! Is this a test model, or can I buy this one?" I asked excitedly.

"It was paid for, Olaf," he said, his tone much more serious.

"What do you mean? How could you have known I was going to be here?" I asked, my mind going a million miles an hour.

"Akamu is a good friend. He said you'd be by, so I made this for you. I actually have another one I was asked to make, but I need to ship that one. You'll have it in a month or so," he said, smiling.

"Please don't tell me that you guys are part of the facility that ass Todd tried to take me to," I said, nervous I had somehow fallen into a trap.

"No, Olaf. We are not. If anything, this is the end of the line for our dealings, except for the piece I'm still building for you," Rick said.

"Olaf, do you have any clothes?" Stan asked me.

"Truthfully, no, Stan. I don't. I've no clue where my luggage would be, and I'm not about to go looking for it. Know any place that I can pick up an outfit or two?" I asked, realizing the situation I was in. I had no clothes and none of my toiletries. I wasn't about to replace it all, but figured, with a couple outfits and a nice hotel, that would suffice.

"Right around the corner. We can get you fixed up, as long as you like Hawaiian shirts and board shorts," he said, gesturing to the right.

"Well then, I think we have our next stop. Nick, thank you so much for my cane! This is amazing!" I said, walking toward the door. "Can you tell me anything about what you're still making?"

"No, I cannot tell you about it quite yet. I just promise that she's just as special as the one in your hand. If anything happens to them, let me know, and I'll do what I can to fix them," Nick said, walking toward us. "I'm very proud to be able to help the people I do. Let me know how you are, Olaf, and how she works out for you."

"I promise you I will," I said, and we left the store.

I could not believe the difference! I could actually walk, almost at a normal pace. Considering I solely had used a walker to this point, with minimal success, this was a revelation to me. Being mobile again gave me a sense of freedom that I hadn't had in almost two years.

"Looks like you have your stride back, son. I'm so happy to see that! Sorta sounds like you have had a rough road lately," Stan said. "You seemed awful nervous back there. You aren't in some kind of trouble, are you?"

"I completely understand why you'd be concerned, Stan. Suffice to say, my family took me out of the hospital after treating me horribly there. They are trying to save face by bringing me here to do some rehab at some facility, but they left me at the airport and told me nothing about the rehab. I have zero desire to see those folks right now. I hope this answers your question," I responded.

"Your family just left you at the airport? You had no idea that man was coming to pick you up? Jesus, Olaf—I don't blame you a bit for feeling like you do. After we get your clothes, do you know where you want to go?" he responded, concern rich in his voice. "I cannot believe they just left you there. Even my no-good son wouldn't have done that. What the hell is wrong with people?"

"Is there a nice hotel close by that you would be willing to drive me to?" I asked, relieved that Stan understood my predicament.

"Yes, but it's pricey. The Seashell is on the beach. It's a five-star affair, my friend. If you can afford it, that's where you go."

"Well then, that sounds like home for at least tonight. Ready to help me find some swanky clothes?"

"I cannot wait, Olaf."

With that, we entered into The Shark, a store specializing in men's clothing. There, I bought three shirts, three pairs of shorts, a pack of boxers, and a hat. I figured this to be enough clothes to get me through until I decided what I was going to do. No matter what, this was important to me.

Stan then drove me to the hotel and helped me get my new duds up to my room. I was getting better with the cane, but by no means was I completely steady enough to walk smoothly and carry something in the other hand. Seems simple, but I'll tell you, dear Reader, it's anything but.

"I think that's it, Olaf. Anything else I can do for you tonight?" Stan asked.

"Not tonight, no. But, Stan, would you have breakfast with me in the morning? My treat," I said, thinking I desperately needed to do something out of gratitude for this man. He had done so much for me, and I was a complete stranger.

"I would be happy to, Olaf! What time?" he beamed.

"How about 9:30? I'll ensure we have a table. Oh, and Stan, one other thing… Please, if anyone asks where I am, would you please just let them know I'm safe? I need some time to think how I go about moving forward. The whole lot of 'em have been awful to me," I said carefully.

"Of course, Olaf. I can next to guarantee questions will be asked. I'll handle it. I am a Marine. What I'm asked not to tell, I don't tell," he said intensely. "I would be happy to meet you in the morning, but could we meet earlier? I need to be at the airport by 10:00."

"That's a deal, soldier. 8:00 it is," I said and shook his hand.

After I got our reservation set up, I found a couple mini-bottles of scotch and poured myself a drink. I then walked out onto my terrace and sat on a nice lounge chair facing the Pacific, sipping away at my libation.

I could not believe the developments of the day. From the morning with Coach, to the horrible shower at my parents' house, to being left at the airport with some random person named Todd. I'll tell you, dear Reader, even if this facility could make me fly and be free of pain forever more, I was not going. The lot of the people involved, Annie and Father included, needed to learn what I did not want— what I would not have.

I watched the sun set, finished my drink, and went to bed. I fell asleep to the sound of the tide withdrawing into the sea; it reminded me of home, and it made me smile.

****

The next morning, I again was treated to the wonders of bathing and getting dressed. I didn't have the same kinds of pain I had the day prior, but it still was a challenge. However, my cane made a significant difference in almost every facet of my life. It helped me to walk, obviously, but it also steadied me when I was getting dressed. I could not believe the change.

I made my way downstairs and met Stan for breakfast. He was appreciative of the invitation and the hot meal. As we were about to part, I asked him, "Stan, you know that park on the Big Island—the one with all the custom lights? Do you know where it is? It has to be close to a shore."

"Of course! It's on the shore facing us, on the south side of the island. It's a prohibitive distance by boat, but you could be there in about an hour, considering the flight and a short drive. How do you know about that?" he asked, a quizzical look etched into his face.

"My grandmother created those lights. I'd like to see the park again."

"Wait…you're *that* Olaf? Jesus God Almighty," he said as his eyes lit up.

"Do you know me somehow?" I asked. I was disturbingly confused.

"News of the shooting in your house made it through most of the islands. You are *revered* here for saving your family. My dear friend, it is an honor to have been able to help you. Is there anything else I can do for you?" he asked, tears in his eyes.

"I'm just a man. I'm not sure why my story is known here," I said. I was very uncomfortable.

"You're a man, yes, Olaf. You selflessly sacrificed yourself to save your wife. That's not just a man, my boy. That's a *man*. Be proud of yourself, and know what you did, few would have done had they found themselves in your nightmare," he said. "I know where you need to go. Do you trust me?"

"You've given me no reason to distrust you, Stan. Please though, if your thought is to return me to my family, I am in no way ready for that."

"I am honoring your request, though it makes me sad, Olaf. They have to be worried about you," he said, leaning in.

"Perhaps, but the things they did to me, collectively, does not earn them the right to be in my life right now. I miss my daughter tremendously, but I cannot see Annie. I cannot fathom speaking to Father. I do not want to see my former physical therapist. I'm not ready to face any of it," I said, wiping a tear from my eye.

"Then listen to me, Olaf. I will take you someplace where you will continue to enjoy your freedom and start to get better, but just understand that this is a small island. People don't stay hidden for long—especially when they are trying to stay hidden. Given your check-in at the hotel alone, I guarantee that several people are circulating your whereabouts. I will take you someplace that would be honored to help you, and I will come back there after my shift at the airport to bring you here. Is that okay?"

"Yes, Stan. I just hope that you truly are a man of your word."

We got into his car and drove a short distance to a brick building that had large open sections on all sides. As I looked closer, it was a boxing gym.

"Come on. You have to meet someone," Stan said excitedly. We walked in and all activity stopped.

"Where's Joe?" Stan asked the collective.

A short man emerged. "Found 'im. Now Stan, who the hell is this, and why are you interrupting our session?" he said angrily.

"This is Olaf. You know… Madelyn Dolby's grandson?" Stan said suggestively. The tiny man's eyes lit up and he ran toward us.

"*You* are Olaf Waniglia? *Iron Hands Waniglia* is in *my* gym? This is incredible! My man, what can I do for you?" Joe said, nearly breaking my hand when we shook.

"Yes, I am Olaf Waniglia. I need some help rehabbing. Can you do that? My right leg…"

"The one that was shot to smithereens? Yes, we will help you rehab. How long do I have you today?" Joe asked, anticipation rich in his voice.

"How about until 3:30 this afternoon?" Stan asked.

Joe's eyes got wide, and he took turns looking at me, then to Stan, and back to me. "OH HELL YEAH! I have clothes, wraps, and gloves for you in the back. Go, change. Let's start this dance *right*!" he shouted like a bewitched clown at a carnival. "Boys! Back to work!"

"Good luck, Olaf. I'll see you this afternoon," Stan said. I nodded and headed to the back of the gym with Joe.

"It truly is an honor to meet you, Olaf. I will do whatever I can to help you," Joe expressed genuinely.

By the end of that day, dear Reader, I was steady on my feet enough to use a speed bag. I went back the next day, and by the time I left, I was able to hit a heavy bag, stepping into my punches. Joe's process was remarkable, and he was impressively knowledgeable about the human body. He used specific movements, and specific stretches to strengthen the area around my knee. He also had me do movements for my chest and core.

These were not your garden variety pushups and sit-ups, dear Reader. They were movements that combined tribal dance and tai chi stances, which couldn't have been more opposing. I had never seen, nor done anything like this, and I could not believe the results.

As I walked into the gym on the third day, I was barely using my cane. By the end of the third day, I did a clinic for the guys in that gym, and worked one-on-one with many of them to improve their power. In three days, Joe had gotten me as close to "normal" as was possible. I could walk without the cane, but every so often, my balance was an issue so I continued to carry "her." In the gym, I was nearly back to what I had been before the shooting, in terms of my boxing ability. I was miles ahead of where I had been in the hospital, and I was eternally grateful.

Knowing my body was moving in the right direction, it was time to resolve my issues with my family. In my conversations with Stan and Joe, I learned there was a small airport that offered charter flights to the Big Island. So, I booked a round trip flight and car service so I could go back to the park with my grandmother's lights. After I washed up and had some dinner, my car took me to the little airport, and I departed Maui. I figured the best first step in this process was to go to the place where our family began.

It was twilight; the sun was almost completely swallowed by the Pacific. I made my way into the park, where the lights had begun to twinkle. I found a bench under one of the lights and sat down. The energy in this place was different; I could feel it all around me. There was an undercurrent of warmth that gently passed through my body; it was as though I was being hugged both inside and out. I did not feel this when we were here after the wedding, and to me, that was comforting in a way I desperately needed. It seemed to me that what I sought—to begin healing my mind—was found in this place.

Not long after I sat down, I heard a familiar voice to my left.

"This is a beautiful place, no?" Akamu said softly. "May we join you, Olaf?"

"Of course, Akamu," I said, my nervousness instantly cutting through the calm I had just achieved. I didn't know who the "we" entailed. He sat, and Fanny walked over and hugged me. "Are you okay, Olaf?" she asked, her voice dripping with sadness. She took a deep, sad breath, and sat next to Akamu.

"That depends, Fanny. Physically, I'm making massive strides. Emotionally, I'm just getting started. That's why I'm here now. I needed to go back to the beginning," I said. I could feel myself getting emotional; tears were in the corners of my eyes.

"I need to say this, my dear friend," Akamu began, "You have every right to be very angry. What was done to you by those charged with your care was abysmal. It was taken way too far."

"You all left me at the airport, Akamu. How the hell am I supposed to feel about that? After everything that happened, you all *left*. I had just begun to allow myself to trust what was happening, and it all came crashing down," I said, tears streaming from my eyes. Both Fanny and Akamu were crying too.

"I don't know what to say, Olaf," Fanny said and walked away crying.

"I don't either, Olaf. Again…" Akamu paused to gather himself. "You have every right to be angry."

"Never in my wildest imagination would I have ever thought Annie would abandon me like this. I would have scoffed at the notion Father would be a part of anything of the sort. *No one—not one soul—was there for me.* I fought to remain alive. I fought to move forward. I did all this fighting, and when I looked around, I was *alone*," I said, exasperated. "I'm terribly sorry, Akamu. I have to go."

I got up and walked back in the direction of my car. I was then whisked back to the airport, where I waited for just over an hour for my flight back to Maui. I stewed in this horrible mental space the entire time. It didn't surprise me when Akamu found me at the park, but he was oddly unable to help the situation.

Once I was back at the Seashell, I sat out on my patio for a couple hours. In the beginning, I knew I needed to calm down. I had an irresponsibly large drink. I then closed my eyes and deeply breathed in the salty Pacific air until my heart and mind stopped racing.

When I retrieved myself out of the emotional spiral I had fallen into, I became analytical. This was never going to get better unless I let it. This, dear Reader, was the truth. So, in order to let this—my life, my family, my recovery—get better, I had to let go of anything inhibiting healing, anger being at the top of the list. I could not possibly remain angry if I ever wanted to find forgiveness in my heart. You see, dear Reader, there was one other nasty part to this— much harder to determine a resolution for—and that was hurt. I saw the two as mutually exclusive; anger was something I had chosen to express myself, but its purpose was to mask the hurt I felt.

As hard as I knew it would be, I decided to go to Rupert's the next day and just listen. I would not stay, and if things got too hard, I would leave. So, I called Rupert's house and relayed this to Michael, with the clear instruction I would be there for no more than thirty minutes, and I would do nothing but listen.

The next morning, Stan and I had our customary breakfast before he delivered me to Joe's, where I did a two-hour session. He did not like the abbreviation compared to what we had done the previous days. I then told him that I intended to come back in the early evening. He smiled widely, greatly pleased.

I then went back to the hotel, showered, and changed. I'd arranged for a car to take me to Rupert's house. The driver promised he would wait for me, with the engine running, ten feet from the door. I, in turn, promised him I would be back in thirty minutes.

So, my heart beating out of my chest, I got out of the car and approached the door. I paused before knocking, wondering if I were making a colossal mistake. I took a deep breath, looked at my watch, and knocked. Michael opened the door, a look of solace blanketing his face. It was a stark departure from the look I was greeted with on the plane. I nodded at him and he directed me toward the patio. Doc came rumbling down the hallway when he heard me. It was so good to see my dog again, dear Reader. I honestly felt he was the only one in that house I could trust.

Everyone who had travelled was sitting on the patio, along with someone else I didn't recognize. Addie ran over to me and attached herself to my waist. I bent down, overcome with emotion. I hugged her tightly, then wiped tears from her eyes.

"I miss you Daddy. Where did you go?" she asked as I wiped the sadness from her cheeks.

"I'm not far, sweetheart. I promise you," I said, doing all I could to keep it together.

I stood up, held Addie's hand, and walked out to the patio. I looked at my watch—twenty-eight minutes left. As I neared the patio, almost everyone stood up. It was in that moment that I realized I was not looking forward to this at all. There was a seat near the entrance to the patio, where I sat down, and pulled Addie onto my lap. Doc laid down next to me.

I cleared my throat, and said, "I'd like to hear what you want to say, and I hope that it is understood how today is going to go. I'm here for twenty-seven more minutes."

There was stone silence for the next three minutes. Most of the people either looked at me, or looked down at the fidgeting hands in their laps.

Father was first to speak. "You didn't go to therapy. I'd like to know why."

"If that's the first thing you want me to know, Father, I'd prefer you not say anything else until I'm good and ready for you to hear what *I* have to say. No one has anything to say?" I asked calmly, but firmly.

"Sweetheart, I don't think any of us knows what to say," Mother said sadly.

"I agree, son. I truly am not sure what I should say to you," Nol said.

Annie cried. Normally, this would have broken my heart, but this time I found I couldn't understand the emotion.

Rupert quietly said, "Olaf, without understanding how you feel, how can anyone make this better?"

"At this point, Rupert, that is irrelevant. I'm quite confident Akamu has told the lot of you what I said yesterday at Grandma's park. I'm not going to repeat that. Eighteen more minutes," I responded.

"Olaf... I.... I don't... I don't want to... I can't lose you," Annie cried. Sadie immediately got up and hugged her tightly.

"Olaf, I..." Father began.

"Father, you had your chance. I know where you stand, and again, I care to discuss this with you when I'm ready. Right now, I'm not," I said flatly, interrupting him.

"I'm sorry, kid. I should have stopped this crap before it started. I'm truly sorry," Coach said sadly.

"Jesus, son. I am so sorry," Nol said. "I should have helped you. Lord knows how much you have helped me through the years. I get it now, and I understand."

"Olaf—anything at all I can do, you ask," Gerard said, smiling.

"Sweet Honey Boy," Fanny began, "I know how you feel. I love you. Everyone here loves you. We made a few mistakes, and at least for my part, I am so very sorry."

The person I did not recognize stood up, glared at me, and said, "Olaf, we worked very hard on your rehabilitation program. You're coming with me, right now, and we are getting started."

"Sir, you come even one step closer to me, and I will put you in the hospital. Go ahead and test me," I said threateningly. Doc perked up when he heard my tone. "I came here to see the group who let me suffer in Charleston, to see if there was even a shred of remorse. This same group told me your program, sir, was not an institutional one, and I clearly see now that it is. Y'all, if I ever see that man again, I'm flying home, and none of you will see me for a good, long while. If this is a cost issue, I'll pay for time spent on the program. I am rehabbing on my own. There is not one chance any of you will have a say in that area of my life ever again. Y'all have a wonderful night."

I then hugged Addie, kissed her on the cheek, and said, "Sweetheart, your Mommy needs a hug. Can you do that for me?"

"Yes, Daddy," she responded and ran over to Annie, who scooped her up. I got up, and the glaring man ran toward me. Doc jumped to his feet, growling fiercely.

"Wow, sir," I responded, and stepped into a vicious right to his jaw. He was unconscious before he hit the ground.

"Y'all had a choice tonight. This shows me where I stand in your world," I said.

"Christ, kid. You knocked him out," Coach said.

"I warned 'im," I said, straightened my hat, grabbed my cane, patted Doc, and headed for the door.

I had almost made it back to the car when my shirt was grabbed from behind, and a pair of arms wrapped around my chest.

"I cannot let you go," Annie said, her voice muffled.

"For now, you have to," I said.

"No, babe. I can't. Please, if you won't stay, let me come with you. I have too much to say, and being away from you is torture. I waited for over a year for you to wake up. The least you can do for me is hear me out," she said, holding me tighter as she spoke.

"What about Addie?" I asked.

"She'll have a sleepover with Grandma. Please, Olaf," Annie implored.

I stood there for a second, thinking. At minimum, she deserved a chance to explain herself, and no matter how hurt I was, I needed to give her that chance.

I looked back and saw Mother holding Addie. "You okay with her tonight?" I asked.

"Always, my precious son. Can she give Mommy and Daddy kisses goodnight?" Mother asked.

"Of course," I said. So, Mother walked her over to us, and Addie took turns giving us kisses.

"Goodnight Daddy," she said, "You hit that man really hard."

"Well, tiny one, that happens sometimes," I said and winked at her.

"You're going to come back, right, Olaf? I'd like some time with you too," Mother asked.

"Yes, after rehab, tomorrow afternoon. I'll send Annie back before rehab. I'm completely serious, Mother, if there is a single attempt to take me anywhere I do not care to go when I come back here…"

"You will not be going anywhere, Olaf," Mother said, interrupting me.

So, kisses complete, Annie and I got into the car and headed back to the Seashell.

Annie's eyes lit up when we got to the room. "You've been living *here*? This place is amazing!" she said as she moved throughout the suite.

"For the past couple days, yeah. I didn't have any of my luggage, so I figured this would be a good stop gap given the service," I said. "Would you like a drink?"

"Sure–surprise me," she replied and walked out to the terrace.

I made our libations and joined her on the terrace. It then hit me I had promised Joe I would be at the gym in just ten minutes. So, I excused myself, called him and told him the situation. He understood, but made it clear he wanted at least four hours with me the next day; I agreed. I could practically hear him smile when I did. After arrangements were made with Joe, I changed my reservation in the morning to three, and arranged for the car service to return Annie to Rupert's house when I left for Joe's.

I then took a couple very deep breaths. I still wasn't ready for this conversation, dear Reader, and it was critical to me that *if* this relationship were to be mended, the process would begin here. So, I got a couple thoughts together, and returned to the terrace.

I sat down a few feet from Annie, who then moved closer.

"Won't you sit with me?" she asked sadly.

"Annie, there is a lot that needs to be said. I much prefer to be able to look at you for this conversation," I responded softly.

She started to cry softly, and was quiet for a short while. After it was clear that we were stuck, I got up, got a box of tissues, placed them next to her, and returned to my seat. "I understand that this is hard. It's insanely hard for me too, Annie, but we need to start somewhere."

Annie wiped her eyes with a tissue and said, "I just don't know what to say, babe. How is this hard for *you*?"

"Well, I truly don't feel I was ready to have this conversation yet. Our marriage is very important to me, and I want to do this right," I said and took a sip of whiskey.

"Why aren't you ready, Olaf?" she asked coarsely, furrowing her brow. It was the same damn tone she used in the hospital.

"You watched me suffer for almost a month. You took my daughter away. My dog was nowhere to be seen. You degraded me verbally, just as your mother did in the beginning, the *whole time*. Then, we land in Maui and you disappear. You, of all people, Annie–you are my wife. When the plan in the hospital failed after a couple days, or even a week, you should have intervened. You should have protected me," I said angrily.

Annie cried harder.

I took a big drink, and then continued, "How am I supposed to feel when the person who pledged before God to protect, love, and honor me no matter what, forever, does this? It sure sounds like you guys had resolved to put me in a place that was going to attempt to force me to comply for my rehabilitation. Knowing me as you do, as your husband, how could you *ever* let this happen? I mean, Christ, Annie, I *just* woke up after a year of being asleep. I missed our daughter being born. I missed her first birthday. I missed her first steps. I'm trying like a madman just to catch up, and instead of feeling love and support, I was dejected and maligned. I was a forgotten misfit, a cancer that none of you knew what to do with, so you threw me aside. I'm not ready because the sum of all of this is a mountain of hurt and mistrust, and a question of who the hell you are. Do you need any further clarification?"

Annie could only sit there sobbing. I finished the rest of my drink, and went back inside for a refill. When I returned, the box of tissues was completely gone; its remnants in a pile next to Annie. I sat quietly, sipping my drink, deeply breathing in the salty Pacific air. The silence was solely stifled from a sniff or two every few minutes. This pattern continued for over an hour. I finished my drink and got up to get ready for bed when I heard Annie whisper, "Can I ever make this okay?"

"I'm honestly wondering the same thing. Even tonight, your first reaction was being indignant. If you have become the person I think you've become, I'm truly not sure. The girl I bled for would have never done this to me. I'm tired, and we have breakfast reservations at 8:00. I'm going to bed. You sleep in the room to the right tonight. I'll make sure you're up in time for breakfast. Goodnight."

"Wait…you mean I'm not sleeping with you tonight?" she asked pointedly.

"No Annie, not tonight. Right now, you're a stranger. I don't sleep with strangers. Goodnight."

I woke up, hearing a loud noise. It was 2:17. I wiped my eyes and went to see what might have happened. As I made my way out of the bedroom, I saw that the terrace had a couple new occupants—Nol and Sadie. I shook my head in abject disbelief and headed out to the patio.

"Sorry son—didn't mean to wake you. My fat ass knocked over a chair," Nol said.

"No worries, Nol. I'm gonna go back to bed. I just wanted to be sure nothing was seriously wrong. Y'all have a good night," I responded and turned to go back to bed.

"Wait, Olaf," Sadie said. "Sweetie, you have to tell him," she continued, looking at Annie.

"Can't this wait until morning, y'all? I'm exhausted."

"Just real quick," Sadie said. "Come on, sweetie. You need to say it."

Annie looked up at me with extremely red eyes, and said, "Babe, I'm so, so sorry."

I looked carefully at her, trying to determine if she was being genuine. I wanted desperately to believe her, but I just didn't.

"I truly appreciate you saying that, but you already apologized back in South Carolina. Thing is, at this point you–all of you–need to *prove* you're sorry—not just say it. So far, none of you have done that. Don't mistake me here, I want my family back. I want my friends back. I understand when I was asleep, it was hard on you. Honestly, I do. Here's the thing though, since I've been awake, none of you have acted like friends or family. I *lost* my wife. I *lost* my best friends. Father is *gone*. In their places are people I don't know.

There's this month of my life where I needed you, desperately, and you watched, hell *encouraged,* me to suffer. I've met two people here, on this island, who have been so kind to me, and I'm nothing to them, but they got me whole again. That was *your* job, not theirs. What the hell did I do to have y'all treat me like this?" I passionately imparted. "I'm exhausted, and this ain't getting fixed here tonight. I'm going to bed. Goodnight."

The three offered not one word in response; they just looked at each other. So, I returned to bed and went to sleep.

When I woke up the next morning, I found they were gone, and I had a new roommate—Akamu.

"This is rather unexpected," I said, scratching my head.

"I understand I have a time boundary today. May I just have a couple minutes, Olaf?" he asked sadly.

"Of course, Akamu," I said and sat down across from him.

"You've spoken some profound truths, Olaf. Things that we, collectively, are having a tremendous amount of trouble resolving. Will you be patient with us, and be willing to do a couple things, even if you are uncomfortable doing so?" he asked, leaning in.

I thought for a second before answering. "I am willing to do anything, Akamu, except any form of rehabilitation with the people Father made arrangements with. I hope that is clear."

"Oh trust me, Olaf, that is very clear. You will not be asked to do anything of the sort," he responded, smiling. "Your knockout yesterday has closed that door permanently."

"Well, I warned him. I'm completely serious, Akamu."

"Yes, you did, and trust me my friend, I know," he said smiling. "All of us have taken some hard looks at our parts in this and have come up with a plan. Can you be at Rupert's tonight by 6:00?"

"Sure. Are you able to join me for breakfast?"

"No, Olaf. Not today. I'm being picked up right about… now," he said, and as soon as the last word left his mouth, there was a knock at the door.

"Figures," I said chuckling, and got up to answer the door. When I opened it, I was surprised to see Rupert, who hugged me tightly.

"I am so glad you are okay, Olaf. You're coming at 6:00, yes?" he asked as he hugged me.

"Thank you, Rupert. Yes, I will be there at 6:00. Should I eat before I arrive?"

"Absolutely not. You must come hungry, and this time, you may not have a car on standby to leave. Agree?"

"I solely agree if *you* agree to bring me back here if I ask. Deal?"

"Yes, Olaf. You have a deal."

Akamu and Rupert then departed, and I went to have breakfast with Stan, who was treated to a play-by-play account of the prior day's events. He was shocked at all of what he heard, and by the time he took me to Joe's, he had worry in his eyes.

"Joe, would you come here for a minute?" Stan asked, his voice heavy with concern.

"What's wrong, Stan? Olaf, you ready for a few hours of fun?" Joe smiled.

Stan then reviewed the entirety of what I had told him. Joe smiled when he heard about the knockout. His eyes showed concern when he heard about the plan for 6:00. When Stan was done talking, Joe thanked him, ensured him he would handle everything, and Stan left for work.

Before we got started, Joe called over the entire team.

"Guys, we might have a situation we need to help Olaf with tonight. Who's available?" Joe asked intensely. Everyone raised their hand. I smiled when I saw this. Joe did too.

Joe then crafted a plan to give me an outlet if I needed it. As it turned out, most of the team, including Joe, lived within three blocks of Rupert's place. If anything went awry, I was to walk to that neighborhood, and they would take me to the hotel. Additionally, one of the larger, meaner team members, Haku, was going to station himself just outside of Rupert's house.

"I pray at that time every day. I'll just move over there tonight," Haku said.

I was so touched that these people, who had known me for less than a week, would be so willing to help me. "Thank you, all. This means so much to me, this support," I said.

"This is what family does, Olaf. Family protects family," Joe said. "Now then, we all have work to do. Let's go!"

Our work that day was intense. The physical parts of it all clicked; my power was back! The therapeutic parts were fluid and felt right. I could move without stumbling or pausing. At the end of the session, Joe gathered us together.

"This was an amazing afternoon, gentlemen, and I am proud of you. Before we go, we pray. Our brother Olaf is to walk across hot coals tonight. Please, gentlemen, pray for his safe passage to the other side," Joe said, and bowed his head.

We stood there silent for a minute, and when Joe said, "Okay," the entire team put their hands on my back and shoulders.

"We are with you, Olaf. If you need us tonight, you know what to do," Joe said.

"Thank you," I said, humbled beyond words.

My workout complete and plans solidified, we departed and Stan delivered me to the hotel. As I reached for the car door handle, he grabbed me.

"I'm worried about you, Olaf. I'll be thinking about you tonight. Good luck," he said, his words strained.

"It'll be okay, Stan. I promise you. We have a plan if things go south tonight," I said, putting my hand on his hand. He cautiously smiled, and I headed into the hotel.

My mind was racing like no tomorrow, dear Reader. I had no idea what I was walking into. I got myself cleaned up and had a drink. When it was time, I headed downstairs to my waiting car.

When we arrived at Rupert's house, Haku was already across the street, sitting cross-legged with his eyes closed.

"Many blessings, Olaf," he said, remaining still.

"Thank you, Haku," I said.

When Michael opened the door, he saw Haku and had trouble hiding the quizzical look on his face. "Who is *that?*" he asked.

"A friend. Don't be concerned, Michael," I said, smiling.

As I made my way inside, Akamu met me first. "Would your friend like to join us inside, Olaf?" he asked.

"Um…. I think he's okay for now, Akamu," I said, unsure of how to respond.

"I promise you, my friend, you will not need their protection tonight. At minimum, I could offer your friend a more beautiful place to pray," he offered.

"I suppose we could ask him," I cautiously responded.

"Let's go ask him," Akamu smiled.

We approached Haku, who did not move, nor open his eyes. "Everything okay, Olaf?" he asked softly.

"My friend, may I offer you a better place to pray?" Akamu said. Haku opened his eyes and looked at me. I shrugged my shoulders, not knowing what to say.

"Joe?" Haku said loudly.

Joe approached from about a block away. "He goes in, I go in. That's the deal," he said gruffly.

"That's absolutely fine, sir. I want you to see that we mean Olaf no harm. Additionally, we would like to thank you. You've done so much for this man, who we care deeply for. Please, gentlemen, join us," Akamu said, smiling.

Joe looked at me, and again I shrugged.

"We will go with you, but Olaf can never be out of our sight. Is this something you will agree to?" Joe asked, leaning in to Akamu.

"Of course, sir. I promise you," he said, still smiling brightly and gesturing to make evident their welcome. With promises made, we went back in to Rupert's house. Akamu led Haku to a place just passed the edge of the patio, where a blanket had been laid.

"Here, my friend. This place is special," Akamu said.

"I feel this. Many thanks, kind sir," Haku bellowed and returned to his cross-legged posture on the ground. He closed his eyes and started to pray silently. Akamu also bowed his head briefly; when done, he put his hand on Haku's shoulder and returned to the house.

Joe was escorted through the house by Rupert, who gave him the full tour.

I smiled as I saw the acceptance of these two people, but I also realized they had been essentially separated from me. I was very apprehensive, and was startled when Annie approached me from behind and grasped my hand.

"Come on," she said, and gently pulled me along.

We walked to a room with only a love seat in it. Doc rumbled in after us and laid down next to the small couch.

"Would you sit with me, please?" she asked, her eyes hopeful. I nodded, and we sat down.

Annie took a deep breath, tightened her grip, and said, "You were right about everything you said last night. You're not the only one who's upset about it, either. My parents and your mom are furious about how things were handled. So, the one thing you have to know is they had nothing to do with what happened, and all of them tried to get me to protect you. And, all of them were prohibited from seeing you in the hospital. Your mom about lost her mind when she saw you that day in the beginning. She had to be physically removed from the hospital due to the fit that she threw and wasn't allowed back thereafter. My parents were also told to butt out. In fact, all of them—your coach, Nol, Sadie, Akamu, Fanny—were all explicitly told to stay away."

"Who told them to stay away?" I asked, shocked at what I was hearing.

"Susan and your dad. They drove the whole thing, and they got the hospital to wholly support them. Administration and all; my dad was sick about it."

"Okay…. but a large part of this still makes no sense to me. I wasn't locked away in some remote part of the hospital. Any of them could have grabbed me and taken me out of there."

"Well, this was sort of attempted. Joe filed a lawsuit against the hospital. My dad found a rehab facility for you, and it was their thought to take you there for treatment. The government shut it down, though, and tightened their grip around the whole thing. Because your treatment was paid for by the government, they were the ones ultimately in control. Had you not stayed where you were, you were going to be transferred to a hospital in Washington, D.C. where we knew you'd never recover."

"The government could not have done that if I refused, Annie. Had I known what was happening, I would have discharged myself. Bear in mind, this all happened because of a stupid, degrading button. The government didn't do that. The government didn't hold a gun to your head and berate me as I struggled to stand. The government didn't force you to laugh at me when I struggled in the hallway. You did those things. No one else—that was you."

I took a couple deep breaths, then continued, "A huge question in my mind has to be answered at some point. Simply put, why did you do this to me? I don't accept that the government, or Susan, or Father could have made you do that, or force everyone in my life to abandon me. Jesus, Annie, I thought you died. I thought I lost you. The thing that positively kills me to this very minute is that I think I really did lose you."

Tears were streaming down both of our faces.

I felt someone put their hands on my shoulders. "Olaf, come on. We need to talk," Father said. I stood up and glared at him.

"No, Father. There is no way I'm willing to do that," I scolded.

"Please, Olaf. I want…"

"No. Now if the two of you will excuse me," I interrupted and left the room. I was met in the hallway by Joe and Rupert, who looked very concerned.

"Joe, I need to go to the shop. Now," I demanded, walking toward the door.

"I'm coming," Nol said from across the hall.

"Me and Jonah too," Sadie said.

"I'm in," Rupert said.

"I'm going too," Coach said.

"What the hell? I need to go hit a heavy bag for a while and try to digest what I just learned. Why do you all need to come?" I asked, annoyed.

"You ain't leaving the party without the party coming too, son. I ain't letting you slip away when I can control it. Not again," Nol said.

"Jesus. Haku! We're leaving. You coming?" I yelled.

"No. Blessings, Olaf," he responded quietly.

"We leaving then?" I asked, looking at Joe.

"I'm driving," Rupert said.

I huffed and left the house. When we got to Joe's gym, I removed my shirt, put on some wraps and gloves, and went to a heavy bag in the back corner. I turned my back to the room, and started hitting as hard as I could. I pounded over and over and over again. I got to a point where I stopped, closed my eyes, and yelled, "*Why? Goddammit, why?*"

I took a breath, and started hitting again.

After about ten minutes, Joe stepped in and said, "Olaf, take a break. You're going full bore and need some fluids. Take a break, okay?"

"Okay, Joe. Just one second," I responded and threw several more punches. I was dripping with sweat. I turned around, and the gym was full. The whole team was there, all looking very concerned. Everyone from Rupert's house was there, also notably distraught. There were red, damp eyes everywhere I looked.

"What's wrong?" I asked the team as I squirted water in my mouth.

"There's such pain, Olaf," Joe said. "I've never seen anyone hurting that bad, hit that hard. It's so sad to watch."

"Son, we need to go fishin'. Tomorrow," Nol said sadly.

"I am terrible at fishing, Nol. That hasn't changed," I said and took another drink.

"We're going fishing," he repeated.

"Whatever." I dropped the water and started hitting the bag again.

By the time I was tired enough to stop, it was 9:00. No one from Rupert's house had eaten.

"You need to eat, Olaf. There's no way you can do that much work, that intensely, and not refeed," Joe said. "If dinner at Rupert's house is still available, we should go there."

"I need a shower. I'll just go to the hotel," I responded.

"No chance, kid. You're not alone until you eat," Coach said.

"Your luggage is there, there are showers there, you have no reason..." Annie started.

"I have *every* reason. I won't be rude to Rupert though. He invited me, and I interrupted his event. I'll go back there on account of his hospitality," I declared and wiped my face with a towel.

The car ride back to Rupert's was silent. I'm not sure what people saw at Joe's, but it had clearly struck a nerve. Joe, Rupert, and Akamu rode with me. It sounded like Akamu was choking back tears. He felt something, but I couldn't place it. I just hit a heavy bag—nothing else.

When we got back to Rupert's house, Haku greeted us at the door. His eyes met mine briefly, he lowered his head, and said, "Olaf, there are many who wish to help you. It's very important you listen intently now... forward. You must know in your heart that when you hear truth, you will know truth."

"Haku?" I asked, confused.

"I am going to go home. You are safe, my friend. Blessings," he said and walked away.

Rupert then led me to my luggage—in a room housing Annie and Addie. There was a full bathroom attached to the room, so I showered there. When I came out, Annie was sitting on the bed.

"Olaf, listen…. Our conversation today didn't go as I would have liked it to. I will leave you alone after I say this, but I want you to know I will show you that I *am* the girl you fell in love with ..in any way possible," she said.

"I don't want you to leave me alone, Annie. I want you to *care*. Jesus, you forced your way into a conversation last night that was a continuation of what you did to me in the hospital. That passive-aggressive arrogance has taken the place of the strong person I knew—the person that didn't need that shit. I want my wife back. I'd give anything for that," I replied.

She got up, came over, and embraced me. For the first time in a long time, I hugged her back.

"You are everything to me, babe. I've been waiting to feel your arms around me for too long," she sighed.

"Make me believe that, Annie. Please," I replied and hugged her tighter.

"You need to eat, babe. I've never seen someone work that hard, for that long, without stopping. You have to be starving," she said.

"I know. I should eat. Any idea what was cooked?" I asked.

"Honestly, no." So, we headed toward the patio. Joe intercepted me, grabbed my arm, and sat me down in front of a massive steak. There was broccoli and a baked potato on separate plates next to it.

"You eat now, Olaf. I'm scared you're going to pass out if you don't. Your body…" Joe said.

"I know, Joe. I promise I'll eat."

He sat and watched me eat. They all did, for that matter. The steak had to have been north of two pounds; it was a gorgeous porterhouse. The fillet on that thing was as big as a softball; the T-bone was lean and incredibly tender. The broccoli and potato were delicious too; everything was cooked perfectly.

Joe's eyes were huge once I had cleaned everything off my plates. "Wow, Olaf. That was a huge steak. I think you'll be sleeping real soon. No training tomorrow. Your body needs to rest. Did you have breakfast set with Stan?"

I nodded.

I then woke up next to Annie at 9:30 the next morning.

"Stan!" I exclaimed and jumped out of bed. I promptly fell down and pulled myself back up in a complete frantic panic.

"Easy babe. He's on the patio," Annie comforted. "Sleep well?"

"Stan's here? What?" I asked, very confused.

"Yes, babe. He's the reason our daughter is not here at the moment. She held onto you all night. I did too. I haven't slept that good in months," she said, smiling with her eyes. I hadn't seen that since before the shooting.

So, I brushed my teeth and headed out toward the patio to find Stan and Addie. When I got there, I found Addie sitting on his lap; he was reading the paper to her.

"Well, I'll be. The zombie rises. How are you, Olaf?" Stan asked, grinning widely. "Your daughter is so special. It has been a privilege spending time with her this morning. Annie too."

"I'm doing okay, Stan. Not terribly sure what happened after I ate, though," I said.

"Um, you careened over onto Michael's lap. Joe and I carried you into your room. You are much heavier now son," Nol said.

"Yeah, okay lineman," I responded. "I'm not that heavy."

"None of your clothes fit you, Olaf. You basically have been moving your body with your arms alone for the past several weeks. Your upper body is incredibly strong. That's obvious just looking at you. Stands to reason you put on a few pounds of muscle," Annie said, grinning.

"Nol used to throw 400-pound dudes aside like they were made of paper. No way I'm too heavy for him," I said dismissively.

"You were awkward, dead weight, son. Throw a guard my way and I could still toss him, but that's energy transfer. Put that same guard on the ground unconscious, and it'll take six dudes to lift him. Happened all the time in camp. Crazy stuff," Nol said.

"All, we are preparing breakfast. It will be ready in about five minutes. Would you please start moving toward the dining room?" Michael asked distinctively.

"I didn't hurt you last night, did I Michael? Sorry I…" I started.

"Nonsense. That was the best belated birthday gift I've gotten yet," he interrupted, smiling demurely. He then disappeared into the hallway.

I got up, and Stan grabbed my arm. He waited for everyone to leave, then said, "Olaf, I think you need to hear your dad out. I know how you feel, and he knows too. Thing is, I truly think he wants to make things right. May be worth it. You can't take your precious daughter's grandfather away."

I nodded, and we headed to breakfast.

As breakfast was underway, Rupert stood up and announced, "We have a full afternoon and evening. Everyone be ready to leave by 2:00 sharp. Cars will be out front."

"What's going on?" I demanded.

"You may not ask questions, Olaf. You may solely do as you are asked. Trust me, kind sir," he replied. His grin told me to take his word for it.

After breakfast, I headed toward my room, but was stopped by Mother. "Olaf, can we talk?" she asked.

"Of course, Mother."

We made our way to the patio and sat down. Michael brought us coffee and winked at us before disappearing once again into the hallway.

"Son, you look so much better than the last time I saw you. Do you feel better?" Mother asked intently.

"I'm getting there, Mother. Why do you ask?"

"Well, I was cut out of everything, and I have literally no idea what is going on. I saw you at that gym last night, and could not believe what I was watching. That was the first time I've really seen you in months," she said, taking a sip of coffee.

"Annie told me you weren't allowed in the hospital. Thank you so much for caring enough to get thrown out, Mother," I said chuckling. "I think you know everything. My routine the entire time was this—wake up, crawl to the bathroom, crawl to my walker, go to the cafeteria, eat, sleep in the cafeteria, find my walker, go back to my room, sleep 'til morning. Along the way, I'd get treated like dirt by everybody. When we came to Hawaii and everyone disappeared, Stan helped me out of the airport and introduced me to Joe. Joe then completely rehabilitated me. That's the whole story. What about last night was so awful? I don't understand," I said and reached for my own cup of coffee.

"I cannot believe they did that to you, Olaf, for all that time. I hated being away from you. I knew you needed me. You needed *someone*. I couldn't get beyond the front doors of the hospital. It was unreal," she said and reached for a tissue. "The thing about last night was the way you were hitting that bag. It looked like you were trying to force something out. I've never seen someone physically express themselves like that before. There was not one person in that gym who wasn't crying, Olaf. We saw firsthand how deeply hurt you were. It was crystal clear. Your Father was positively beside himself."

"I'm not sure what to do about Father. It's going to take a long time for me to look at him as anything other than a monster. Susan, man, is that a disappointment—given I saved that woman's life and child."

"He loves you very much, Olaf, but he made a grave mistake. In fact, *multiple* grave mistakes. I think you just need to give him a chance. Lord knows, son, he and Annie are on extremely short leashes these days with me, Franklin, and Helene. The three of us are still trying desperately to resolve our own disappointment. I had no idea the plan was to essentially house you at that facility. I cannot believe this was done behind our backs. Coach, Nol, Akamu, and I seriously thought you were to come here, get some top-notch treatment, and live *here,* with all of us. You were going to have a room to yourself, but when we got here and you never showed up, they told us what their plan was. All of us came down hard on your Father, Susan, and Annie. Susan left–I don't know what happened there. When you went missing, though, the lot of us about lost our minds."

"I just could not believe that everyone left the airport, Mother. What did they tell you when I wasn't there?"

"We were in two separate vans. I thought you were in the other van. Coach and Nol thought the same."

"Jesus. This is positively sadistic."

"Yes, son, it is. But, we are a family, and family is worth fighting for even when something like this happens. It warmed my heart to see you, your daughter, and your wife in a giant snuggle mound. There is love there, Olaf, if you can just allow yourself forgive."

"I'm trying, Mother. Stan and Joe have been a solid foundation for me here, and both have told me the same thing, but in their own ways. Who'd have thought that two strangers would be so kind to me?"

"I thank our lucky stars that they found you, Olaf. They are such wonderful people."

As soon as Mother said this, Father joined us. Oddly, he did not sit next to Mother, and she did not seem surprised.

"Olaf, I…" he started.

"Father," I interrupted, "I'm going to ask you questions. You may not say a word outside of the answers to those questions."

"But Olaf..." he nervously interjected.

"First question—*WHY?*" I insisted forcefully.

"I... I thought I was helping you," he said and put his head in his hands.

"You arrived at this conclusion as you watched me suffer? Explain yourself," I said and leaned in.

"Yes David, I would like the answer to this as well," Mother said slyly.

"I thought you would benefit if you asked for help. Susan..."

"When I didn't ask, and you removed everything and everyone from my life, how, as my father, could you stand to have been a part of this beyond the first couple days? I *died*, Father. I woke up, and this is how you show you're grateful that I was alive? By woefully ignoring my struggle, disrespecting me as a person, and instructing the hospital to neglect me? And lying to my face back home—fully intending for me to be institutionalized here? What was your logic there?" I said, tears again finding their escape down my cheeks. Both Mother and Father were crying too.

"Olaf...." he said.

"I need answers, Father," I said, wiping my eyes.

"I... I'm not sure that I have any," he said, shaking his head in disgust.

"Well then, I guess this conversation is over. When you have answers, find me. Until then, stay the hell away from me."

"Olaf, I am so..." he started.

"You do not deserve the right to complete that sentence. I'm not sure who you are, but you are not the man I knew my father to be before I was shot," I blasted back at him. I then got up and walked off the patio toward the beach.

I walked along the shore, my feet in the surf, for quite a distance; I think it had to have been close to a mile. I saw in the distance a familiar sight. I saw an arch made of wood. So, I proceeded, thinking that, at minimum, a conversation with Akamu might really help me to find some perspective on all this insanity.

When I got to the arch, though, Akamu was not there. Instead, the blanket that Haku had used for his prayer was spread out over the sand. I figured this was a place to stop anyway, so I sat on the blanket and closed my eyes.

I know what you're thinking, my dear Reader. "Yeah, yeah Olaf. Here we go with the lightning flashes and the crazy ocean and all that nonsense, right?"

Nope, not this time, dear Reader. I literally just sat on that blanket with my eyes shut. The gentle sound of the ocean in the background was very calming and exactly what I needed to clear my head and begin to think a little bit more deeply.

In the truest sense, there are some actions we all do that have no answers for "why." There are those things in life that are tragic, and the tragedies themselves are not bound by logic. These things happen. No human mind is perfect; one may perhaps argue the soul is, but we're not venturing into that vortex of thought here, dear Reader. Put plainly, for whatever reason, Father, Susan, and Annie did *this*. I'm positive, in the beginning, they had a reason why they were doing what they were and in turn a pattern was formed. I almost assuredly helped *create* the pattern with how I responded to it. This part is easier to understand because I was the one reacting; I simply don't do well if I feel I'm being disrespected, and this was precisely why I reacted as I did. I positively owned the creation and persistence of the pattern that was used because of my behavior. They stayed in this pattern until external forces pressured them to change directions. In truth, what they chose to do in Hawaii was worse if I truly look at it, but that's irrelevant because it never happened. The fact remains they did what they did in South Carolina, and quite likely, none of the participants are able to answer a "why" question with any validity whatsoever. Even if they did answer, it wouldn't have made me feel better.

The trio's actions were bound by a common thought, no matter the reason for it, in the end. The result of this was profound; relationships beyond my own were tried mightily. My parents' marriage had been tested in ways I would imagine neither of them ever thought could occur. Father's partnership with Franklin was severely compromised. Annie's relationship with her parents had become a casualty as well. I hadn't spoken with Helene or Franklin yet, but I could only imagine what they might say after everything we had been through as a family.

The one thing I could control, in the end, was how I reacted to this. I was better physically. I had learned some key behaviors I had to discuss with both Annie and Father if those relationships were to be healed. No matter how hurt I was based on the events of the past couple months, I loved my wife, and Father was always and forever going to be my father and Addie's grandfather. I was not in any way willing to fracture my family in the name of self-righteousness. As a result, I had to have the courage to step into uncomfortable conversations to give them a chance.

I took a couple deep breaths and opened my eyes. Out of the corner of my peripheral vision, I saw a robe blowing in the wind.

"Hello, Akamu," I said calmly.

"Hello, my dear friend. How do you feel?" he asked. I could hear the smile in his voice.

"Well, I believe I have a much better perspective on all of this. By no means would I consider the issues to be all resolved, but I feel I'm in a place to begin that process," I said, closing my eyes again.

He put his hand on my shoulder. "Olaf, that's all you can possibly expect of yourself. You have been through a horrible experience. People dear to you have done things that hurt you deeply. You cannot expect to find forgiveness easily. The important thing is that you allow yourself to take steps forward, even if they are small."

"I agree, my friend. I apologize if I was too hard on you. I didn't know how things had played out at the airport," I said, finally turning my head to look at him.

"You had every right to say what you did, Olaf. In every possible sense, we all could have done something, collectively, to change your experience. For my part, I inexcusably gave in to helplessness and cowardice. As your friend, I owed you much more than I gave. For this, Olaf Waniglia, I am deeply sorry," he said, his grip on my shoulder tightened.

I put my left hand on his. "Thank you, my friend."

"I am here to retrieve you. We are to make our way back to Rupert's to get ready for the item at 2:00."

I looked passed Akamu and suddenly noticed that the arch was gone. "Where…"

"We should head back, Olaf," Akamu said, smiling.

Together, we walked back to Rupert's, and I was instructed by Michael to change into the clothes on the bed in my room. I headed there and found a dress shirt and khaki shorts. Confused, I changed into my clothes and walked to the front of the house where I found four shiny, black cars, and everyone dressed in similar attire.

"Our guest of honor has arrived. Shall we?" Rupert asked gallantly. The lot of us got into the cars. I was sitting next to Addie; Annie was on her opposite side.

"Where are we…?" I began.

"Ah ah, Olaf Waniglia... No questions," Rupert interjected.

I sighed and Addie laughed.

We arrived at the airport and boarded Rupert's plane. In the back of my mind, I had already determined that I was not going to be the last one off the plane this time. Lesson learned there, my dear Reader.

We landed somewhere I did not recognize. I walked out of the plane after Mother, who grabbed me as soon as the plane landed.

"This time, you and I do not get separated, son," she said, smiling.

"Agreed. Thank you, Mother."

"I'm following you two," Nol said. "Ain't no way y'all leave my sight this time, son. No way, no how."

I smiled knowing I had recovered at least part of my life. I had Mother, I had Nol, and I had Akamu. The rest were on parole, pending my steps forward.

"Into the cars, please," Rupert bellowed from behind us, pushing us toward two limousines. I rode with Mother, Father, Nol, Sadie, Jonah, Stan, Addie, and Annie. The other car held Rupert, Michael, Joe, Coach, Akamu, Fanny, and Gerard—or so I knew anyway.

We drove an hour or so to a small village. I had tried desperately to try and figure out what direction we were driving in, to no avail; I had no idea where we were. We arrived at the center of the village. The houses there surrounded a common area in the middle. We got out and walked to a small pavilion that had lit torches on each of its corners. A man in traditional Hawaiian dress was sitting on an ornate carpet. He motioned for us to join as benches were set up facing him.

"Welcome, my friends. My name is Iokua. It is a pleasure to be with you today. You don't realize it, but we have met before. It is my hope that, by the time we part, you will feel as you did on that day as a family. Olaf, will you join me up here please?" the man asked with outstretched arms.

My balance for whatever reason was shaky that day, so I was using my cane. I had zero idea how I was going to gracefully sit on the floor—or get back up for that matter.

"Sir, I'm not sure I will be able to sit on the floor with you. Can I just stay here?" I asked.

Iokua smiled and said, "Just give it a shot, my boy." So, I got up and made my way to the carpet. As expected, I had no balance and my feeble attempts at bending resulted in me leaning heavily on my cane.

Nol got up, met my eyes, and winked. "We got this, son," he said and walked behind me. "Bend at your waist, and keep your legs straight. I'll lower you down." I did, and he eased me to the ground.

Iokua smiled brightly. "You see what family can do, my friend?" He took a deep breath, and his gaze became much more serious. "Olaf, you have accepted death and touched it. It was in that place you met your grandmother for the first time. Would you agree with me for this reason alone, you can find a blessing in the chaos?"

"How did you...." I began.

"My dear boy, the line between life and death is not a chasm, but rather a wisp of a breath. Your grandmother is connected to these islands. Though she no longer breathes the air here to live, she still lives here. This is her home. She told me everything I needed to know to help you. All of you," he said.

"Wow, I guess I don't know what to say. Yes, I suppose meeting my grandmother was a blessing," I admitted timidly.

"You know how it felt to have your life pushed to an extreme. But, do you know how that felt to all of these people?" Iokua said, looking toward everyone seated on the benches.

"I'm sure it was very hard, but… honestly…" I began, trying to find the right words.

"I lost my ability to heal others, Olaf. I had to focus exclusively on myself. I was deeply and profoundly shaken," Akamu said sadly.

"Life didn't make sense anymore. I never thought you'd wake up, and when you did, something in me didn't know what to do. I cannot believe what I did, what I said…" Annie added.

"Part of me was dead the entire time you was asleep, son. I didn't go fishin' once," Nol said sadly.

"That's true, Olaf. No matter how many times I drove him to the marina, he wouldn't get on the boat. It's not even in the water right now. We put it on a slip in storage," Sadie said.

"Jesus. I had no idea," I said, shocked.

"We shot at the range so much we constantly smelled like gunpowder, Honey Boy. I was scared, then angry, then scared again, and I used an assault rifle like a teddy bear. Our boys thought we had gone completely off the rails," Fanny said, chuckling.

"Yeah. Ray, our oldest, actually called a couple assisted living homes thinking we had lost our minds," Gerard added.

"I lost my passion for training, kid. I stepped down as head trainer at the shop," Coach said.

"Coach?" I exclaimed, shocked. I couldn't believe what I was hearing.

"Don't worry, kid. Joe here has been amazing. He's flying to Charleston next month and is training with us. I will resume my insanity at the shop, don't you worry," Coach said, smiling snidely.

"You see, Olaf?" Iokua said energetically. "You see that you were not the only one struggling to be truly alive?"

"Olaf, I…" Father began. "I found I couldn't treat people anymore. I literally stepped away from all of my patients. Franklin labeled it as 'Bereavement Leave,' and I think saved my license."

"What?"

"It's true, Olaf," Mother said.

"Yes, it is, but my partner has not one damn excuse to keep this shit up. It's time to get back to work, David. Save lives," Franklin said, walking in with Helene. "Sorry we are late. Flight issues."

Rupert got up and hugged them both, then sat next to them. Addie ran to Helene and sat on her lap.

"All of you have struggled to find your way to what you knew your life experience to be, prior to that awful day. Words have been spoken and actions have been taken that are departures from all of your lives. It will take time for wounds to heal, but they will. The key here is that you are a family. There may not be bloodlines running through all of you, but your lives twist together like the trunk of a palm tree. Just like that palm tree, there are times when the wind blows and the trunk bends. Your family has been tested, but by no means has it been broken, even if it feels that way," Iokua pontificated. "I am in no way saying all has been healed. Please don't mistake me. These things take time. The key, for all of you, is that you *allow* yourselves to heal. You *allow* others to find their way without judgment. Perhaps most importantly, you accept the past is not the present, and *allow* the present to unfold without holding it hostage in the past."

He paused, then looked at me, and smiled. "Olaf, there is a reason I have asked you to come here. Please close your eyes and take a deep breath," he said.

I did, and felt him, or someone, put their hands on my shoulders. As soon as they did, I was sitting on that beach with the violent waves and empty sky—the same one where I had first seen my grandmother. She appeared at my side again and sat down.

"Hello, my wonderful grandchild," she said, smiling. "How are you?"

"Well, you tell me, Grandma. Am I dead?" I asked naively.

She chuckled and said, "No, my sweet Olaf. You are here because you want to be. What you've experienced since leaving here has been exceptionally hard. I was with you every second, dear one. I saw how horrible you felt. I saw what David and the lovely Annie did, and felt so bad for them. They had no idea what they were doing."

"Grandma, how is it I can talk here now? And… where is *here*?" I asked.

She smiled. "You are stronger, Olaf. When you were here before, you were so very weak. This place is merely one for you and me to talk. There is no official word for it."

"So, then, I can come back here and not die? Am I in a coma? I don't understand… I'm so sorry," I said, shaking my head.

"No apology necessary, Olaf. Do you recall Iokua saying the distance between life and death is merely a breath? You are not dead. You are not in a coma. You are just here… with me. Would you please take a walk with me?" she asked politely.

"Of course. Just please promise me there will be no massive water tests, please."

She laughed and extended her hand. I got up with her help, and we walked toward the tree-line. We strolled through the trees to a small clearing. Once there, I saw the same pattern in the trees that Grandmother's lights had been in. They weren't physical lights, but orbs of light, coursing and changing shape as though they were stars with active magnetic fields.

"Are these..." I began.

"Yes. They are exactly the same pattern as the lights I created for Christopher," she said, intriguingly answering the question I had yet to ask.

"Do they have a significance beyond what you initially intended? This was the pattern of your first walk with Grandpa, right?" I asked.

"They are indeed in the pattern of our first walk, yes. The significance, though, is more universal. This, for me, was a path of love. It was insignificant at the time, but as so many others have taken the same path, I saw it as something more than simply an outline of our first walk," she said as we made our way to each one.

"Do the colors mean anything in particular?" I asked, trying to understand all I was being told.

"Well, originally, they did. Truthfully, I just like how they flow from one to the other," she said, smiling. When we reached the final light, we stopped, and she turned toward me. "Olaf, my sweet grandson, I cannot possibly say how happy I am to see you stronger than you were. Please promise me you will be patient with yourself as you go back to your life," she said kindly.

"I promise I will, Grandma," I said.

"Now then," she said, "I need you to promise me one more thing—kiss your wife."

As soon as she finished her sentence, I was standing under the light in the park that matched the orb I had just been standing under with Grandma. Annie was holding my hand.

"What in the world just happened?" I asked her.

"Well, you got up, grabbed my hand, and walked me by every one of the lights. That guy in the pavilion told me…" she began.

I interrupted her with a lengthy kiss, as instructed by Grandma.

"Promise me that wasn't a kiss goodbye, babe," she said, catching her breath.

"No, love. It's a 'Hello' kiss," I said, smiling.

"Well then, *say it again*," she whispered and leaned in. We kissed. She embraced me tightly; I could feel her heart racing.

"Olaf, I love you. I am so…" she began.

"Babe, no more 'sorries.' I know you're sorry. I am too. I also know as we stand here, right now, the only thing that matters is you and me, and how *we* decide to move forward. We can live in a world of hurt, anger, the past. Or, we can treat every second of every day as a gift and share it. I much prefer the latter," I said, interrupting her.

"Walk with me?" she asked, smiling.

"Of course. You lead the way."

We walked over the bridge where my grandparents' initials were, then back to the beach where we were married. Akamu was standing there, along with the rest of our friends and family.

"Um…?" I said, confused.

"Relax, my friend," Akamu said. "Just listen."

Iokua stood up and said, "My friends, welcome back to this wonderful place. It was here marriage bonds were formed and this family grew. It is my hope that today, these bonds will be strengthened, and this family will once again move forward as one."

"Amen, my dear friend. Thank you so much for all of your help!" Akamu said. He continued, "Olaf, Annie, it is here that, should you choose, you can say something to add to your wedding vows. You can also say the same thing you did before. This is all your choice. Annie, you asked to go first, so please say what you would like, sweetheart."

Annie grabbed both of my hands, took a deep breath, and looked into my eyes. "Olaf, I promise you I will remind you every day you are loved. I promise to be a partner to you in every possible circumstance. I promise to protect you, to be your voice if ever you cannot speak. I promise, above all, to love you for the rest of time."

I smiled. I could see that she meant every word.

"Olaf, would you like to say something?" Akamu asked.

"Yes, and I need to say quite a bit, to all of you. Is that permitted?" I asked.

"My dear boy, you know that it is. Go ahead," Akamu said, pleased.

"Annie, I promise to be your partner. I promise to ensure you know you are loved every second of your life. I promise to do every damn thing I can to remain conscious and keep you from needing to be my voice. I promise to be your 'you,' to love you wholly for the rest of time."

I kissed her, hugged her tightly, and said, "I'll be right back."

"Okay babe."

I walked over to Akamu. "I promise to help you in any way I can to find your rhythm again, my friend. I truly owe you that."

He smiled from the depths of his heart. "Thank you, my dear friend."

I then walked over to Nol. "I promise to go fishin' as soon as we get home. I promise to endure all your shit talk and cook you pie. I promise to help you to be Nol again."

"Dammit son, don't you dare make me cry," he said, wiping his eyes.

I looked at Sadie, who was sitting next to Nol and said, "I promise to be the friend you deserve, Sadie." She said nothing; she just stood and hugged me tightly.

I made my way over to my parents, and said, "I promise to come over and help with the orchard. I promise to make shepherd's pie at least twice a month for the next two years for family dinner. I promise to help both of you in any way I can."

Father stood up, tears in his eyes, and hugged me. He had only done this a handful of times in my life, mostly when I was in diapers.

Mother also stood, and kissed me on the cheek. "I'm so glad you're feeling better, son. I'll look forward to making that shepherd's pie with you. Extra peas and carrots."

I walked over to Franklin and Helene, where I shook Franklin's hand and kissed Helene on the cheek. "I promise... we'll talk."

"Good enough for me, son," Helene said. Franklin nodded. Next was Fanny and Gerard.

"I promise to let you teach me how to shoot. I think maybe I get it now."

"That was my plan anyway, Honey Boy. That new cane you're getting has a gun in it," Fanny said, smiling.

"Yeah, we're taking you to the range, Olaf. Gotta make sure you don't shoot your foot off or anything," Gerard grinned.

"Um…. I'll get there, but I'm not completely comfortable with guns. You both know this, right?" I asked nervously.

"You should know how to shoot anyway, Olaf. I'll help too," Helene said.

"Seriously?" I asked.

"My Daddy had me shooting by the time I was eight. I still shoot, just not as frequently," she said.

"I had no idea."

"That's the point, dear boy," Helene said, grinning.

I walked over to Coach and said, "I promise to let you kick my ass in the shop."

"Damn straight, Kid," he said, with more intensity than humor, and slapped me on the shoulder.

Joe and Stan were next in line, "I promise to remain in your lives."

"That would mean the world to me, and the team, Olaf," Joe said kindly.

"I would love that, Olaf," Stan said with sincerity.

"You both helped me get my life back. I cannot thank you enough." I was surprised by how sentimental I felt about both of these men. "Rupert…Michael," I said approaching the duo, "I promise you a visit that isn't this filled with drama."

"We love our time with you, however it comes to us, Olaf," Rupert said. Michael nodded and grinned ear to ear.

I walked over to Iokua and shook his hand, "Thank you so much, for helping us "

"Please, Olaf. I was more than happy to do this. How was your grandmother?" he asked, smiling.

"She was wonderful. I wish like anything I knew how I was talking to her and seeing her world."

"Maybe one day we will talk about it. When we are done here, I have something to show you," he said, a knowing look in his eye.

"More surprises. Just what I need," I said and rolled my eyes.

Lastly, I walked over to Addie, picked her up, and told her, "I promise to be your daddy. I promise to tuck you in at night, to read you bedtime stories, to teach you all kinds of things, and to be everything you will ever need me to be. I love you so much, tiny one."

She giggled and hugged me. I put her down and returned to Annie.

"I think that's everything I need to say, Akamu," I said.

"Well then, by the power vested in me, I am pleased to accept all of the promises made today in support of this wonderful family," he said. "Iokua, we are yours."

"Everyone, follow me!" Iokua bellowed.

We crossed back over the bridge, then along the tree-line out in a different direction than we had been. We arrived at a moderately large brick house; it looked to have two floors and had a porch that wrapped around the whole building. The style of the house was different than those in the village.

"This house predates our village by about ten years. In fact, Louis Dolby gave us the land to develop. This house was Mr. Dolby's," Iokua said. "It was recently put up for sale. I thought perhaps you might like to take a look at it, Olaf."

"I'd love to. Can we go inside?" I asked.

"I didn't know this was here," Father said introspectively.

"We can absolutely go inside. It so happens I am the one handling the sale," Iokua said excitedly.

We walked into the house, which looked to have been abandoned for some time. It smelled musty, but was incredibly grandiose. The staircase was ornately crafted in dark wood, maybe mahogany. The rooms all had impressively tall ceilings, and most of them had tray inlays outlined with wood moldings. It was a gorgeous home, no doubt about it. It needed some love, though.

"I wonder what Mr. Toth would need to do to fix this place up," I thought out loud.

"He will be here tomorrow. Here," Iokua answered and handed me an envelope.

The letter read:

Good Day, Olaf—

I had heard of the Dolby place years ago, but never thought I might get to work on it. I was sent pictures, but want to see the place on my own. From what I am seeing, the

*work is almost exclusively cosmetic. I think the foundation
and overall structure is sound. It's a good purchase if you're
willing to take it on.*

Looking forward to seeing you.

Hollister

"How did Mr. Toth know about this? Who is selling the
house, and for how much?" I asked. I was beginning to become
accustomed to this perpetual state of confusion.

"Well, truthfully, *I* am selling the house," Iokua said. "The
price is something I will discuss with you if you are interested. I have
been the caretaker of the property for many years. I knew when the
right person came here, it would be time for me to offer it for sale.
When I knew you were in Hawaii and got Rupert to agree to come
here, I reached out to Hollister with the pictures. The community
would continue to care for the exterior of the property as this has
meant the world to us. It would mean just as much for Madelyn's
family to own it again. Take a look around. David, you will find your
mother's room upstairs. First door to the left. Olaf, if you go to the
master suite, you will find that it overlooks the park and has a clear
view of the Pacific as well."

I looked at Annie and said, "We haven't talked finances at
all, babe. Is this something we can do?"

"We've done quite well over the past year or so, babe. We
should be just fine," she said confidently.

"Olaf, I'll sell you the place for $1, if you solely do a couple
things," Iokua said.

"Dear Lord! What things, Iokua?" I asked, flabbergasted.

"Well, pay the taxes and overall expenses for the property,
help us to maintain the park and your grandmother's lights, and agree

to contribute to and participate in at least one big feast per year," he said and winked. "To know the house will get the updating it deserves and have a family caring for its legacy is good enough for me. Our village exists because of your great-grandfather. We got our land for free. Two entire generations of families were able to establish their roots here, and that is so much more precious and valuable to me than anything. I don't feel right asking for anything more."

"Well sir, I think you'll change your tune on that once you try Olaf's meals. I'm comin' for the feast if he's cookin'. I promise y'all will be asking him to cook for you when he's here," Nol said.

"I'd be very willing to do a 'your house-my house' thing if you chose to come here from time to time," Rupert said. "If you're on the islands, I will find a way to be with you and your family, Olaf."

"It would mean everything to me to have a piece of Mom's life in our family, Olaf. I lost her when I was so young. This, in part, gives me some of her back," Father said emotionally.

"Iokua, you have a deal, contingent on one request," I said, extending my hand toward him.

"What is that request, Olaf?" Iokua asked, a hint of concern in his voice.

"Please try to help Father to find *his* way to talk to Grandma," I said.

He grabbed my hand, leaned in, and whispered, "I will help, but I think you will be much more instrumental there than I will be. Just a hunch."

"Well then, we are agreed. Annie, come with me," I said and grabbed her hand.

I took her out the front door, picked her up, and carried her over the threshold. "We need to be official-like here in the Dolby house," I said coyly.

Annie leaned in and kissed me. "This is amazing, Olaf. To have this be a part of our family is really something special."

We spent the rest of the afternoon looking around the house, the park, and the village. We met quite a few people who had been at our wedding reception. All were excited to learn we were buying the house, and would be a part of the culture in the village.

The next day, Mr. Toth arrived with two of his top designers, and a crew of six guys, to create a plan. They managed to get everything drawn up within two hours of arriving. I gave my 'OK' to the plan, and work started literally the next day. Within three weeks, all the work was done, and all new furniture was in place. Annie, Addie, Nol, Sadie, and Jonah spent the last week of our time in Hawaii in our new house. It was surreal to live where Grandma had grown up. I could feel her presence everywhere in that house.

I had no idea my time in Hawaii would take such incredible twists and turns, dear Reader. I arrived there broken and abandoned. Two strangers healed me physically and emotionally. I made major strides forward with my family—after essentially thinking that all was lost at varying points of my time in Maui. I became a homeowner, in a home profoundly meaningful to so many, including me.

I *got* my life back. I *got* my wife back. I *got* my family and friends back, and made new friendships along the way. This was a major turning point in my life, dear Reader.

A New Beginning

Returning to Charleston was a mix of emotions. On the one hand, it was tough leaving everyone in Hawaii. If anything, the relationships made there guaranteed we would be back with a certain frequency. On another hand, I hadn't been to our house since the shooting. I hadn't actually lived in our home with our daughter. Still yet, I was excited to see the farm and the Rodriguez family again. I was excited to get back to work in my office. I was nervous to return to the hospitals, especially the one I was last in as a patient.

Directionally speaking, it made some sense to stop at the farm before heading home, and that's exactly what we did. Addie immediately ran to José, who scooped her up.

"It's been such a long time, Mr. Olaf! How are you feeling?" he asked as Addie stole his hat.

"All in all, I am well, José—thank you for asking. How are you? How are things going?" I asked.

"Well, incredibly, everyone is doing great. My father, the boys, Maria, Carla, Jorge, Manny, Manuel, we are all great. The crops have flourished, even when Mother Nature hasn't been kind. The contracts have been met at every point, with some surplus provided from time to time. I have nothing to complain about. And, we are all American citizens now! I cannot believe how much you and your family have done for me and mine. I swear, Mr. Olaf, I am eternally grateful," he said, and tickled Addie who giggled uncontrollably.

Hearing us outside, Carlos and Julio emerged from the garage, both covered in grease.

"Mr. Olaf! Welcome back!" Carlos yelled as he approached.

"Nuestra supervivencia! Gracias a Dios," Julio echoed.

"What did he just say, José? My Spanish has gone to pot," I said, trying desperately to remember at least part of my Spanish chops.

"He said, 'Our survivor! Thank God!'" José said, smiling. "I cannot say it any better, Mr. Olaf. I am so glad you are okay and here with us again."

"You know, I am too. This has been a crazy decade!" I said, and hugged Julio, who had just joined us. "Muchas gracias, Julio!" I said as my back was summarily covered in grease. "Thank you all for continuing to grow the farm. I truly cannot say enough."

"It is our pleasure, Mr. Olaf. Would you come for dinner soon? Maria would love to cook for you again," José said.

"I would love to. I miss Maria and her cooking so much, and I'd love to spend time again with your father. He is incredibly insightful on so many topics. I'm so glad his health is good," I said, relishing in the thought of another dinner with their family. The last one—over two years ago—was incredible.

"I will let her know, and we will celebrate your return, Mr. Olaf. It will be fun! I have to get back to the cotton. Again, it is so good to see you healthy. Be well, my friend," José said sincerely.

"I cannot wait. It is wonderful to see you all again!" I said, and Annie led me into our office.

"Apologies for your desk, babe. That's been Addie's coloring station for quite a while now," she said. Looking at my desk, it was an odd array of broken crayons, stickers, dolls dressed in silly clothing, and a sippy cup. I had to smile when I saw it; I couldn't remember what state I left the thing in last.

"No apology necessary, love. We'll have to get the tiny one a desk of her own for the times we both are here," I said.

We stayed in the office for about a half hour. Annie had some phone calls to make, and I spent the time getting my desk un-kidded and organized to start the catch-up process. I had four different projects in-flight at the time of the shooting. It was going to be a challenge to get back on track with each of them.

As we were leaving the office, Annie stopped at the door and put her hands on my shoulders.

"Every step we take together reminds me how much I love you, babe, and how much you do for me. It took you being here with me to find the same joy I used to have here. It's been missing," she said and kissed me.

For the first time since before the shooting, I heard Annie's *vox corporis*. She said, "*Olaf, if you remember what I told you the first time we conversed, our essences are connected. When one is without the other, something precious is lost that is not automatically returned. This is why it has taken so long for her to return to being the person you know her to be. She needs you desperately, Olaf.*"

I squeezed Annie tightly, knowing what I had just heard was critical to me making sense of the entire series of events and moving forward for good.

"My God babe, you're going to break my ribs. I cannot believe how much stronger you are," she said, her laughter strained.

"Sorry love. I just wanted you closer, that's all," I said, smiling.

She leaned in and whispered in my ear, "Trust me when I say I would love you to be much, much closer." She kissed me again. "Let's go home. You won't recognize it. Peanut, you ready to go?"

"Yes Mommy," Addie replied.

So, off we headed to our house. I must admit, dear Reader, I was more than a little apprehensive about going back there. I had knots in my stomach; I really didn't know how in the world I was going to feel comfortable there.

When we pulled into the garage, my nervousness was at a fever pitch. I must have shown it all over my face and in my mannerisms. Annie very gently put her hand in mine and said, "I got you. I know this is really hard, and I am not letting you do this alone. I am right here, babe."

I had no words. I just looked at her and smiled. As we took our first steps into the house, Doc attached himself to my left side, and Annie was on my right. At first look, things were the same.

"When you're ready, we can go in the living room. Not until then though. If you'd like to sit on the deck a minute, we can do that. The Intracoastal and some whiskey will remind you just how special this place is," Annie said comfortingly.

"I think I should go there, babe. I need to get this insane feeling out of my belly," I said, though I was literally shaking.

"Babe, my God you're shaking! Seriously, let's go to the deck first. I don't want you to be so nervous," she said, leading me out. I sat down in my favorite chair, and she brought me a large glass of whiskey–there had to have been a fifth in that thing! I sipped and watched a pod of dolphin hunt. A little bit later, a manatee made her way by. She looked up, and almost seemed to say, "Welcome back," as she meandered by.

Doc remained glued to my left side. He knew I was nervous, and I tried to calm his nervousness with a pat every now and again. Thing is, I could feel the scars from his bullet wounds, and in a cruel way, it never really let me relax. It also introduced an undercurrent of guilt that would not let go.

Addie came outside with her Shooshoo in tow and plopped down in a chair next to me.

"See any fishies, Daddy?" she asked adorably.

"As a matter of fact, tiny one, I have. Some dolphins and a manatee so far. See anything in the water?" I asked.

"There's a turtle," she said as a sea turtle curiously studied us and disappeared below the surface.

"Yep–good eye kiddo!" I said excitedly.

"What are you two doing out here?" Annie asked, approaching us.

"Watching for fishies, Mommy. What are you doing?" Addie responded.

"Well, I'm gonna watch for fishies too," she said, pulling up a chair. She gave Doc a pat and grabbed my hand. A couple seconds later, I heard the sound of car doors closing and Nol, Sadie, and Jonah appeared on the deck. Addie jumped up and ran to Jonah, and the two disappeared into the house. Annie and Sadie followed them, talking the entire way.

"Drinkin' alone? That ain't right son," Nol said, producing a six-pack of beer from a bag. He then opened one and poured it into a pint glass he also produced from the bag.

"I am not handling this house thing all that well, son," I said and took a big sip of whiskey. "And, I'm all kinds of guilty feeling Doc's scars. None of this would have happened if I would have been more careful."

Nol took a sip of beer and shot me a look as though I'd killed his kitten.

"'The hell you talkin' boy? That sumbitch got away from three cops with guns drawn, son. Killed one of 'em, and two others before he came here You saved his wife's life, Olaf. He was a bad, bad dude, and you stopped this menace with your hands after being shot to hell. Your dog there probably gave you a chance to do what you did. Yeah, he got shot. Look at 'im, son. His tail is waggin', and Addie puts clips n' bows on his ears n' shit. He didn't die, son. You sure as hell didn't either," he said and took a big swill of beer.

"You been in that room yet?" Nol asked after a moment of silence.

"No son. I started shaking when we walked in the door," I said shamefully.

"Git up and come on. You gotta see what Toth did," he said, getting up and offering me his hand.

"I dunno, Nol, I..." I began.

"I will carry yer damn self into that room if you don't git up. Git up, son," he demanded.

"Jesus, Nol," I said and grabbed his hand to help myself stand up. We walked into the house, where Annie then grabbed my hand, told me to take a breath, and led me slowly toward our living room. Sadie and Nol walked in front of us. Jonah and Addie were playing on the floor in the living room, which looked nothing like it did on the day of the shooting. The furniture was all replaced, the flooring was redone, the entrance to the room was bigger and more angular looking, and the lighting was all in the ceiling; the lamps were gone.

"What you can see are obvious changes—the furniture, the lighting, the overall design," Annie said. "Thing is, Hollister went way, way further. Every window was replaced with bulletproof glass on the first floor. This includes the doors to the patio. Every window and exterior door is protected with magnet locks that withstand over one-thousand pounds of pressure each, like your office door. If you look to your right, you will see an opening. That leads to a stairway taking you either upstairs or to a safe room that is triple-steel encased. From the safe room, you can see every square inch of the house, and it has a unique phone whose line cannot be cut from the outside. Fanny insisted that some of her and Gerard's hiding places for guns be built into the house. Hollister agreed to build *half* of them, and agreed they weren't *necessarily* a bad idea. They are empty currently, and we can talk about whether they ever get filled or not. Thing is, I don't see anyone getting into this house, so I'm not sure how necessary it is. Dunno…"

She continued, "The asshole came in through the front door. If he tried the same thing today, the security system would have alerted us—as well as the police and the security company—much sooner. It was upgraded. We can now see every square inch of the outside of our home on any TV and can send the video feed directly to the security company so they can see what is happening. Apparently, they have a security team that works with the police and can get here quicker than the police can. Supposedly, anyway. Last thing, the bedroom doors have been upgraded and outfitted with those magnet-lock things. The doors themselves, and the door frames, are resistant to bullets and crowbars and things. The security system will automatically turn on the magnets if a threat is perceived, but we can control them if we need to from panels in our room. In short, this place literally has become safer than our bank."

"I insisted on testing the doors and windows when they were installed, son. I haven't been sorer in years. I was dripping with sweat by the end of that day. I couldn't budge a single one of 'em," Nol said.

I looked around and could not believe what I was hearing and seeing. The room wasn't recognizable. I tried to find similarities, but they were gone. I hugged Annie tightly; I was completely overcome with a variety of emotions. On the one hand, the house was safer by a mile, and nothing like the shooting would be likely to happen again. On the other, we were both shot *in that room*.

"My ribs, babe," she strained.

"Sorry love. I'll work on that," I said and took a step back.

She promptly attached herself to me, squeezing *me* tightly. "You don't back away until I'm good n' done with you, Olaf Waniglia. I'm not done yet," she said.

I looked down and saw Doc had pink bows on his ears and an action figure on his back. He couldn't have looked happier; he seemed to be smiling and his tail was wagging slowly.

In this room, terrible things happened. Simon died where I was standing. I sat and breathed what I thought was my final breath in a pool of blood where the kids were playing. But, in this room my daughter now played with her pal on the floor. Doc wore new fashion accessories. My wife attached to me, squeezing so hard she was quivering. In the end, though, the terrible things that happened were insulated and in the past. Many happy memories were being made just as I stood there. *That* was what I knew I had to focus on.

Later on, I cooked for the first time in over almost two years for our families. Spending time with them was comforting, and my first night home ended up being a memorable one. The next day, Nol put his boat back in the water, and the lot of us went out with my father-in-law. The typical cadence of chastising my fishing acumen was lessened, surprisingly. I thought for sure the group would enjoy playing that up again. Later that night, all of us had dinner at the Glaush's, and both my parents and Nol's parents joined us. It was the first time the entire group had been together since our combined wedding, and it was a joyful gathering.

The next week, I slowly got back into my work schedule— though I was mindful of both my family and my health when I did so.

I caught myself up with Fanny in my practice, and called every one of my patients. I talked with doctors at the hospital about what they may need my assistance on. I settled some business at the farm and got my projects back on track. I met with Mr. Toth to discuss his latest business endeavors, Joe Lating to talk about the house in Hawaii and my time in the hospital, and Mr. Bace to talk finances. In short, it was a busy week and it was taxing, but by the end of it, I was nearly caught up after over a year of being away.

Speaking of Fanny, she and Gerard invited us to come to their house for dinner that week. After arriving, I was handed a large box with a 'Walking Sticks' return address on it. Inside, I found an intriguing cane and a letter. It read:

> *Hello Olaf!*
>
> *Well here she is—what I promised you—and boy does she pack a punch! She is a cane with a built-in 45mm gun. You can load a total of 15 rounds in the body through the shaft opening on the side facing you as you hold her. The trigger is hidden unless the safety is released, and it is in the notch of the handle. I've built this to Fanny's design in terms of what the cane was supposed to do. I then had a buddy of mine, who builds firearms, build the mechanism for the gun and added what I thought you would like in terms of the look. If she's never loaded, you could still knock a guy out just hitting him with the butt-end of her. It was a pleasure meeting you, Olaf, and I hope I see you again sometime. No matter what, let me know what you think of your new beauty!*
>
> *All the best,*
>
> *Nick*

The cane itself was angular—if that makes sense. The body and handle were not rounded, like a traditional cane was. My other cane was rounded, and its size grew from top to bottom—so the bottom was the thickest part of it for better stability. This new cane was uniform in terms of size, but the shape of the handle and body were trapezoidal in shape, with a brushed metal accent running along the length of the left and right-angled edges. The handle fit my hand as though it had been built for me, and there was no part of this tool made cheaply; both Fanny and Gerard looked longingly at the craftsmanship of the weapon.

"Olaf, we have always believed soundly in our right to defend ourselves, especially because both of us saw friends or family taken for no reason. Now, I know how you feel about guns, and I respect that," Fanny said carefully but with conviction. "Thing is, I personally don't want you to break your hands again while someone is shooting at you or your family. At minimum, this evens the playing field, though I pray that you will never, ever have to pull that trigger. I love you, Honey Boy. Y'all used up two lives already, and y'all only have but one left."

Gerard then added, "This is the least we can do for what you have given us as a family. It may seem like a strange gift, but truthfully Olaf, I never want the man that gave me my life back to ever be faced with losing his. That ain't fair, my dear friend. I promise y'all, we will teach you everything if you want to learn, but this will be the only time you hear me say that. No pressure whatsoever."

I walked over and hugged them tightly. "You are dear, dear friends. Thank you so much for this gift. I will gladly accept it, and will absolutely accept your offer to learn. I can't promise I will ever load it, but I will learn. I should have listened to you, Fanny. If I would have, I may have had the last year of my life, and seen both my daughter's birth and her first steps. Tell me where to be and when, and I will learn."

They then showed me all of the hiding places they had for weaponry in their house. It didn't matter where one might be; all you had to do was reach down or to either side in most rooms, and you would find some form of gun. It was obvious to me both had been scarred in the past, and as a result, they learned how to protect themselves and the boys against just about any threat.

"Have you ever had the need to use any of these weapons?" I asked, surprised at what I was seeing.

"Unfortunately, yes," Gerard said. "There was a young man several years ago who threatened Ray. I never found out the details, but a knife was pulled on Ray in the family room. That young man then had five guns pointed at him, one of which being Ray and our youngest, David, being another. I never saw the kid again, and we, knock on wood, never had to draw the weapons since."

"When the nonsense with that Simon person happened, the boys came home, cleaned every gun in the house, and stayed for two weeks. Ray's wife and Bobby's fiancé came and helped too. The boys took turns staying up in twos through the overnight. It was wonderful having the family home again, but I would have much preferred a different reason for it! We were all so tense, all the time. Guns were drawn when the mail was delivered. Dear Lord, if that mail carrier knew," Fanny said, chuckling.

Over the next several weeks, the McNutters taught me and Annie how to use my cane and other guns safely. I can't honestly say I was at all comfortable with the idea, dear Reader, but I saw their reasoning and learned. My accuracy with my cane became quite good; I was accurate to almost fifty feet with it. This was almost the exact distance from my office door to the front door of my building.

Oddly, my parents strongly supported this. I was very much of the mindset that the house was bulletproof, so I didn't see the reasoning behind the use of guns. Mother very pointedly said, "The farm, the hospital, and the front of your office do not have the same protections, my son. Your father and I want you to be safe. As long as you have that cane, and know how to use it, you at least can play the bad guys' game."

"I have to agree, Olaf. This seems logical to me, even though I see your concern," Father said. "Just make sure the folks at hospital security are aware—there shouldn't be any issues."

Father and I worked on mending our wounds together, and though it took a couple months and many conversations, we were able to move past all of the nervousness and awkwardness that were artifacts from the end of the Hawaii trip. I made a point to work with him in the orchard nearly every day. As time went, our conversations evolved; in the beginning, they were constrained to the orchard and the hospital, with large patches of awkward silence. Over time, we talked more about life and family and both the tension and the silence disappeared. He offered apologies from time to time, and at the time of his final apology, I had absolutely forgiven him. However, the punishment of shepherd's pie on a regular basis remained for quite some time; it was simply too much fun for Mother and I to torture him. Annie and I made massive strides forward; the closeness we enjoyed early in our relationship returned quickly. In what seemed like two blinks, and maybe three deep breaths later, she was pregnant again. Perhaps ironic, nay shocking, Sadie informed us of *her* pregnancy two weeks later. Nine months following, my son, Louis Stanislav Waniglia was born, joining Addison Grace. Nine months and three weeks later, Nol and Sadie's daughter Elizabeth Rae was born, joining Jonah Richard. I had the immense pleasure of feeding my son his first bottle, changing his first diaper, and rocking him to sleep for the first time. It so happened that Addie was sitting with us on that rocking chair, and she too fell asleep. I will never, ever forget that magical moment, dear Reader.

A Connection Long Overdue

One afternoon, shortly after Louis was born, we were at my parents' house and I was helping Father in the orchard at harvest time. We were midway through working on the peaches when I heard my grandmother's voice.

"Olaf, I would like to talk to my son. Would you mind helping me?" she asked.

The environment around me did not change in any way, so I searched my brain to find a way to accomplish this.

It seemed Grandmother heard my consternation, and said, "I'm right here, my dear grandson. Show your dad this."

Well dear Reader, I was still stuck. Regardless, I said, "Father, would you mind closing your eyes for me?"

He looked at me quizzically and asked, "Why exactly do I need to do such a thing, son?"

"Well, suffice to say, I believe you will appreciate the result," I said, not knowing in any way whether I was being truthful.

He shrugged and closed his eyes. I did too. I quickly found myself with Father and my grandmother in the "blue room" with the orbs looking like Grandmother's lights in Hawaii.

"Hello, son," she began. "Thank you for joining me here," she said as she approached us. "Olaf, thank you for your help—and congratulations on Louis' birth! He is a special person, Olaf. One, without question, you, Annie, and Addison deserve."

"Mom?" Father said, his voice breaking up.

"Yes, David. It's me. Please don't be sad. Too many tears have fallen from your precious eyes on my behalf," she said and hugged him.

"Where are we?" he asked, wiping his eyes.

"Olaf has also asked me this question, and about all I can come up with is it's a place for us to talk. I hope that's a good enough of an answer for you," she said comfortingly.

"Of course it is. I just... I just can't believe it's you. I've wanted this for so long, but never thought it possible. I lost you so..." he said and buried his face in his hands.

"David, you never lost me. I *promise* you, son. I watched you grieve and I helped you. I was there, son. I was with you, just as we are together here. Do you not remember your dreams, David?" she asked reassuringly.

He took a moment and thought. His face then brightened.

"You were in my dreams. I remember now! We talked. You promised me you hadn't left, and told me how sorry you were. But, then you *seemed* to leave. Dad said the same thing—there was a point where you just vanished. We couldn't feel you around anymore," Father said, his frustration apparent.

"I had to, son. I had to let you and your father grieve once I knew you were strong enough. Just because you didn't see me, though, never meant I 'left.' I've *always* been with you, David. You can credit Olaf for giving us a way to talk now. But, just because up until this point you *felt* I was away from you, doesn't mean this was the case," she said, exactly as a mother makes a point to a child.

"How am I getting credit for this, Grandma?" I asked, confused by this latest wrinkle.

She smiled and said, "Olaf, have we not met here before?"

"Yes," I cautiously responded, completely unaware how I could be responsible for any of this.

"Well, my sweet grandchild, how then do you feel you are not responsible for this?" she asked, approaching me.

"I'm honestly at a loss, Grandma. The first time we met was after the shooting, and you taught me how to look at life before returning to consciousness. The second time was in Hawaii, after all the family turmoil. I can't honestly say how any of this is possible," I responded, trying to figure out the riddle I was being presented.

"Olaf, tell me about Gerard—how you healed his back," she said playfully. Father seemed to be intrigued just watching us go back and forth.

"Well, he was willing to be healed, and I listened," I said, still at a loss for words to explain this.

"There you go, my dear grandson. That's your answer," she said happily.

"Mom, can I ask you a few questions?" Father interjected. I was relieved he did, dear Reader! I was at a complete loss. I have to believe Akamu would have been amused to watch me squirm.

"Of course, David. What questions do you have?" she replied happily.

"Did you suffer at all at the end of your life?" he asked, heaviness in his voice. "This has been something that has haunted me for most of my life. I can't seem to resolve this feeling."

"Physically, no. Emotionally, yes. I could feel my life quickly slipping away, and I could not stand the thought of leaving you and your dad. I didn't know what to say, David. Looking at this with different eyes, I see I could have done so much more for you had I handled this differently. I am so, so sorry, son," she said apologetically.

"Mom, I have watched many people pass away in the hospital. In almost every, case the person turns into themselves very close to the end. Your end came quickly, and I have to believe you needed to do what you did. Yes, it was hard on all of us, for many reasons. But, you shouldn't apologize. Considering it all, you shouldn't have done anything differently. I would have given anything to have you in my life back then. What I should have realized is that I did," Father said.

She smiled, approached and hugged Father. As I watched their embrace, it was as though Dad allowed pain he had held in his mind to dissolve. I saw my familiar "light waves" appear around us and mentally asked for the outcome all needed most. Instead of entering his body, they slowly began moving toward, and then up above his head. Something dark looked to be gradually pulled from the top of his head and consumed by the light.

"Thank you, Olaf," Grandmother said softly.

"Olaf, what just happened?" Father asked, his voice laced in confusion. "Something just happened in my brain I think."

"Well, how do you feel, Father?" I asked intently.

"I feel different. I feel... lighter," he said.

"Olaf did what Olaf does, son. He just healed decades of hurt David, the parts of your anger you never let go. It was magic to feel that, Olaf. Thank you for including me! Now, I think you need to kiss your wives," she said playfully.

As soon as her sentence ended, we were looking eye to eye with our spouses.

"Olaf, what did you do?" Annie asked impatiently.

"Why do you ask, love?" I chuckled.

"Tell me you weren't with your Gram again. That broad is responsible for some strange things lately," she said, wrapping her arms around my neck.

"David?" Mother asked intently.

"Si, I… I just talked to Mom. Olaf… He…" Father said, tears falling down his cheeks.

"Papa, why are you crying?" Addie asked and started sniffing.

"Aw peanut, I'm just so happy. That's all. Nothing is wrong, princess. I think Daddy deserves a bug hug. Would you help me do that?" Father asked comfortingly.

"Huh?" I asked, my confusion peaking. Father hadn't hugged me except for maybe three times total in my life. All the other times a hug was required was resolved with a pat on the back and a handshake.

"I need details you two," Mother asked sternly. "You talked to your mom, David? How is this possible?"

Well dear Reader, I wish like hell I was making this up. As soon as Mother finished speaking, the room changed; it seemed like, all of a sudden, she and I were on a hill with a stone fence surrounding the area.

"Olaf," Mother panicked, "why in the world are we in Ireland?"

A tall figure approached us. Mother covered her mouth. Tears streamed down her cheeks and caressed her hands.

"My sweet Sierra Grace, it's been donkey's years! Grandson! Been too long, this has. How are you, Seesey?"

"Daddy?" Mother asked, still sobbing. "How?"

"Ask your boy later. Now, we talk. First, you are well, yeah?" he asked, his voice laced with Irish charm.

"I'm good, yeah. I just… I can't…," she began, her voice reflecting an Irish accent I had never heard before.

He approached and embraced her. He hugged her tightly, and she submitted to the embrace like a small child. His arms completely consumed her—he seemed to be hugging her sadness away.

"Lass, I need you to just know one thing. I have never, ever stopped loving you. I've also been with you straight away, through all of it. The cancer—your family saved you, and I am forever in their debt fer doin' so. I was there when this fine lad was born, and was touched when you gave him my name. I never left you, Seesey, an' I never will. Know this in yer heart, dear one. Know it true," he said, looking into her eyes.

"Wait," I interjected. "I was named after my grandfather and never knew this?" I asked, shocked. For whatever reason, this hit me like a thousand bricks. The emotion of the moment was heavy, and I sank my head into my hands. I knew the loss Mother experienced was deeply painful. It was powerfully meaningful to me to carry the name of someone who meant so much to her. But, it carried a heaviness I now felt deep inside, almost as though I was somehow fraught with Mother's sadness.

Well, as it turns out, this is exactly what was happening. Mother seemed to brighten—I literally was pulling decades of pain out of her, and it was coming straight into my chest. The weight of the emotion was all consuming.

"Olaf, what's happening? I feel so different, almost as though I'm lighter. You look to be suffering though," Mother said, her voice wrapped in concern.

"Lad, what you seek is just over the pass there," Grandfather said frankly, pointing toward a nearby hill.

I nodded and walked up the hill. As I got near the top, I saw my familiar light waves gliding along a wide river. Mentally, I asked for the best possible outcome to occur for all. When I did so, the light waves left the river and headed in the direction of Mother and Grandfather.

This both confused and dejected me. I felt awful, dear Reader. The weight of the sadness I had taken from Mother was consuming. I truly thought I was to be the recipient of the light waves' wonderful healing, but this was not to be.

I was drawn toward the water. As I got closer, I got heavier and much weaker. By the time I got to the water, I could no longer stand. I fell lifelessly into the river.

As soon as I hit the water, the river became more active. I was suddenly being tossed back and forth in violent rapids. I completely lost my bearing—I just knew I was speeding up. I did not fight the current. I submitted to the river and wherever I was being taken.

The water sounds seemed to be diminishing as I sped up. I knew this meant but one thing: I was headed for a waterfall. I was confident this was no ordinary river—or waterfall for that matter. Indeed, as I went over the edge, I could not see where the water was going.

I heard familiar singing far in the distance. The beautiful woman in the ornate dress—the one who ushered me through my post-shooting existence—was not far from me. I was oppressively heavy; the only thing I felt I should do is submit to wherever I was heading, and this is exactly what I did.

I'm not sure how long I fell. It could have been several minutes, but I'm not sure. As I fell, the singing in the distance got much louder. Not unexpectedly, I saw the singing woman. Her dress flowed like the water in the river around her. When I got close enough to see her face, she smiled and approached the waterfall.

As soon as I was directly across from her, she reached out and pulled me close to her.

"My dear one, it's my turn," she said gently. Her ice blue eyes smiled as she spoke.

The longer she held me, the better I felt. All of the heaviness eventually left me.

"You didn't just take all of that horrible sadness, did you?" I asked, panicked this angelic being had just interred my heaviness.

She smiled, and gently said, "No, dear one. I just moved it to where it should have been. It was not your burden to bear. Such sadness has no place here. I am so proud of you, dear one," she said and held me tighter.

I can't explain properly what this felt like, dear Reader. This wasn't a human hug, but in practice, it was similar. The tighter she held me, the less human I felt. I didn't have a body, per se. It was as though my soul briefly merged with her being.

She slightly released and shot an intense gaze my way.

"I am here, dear one. When you need me, I am here. Know this," she said with quiet intensity. She smiled, and let go.

I once again fell, and when I landed, I was in the Intracoastal, just off my deck. I looked up to see a bunch of incredibly worried people. Mother was holding Louis, Father was holding Addie's hand, and Annie was visibly upset.

"What just happened? How in the world did we get back here? We were at the orchard last I checked," I asked as I wiped my face.

"Babe," Annie began, "are you okay? Why were you just with dead people?" she asked and wiped tears from the corners of her eyes.

"I promise you, love, I had no idea this was going to happen. I heard my grandmother when Father and I were in the orchard, so I was aware of that conversation. The conversation with my grandfather was unexpected in a couple ways. I didn't hurt anyone, did I? I'm not sure how I got out here," I said and pulled myself up onto the deck.

Annie grabbed me and hugged me tightly. I could feel she was crying.

"Sweetheart, what's wrong?" I asked, concerned somehow I had done something disturbing to cause this reaction.

"Mom told me what happened to you when you learned about your name. You said, 'I need all of you to go into the living room,' but you were so sad. The last time I heard you that sad was in Hawaii. My brain went right back to that gym where you beat the life out of a punching bag with a whole village watching. I can't stand thinking you were so sad babe," she said, and squeezed me tighter.

"Olaf," Mother began, but seemed to be at a loss for words.

"I... I don't know what to say," Mother said.

"I do," Father said. "You did something for me today for which I will never be able to thank you properly. Son, never in my live have I felt relief in ways I do now. Hearing my mom's voice again took decades of hurt away. I haven't felt like this—this light—ever.

It's *profound* to me, Olaf. I will never be able to thank you for what you've done. That said, I'm as worried as Annie. Are you okay?"

"Father, I—" I began, but was interrupted by Mother.

"Olaf, you fixed my hurt. You fixed my heart. Seeing Daddy again—I can't tell you how grateful I am to have had that conversation. The place we were was a park where Daddy and I used to walk. The river you walked toward is one of the most beautiful I've seen. I take it you fell into that river in that place, whatever it was, and in this world, you fell into the Intracoastal?" Mother said analytically.

"Not exactly Mother," I said and smiled. "I'm still not sure how I got here physically."

"You said, 'Babe take me home please,' and I drove you here. You struggled to get out of the car, and practically crawled out to the deck. I begged you to talk to me. I *begged* Olaf. You just fell over, into the water," Annie said, her face still buried in my chest.

"Annie, my love, will you look at me?" I asked and gently rubbed her back.

She turned and looked at me with heavy, red eyes. Tears were all over her face.

"Love, I'm not sad. I *promise* you. I can't tell you where I was, nor what all of this was about. I *think* it was what Mother and Father needed, and I was just there to help. I too had help, but that's a whole different conundrum. You were a big part of that help," I said, wiping her tears away.

"Why did you get so sad though?" she said with a scratchy voice.

"Well, all I can possibly say is it was part of the process. I wasn't sad for long. Promise," I said softly.

"Why are dead people pulling you into weird places?" she asked as fresh tears fell.

"Have her close her eyes, dear one. You too," a familiar voice said.

"Annie, my love, please close your eyes. Mother, would you and Father take the kids inside?" I asked carefully.

"Olaf, why?" Annie responded defiantly.

"Annie, just close your eyes. Please," I implored carefully.

Annie took a deep breath and closed her eyes. I did too, confident something interesting was about to happen.

"Olaf, where are we?" Annie asked, panic evident in her voice.

I looked around and saw something familiar: we were by the singing woman's waterfall. I could not place where we were standing though. The "ground" was hazy and transparent, almost as though we were standing on a cloud. Every time I had been in this place, I fell facing the waterfall and was pulled from my descent into the singing woman's arms. I may have seen this surface after the shooting, but I didn't remember it.

The singing woman approached us, her dress elegantly drifting back and forth.

"Hello dear ones. Thank you for joining me here. I felt it important to do so," she said.

She glided in front of Annie and softly grabbed her hands.

"Please, dear one, know your Olaf has not been hurt. You also must know it is you who allow Olaf to do what he does," she said.

Annie looked at the singing woman and asked, "Thank you for saying that, but where are we? Who are you? And, how in the world am I allowing Olaf to do this?"

The woman smiled and said, "My dear one, if I told you the answers to your first two questions truthfully, it would make little sense. This place is a healing place. This is where Olaf healed after the horrible violence. Much of how he healed had to do with you."

"Me? How?" Annie asked, intent to understand.

"This is where Olaf heard you. It is where you remained connected to him. Do you remember what you used to say at night, dear one?" the woman gently asked.

"I used to say, 'Olaf, know I love you wherever you are.' I'd say that and Mom and I would cry ourselves to sleep," Annie said sadly.

The woman smiled warmly and pulled Annie close.

"Dear one, your words were so much more than a means to end your day. They carried weight. They created this place, and allowed me to be present here, in the way you both have needed. I was there to help you sleep. I was here to help Olaf heal. Well, me and his grandmother—one of your 'dead people,'" the woman said with a slight and unexpected chuckle.

The woman let Annie go, but Annie held on.

"You helped me sleep? You helped Olaf heal? Please, I have to know, are you an angel?" Annie asked intently.

"Sweet Annie, what I am is similar to what a comet is in the universe. A comet is something created at the beginning and travels a path based on that beginning. Please just know I am here. This is more important than the who, what, or where in question. I hope this is an acceptable answer for you," the woman said softly.

"Okay, I understand," Annie began. "I have just one more question though. If we are here with you, what are our bodies doing? I can't imagine this is any different than what Olaf just did with his grandparents."

The woman smiled. "Your bodies are safe, dear one."

She then turned to me and said, "Olaf, thank you for helping me. It was a true blessing to have this conversation."

"It is my pleasure," I said. "I have one question too, though. Was this surface here the whole time?"

"What surface, Olaf?" she smiled brightly.

I looked down and began to fall. Annie fell too, but wasn't panicking. The thought formed in my mind we were going to land in the Intracoastal. Instead, we sank into our couch.

When we both came to, we were holding hands. Mother was rocking a sleeping Lou, and Father was on the floor helping Addie with a puzzle.

"Well you, you're off the hook," Annie said and embraced my arm.

"You kids are with us?" Mother whispered. "I figured something was happening."

"Man, what a day," I said. "I am profoundly honored to have helped in whatever way I could. Love, I'm just glad you got a taste of the experience. That woman was a major part of my after-shooting existence."

"Were you just with an angel, kids?" Father asked intently.

"No Papa. They were with the singing lady in the sky," Addie said as she played with a doll. "She helped everybody."

My jaw dropped to the floor, dear Reader.

"Peanut, can you tell me about the singing woman?" I asked, trying to contain my astonishment.

"She's nice. I like her dress Daddy," Addie said happily.

I was stunned. I measured the words in my head carefully before speaking again.

"Sweetheart, when did you first meet her?" I asked, kneeling in front of her.

"When you were hurt Daddy. She held my hand and showed me where you were by the waterfall. You were sad, Daddy. She told me Mommy and me were helping you not be sad and get you better. She still sings to me sometimes. I love her Daddy," Addie said in her tiny voice.

"So, the lady we just were talking to has a relationship with our daughter?" Annie asked exasperatedly.

"She sings to Louie too Mommy," Addie said without missing a beat.

Annie shook her head in disbelief. I was stunned silent.

"Well, it sure sounds like your singing woman is an angel and that's pretty fitting," Father said. "You needed Heaven's help to heal, Olaf. I still cannot believe what you survived, *and* that you're walking. It's surreal, son."

"That's true Father, but I did not know she had communicated with the kids. This is both so special, and in a different way, intriguing. I've never been able to figure out what that place is or who, or even what, she is. I know she helped me now twice when I desperately needed it. She gave credit to Annie for her existence. I just don't know Father. No matter what, she is a benevolent being with what appears to be nothing but good intentions. It's almost as though she is a physical representation of a *vox corporis*," I said, reaching for an explanation lying just beyond my brain's ability to comprehend the situation.

"Regardless babe, she took care of all of us," Annie said and leaned into me. "If she had any part in giving you back to me, I am eternally grateful to her. Someone or something with that capacity can absolutely have a presence around the kids. Maybe she is responsible for helping Lou sleep when we both needed it. She introduced our daughter to her daddy. Even if you can't understand this, accept just how special it is. This is what is important, you."

Mother got up and gave Annie a kiss on the cheek.

"Spoken like a messenger of the gods, sweetheart," Mother said and smiled.

She then turned to me and said, "Olaf, it's been quite a day, and none of us have eaten. Let's go grab a bite before our bellies decide to eat us from the inside out."

We gathered ourselves and headed to dinner. Conversation was sparse that night. The only time we really spoke was to order our food. The events of the day cast each of us into a shadow of introspection.

That night, when I was tucking Addie in, she looked me in the eye and said, "Daddy, I love you. Thank you for opening your eyes."

I didn't know what to say, dear Reader. I kissed her and managed a slight smile. I managed to get out of her room just in time before my emotions got the best of me. Annie intercepted me in the hallway after getting Lou settled in his crib. She said not one word, dear Reader. She took my hand, led me to bed, and held me until morning.

Vickery Applebottom, Weedy Cankerblossom

The next year of our lives was dedicated to adjusting to having two kids. Addie was two steps into life as a three-year-old when Lou was born. I had never had the privilege of the sleep deprivation that comes with a newborn baby; I never truly understood the test this represented for the whole household. With Addie, Annie had both my and her mother to assist, so she never really got to the level of sleep deprivation we experienced with Lou. He was the first baby she raised without a grandmother as backup. Even though Annie had me, I was no substitute for a willing grandmother, dear Reader. Especially in the beginning, I was figuring out how to simply handle a newborn. I caught on quickly, but did not shoulder as much of the responsibility Helene or Mother had taken on. I have to imagine the circumstances surrounding Addie's birth had something to do with this. We did get a grandmother assist, though, and this marked an important part of Lou's life. Addie went and stayed with Helene and Franklin for a couple days right at the end of the sleep deprivation period. I like to say they are credited with Lou sleeping through the night—he slept a solid eight hours the second my daughter returned from her stint with Gramma and Grampa Glaush.

Watching Lou grow into a functioning person was one of the most amazing things I had witnessed, and it truthfully had nothing to do with any part of my ability. Seeing him simply become mobile was amazing. It was unnerving, but it was thoroughly incredible. From there, seeing him begin to communicate with his simple verbalizations, and then progress to words and word fragments, was a study to me. Every experience with him as a baby, and then a toddler, was something I relished.

Seeing how Addie loved her brother was profound unto itself. She helped Annie and me in any way she could, and at her age, it was almost surreal. Be it getting him a fresh pacifier because he threw the one he was using and Doc shredded it, or giving him food when it was ready, or just playing with him on the floor, Addie did it all and then some. My little girl showed, at a very early age, she was both wise and capable beyond her years.

Our family got much stronger. It felt as though the final piece was in place. Lou seemed to complete us in a way; his birth came after some serious tests in our life, and subsequent tests *mostly* failed to appear after he joined our little tribe. I won't look too deeply into this, dear Reader, as I would be reaching into a bag of hypothetical nonsense that would not serve you well. However, it's a simple fact that things changed when Lou was born; perhaps this was an interesting alignment of life, and perhaps it was just coincidental. I'll defer to your judgment as to which it may have been.

We built in quarterly trips to our house in Hawaii as soon as Lou hit the ripe age of six-months old. Two trips per year were to be non-working for the duration, as much as possible. The others were free game for work, and work we did. The house was set up so Annie had all she needed to continue running the farm from the Dolby house seamlessly. I extended my practice to both Hawaii and Maui and had a steady stream of patients whenever I was on either island. I ended up treating every adult in our village within the first two trips after the extension, and had touched multiple familial generations on three of the islands within the first year. I never extended my practice physically to the other islands, but I often would receive referrals from family or friends taking me to Kauai, Oahu, and even a couple folks on tiny Lanai. Rupert was invaluable to me for those trips; he flew me everywhere I needed to go in exchange for a single cooked meal, and so long as dessert was some form of fruit pie.

Akamu and I began sharing the practice as it grew from tiny to not at all tiny. When I was in Hawaii, he and I worked together more often than not. When I was in Charleston, we talked many times a week; in fact, we found working together so effective, he travelled to South Carolina a couple times a year, and we worked together there too.

When Addie started school, an entirely new dynamic was created with respect for time. Annie's role at the farm had greatly expanded to one requiring her to work almost six days a week. My role was mostly a stabilizing one, and I worked on accessory business ventures when it made sense to do so. I still ultimately made the executive decisions for the farm, did all things financial, and worked new angles we decided were outside the scope of Annie's business relationships. My practice and time at the hospitals increased like wildfire in a drought by the time Addie started kindergarten. So, though there was some flexibility in both of our schedules, it was miniscule, and creating the required time to get her to and from school on time became an impossible task. Both grandmothers helped with Lou, but this too was a challenge as neither Mother, nor Helene had complete freedom of time in *their* schedules. Annie and I were faced with impossible time snafus when an interesting character entered our lives.

I was in my office documenting a patient's appointment when Fanny appeared in the doorway.

"Olaf, there is a gentleman here who asked to speak with you. He has an accent and is extraordinarily well dressed. Is it okay for him to come back here?" she asked.

"I suppose so… are you concerned, Fanny?" I asked, getting the sense that she was.

"No, Honey Boy. It's just… he's not in the books, and I don't really know why he's here. Your cane is loaded, right? Just want to be sure," she said, her voice more agitated.

"Um, no. My cane is not loaded right now," I said carefully, fearing what Fanny's retort may be.

She reached into her pocket and produced three bullets. "Here. You load it, or I will. No chances, Olaf. I don't like strangers."

I nodded and loaded the bullets into the cane. Fanny stood and watched me like a hawk while I did so.

"Honey Boy, no chances. Take the safety off and have it close. I'll send him back and will be ready if you need me," she said, every bit the drill sergeant.

I did as I was told and brought my cane closer to me. It made me profusely nervous to have it loaded, with the safety off, in my office. Regardless, I understood Fanny's concern and kept it close as the gentleman walked into my office. On first look, he was in his late 40's or early 50's and indeed was immaculately dressed. He was wearing a vest with dress pants, a gloss white kerchief stuck out of his vest pocket, and the chain of a pocket watch led to a lower pocket.

"Hello sir. Can I help you with anything today?" I asked nervously.

"Actually, Mister Waniglia, I am here to offer my services. My name is Vickery Applebottom. I am a nanny, and based on a phone call I received two days prior, I believe that I can assist you," he said with a refined British accent.

"A nanny?" I responded, shocked due to the difference between what I had prepared for and what the gentleman actually was.

"Yes, sir. I received a call from a dear friend of mine whose father you helped immeasurably over the past year. This same friend told me that you were extraordinarily pressed for time because of your responsibilities to your family. It so happened that I recently moved here to Charleston with my wife, and feel that I would be an asset to you given your responsibilities. I have watched children both young and old, royal and common, in London. It would be my honor if you and your wife would consider me to help you," he said with soft, refined confidence.

"Out of curiosity, which friend of yours referred me as a potential client for you?" I asked.

"Joanna Paveda. Her father is Gregory Nelson. Joanna told me that you effectively cured her father of depression and removed all of his pain. In her mind, you made it possible for her children to have their grandfather back. If this is true, Master Olaf, I can think of no other man that I would like to help more," Vickery said kindly.

Greg Nelson had come to me as a referral from my father-in-law in the hospital; he had fallen at a construction site and broke his back. He was unconscious when he arrived, and Franklin wanted me to be sure that his back was the only thing that they needed to address. Per his *vox corporis*, it extended to his brain as well, but the sole item affected was the area that affected his mental stability.

Unfortunately, there was no medical fix for that item, and that was where I came in. Once Greg's back was repaired, and he was fully conscious, a deep depression set in. It was so severe that Greg stopped communicating and eating once he was discharged. His family brought him to my office, where, after six appointments, I was able to rid him of remnant back pain and resolve the anomaly in his brain. On the date of his final appointment, both he and his daughter cried so hard that I talked about the kids for an extended time as I tried to calm them down. Apparently, that conversation did more than stop Joanna from crying.

"Yes Vickery, that is a true account of what happened. I'm surprised, though, that Joanna recommended me to you. We only really spoke once about anything other than her dad's treatment," I responded.

"Well, Mister Waniglia, it seems that your actions did the talking. Is there any possibility that I might stop by early this evening to meet your wife and the children?" he asked unassumingly.

"That would be perfect, Vickery, and please, call me Olaf. I'm not fit for 'Mister,'" I said and stood to shake the gentleman's hand.

I called Annie to tell her the latest, and she was mildly receptive to the notion of a nanny, though the fact that he was British seemed to be a point of contention.

"So the guy is from, you know, over *there*? Europe?" she asked suggestively.

"Well, yes babe, he is. Is that a problem?" I asked, confused as to what the problem may be.

"You just can't trust those Europeans," she said with utter seriousness in her voice.

I started to laugh. "And why might this be, love?" I managed to get out.

"You know," she said flatly.

"No, love, I have no idea why you might feel this way," I said, still chuckling.

"Olaf Waniglia you silly man," she said dismissively.

I never found out what in the world Annie's hang-up was with European people. Regardless, Vickery arrived at our house at 5:30, and was promptly greeted by Addie.

"Well hello there darling. What might your name be?" Vickery asked.

"I'm Addie. What's your name, and how come you're talking funny?" she replied innocently.

"My name is Vickery. I'm from a place called Britain. That's why I have an accent," he said patiently.

"Oh. I like that," she said and ran off toward her room.

I was holding Lou, and Annie soon joined us.

"Why hello there young man. What is your name?" Vickery asked.

"Lou," my son replied shyly.

"Louis? My goodness, that was my father's name. Why I say, Master Louis, it is wonderful to meet you," Vickery said and looked at Annie. "And you, my darling, you must be the lovely Annie. It is wonderful to meet you as well."

Annie was visibly surprised by Vickery's kindness. "Thank you, sir. It is nice to meet you as well," she replied. "Let's go in the family room and sit."

So, we made our way to the family room, where Addie had assembled all of her dolls and stuffed animals into an orderly display, based on type. She grabbed Vickery's hand and led him to a chair nearby. She then verbally catalogued each of the characters and introduced Vickery to Doc, who was sound asleep on his bed right next to Addie.

"Well, I'd say that this is a good start," Annie said. "Can you tell us how this might work? I've never really thought about a nanny before."

"Of course. I live but fifteen minutes away. I can be here as early as you need me to be, and I can stay late if that is the need as well. My wife may accompany me from time to time, as she likes to watch the children and knit things. Our own children are grown, and I believe she misses the opportunity to see the innocence of the young. Are we good so far?" he asked.

"So, you can be flexible then? Are you comfortable taking Addie to school and picking her up? And… are there any references you could provide?" Annie asked intently.

"Of course! I'd be happy to give you a couple families that I have worked for in the past. In terms of the cadence you mentioned, I'm more than happy to do whatever you two need," Vickery responded enthusiastically.

"That would be amazing. It would help so, so much," Annie said.

"What would be your fee, Vickery?" I asked, thinking that this would be the sticking point.

"Well, if you'd be willing to entertain something of a trade, my fee would be a flat $1,000 a month, no matter how much of my time is used. I don't need to do this for a living. I just truly enjoy the children," he responded.

"A trade?" I asked intently.

"Would you be willing to travel to London to help my brother? I certainly wouldn't ask that this take place with any set frequency nor duration. He is someone that I feel you could help, Olaf," Vickery responded, his tone hopeful.

I thought about this for a couple seconds, and wondered how I could add Britain to the list of places that I travelled to treat people.

"I'd need to really look at the schedule before I answer, Vickery. I know that the next several weeks are completely and totally full," I said honestly. "I wouldn't want to enter into an agreement that I'm not sure I could fulfill."

"Babe, if Vickery can help me, I can hold down the farm for a couple days. I did that for almost two years, ya know. I'm sure Fanny could work her magic, right?" Annie asked, hope rich in her words.

"Tell you what, let me call her. She knows my schedule better than I do. Be right back, y'all," I said and headed off to call the amazing Mrs. McNutter.

We settled on a three-day segment that had lighter hospital and patient time. I had originally set this time aside for a project I was discussing with the Poe Foundation, but the time itself was just my own that I could easily move. I returned to the conversation to find Vickery on the floor playing with a truck set with Lou. Annie was watching the whole thing, smiling warmly.

"Well sir, I think that I have some good news. I can travel to London in three weeks, if that works. I'd really like to meet your bride if she is going to be here from time to time. Would that be possible too?" I asked.

"Of course, Olaf. She would love to meet you all as well," he responded and drove a toy truck up to a filling station.

The next day, we met Mrs. Olivia Applebottom, a charming woman similar in age to Vickery, less a couple years. I don't think I ever saw her not smiling during our meeting. There was a genuineness about her. There was something so charming between the two of them, and it was obvious they were extremely happy together.

Vickery gave us a list of three families he had worked for, and all of them had glowing things to say about him. One lady, Mrs. Gilbride, told me that I should prepare myself for some of the most ornately knitted items I have ever seen, and that both Vickery and Oliva still stay in touch with her children. Another, Mrs. Preston, told me that it still makes her sad that the Applebottoms were no longer a constant presence in their lives. She told me to tell them "hi" for her, and to thank Olivia for her scarf. It seemed, based on those two calls, that we were in good hands. I had no idea that true saints had entered our lives.

Over the next three weeks, we learned the magic of the Applebottoms. Vickery took over responsibility for getting Addie to school, and took care of Lou from morning until late afternoon. In that time, Olivia knit him a comforter big enough for a full bed out of the softest material I had ever felt. Addie was knit a throw blanket that she began sleeping with every night. Doc was knit a blanket that he slept on or under every single day, no matter where it was he was sleeping. Vickery worked with Lou daily on potty training, reading, the alphabet, and counting to 50. He additionally respected every request we gave him, from nutrition to naps to everything in between, and he gave us so many helpful insights wherever he felt it appropriate. He began having Addie read to him and Olivia every day. In just three short weeks, our kids took massive strides forward. Three weeks, dear Reader.

In this time, I got to learn more about the Applebottoms and gained a much greater appreciation for the gift of their help. Vickery's first job as a nanny happened with a family he'd only describe as "royal." He taught me more about British culture in one conversation than I'd ever learned in school, and I found that to be a shame.

This first family were sadly required to let Vickery go after but three years. Vickery grew visibly emotional when speaking about the children, who were transferred to a full-time military school at the discretion of their father. At that time, the older boy was six and the younger boy was four. I could see tears in Vickery's eyes when he spoke of the boys; it was clear he considered them to be like his own kin.

"I couldn't say a word about this, Olaf. Not one word. I was the commoner there. I did the best I could for the boys in the time I had them, which was at least a decade too short. I've been communicating with both for a few years now. We all had a good cry as we caught up. Their childhoods were lost, Olaf. I still find it to be one of the saddest possible outcomes for two children who were still finding wonder in the world. They were still discovering life. So, so, sad," he recalled, frequently wiping the evidence of heartbreak from his eyes.

The Gilbride and Preston families were vastly similar. Vickery was introduced to older children in both cases.

Mr. Gilbride was transferred temporarily across the world, leaving Mrs. Gilbride alone to navigate the lives of two extremely busy children alone. She couldn't leave her job as an attorney because she was in the middle of a huge case. So, Vickery was referred to her and the Applebottoms rescued another family.

"Ah Joe and Minnie Gilbride... they are such beautiful souls. Teenagers are interesting creatures, Olaf. They believe themselves to be adults, in many cases, with nothing left to learn. We worked tirelessly to help them just be children. It was the most important thing to me, hands down. They were dealing with the emotion of their father being on the opposite side of the world. Their mother would basically come home and collapse after long days in court. Thankfully, Mr. Gilbride is home now, and Mrs. Gilbride has become a judge. The children have grown into such wonderful people. Joe is an engineer and Minnie is a teacher. Minnie is getting married next year. I know myself well enough to say I will be a tearful mess on that occasion, a blubbery fool to be true," Vickery said as he dressed a doll for Addie.

The Preston children lost their father to cancer when they were ten and thirteen. Mrs. Preston had no family closer than a three-hour plane ride and was unwilling to remove the children from their friends.

"Ah, the Preston children. Losing their father... I cannot begin to imagine the grief. Emmanuel and Josie are such strong people. They almost didn't allow themselves to recognize his death. My greatest challenge was to get them to use their strength smartly, without becoming empty, emotionless individuals. My greatest achievement to date has been softening those children emotionally while making them even stronger. They needed to be strong to move forward as healthy people. At the same time, they needed to know it was okay to shed a tear every now and again—to accept pain and sadness and process it smartly. Even today, I still get calls from Emmanuel. The conversations usually start the same way, with him stammering, then ultimately asking to make sure he was looking at a situation the right way. We always outline the situation and I ask questions, but he eventually addresses his own concern through the discussion.

I love hearing from the children, all of them. I know I have a place in their life, and I believe to my core this is my purpose. I am positive Olivia feels the same," Vickery said as he put Lou's blocks away. "I must say, Olaf, I find joy in being with your children in a completely different way. Your daughter enriches us with her smile. Addison Grace is a beautiful person. You and Annie have done wonderfully to create such a special girl. Louis, my goodness. He is growing into such a thinker. There are times he asks me things, and I need to take a moment to prepare an answer. I love the challenge, Olaf. I love your family. To be with you is joyful, and I'm not sure if there is anything better in life."

Vickery and Olivia installed themselves as the keepers of our family. I must say, dear Reader, I would have had it absolutely no other way.

Given that three weeks had passed, it was time for me to fly to London to help Vickery's brother, Owen. Vickery had given me little indication of what was wrong; he always said, "I feel you can help him." I didn't know what that meant, but I figured I would see what I could do.

I arrived at Owen's home by 3:00 in the afternoon. He graciously invited me in, and almost immediately, his *vox corporis* spoke to me.

"Hello, Olaf. Thank you so much for coming here. Owen indeed needs your help. I will fill in whatever gaps he leaves," he said.

We went in, and he offered me a cup of coffee. It smelled as though he had just made a fresh pot, so I graciously accepted. Our mugs in hand, we went into his living room and sat down.

"So, Olaf, how is my weedy cankerblossom of a brother these days? I miss that bloke like mad," he said.

"Weedy what? Vickery is doing well, Owen. I just hired him to be a nanny for my children," I responded, chuckling.

"Cankerblossom. It's from Shakespeare. Vickery and I trade unique Shakespearean insults from time to time, but he will always be a weedy cankerblossom to me. You are quite lucky to have his help. He actually was a nanny for royalty in the beginning. He is quite good with children," Owen said and took a sip of coffee. I noticed that a sadness seemed to settle over him as he finished his sentence.

"Owen, are you alright?" I asked, as he now was looking down.

"It's just... I...." he began.

"Olaf, Owen's wife and son died tragically two years ago in an airplane crash. He has never allowed himself to grieve enough to begin to heal. He turns to both drugs, prescribed by his doctor, and alcohol to cope with the sadness, but it solely masks how badly he really hurts. The combination is horrible for his heart too—time is genuinely of the essence here. He will listen to you. Be persistent," Owen's *vox corporis* interjected.

I was deeply saddened to hear this, and it made sense to me now why Vickery hadn't told me what was wrong. He lost his sister-in-law and nephew; the topic had to be unbearable for him.

"Owen, do you know what it is that I do?" I asked gently.

"You help people. That's what Vick said, anyway," he quietly responded.

"That's right. You've endured something unbearable, my friend. I can help you," I said carefully.

He looked up; his eyes were puffy and red. He was pursing his lips tightly together, doing all he could not to allow the emotion to bubble up over the surface.

"While I can't promise that I can make you completely better, or quickly, I can make you better if you trust me. Do you trust me, Owen?"

He nodded, and took a long sip of coffee. I too took a big gulp, knowing that this was not going to be easy.

"Tell me about you. Where do you work? What do you enjoy doing?" I asked.

"I'm a photographer. I do work by appointment, and I also do freelance photography and sell the photos to different types of publications," he said and scratched his head. "What I enjoy? I don't know that I can answer that, Olaf. I don't…. I don't really enjoy anything anymore," he said. The realization of that truth seemed to be impactful to him.

"I am going to do all I can to resolve that, Owen. Tell me this, though, at one time was photography something you enjoyed?" I asked and leaned in.

He thought for a couple seconds, took another sip and nodded. "I've been taking photos as long as I can remember. It lost its luster when... *that day....*" he responded and put his head in his hands.

"What about *that day* took the joy out of a lifelong passion, Owen? I completely understand the loss and how hard that is, but I'm not sure I understand how the two are related," I said analytically. I needed Owen to hurt again, and I prepared myself for his response.

He lifted his head and his eyes narrowed. I could almost feel the anger brewing.

"My passion for what I do died when I lost them, Olaf," he said, raising his voice. "How are the two related? The most beautiful thing I ever photographed was my wife holding our newborn son. That's how. My most amazing, most beautiful subjects I've ever had are *gone*. They were taken from me, Olaf. They..." he started to cry, unable to finish his sentence.

"Yes, Owen, they were. But, please, answer me this, would your wife want you to hurt like this if she were standing next to you? How could she possibly feel right about something that means so much to you becoming lost because of their deaths?" I asked gently and handed him a tissue.

He looked up at me with red eyes; it appeared that he didn't know what to say.

"*This is working, Olaf. Please don't stop,*" his *vox corporis* said intensely.

"If you let me, I will show you how to speak to your wife again," I began. "She will tell you the answers to those questions, Owen. You see, a very wise man showed me that the distance between life and death is much smaller than most believe. It is a choice, though, to see it that way. At the moment, your family is lost to you. If you choose a different path, your family and their memory does not have to be gone, nor painful."

"But…. How…" he stammered.

"Grab my hand," I said stoutly.

He did, and what Iokua told me about my ability to assist those in communicating with loved ones who had passed got its first test. In true, strange fashion, he was right. The environment changed to what looked like a hilly set of plains. Tall grass swayed as a gentle breeze caressed it. Opposing us was a woman in a long, flowing dress. She smiled and walked toward us. Owen's eyes lit up, but he was unable to speak.

The woman looked at me, put her hand on my shoulder, and said, "Thank you, Olaf. You must promise me you will help Owen become stronger again "

"That is my intention. What is your name?" I asked.

"I am Sophie," she said. She then walked to Owen, whose eyes were expressively sad. "My sweet husband, you must find joy again. To answer Olaf's questions…. I wish your hurt did not run so deeply. It makes me sad knowing you have not allowed yourself to move forward. You must, dear Owen. Your photography…. you are brilliant, my love. You may not allow something so precious to be stifled for any reason. Promise me you will work on this," she said emotionally.

He nodded, eyes laden with sadness.

"I will look forward to seeing you again when you are stronger, my sweet Owen. Bless you, Olaf. Be well," she said and walked away.

With each step she took away from us, the environment transitioned back to Owen's house.

"What the hell just happened, Olaf? Was that really my Sophie?" Owen demanded, tears streaming down his face. "Why couldn't I say anything?"

"Yes, Owen, that was your wife. You couldn't say anything because you are so weak emotionally, and your body is beginning to fail. If you change these two things, you will be able to converse with her again," I said. "As painful as it will be, you have got to let yourself grieve. No more drugs, no more booze. It's time for you to live again, Owen."

"*You just saved another man's life, Olaf. Would you please look at his heart? He is now receptive to you doing so,*" Owen's *vox corporis* said.

Before I could say a word, Owen got up and ran into another room. I heard shuffling and stifled cursing. After a minute or so, he returned with his arms full.

"Take it all. I will give up anything you ask to see Sophie again. Anything, Olaf," he said passionately and set down three pill containers and four bottles of alcohol.

"This is just part of it, Owen. Stopping the pills and drinking will begin to help your body. Thing is, you need to live. You need to find passion again. You need to find joy again. It's not enough to simply stop the bad. You need to start the good too," I said.

"Hold on," he responded and again dashed into the other room.

He returned shortly thereafter with a leather knapsack.

"Will you come with me?" he asked.

"Of course... where are we going?"

"You'll see."

We drove a short distance and boarded a train that took us due East. For the duration of the thirty-minute train ride, Owen sat silently and looked to be deep in thought. His expression was intense and active; something was stewing.

We arrived at a town called Grays. It was an interesting place, mixed with notably historic buildings and newer, trendier shops and restaurants. We took a cab to the Chafford Gorges Nature Preserve. Owen got out of the cab, took a huge breath, and said, "We just have a short walk from here."

We walked along a path that led us passed a small lake, then through a dense, but small, forest. We arrived at a clearing that faced west, and Owen fell to his knees.

"I swore I'd never come back here," he said, his spirit broken.

"What happened here, Owen? Why is it hard to come back?" I asked. I looked around and couldn't determine what about the area might cause him so much sadness.

"This was the last place I photographed them. It was the best picture I ever took, by a mile," he said, wiping his eyes. "You told me to grieve. Well, this is where I start."

I sat down in front of him. "What about that photograph was so special? Was it Sophie's expression? Something your son did?"

"It.... it was just the perfect evening. The sun was setting, as it is now. You see how this area becomes flooded with deep ambers from the sun? This is the only place on Earth I've found like it. Sophie was holding Edward, and he was reaching for the sun. It was just so magical. My beautiful bride and my son, bathed in gorgeous amber light. We took several pictures here and had dinner in Grays. The next day... the next day, they were taken from me," he said, tears streaming down his cheeks. "I never in a million years thought I would ever see this again. It's still the most beautiful natural light I've ever seen. Look at it, Olaf," he said and reached inside his knapsack.

Owen pulled out his camera, put a lens on it, and started milling around. He seemed to find something that caught his eye; he took several pictures from different angles at one spot.

"Olaf! There's a baby fox asleep in the brush! I got some great photographs of the little guy!" he said excitedly.

He then took several steps backward and faced the sunset. He smiled, raised his camera and snapped a couple pictures.

"Beautiful sunset. I haven't seen one this dynamic in a while," he said, and put his camera back in his knapsack. "We should eat. You hungry?"

"*He found his passion again, Olaf. It solely took him being un-medicated, sober, and seeing Sophie. It's remarkable how fast this has happened! Thank you! Please look at his heart before you leave today. It is very weak and damaged. He is now completely able to be healed. Your ongoing influence and his relationship with Vickery will help him immeasurably. Your grandmother is quite proud of you,*" Owen's *vox corporis* said enthusiastically.

"Yes, I am hungry so supper sounds perfect. I have to ask, how are you feeling, Owen? It seems you are in a completely different place mentally than when we first arrived," I said, heeding what I just heard from his *vox corporis*.

Owen scratched his head and said, "You know, I haven't felt this good in a long time, Olaf. I've been so sad… it was hard for me to see anything but grey. I'm seeing things the way I used to—in color and such incredible detail. I seriously haven't seen this clearly…" he said and lowered his head briefly. "I miss my family. Knowing I'm making Sophie sad though… it's time. Time for me to live again."

Owen no sooner finished his sentence, when he fell forward. I caught him before he hit the ground and went immediately into the cadence I used at the hospital. I addressed his *vox corporis* with a tremendous amount of intensity.

"Okay, I have to believe it's his heart. Help me… am I right?" I asked feverishly.

"*Yes, Olaf. This was my fear. You can save him. Focus,*" his *vox corporis* responded.

This was new territory for me. I had never done a healing session on someone who was unconscious and actively dying. I had spoken to a myriad of *vox corpora*, whose people were mostly medically stable. So, I closed my eyes, took a deep breath, grabbed his hand, and focused all my energy on his heart.

The environment changed in an interesting way; we were back on the hill with Sophie again. She looked at me, and nodded in approval. Oddly, Owen was "conscious" here; he was looking around. Sophie saw this and approached us.

"It's not time for this, my love. You must accept Olaf's help," she said.

Owen looked at me, and I put my left hand on his chest, to show him what I was going to do. He nodded and closed his eyes. Almost immediately, I saw his heart. It had stopped, and I could see damage all throughout the organ. My helpful streaks of light appeared all around me, and all seemed to be more active; they looked to be almost energized. Sophie smiled and touched one of them. I focused on the one she had connected with, and slowly moved it into Owen's chest—into his heart.

It started to beat again.

I looked at Sophie and asked, "Would you mind, a couple more?"

She smiled and touched two more light streaks. I focused on those two beams and put them on opposing sides of Owen's heart. They surrounded the organ, and in opposing ways, wove around Owen's heart, eventually dissolving into it after several rotations.

I no longer saw any damage on Owen's heart; in fact, it looked completely healthy. I also no longer saw Sophie. I heard her say, "Thank you, Olaf. Blessings," from what seemed like a distance.

I then heard my grandmother's voice say, "I am so proud of you, my precious grandson. You must let go now."

I nodded and released Owen's hand. I woke up in what looked like a hospital mere moments later—a worried Owen sitting next to me.

"Jesus Christ, Olaf! I thought you died!" he yelled.

"How are you feeling, Owen?" I asked weakly.

"I feel like a million bucks! The ticker is beating away. I swear to you, I have not had any pills or anything to drink, even though I could have, thinking I had somehow killed you," he said, his tone calmer.

"How long have I been here?" I asked, thinking it had only been minutes since we were in the nature preserve.

"A day and a half. You passed out there in the field. The folks here said you showed signs of extreme exhaustion. I've phoned Vick and your wife is aware. Per the doc here, you cannot be released unless you are conscious for at least twelve hours," he explained. "What the hell did you do to my heart, Olaf? It hasn't felt like this in years."

"A day and a half? I could have sworn... Aw hell, it doesn't matter. Part of what I can do is heal, if the person is receptive. You passed out and your heart stopped. I started it and fixed the damage as best I could. Do you remember Sophie being there?" I asked, taking a sip of water.

"Vaguely. It's almost as though it was a dream. Oh! I forgot! I have to show you something!" he said excitedly and reached into his knapsack.

"The photo I took when I was with you is up for an award! The one with the baby fox, you know? I looked at the film and knew it was a gem, so I submitted it. I sent a few of the others off to the publications I work for, and every photograph was purchased. That hasn't happened since before Edward was born. Thank you so much, Olaf. I cannot say this enough," he said and handed me a proof of the baby fox photograph.

The picture was stunning! The light accented the tiny fox in a way that it almost appeared to be glowing. He showed me the other photographs as well, and every one was masterfully taken. Owen had a superhuman eye, and both his angles and perspectives were immensely creative. As I looked at more of his photographs, he had an intriguingly identifiable style. The man had talent!

After my requisite twelve hours of consciousness, I was released from the hospital. The doctors and nurses were all so polite and seemed to care in ways I truly appreciated. It, in some ways, showed me what health care was meant to be like for the patient, and I took many notes from the experience.

Owen and I had a final breakfast on the day I was to fly back to Charleston. Before I left, I honored a promise and again connected him with Sophie.

"Hello my sweet Owen. I am so proud of you," she said kindly.

"My Sophie," he said sentimentally. "You are the reason I'm alive. Every day, for the rest of my life, I will love you. I hope, wherever you go, you know this."

"Of *course* I do, love. Question is, do you feel how much *I* love you? I have never stopped, and never will," she replied and put her hand on his face. "I am always with you, Owen. *Always*."

The two embraced. When they separated, both turned to me, and nodded a knowing 'Thank you.'

Shortly thereafter, Sophie began her walk away and the environment returned to Owen's house.

"That is a gift, Olaf," Owen said. "I cannot believe I just talked to Sophie again. Thank you so, so much for giving me this gift!"

"It was my pleasure, Owen. I am just grateful I could help you. Any time you need me, for any reason, call. I will always be here for you if you need me to be," I replied.

"Tell you what, I will come to Charleston once a year, and you come to London once a year. If nothing else, we will have a fun couple days, and I'll show you more of my favorite places to take photographs. Also, I am sure I know a few people who could use your assistance," he said, extending his hand.

"That, my friend, is a deal," I said and shook his hand, bidding him farewell.

****

I returned to Charleston and received a warm welcome home. Vickery was at the house when I arrived and gave me an unexpected hug as I walked through the door.

"You saved my brother, Olaf. Thank you! He told me what you were able to do, and it astounds me. You are a remarkable human being!" he said, releasing me from the heartfelt hug.

"That was our agreement, no?" I said, smiling.

Addie and Lou came running when they heard my voice. I got impeccably colored pictures from them and wonderfully special Daddy-hugs to boot. Annie came home early and was in tears by the time she made it into my arms.

"I cannot handle you in any more hospitals, babe. Are you okay?" she asked, wiping her eyes.

"I'm okay, love. I promise. Just a little tired," I said and wiped her tears, then kissed her.

"On the deck. Sit. I'll pour you booze," she said, still noticeably upset.

"Whoa there, Annie Louise. I don't let y'all go until the tears cease. This is 100% up to y'all. Just sayin'," I said and held her close to me.

We stood there for a good couple minutes while she gathered herself. In that time, Doc attached himself to my right leg. I could tell he was worried too, in his own way.

"I'm going to need to inspect you for damage, sir. You best be awake for the inspection. Just sayin'. Now then, go on the deck and sit down like I told you. Nap if you must." After a brief pause, her tone became much more serious. "No more, Olaf Waniglia. I cannot have you hurt, I cannot have you sick, I cannot do this. *So don't do it.* Got me?" she said, grabbing my collar.

"I'm okay, love. Honestly. I don't know what happened after Owen was better. This was completely different than anything I've experienced. He was dying, then I was with his wife, and then I was in the hospital. Poor Owen thought he'd somehow killed me. I've certainly had my dances with the dead my love, but this one takes the prize for the strangest ever. I promise—I'll talk to Akamu about it. I'm sure he can shed some light on this," I said and kissed her.

Vickery approached us and said, "Olaf, the person you just mentioned, Akamu I believe, is on the deck. Charming fellow. Ah, and me and the missus are cooking dinner for you all tonight. My way of further expressing my gratitude."

"Figures 'Akamu the Great' is here, right when I needed him. Thank you, Vickery. I cannot wait to see what you guys are cooking!" I said, kissed Annie one more time, and headed to the deck.

"You got *stuck*, Olaf Waniglia?" Akamu asked playfully.

"Apparently so. I never thought when I released Owen's hand that time would be impacted. I didn't have a single clue suggesting such a thing. What did I miss?" I asked, leaning toward him. "It's so good to see you, by the way, Akamu. Thank you so much for doing this. You are always here when I need you."

"It's my pleasure, Olaf. No magic here though. Annie called me when you were hospitalized. I timed my visit based on when she said you'd be home. I wish I still had the connection to you I had in the beginning. It would make this so much simpler!" he said and took a drink of something colorful. "Now then, tell me what you saw."

I recounted the experience, thinking about every possible angle.

"You said he was unconscious, correct?" Akamu said, furrowing his brow.

"Yes, his heart had stopped. I caught him before he hit the ground."

"This is not something I've ever done, Olaf. Anyone I've healed has been conscious. Remember the toll healing Gerard took on you initially? The fact that you were in two different planes, the healing plane and the spiritual plane, simultaneously... Honestly, it's something of a miracle that all you were was tired, Olaf. It will be interesting to see if this integration happens again, to see if you notice any differences," he said and took an extended drink of his colorful beverage. "You didn't intentionally enter the spiritual plane, did you?"

"No, I just focused on his heart. Could it be the two worlds merged because he was technically split between them? I mean, truthfully, a stopped heart can only be stopped for so long before one dies. What the heck are you drinking, Akamu?" I asked, and took a sip of the whiskey Annie had just brought me. She was not at all happy hearing this conversation.

"You mean you were there with the guy's dead wife? Akamu, doesn't that mean Olaf was dead?" she asked intently.

"No, my dear girl. I just believe our dear Olaf here may have discovered a wrinkle that needs to be communicated to the others. Oh—and this is Kool Aid, dear boy. Addison Grace supplied me with said beverage."

"So, let me get this straight," Annie begins. "Guy's heart stops. Olaf goes to do his thing and help. He then ends up with the dead guy's wife, helps the guy, and loses a day and a half, but doesn't notice the time difference? You can do some crazy things, you, but this takes it for me. That broad didn't touch you, did she? I won't have some dead lady makin' moves on my hubby. Uh-uh. Not happenin'.""

Akamu laughed hysterically in response. "Oh, my sweet Annie, you touch my soul," he said, wiping his eyes.

"Yes, love. That's what happened. I cannot explain the time difference. Maybe Iokua would have an idea? Dunno," I said. "…And no, Sophie did nothing inappropriate whatsoever."

"Ah, so this broad has a name too, huh?" Annie postulated.

"Annie Louise… seriously. She was there for Owen, not me," I said, grabbing her and bringing her over to me.

She looked down at me and said, "You're mine, Olaf Waniglia. Here and everywhere. This includes wherever dead people are."

"And you're *mine*, Annie Waniglia. Here and everywhere."

Vickery appeared at the entrance of the deck and announced that dinner was ready. They made the adults homemade bangers n' mash and homemade macaroni and cheese for the kids. The food was out of this world delicious.

Vickery became a fixture in our lives, and by extension, his wife and brother did too. Owen photographed the kids with the Intracoastal as a back drop as the sun began to set. To date, it is still the most remarkable picture I have ever seen.

You will see sprinklings of the Applebottoms through the rest of this story. As time flowed lazily by, they became family. Olivia made our closets full with the most comfortable sweaters imaginable. I still wear them every time I get cold. Every dog we've had—and you shall meet every one in due time, dear Reader—has loved and taken ownership of the blankets she made for us.

Vickery was a confidant in the way an older brother would be to me. He was the perfect combination of a life coach, a teacher and a father-figure to our children into their adult lives. In short, the mark this family made on us was profound, dear Reader. I'm still not sure about the "Weedy Cankerblossom" thing, but Vickery was a blessing and his wife was the closest thing to a living angel I ever encountered.

The World According to Jolene and Jebodiah Crawsnatch

I had tens of thousands of patients throughout my career. Jolene and Jebodiah Crawsnatch were so unique, I felt they deserved their own chapter. I met these two when the children were in middle school. Addison was among the best junior tennis players in the South and Lou had developed a love of the farm and enjoyed helping both the Rodriguez clan and Annie any way they needed. Vickery and Olivia remained fixtures in our lives despite them giving our children every possible tool to be independent. I'm convinced it had something to do with a monstrous knitting endeavor Olivia cooked up and engaged the whole family in. We were captive labor. I digress and apologize...

Jolene and Jebodiah Crawsnatch were referred to me by a colleague in the psychiatric community because he felt he had done all he could for them, and it was court ordered they attend some form of therapy on a monthly basis. In other words, said colleague was giving up in utter defeat without telling me why. I'll simply say this about the pair: they complimented one another quite nicely.

In my first meeting with the Crawsnatch family, I asked Jeb about his last name.

"My daddy made it up on the day I was borned, doctor man," he said proudly.

"Your father made it up?" I asked, very confused by this response.

"He done said I was fit 'n borned out a crawsnatch, doctor man. Ain't that damn hard to understain', doctor man," he said confidently.

"I punched my sister las' Tuesday, doctor man," Jolene chimed in.

"You punched your sister, Jolene? Why did you do that?" I asked, surprised.

"She done smacked me wit a switch, doctor man," she responded, furrowing her brow.

"Do you know why she did that, Jolene?" I asked, trying to understand this pair as best as I could.

"She say Jolene da debil, doctor man. Smack 'er wit a switch, doctor man," Jeb interjected.

"I see. You both can call me Olaf, if you like," I said, hoping to begin to make sense of them.

"I done had me a pig named Ollie, doctor man Olaf. He done run off, doctor man Olaf," Jeb proclaimed.

"Really? Did you ever find Ollie, Jeb?" I asked, practically fearing the answer.

"Yes'm. Ollie done turned mean, and ate one of Daddy's fingers, doctor man Olaf. So, Ollie done gitted shot, doctor man Olaf. Tasty bacon, doctor man Olaf," Jeb replied.

"Were you sad that Ollie died, Jeb?" I asked, wondering what the response might be.

"Naw, doctor man Olaf. Ollie neva' like Jolene, doctor man Olaf. Ollie done bad thangs and thus'n getted cooked up, doctor man Olaf."

"*Hello, Olaf. This pair may have the fewest brain cells of any two people on Earth, but it's not in any way their fault. So you know, they both come from parents who are brother and sister. Please understand what you have here may not be fixable, nor changeable,*" Jeb's *vox corporis* said. His voice had a southern inflection for sure, but spoke incredibly well.

"*Hello, Olaf,*" Jolene's *vox corporis* said next. "*I agree. This is a case where the two may not learn anything at all and are unlikely to change in any way. They aren't violent, but they cannot work as their brains have sizable malformed areas. Truth be told, it's a miracle they get up and function every day. Their existence is not easy in any way.*"

She continued, "*The state provides their income and requires a therapist to certify they remain non-violent, to continue the flow of state money and keep them out of managed care. They would not be able to remain together if sent into the care system. This said, their parents are equally challenging, so your work is not going to be easy simply because their home life will counter everything you tell them. Just look at how Jeb's last name was chosen. This really did happen as Jeb explained.*"

I thought about this for a moment, and figured I would continue to learn as much as I could about the pair. When I next looked at Jolene, though, she was sucking on Jeb's thumb.

"Jolene, why are you sucking on Jeb's thumb?" I asked, puzzled beyond belief.

She shot me an angry look and replied, "I love my Jeb like I wan', doctor man. Don't you tell me no different, doctor man."

I began, "But, I just…"

Jeb interrupted me, saying, "Why you like 'at, doctor man? Ain' neva seen someone love befoe, doctor man?"

"I apologize, you two. I guess I have not seen the way you love one another, no. Please forgive me," I said apologetically. This seemed to placate the situation, but it showed me I needed to be much more careful when I addressed them.

The first session ended without much fanfare, and I set their schedule according to what the state needed for their reporting. This meant I would see the Crawsnatch family every week. It also meant I would learn more from these two people than I ever thought possible.

The next session, which was almost exactly a week after the first session. It began with a 5-minute session of laughter. The two came in, sat down, and Jeb said the word 'bitterwhipple.' The two then laughed hysterically for 5 minutes. Tears were flowing, noses were running, and hysterics were being had for reasons unknown.

When they finally calmed down, I asked, "Jeb, can you explain what 'bitterwhipple' means?"

They looked at one another, and a second session of hysterical laughter erupted. During this session, Jeb's *vox corporis* said, *"Well Olaf, I'm not sure you'll get much more than this. 'Bitterwhipple' seems to tie into something of a sexual nature, but the meaning changes from instance to instance, and what it means today makes absolutely no sense. It's not even worth explaining."*

"Yes, it is about something sexual, but they aren't agreed in terms of its meaning. Jolene is associating it with the top end of a human, and Jeb the lower. It's lunacy that they find humor, even though they're understanding of it is not congruent," Jolene's *vox corporis* added.

"Were they intimate last night?" I asked as the two slobbered their way through their laughter.

"Well, not exactly in a conventional sense, no. In fact, they have never had intercourse, Olaf. Their definition of intimacy doesn't even involve kissing," Jeb's *vox corporis* said.

"That's right. The way they maintain their intimacy has nothing to do with intercourse or anything of a sexual nature. Their intimacy involves sucking

fingers, often times humming while doing so. This resonates deeply with both of them. Thing is, beyond this, they essentially have no physical contact aside from a random hug once every couple months," Jolene's *vox corporis* added.

I found this to be quite interesting, and decided to make it my focus of understanding.

Once the laughter slowed down to a random chuckle here or there, I asked, "Jeb, would you tell me about Jolene please?"

Both shot me a look of confusion.

"What dat mean, doctor man? What you tellin', doctor man?" Jeb asked angrily.

"I don't mean anything by this. I'm so sorry if I've upset you. I'd just like to know what you would say about Jolene—like how you feel about her. So, Jeb, can you tell me about Jolene?" I asked carefully.

He thought for a moment, looked at Jolene, and said, "Jolene my girl, doctor man. I like when she punch people, doctor man. Make me smile, doctor man."

"I remember you talking about Jolene punching her sister from our first session. Jeb, can you tell me something different about her that you like?" I asked.

"She da best, doctor man. I like ha ha time wit 'er, doctor man," he said, looking at Jolene.

"Ha ha time da bes' wit Jeb, doctor man. Da bes', doctor man," Jolene interjected.

"Tell me about ha ha time, Jeb. What is ha ha time, and why do you like it with Jolene?" I asked carefully.

Jeb looked at me as though I'd just asked the most asinine question possible.

"Ha ha time, doctor man. You know, ha ha, don' you, doctor man? It fun wit Jolene, doctor man. Make me happy, doctor man," Jeb responded.

"Do you mean you like to laugh with Jolene, Jeb?" I asked, still unclear as to what "ha ha" time might be.

"Ha ha time, doctor man. Call it what you wan', doctor man. What 'dis *laugh*, doctor man? What dis mean, doctor man?" Jeb asked, starting to chuckle.

"*Laugh*, doctor man," Jolene added, and joined Jeb in his chuckling.

In no time at all, the two were in hysterics, randomly saying "laugh" to each other.

"*Olaf, 'ha ha' time can take multiple forms, and this is one of them. A word often sets them off, or anything they find to be odd,*" Jeb's *vox corporis* said.

"*Yes, Olaf. This hysterical laughter happens at random. They seem to feed off one another. When one starts, the other follows. What's interesting is they both don't have to experience something 'odd' to respond like this. It's good enough that one starts to laugh for the other to follow,*" Jolene's *vox corporis* added.

I found this to be touching, if nothing else. For these two people to be able to find shared joy seemingly out of nothing was a gift. Imagine, dear Reader, the quality of life you would have if simple, random parts of your day made you belly laugh. Better yet, imagine being able to share a laugh with someone you're close to without needing to understand the context in order for you to respond as they are. Can you possibly imagine the closeness you would have with that person? Can you imagine the positive impact on your life this would have?

As the "ha ha" session settled down, I turned to Jolene and asked, "Jolene, can you tell me something about Jeb that makes you happy?"

She looked at Jeb, looked at me, and then looked back at Jeb. He nodded and she said, "Bitterwhipple."

The session that day ended with the two laughing so hard they each wet themselves slightly. The aide who transported them to and from my office looked at both and said, "Well doc, looks like you had a mighty productive session today. Hell, takes a bit for them to tinkle."

I smiled and responded, "Honestly, I learned quite a bit about them today. Wasn't as bad as it looks."

The aide looked to be confused. "It took two sessions like this for the last guy to give up. Hopefully you're more patient," he said.

I nodded. "I promise you—I'm nowhere near the end of my rope," I said, grinning.

Our next session began with just Jeb, who walked slowly into my office. Fanny looked at me sadly, shook her head in obvious disgust and walked away. I found this to be disturbingly curious.

"Jeb, where is Jolene this morning?" I asked, concerned.

He looked at me for a couple seconds with a completely vacant stare and said, "She ain't here, doctor man."

"I see this. Is everything okay, Jeb?" I couldn't figure out what was going on, but it was obvious something had happened.

Jeb scratched his head, then laid down on the couch. It was obvious to me something had happened, even if he couldn't say what.

"Olaf, Jolene was taken into protective custody last night after a brief stint in the hospital. Her mother got confused and thought Jolene was there to have an affair with her father. They were in the middle of dinner. Jeb watched it all unfold, seemingly unable to comprehend the situation. At this point, he just knows Jolene is gone, and it's having a massive impact on him. His ability to communicate is stifled. There is no hint of happiness. Jeb is lost, Olaf. Please help him any way you can," Jeb's *vox corporis* said, his words heavy with sadness.

I was deeply saddened to hear this. If I had learned anything about the Crawsnatch family, it was that they needed one another. I remembered the effect of being separated from Annie, and this lit a fire in me. I was going to help this family any way I could. Jeb went to sleep on the couch. So, I picked up the phone and called Joe. The state provided protections for people like Jolene, so I needed Joe to assist me in getting access to her as her therapist. I also enlisted Fanny's help to contact the hospital and see what she could learn. Both were eager to contribute; Fanny especially. This entire circumstance did not sit well with her at all.

Joe got back to me first. He couldn't do anything himself, but found out that I could. Because I was Jolene's state-sponsored therapist, I had clearance. Joe gave me the number of the facility where Jolene was being held, and I called as soon as I hung up with him.

It turned out my sense of urgency was absolutely necessary. Jolene had gone into a state similar to Jeb—unresponsive for the most part, seemingly lost. I made arrangements to see her and bring Jeb with me. This was a sticking point as the terms of her protection included a separation from everyone in the family. Jeb was perceived to be a part of the problem because he didn't intervene when the assault took place. After I explained the situation, I was granted a 'monitored' visit. Aside from having someone in the room, I had no idea what this meant.

I contacted the aide who transported them and had Jeb picked up. I was not allowed to transport him myself, so I led the processional to Jolene's location. Man, oh man, I was not well prepared for this. You see, dear Reader, I was just given an address. Nothing else.

When we pulled up to the building, it was unmarked, and I saw nothing out of the ordinary. When we went in, though, a nightmare from my past returned. I was back in the same psych ward Dr. Small had put me in, and the inmates there knew I had returned. Well, some part of them did anyway.

"Welcome back, clown. I look forward to tasting that heart of yours. Come a little closer, clown," a demonic voice said.

A chill ran down my spine, and I started shaking. I had long healed physically from this experience, but mentally I was far from being able to navigate this with a clear head. Thing is, I had to if I was to help Jolene.

"Mr. Waniglia? Are you okay?" the aide asked.

"I'll be okay. I had a horrible experience with this place several years back. I just hope Jolene isn't in with those who were committed," I said and wiped sweat from my brow.

We signed in with the front desk and were led to a back room. We sat there for maybe five minutes. In that short amount of time, I heard many more disturbing bursts of insanity, each with a different voice. I could not resolve this; every *vox corporis* I had encountered to this point was rational and kind. I had to believe that what I was hearing were the truths of individuals in the facility, and it was the first time I recognized evil and darkness in this form.

"Your soul is so tasty, clown. With each bite, I drool more."

"You returned. I will enjoy torturing you, slowly and deliberately. I cannot wait to make you bleed. Submit to me, and the torture ends. Or, does it?"

"You may never leave, clown. You will never leave this place again. Welcome home. The damned always return. I cannot wait to break you and watch you suffer."

"You have given us new souls to feast upon. You are not to be spared."

I did my best to keep my emotions in check amid this verbal assault. It brought back such horrible memories. I got a sense something was amiss, so I asked the aide to go back to his van and have it ready to leave in a hurry if need be.

"Uh doc, you want to tell me what the hell is going on?" the aide asked in a panic.

"This is a horrible place. It wouldn't surprise me if we needed to leave quickly. That said, I would prefer you be ready to go with Jeb, at minimum to protect him. I'm, of course, looking out for your safety as well," I said, and put my hand on his shoulder. He was shaking.

I handed the aide a piece of paper from my pocket and said, "Go find a phone and call this number. Ask for Joe. He is expecting your call. Tell him to start plan B. He will understand."

The aide nodded and left the room. Jeb sat next to me in a seemingly semi-catatonic state as this exchange took place. He was breathing and his eyes were open, but not much else was happening. His eyes were fixed on a point across from him, emotionless.

Almost immediately after the aide left to go back to his van, a tall, slender man in a white coat entered the room. His expression was dark; his greeting matched.

"Olaf Waniglia… I thought for sure we had killed you. Huh. Welcome back," he said sadistically.

"I am here to see Jolene Crawsnatch. I am her state-sponsored therapist. As such, you are obligated to produce my client," I responded coldly.

"Mr. Waniglia, can't we have a little fun? I mean, honestly... We do have history, you and I," he responded cynically.

"I'm not here to play. I'm here to see my patient. Please make her available to me," I responded, again doing all I could to restrain the war of emotion that raged inside me.

"Your patient is on her way. So, tell me, Mr. Waniglia, how did you become a therapist after your time at our little camp here?" the gentleman asked, leaning toward me.

"Well, I guess you're just not as talented as you think, sir," I said, glaring into his eyes. I could well play the same game, dear Reader. Perhaps this was due to my time here.

This response seemed to temper the man's aggression. He sat back, now silently, until Jolene was led in a couple seconds later. Jolene's demeanor matched Jeb's—seemingly catatonic, with fixed eyes and slow, lumbering movement. That is, dear Reader, until she got next to Jeb. It happened almost simultaneously, dear Reader. Both Jeb and Jolene 'woke up' and embraced. I had never seen them show affection traditionally. It was special, and showed me something that bonds me to this couple to this day. They needed one another to truly *live*.

"You just rescued two completely lost souls, Olaf. The fire had completely gone out in Jeb, and it's roaring as strong as ever. Thank you for enduring what you have to simply reunite them!" Jeb's *vox corporis* said enthusiastically.

"Yes, Olaf. You just allowed Jolene to feel again. You have no idea how profound this is to her. Thank you, Olaf—so much!" Jolene's *vox corporis* said happily.

The man in the white coat stood up suddenly, and I instinctively put myself between him and the embracing couple.

"She is in protective custody, Waniglia. She cannot be in contact with that man!" he said and began to move toward us.

"You will return to your seat, sir. As their therapist, I am responsible for their well-being, and the protective custody item was addressed legally. If you compromise me or my patients in any way, I will show you what I learned in camp," I said and prepared myself for war.

In the background, I heard running. I could tell it was multiple people. The man continued to move forward. He seemed to be pulling something from his pocket. I moved backward, heeding the steps I heard. I essentially was being cornered between the sadistic doctor and the door. I had no idea what I was in for, but no one was going to lay a hand on me or my patients without some violence.

The man produced a syringe and lunged toward me. I knew all too well what the cocktail probably contained, and it was not going to find its way into my or my patients' bodies. I dodged the man's lunge and moved the embracing couple—yes, dear Reader, they were still embracing—closer to the door. The steps grew closer. I had to be mindful of who might be running toward us, and be prepared for more syringes headed my way.

The steps got closer.

The man lunged at me again, and I hit his hand hard enough to knock the syringe to the floor. I backed up further, pushing Jeb and Jolene closer to the door. The doctor made another attempt to come at me, and I cleanly punched him in the face. I caught his nose squarely, but he didn't fall.

The steps got closer.

Blood began to fall from his face. He grimaced and dove toward me.

The door flew open.

The man grabbed me, and I punched his throat, but at an odd angle. He crumpled to the ground, grasping his Adam's apple and trying to get a full breath in.

"OLAF!" Joe shouted as he ran into the room. He was accompanied by three police officers, who all had weapons drawn.

The man found the syringe on the ground and plunged it into my leg. I felt the needle and kicked with my other leg.

"Joe! He just…" I said and lost consciousness.

"Olaf, stay with us," I heard. I could not feel anything. I couldn't open my eyes.

"Babe! Please!" I heard Annie implore.

****

After some amount of time, I heard the familiar beeps of hospital monitors and blinked my eyes open. I was alone. I had a feeding tube down my throat, a ventilator covering my mouth, an IV in my arm, and sensors everywhere—including some wires going into my chest. I reached for the nurse call button, but couldn't lift my arm high enough to reach it. I sat there for a couple minutes before Dr. Glaush walked by and caught me awake out of the corner of his eye.

"Olaf! Can you hear me? NURSE! GET IN HERE!" he yelled and ran into my room.

I nodded, which hurt like hell, dear Reader. That damn feeding tube was doing me no favors.

"Hold on, son. We need to be sure you're stable before we disconnect you. This was a nasty one, Olaf. Really nasty," he said, which was uncharacteristic for him. My father-in-law was never the matter-of-fact partner; Father was.

No fewer than eight people feverishly rushed into the room. A couple went to the monitors, and the rest surrounded me. One of them was my former therapist, Susan. She grabbed my arm softly and said, "I am so sorry this happened to you again, Olaf. I hope you are okay with me being here."

Years had passed since the nonsense Susan had put me through. I was not concerned whatsoever with her involvement as a result. I reached out for her hand. She smiled, though there was a reflection of sadness in her expression.

After several minutes, I was determined to be stable enough to remove the feeding tube and ventilator, but nothing else. I despise those things, dear Reader. I know they serve a purpose, but I can't stand when they are removed.

"Okay Olaf. Can you talk?" Dr. Glaush asked cautiously.

"Yeah, Dad. How long have I been down this time?" I asked with a scratchy throat.

"Ten weeks. That cocktail was stronger than anything I've ever seen, Olaf. Your heart stopped almost immediately. Joe saved your life, son. It's been a wild ride yet again. Why the hell did you go there by yourself? I mean, seriously Olaf," he said angrily.

"I never had the address of the psych ward. The place is unmarked. I had no idea where I was until I heard some familiar insanity. That's why I had the aide driver call Joe. I had a bad feeling about it, and we planned for things to go bad," I said amid a flurry of coughs. One of the nurses got me a big jug of ice water.

"I never thought about that. Hell, I wouldn't have known it by address either. I only know that place from the inside. Well son, it was the final chapter for a couple of those folks," he said with a serious tone.

"What do you mean?" I asked, my curiosity rising.

"Well, the ass who injected you is dead and one of his ridiculous associates too. The whole place was audited from the top down and is under the state's control now. None of their leadership remains. In fact, two of them are in jail," he responded.

I could not believe this.

"What?!" I asked, followed by a volley of coughs.

"You aren't going to believe this, son. When you kicked, after you got injected, you snapped the guy's neck. Think football on tee, son. His idiot associate comes running down the hall with another needle, and apparently didn't hear the officers say, 'Drop the needle,' and got lit up by three police officers. He is with us no more. The world is less two idiots, thank God. Lating tells the story best though," he said with a chuckle.

"Is Annie okay? Where is Doc?" I asked, knowing that these stints never set well with her. I also couldn't believe my dog was missing from the equation.

"She will be, son. She will be. Akamu has been in town since the second day you were here, and has kept her completely on the straight and narrow. It was rough the first twenty-four hours, son. I think he was as responsible for you being alive as we were. It was fascinating to watch him work. He should be here shortly. Doc is at home with the kids and Annie. I think this time he knew where he needed to be. Oh—and your patients—Joe had a release for the woman, and they are home and safe. They kept saying, 'Doctor man saved us, ya know. Doctor man done kicked sumbitch. Doctor man did,' over and over and over. It's kind of a thing now. Nol, um, *loves* it. Just be ready," he said, barely able to contain himself.

"Jesus. What is my prognosis? And, am I in trouble for the dead guy?" I asked, probably less serious than I should have been given the weight of the situation.

"I don't really know your prognosis because I did not expect you to be awake now, or really, um, *ever*, if I'm being honest. And, no. You defended yourself, and technically, you died. You were medically deceased six times. But, who's counting? In one of these events, we had stopped resuscitation and you came back a minute later." Dr. Glaush said, and put his hand on my chest. "You are human, Olaf. Not feline. Best I can tell, you've used up a bunch of lives you didn't have in the first place. Please son, no more. I'm not sure how many more times we can restart that ticker of yours. I'd like to do an image of it once we can move you and remove the thing attached to these wires in your chest. You have a device electronically managing your heart. You're in the ICU, son. This isn't a trivial situation."

"Y'all, can I have a minute?" I asked with the weight of this becoming insurmountable. The staff respected my request, and everyone left. Well, everyone except Susan.

"I'm not leaving, Olaf. I'm sorry, but I won't," she said softly and handed me a tissue. "You taught me such valuable lessons, and this is one of them. If nothing else, I am going to watch your vitals and will be here if you need me."

Tears streamed down my face. I was touched by what Susan said, and it amplified the horror of the reality I just caused my family. *Again.* It all hit me square in the jaw, dear Reader. I was down for the count emotionally.   About a half hour later, Akamu arrived with Gerard guiding him.

"Well look at this. Mister Olaf, you're awake! Dad! Look!" Gerard said excitedly.

"My dear friend, how are you? The extent of your situation this time was rather grim. No matter! I want to hear how you are," Akamu said kindly. He had recently turned the ripe old age of 88. It was harder for him to travel, so I knew just based on his presence, I was not in a kiddie pool health-wise.

"Ain't y'all a sight for sore eyes!" I began, but was overcome with emotion and my waterworks started again. I was a blubbery mess.

"Hey now," Akamu began commandingly, "you best be crying tears of joy Olaf Waniglia. Any other tears needn't apply here."

"It's just..." I began.

"It's just this, you are alive. The rest is irrelevant right now. I need you to hear me say this, Olaf. You are alive. Your family is safe. Your friends are near, and they all love you. This is not something to shed tears of pain, nor sadness over. So, Olaf Waniglia, if those not be tears of joy, you have no right to continue letting them fall," Akamu said, interrupting me.

"I hear you, Akamu. I do. These are *not* tears of joy. These are tears steeped in fear. They are tears laden with guilt. They are tears of regret. I'm sure this will change, but for right now, I need to process all of this. What I heard at the psych ward. What I have just done to my family, again. What this means to my health. I have wires going into my heart, Akamu. I just don't know where to start," I said and sank into my pillow, defeated.

"Olaf, take a breath. You've been once again exposed to something we have never discussed— evil. You were dosed with a mixture of medicines intended to kill you. You once again took a life, and have been separated from your own for weeks on end. Okay.

You have a right to lament these things, but none of them are as important as this moment. These things have passed, Olaf. You need to focus on healing your poor body, especially that heart of yours. You can, but only when you accept the present and allow the past to teach you, and then wither into nothingness. This is your charge, my dear friend. You know as well as the best healers on this planet how the body heals. It starts with acceptance. Olaf, you need to accept and appreciate. Fear, regret, guilt… These things only have power when we give it to them. Can you please take a few breaths for me?" Akamu asked softly.

"Mister Olaf, Dad is right. You have done so much for so many. It's your turn to allow us to help you. Please let us," Gerard implored.

I nodded and struggled to wipe my face. I was weak in ways I'd never felt, dear Reader. My arms were heavy and awkward. My face alternately burned and froze. My heart—God alive—was practically a robot. This was not one of my more shining moments.

Susan saw my struggle and came to my rescue. She gently guided my arm down to my side. She carefully wiped my tears, smiling as she did, and gave me a drink of water.

"Olaf, close your eyes and breathe," she whispered, and offered another smile.

I did as I was asked. I closed my eyes, breathed a few times, and crashed.

I woke up to a bunch of faces huddled around me. Dr. Glaush, Father, Akamu, Susan, and two others I didn't recognize all looked at me intensely.

"What happened?" I asked, though I had no voice.

"Son, you had a little challenge. You've been out for two days. We need to change things up, so we are talking about relocating you," Dr. Glaush said. It was obvious he was exhausted.

"Relocate me? Where?" I was barely able to speak.

"Hawaii. We're just not sure you'll survive the flight. Or, the car ride to the airport for that matter. This is what we're discussing currently—how to keep you alive from here to there. We're thinking induced coma, but there is dissention among the ranks here," he said, stress woven through each word.

"Why can't I stay here?" I whispered.

"Olaf, you'll die if you do," Father said emotionally. A solo tear found its way down the side of his nose.

"Akamu?" I asked and fixed my stare on him. Father was making me incredibly sad.

"It's my thought we could use some island magic here, my friend. There is nothing better than tapping into some good old Dolby assistance. We really are concerned about getting you there though. You are so unstable," he said, furrowing his brow.

"Who are you people?" I asked, pointing my gaze at the unfamiliar faces.

"We are specialists from Cleveland. Our opinion was sought in terms of your care. I am Dr. Gee, and this is Dr. Brown. It is a pleasure to meet you, sir. I just dislike that it is on these terms," one of the men said.

"I agree, Mr. Waniglia. I have followed your work for several years now. It is a privilege to be able to help you," Dr. Brown said kindly.

"Who doesn't like the Hawaii option?" I asked, my voice improving slightly.

"Well, Gee, Brown, and Susan are in that camp. I'm on the fence," Father said. "The problem is getting you there alive. The counter to that is, literally, we are losing you here. Quickly."

"What does Annie say?" I asked, the heaviness of the topic finding its way into my mind.

"Annie is already there, Olaf. She, Mother, Mom, the kids, Vickery and Olivia, Nol, Sadie, their kids, Toth and Lating are there. Of course, Doc too. They got there yesterday. Rupert is hosting a dinner for everyone tonight," Father said. "Mom" in this case was Mrs. Glaush.

"Can you get me home alive? By the Intracoastal?" I asked, hoping my time wasn't already up.

"Geez, we never even considered that as an option. All? Thoughts?" Dr. Glaush asked, his intensity rising.

"Olaf," Dr. Gee began, "the issue is transporting you anywhere. Your heart appliance isn't something that has any tolerance. If we could get you from here to anywhere without you moving, there would be no issue."

"Call the boys at the farm. Carlos could design something. Can you guys keep me alive for a couple days?" I asked, my panic level rising.

"I'll call him Olaf. Right now!" Father said and rushed away.

"We will keep you alive, Olaf. Brown and I will coordinate with Susan and Akamu and we will give you every fighting chance. Thing is, you really need sleep—really good, restful sleep—without crashing and without medication. We need to give that heart of yours a bit of a rest, but our medical options are running thin. I'm watching your blood pressure rise in a way that's making me uncomfortable. Can you please try to relax?" Dr. Gee implored.

"Doc, honestly, the last time I closed my eyes, I lost more days. I'm, well… scared. First time in my life, all. I'm scared my time is up. My kids are too young," I said and tears began careening down my face.

This was different from the shooting, dear Reader. I had accepted death then; I felt I deserved it. This time, I felt life was being pulled from me, and in the same way, I was being removed from my family. I simply could not fathom this, and felt I couldn't control it from happening.

"Whoa there Olaf. You ain't dead yet, and you ain't dyin' on any of our watches. One of us will be with you, along with two nurses, at all times. Please, close your eyes and relax. Dr. Brown is right. Your blood pressure and the overall stress in your heart is unsafe," Susan said, every bit the mother.

"Susan's right, my friend. I'm seeing your poor heart get weaker. Please, Olaf. Relax. There is someone who has been carefully watching over you, who needs to have a conversation. It's time, Olaf. Most of us will leave you now, and you must relax. I can honestly say, if you don't, time will not be your friend," Akamu said sadly.

I knew two things from this exchange. First, things were *bad*. Second, this was not going to be an easy conversation. Regardless, I nodded and slowly—deliberately—closed my eyes. I measured my body's response with each micro-movement of my eyelids. I was not going to allow my body to crash again, dear Reader.

It took several minutes for me to relax physically. But, my mind never calmed. It raced, measuring every minute feeling in my body. I realized I was not hearing *vox corporis* conversations anymore. I began to feel how much the machine in my heart was working. I felt how weak I was, and experienced weird temperature variances all over my body. The sum of it all was a whole bunch of horrible.

As my mind sank deeper and deeper into a pit of despair and over-analysis, I heard familiar singing. I still could not understand the lyrics, but the music was soothing and gradually removed my mental angst.

"That's right, dear one. Please just listen a while longer," the singing woman said softly. It was as though she were singing to distract my mind from the judgment of my existence. It was working.

Her song resumed, ebbing and flowing sonically like the movement of an angel wing. It moved in and out, up and down as though it were tracing the individual fibers of each feather as they moved through the air. As it got close to the angel's 'body', the song got louder, and more consuming. It was such beautiful sound, dear Reader; words cannot even begin to describe.

"Now then, dear one, we have to carefully observe what you are ignoring: life. You see, you are allowing your existence to be consumed by the elements of physicality, which have no bearing on who you are. Until you embrace your essence—the very core of who you are—your physicality will continue to decline and you will transition to a different existence in the worst of circumstances. This is not predestined, dear one. It is, however, your choice," she said stoically.

I felt as though she were directly above me, almost as though we were facing one another with our bodies in perfect alignment. When she finished talking, she touched—or maybe kissed—my forehead. As soon as she did, she was gone.

My essence. She was right, dear Reader. I focused on everything going wrong with me physically and forgot who I was. I did all I could to settle my mind, and I slept.

I awoke to find Carlos measuring my bed and scribbling something feverishly on a pad of paper.

"Señor Olaf, I'm sorry I woke you. I won't be too much longer," he said.

"It's okay, Carlos. Do you have any ideas?" I asked hopefully.

"Yes! I just needed proper measurements. I needed to see how big the heart machine was. I will have this done before dinner. I have help," he said and smiled.

"Thank you, Carlos," I said, feeling overcome with sentimentality.

"No thanks necessary, Señor Olaf. None at all," he responded. "We'll be back tonight."

I found this to be incredible, but I didn't focus on the details. I instead focused on how I was thinking. A myriad of medical personnel came into my room that day. I evenly answered their questions and allowed them to poke and prod at me. I asked for water any time I had company, and carefully measured each thought in my mind. I was doing an all-day meditation, if you will.

By the time Carlos returned that night, I was relaxed and my heart was a tiny bit more stable.

"This is miraculous, Olaf. Though the change is small, it's the first tick up we have seen. This is a good thing," Dr. Gee said.

"You listened, my friend. Good," Akamu said reassuringly.

"So here is the plan, Olaf. We are going to move you home as a test for a couple days. A small army is already there. We feel this will be a good litmus test for Carlos' platform. Honestly, it is the most genius creation I have seen in my life," Dr. Glaush said.

"It will allow me to see if changes are needed for the trip to Hawaii. I will be with you the whole way, Señor Olaf," Carlos said warmly.

"Thank you, Carlos. I cannot say this enough. You are giving me a shot, and that's what I need."

"Señor Olaf, your thanks are not necessary. You gave our entire familia a chance, and most of all, hope. This is but a drop in the ocean in comparison," he smiled.

Well dear Reader, Carlos' platform worked perfectly. I moved less than one-one hundredth of a millimeter the whole trip. My heart machine didn't move at all. To say this was a success is putting it mildly.

It was so nice to be home. It didn't look much like home, but it sure felt like it out on my deck. The only thing truly amiss was Doc not being with me, and this was a detail I couldn't help but focus on. Doc was glued to my side at all times. That pup saved my life; it wasn't natural for him to be missing in this latest challenge to my health. Being on the deck without him was the one detail weighing on me.

"Dr. Glaush, Doc is okay, right?" I asked while he was checking my heart wires as I watched the Intracoastal.

"Of course, Olaf. Why do you ask?" he responded reassuringly.

"It's just strange that he wasn't with me in the hospital. Being out here... It just doesn't feel right. It's just so strange to not see the rest of my family too. They're okay, right?" I asked emotionally.

"Olaf, listen to me. You *died*. You were not expected to survive the night the day you woke up. We've been taking things in five-minute chunks since you regained consciousness after the last crash. I have to be honest, son… this is *truly* a last-ditch effort. We cannot completely heal you medically because we don't know where your secondary problems are. We need *you* in cases like this. See, we can scan every square inch of your insides and body, trace every path in your body. Based on the sum of those readings, you should not be alive," Dr. Glaush began.

"Think about this, son," he continued, "that needle was two percent fast-acting sedative, and ninety-eight percent lethal injection drugs. Your organs shut down. Your brain stopped controlling your bodily functions. We did everything we could to give you a chance, and that basically fileted your heart muscles. I don't want you to lose hope, because once again you are surviving when none of us can explain how. It's time we tap into the unexplainable portions of what you have shown us and see what happens. I will be by your side as long as you need me to be, Olaf. Just please hear me when I say, you and Akamu are dictating the path forward. Medically, we are happily playing second chair. Let's consider all of this in regard to Annie and everyone who should be here. She couldn't watch you die, Olaf. Your wife and children have Vickery and his wife, your Mom, the Glassburé clan and that angel thing keeping them whole. But, all of that can't take away the hurt in the third dimension."

"I understand," I said. Thing is, something wasn't right. I knew this, dear Reader. I may have been three quarters dead, but something didn't add up.

We stayed at the house for three days. In that time, I improved another two percent. The decision—as painful as it was— was made to travel to my home in Hawaii. Rupert insisted on being the pilot to carry me there, so he flew to South Carolina two days after the decision was made, and was ready for our trip west.

"Olaf, it is so nice to see you," he said kindly. "I promise you, I am getting you to your family. There is no chance you are not kissing your wife and babies tonight."

"Thank you, Rupert. I have every confidence in you. I just can't believe you came all this…" I began.

"I would have flown to the end of the Earth for you, child," he said, interrupting me.

I was deeply touched, but didn't have an opportunity to respond. As soon as he said this, I was carefully loaded into the aircraft. The always-shirtless Michael was in the plane, along with the small army from my house.

That flight was among the strangest ever. Knowing the lot of people on the aircraft did not expect me to survive made the trip part fun, part sadistic. The fun was seeing the look in everyone's eyes when I responded to them. The sadistic was seeing them walk away with a slight disappointment. I knew I was a medical anomaly, but I was still conscious and had a sharp mind seeing all of it. I did all I could to just breathe deeply and keep my mind clear.

The landing was incredible, dear Reader. I barely felt us touch the runway, or slow down. Rupert was a magician with that aircraft!

I was carefully unloaded, and a kind Hawaiian woman put a lei around my neck prior to me being loaded into a van.

"Welcome home, Mr. Waniglia," she said and smiled genuinely.

I smiled, but found no words. I had a notably strange feeling, dear Reader. I really wasn't sure why, truth be told. I was still a medical anomaly in terms of being alive, and this feeling countered the main reason for being in Hawaii in the first place: the "Dolby magic" as Akamu called it. I internalized that this was a last chance for me, and it was a hail mary at best.

In the van were two familiar faces: Stan and Joe. Both looked sad, but tried to keep things light.

"It is so good to see you again, Olaf," Stan said. "You have once again become the subject of a legend."

"Yeah. Olaf—the guy who could not be killed. You okay, bro?" Joe asked painfully.

"I ain't dead you two. Knock off the faces," I responded angrily. I hadn't seen myself in a mirror, so I may have looked like death, but I needed no one telling me so, verbally or otherwise.

The rest of the van ride was quiet. Carlos intensely watched his platform, and Dr. Gee intensely studied my heart monitor.

We arrived at the Dolby house, and I was surprised to find Akamu and his assistant as the only people in the house. There was no sign of anyone in the village either.

"What the hell?" I began angrily.

"Ah ah, Olaf. We have work to do," Akamu said impatiently.

"No, Akamu. I haven't seen my family, my friends, or my dog since I woke up. I need to know where they are, and why the hell they have been missing from my life. I've not so much as had a *phone call* with anyone. NO ONE, AKAMU!" I shouted. As I did, the machines I was connected to started to furiously beep.

"Olaf, I will tell you, but you need to relax. You're going to die if you don't and there is nothing more anyone can do for you. Your heart is too weak. In this agitated state, you are at risk. Stop now, or your life ends. It's that simple, my friend. Make your choice," Akamu responded with a coarseness in his voice that I didn't hear often.

"Do you blame me? God alive, Akamu—it's this Hawaii thing all over again. I land and everyone *disappears*. Thing is, this time it started back in South Carolina! I don't understand. If this is the existence I am saddled with, where everyone abandons me when I need them the most, what the hell do I have to live for? Answer me that, colleague. We have discussed hundreds of cases like mine, and there is one constant. You know as well as I do, I am at that constant. So go ahead, Akamu. Tell me some line that keeps me in this horseshit life that keeps getting taken from me. Say something profound that makes me want to live. Say something… or I swear on what's left of my life, I'm done," I pontificated as tears streamed down my face. I was at a crossroads, dear Reader. I had not one shred of desire left. I was hurt, I was dying, and I had no answers.

"You're right, my friend. You're the constant. What makes you special is your ability to survive this. I know you're angry. I know you're hurt. I know you're confused. Here's what I will tell you. Everyone is close, and have been close. They're not here because they don't want to watch you die. None of them are strong enough. Your mother is faced with losing her son. Your wife is faced with losing her husband. Your children are faced with losing their father. Your friends are faced with losing the rock keeping them steady. In many ways, they feel you are already gone, and it is too painful for them to see you this way," Akamu said carefully.

"What you don't know is the shockwave this sent through the collective." He continued, "You were assaulted once again, and evil had its way. This time, though, each of the people I mentioned *felt* you die. They mourned you, and let you go. They might say otherwise, but this is the truth. Your father is barely able to function, Olaf. Your mother and Annie are shells of themselves. Your children are just sad, and miss you. Addison is furious with her mother, and Louis is searching for answers in his own way. Vickery and Olivia have been instrumental in keeping everyone in your tribe even. They are hurting too, but they are living their charge as stewards of your family. Everyone else is in that bucket too. Amazing couple."

He took a deep breath. "This was different from the shooting, my friend. You were able to be put in a protective coma to heal. Too much of you was damaged to go that route this time. Your brain was damaged in such a way that your ability was compromised, and your ability to receive help from the abundance of healing energy beyond this dimension was lost. This is what I am hoping to work on today. Can we?"

I allowed what I had just learned to soak into my soul. I allowed these truths to find their way into my mechanically assisted heart. Then, in complete despair, I closed my eyes. My eyelids pushed out waterfalls of tears on each side. I felt them travel down the side of my face and disappear. My breath slowed, and I retreated into what was left of my mind.

Ebbs and Flows

A familiar darkness consumed me. I did not feel myself breathing, and my heart did not beat. In the distance, I heard voices. They were saying something in unison, but I could not understand them. I was at peace, and did not do anything but hear those voices. I no longer felt my body. Gone was the pulse of my mechanical heart. In its place was stillness, a comforting, enveloping void. Gone were my tears and my sorrow.

The voices grew louder. They were not speaking English. There was a rhythm to what they were saying. I noticed this, but did not judge it.

"May I join you?" a voice asked softly.

I did not respond as I had no means of doing so. I, again, simply accepted this without judgement.

"Olaf, you are not lost. I am your friend. Please, speak to me. I am Iokua, and I am here to help you. Your heart is broken, my dear friend, but you are not. Please, Olaf, try," the voice said passionately.

I did not respond. I did not care to.

"Olaf, if you will not speak with me, you will listen. You will hear those who love you. Perhaps then you will be inclined to respond," the voice said defiantly.

I heard a chant being repeated with brief breaks between each reprise. I did not pay attention to the number of repetitions.

"Ua ola loko i ke aloha. Ua ola loko i ke aloha. Ua ola loko i ke aloha," the voices chanted.

"Do you hear them, Olaf?" Iokua asked suggestively.

I remained still.

"They are saying this to you, Olaf. 'Love gives life within.' You are *loved*, Olaf. You are not lost. We will continue reminding you of this, and when you are ready, I will be here," Iokua said kindly.

The chanting continued, and I remained still. The darkness remained, but my comforting silence was disturbed by the voices.

"I know you hear me, Olaf. Speak to me please," Iokua asked with more impetus than before.

Leave me alone please, I thought.

"Ah. There you are. Why do you want to be alone?" he asked.

I am alone. I am at peace, I thought.

"You are not alone, and you are not at peace, my friend. Your heart is broken, and you have surrendered. This is not peace, Olaf," Iokua said forcefully.

All have let me go. My body has failed. I have found peace. Please leave me alone, I thought.

"Your body has not failed. There are people keeping your body alive right now, but it's just a bag of bones. No one has let you go. They have mourned you, but they have not let you go. My friend, this is your choice. You are at a door. If you go through it, you cannot come back. We would have to let you go if you make this choice. Please Olaf, carefully consider what I am saying," he implored.

I didn't consider anything, dear Reader. I didn't have time to I heard another familiar voice almost immediately after Iokua stopped speaking.

"I have won, clown. I ate your morbid soul. I broke you, clown. Now suffer, knowing you are lost, and I have taken everything from you," the evil voice from the psych ward growled sadistically.

Before I could react to this, I felt as though I was being pulled feet-first and my speed was increasing. I felt myself begin to panic. I had no idea what was happening, but if I coupled what I just heard with what I was experiencing, this was nothing good.

I felt a sharp pain in my chest that I could have attributed to a stabbing. I then felt a second sharp pain in my side. Then, a third in my head. I had no idea what was happening, dear Reader. I was still in darkness and was being pulled feet-first at a seemingly unbelievable rate of speed. I hurt, and focused on the pain, trying to understand it.

In a flurry of activity, I gasped for air as I started to hear beeping. My chest, side, and head throbbed as though they were bleeding. The pulling motion stopped suddenly, and I heard shouting. My eyes flew open as I gasped for another breath. I was nowhere I recognized. I was with people I had never seen before. They were yelling both at me and each other. I couldn't understand what they were saying, and the pain I felt was getting worse.

"Mr. Waniglia, can you hear me?" a man to my left yelled mere centimeters from my face.

I recoiled and nodded. More yelling ensued. I could see six people surrounding me.

"Where am…" I began.

"DON'T TALK," the man shouted.

A woman to my right was looking at me calmly. She was an oddity here, completely unlike the others. She smiled shyly and looked down.

The man to my left again got uncomfortably close to my face and yelled, "Can you hear me?"

I wanted to push him away, but I could not move my arms. So, I looked him squarely in the eye and yelled, "YES!"

All activity around me stopped. The people in the room seemed to be dismayed with my response, and one by one, left me. The woman was last to leave, and said not one word. I was alone, again, and could not discern where I was. The walls were yellow and equipment was everywhere. I still had throbbing pain in my chest, side, and head, but couldn't move my head to see why. I was either restrained or paralyzed; I could do little but breathe and move my eyes.

I laid where I was for what I determined to be two days. I based this on light I could see in a distant window, across a hallway from where I was. Best I could tell, I was in a room in the middle of a building.

At the start of the third day, early in the morning, I awoke to hear what sounded like a fight. People were shouting and glass was breaking. Heavy objects seemed to be falling down. The commotion drew closer to me. I could not move, and I could not see anything.

I heard shouting, and more glass breaking. I heard running. There were more than two people running. I wasn't sure if they were the ones shouting.

They got close. I got nervous.

"He's in there! He's in there!" I heard, followed by more rushed footsteps and yelling in the background.

Remember the cast of characters from Joe's gym who accompanied me to Rupert's house the first time I returned to Hawaii, dear Reader? In particular, do you remember the massive, but gentle, Haku?

A sweaty, bloody Haku ran into my room. He was shirtless, and had wrapped his knuckles with what looked like medical tape. His hands and chest were bloody.

"We're here, Olaf. All of us. And, some military dudes with guns. They're letting us break stuff," he said, breathing hard.

"Where am I, Haku? What happened?" I asked, completely confused.

"In a minute, Olaf. I gotta make sure the others know you're here. Be right back," he said and ran away.

As soon as he left, the man who had yelled at me when I first woke up ran back to my side and did something that amplified the pain in my chest to a blinding level. I yelled out; the pain I felt was unlike anything I had experienced to that point in my life. I couldn't see what happened. I just felt absurd and unfathomable amounts of pain.

"Get away from him sir!" a voice yelled.

"Or what?" the man coarsely retorted.

"You die," the voice said calmly. It was closer, but I couldn't see anything.

"I die? Try again," the man arrogantly yelled and again did something to make my chest intensely burn.

I heard two loud booms and the man fell backward.

"Gave 'im a chance. Oh well. Mr. Waniglia, we'll have you out of here shortly," the voice said, trailing off. The person had to be walking away.

I was immensely confused and in excruciating pain. My chest felt like it had burning swords twisting my rib cage apart. I was losing consciousness; the pain was worse than being shot, dear Reader!

Joe ran to my side.

"Olaf! Buddy, stay with me. Doc is close. He's real close. Stay with me bud," he demanded.

"My chest, Joe. My chest," I gasped.

Dr. Glaush appeared above me.

"Oh, thank God. What did they... OH MY GOD! WE HAVE TO GET OLAF TO AN ER NOW!" he yelled. "Joe, we need to move all of this equipment when we move Olaf. Call your guys. We need them all."

"I'm on it doc. GUYS!" Joe yelled and ran off.

"What..." I gasped.

"Son, please. Don't talk. Save your energy," Dr. Glaush pleaded. Tears were falling along his nose.

I saw a rush of people from the gym all around me. One guy in camouflage was with them. Dr. Glaush instructed them, and they began to move me out of the room with all of the equipment. Haku looked down at me and forced a smile.

As I was moved through the building, I saw more people in camouflage and a bunch of destruction. It looked like a freight train had mauled a medical building.

"You all are done. Go home and await judgment," one of the camouflage people said in a deep, booming voice to a lady in a pantsuit. She cried and nodded.

I was rushed into the back of a van. All of the equipment I was attached to was held in place by two people each. I drifted in and out of consciousness. Every time my eyes closed, everyone in the van yelled at me. I would startle, the pain in my chest intensifying, and the difficulty breathing started all over again.

"Relax, Olaf. Please try to breathe easy. I know this is so hard on you," Dr. Glaush said kindly. His face reflected a reality I still was in the dark about. I just knew I felt awful and none of this felt right.

The van stopped very gradually, and I was unloaded in front of a large building. Several doctors rushed out and ran next to me as I was pushed inside.

"You've had a rough few days, sir. We will take good care of you, Mr. Waniglia," one doctor said.

"You're in their hands now, son. I have to step away... I'm so sorry," Dr. Glaush said apologetically. I could tell he was crying, and despite the pain I was in, I felt his emotion as clearly as though they were my own tears.

"You got this, kid. We are all praying for you," Joe said sentimentally.

"Find peace, Olaf, any way you can," Haku said kindly.

I was then rushed into a room with a ton of lights, a mask was placed over my face, and I fell back into unconsciousness.

****

"Daddy, open your eyes."

"Daddy."

"It's time to open your peepers. Now, Daddy."

I grunted a little bit.

"I didn't ask you to make noise. I told you to open your eyes. Do it now, Daddy. It's time."

I grunted again, this time a little louder.

I felt pressure on my left hand, and weight on my legs.

"Daddy, what did I just say? I said no noise. Open your eyes."

I considered this for a moment and attempted to blink my eyes open. After several attempts, I was successful. This took a good ninety seconds or so. The room was dark. I was connected to several machines. My pain was gone, but I was incredibly weak. I had tubes going down my throat and an oxygen mask covering my face. I did not recognize the room. My daughter was holding my hand, smiling. A dog I did not recognize was laying between my legs.

"Good job, Daddy! Don't try to talk. Just listen. Okay?" Addie asked softly.

I nodded.

"First thing, you are in a hospital in Hawaii. You've been here for two weeks. Second thing, that is Doc's son by your legs. We named him Angel. He's about nine weeks old. He's been with you since you got here," she said and paused for a couple seconds.

"I'll let Akkie tell you the story, okay? I cry when I tell it," she said and squeezed my hand. Akkie was her nickname for Akamu.

Tears found their way down to my chest. Addie saw this and hugged my belly. Angel saw this and woofed—just like Doc.

"I'm just so glad you're alive, Daddy," she said through a muffled voice.

A couple moments later, Father led Akamu into my room.

"Well now! Welcome to the land of the living, Olaf! I see you've met our friend Angel. He's a mighty special pup, Olaf. He's Doc's son. Did Addie tell you that? How are you feeling?" Akamu asked happily.

I nodded with heavy eyes.

"Forgive me, Olaf. I know you cannot speak. Addison Grace, how is your father?" he asked pointedly.

"He's alive and sad, Akkie," she said, still buried in my belly.

"I'll take both, and tell you a wonderful story! You see, though part of this story is sad, the rest is *hopeful*. It is this hopeful part I choose to look at most closely. Olaf, the second day you were at the hospital back East, you had a really rough day. It was a day most of us felt you leave. This feeling extended to ol' Doc, and he passed on the deck. The next day, Addison found Angel sitting in the exact same spot on that deck where Doc had passed. He was watching manatees swim by, just like his pop used to do. A search effort was conducted for Angel's owner, but no one had ever seen him before. The pound and Animal Protection League was checked, but there were no missing puppies. Annie, with a heavy heart, took little Angel to the vet, where in a spirit of curiosity, a sample of his blood was compared to Doc's. You're never going to believe this, Olaf. Doc's DNA was practically a *copy* of this little critter. His mother had to have been a stray, but no one has seen her. This is nuts because she would have been close to Doc's size based on Angel's DNA! And, she would have had to rear him as a wee pup or he would have certainly died," Akamu said animatedly.

He continued, "Here's where hope is most evident. Angel was placed near you and has not taken his eyes off you even for a second. Addison placed him on your bed at Louis' urging, and he has been watching over you like a hawk, my friend. I am so very sorry Doc has passed, Olaf. He is still caring for you though, through his son. I knew you'd be okay the first time Angel looked at you. He knows what he is here to do—to protect you, just like Doc. You may shed tears for your dear lost pup, of course, but know beyond a shadow of a doubt, you have a miracle staring at you right now."

"It's true, son. That little dog is doing exactly what Doc did the first time you were hospitalized. It's tragic to have lost Doc, but he was old and just like Akamu said, seemed to have passed when we all felt you had, um... had..." Father said, struggling to find words.

"Died, Papa. We thought Daddy died," Addie said into my belly.

I struggled, but managed to put my right hand on Addie's back. I had little strength; this truly exhausted me.

A doctor entered the room, looking down. He gave Angel a pat and grabbed my chart.

"Mr. Waniglia, it is a pleasure. I know you cannot speak, so let me give you as much of an update as I can. When you arrived, you were in full cardiac arrest. The former facility had callously begun disconnecting your cardiac appliance, and your heart was not functioning when you arrived as it had been badly damaged. As a result, you have a new heart," he began, flipping pages on my chart.

He then looked toward Akamu and continued, "This gentleman here has given a cursory history of it, but I'm not sure how... In addition, we have been able to repair damage done to your liver, stomach, brain, and lungs. Those items were not replaced, of course, but repaired surgically. To this point, we are extremely happy with your progress. This said, if you remain conscious for the next four hours, and sleep and wake on your own tomorrow, we can disconnect some of this twisted mess and enable you to speak. In the interim, there are many people who wish to see you. Are you agreeable to a limited number of people coming to see you today? I will solely permit this for two hours. My team needs to run tests for an hour, and you should have an hour to yourself. The dog can stay as he has proven himself to be an asset. Indeed, an angel *is* Angel. Give me a blink if you are good with the plan," the doctor said happily.

I blinked.

"Thank you, Mr. Waniglia. I am also to pass along a thank you from my aunt, Kakalina Kalani. You treated her last year, and she told me how much you have done for her. She passes on her best to you and your family," he said with a smile. "I will send in your first visitors. Um, no, your second visitors. I see your daughter remains attached to you. I'll send them in."

"Your heart has a story, Olaf. A *great* story. I'll tell it to you sometime," Akamu said with a grin.

Lou then ran in and went straight to my right side.

"Hey Dad! How you feeling?" he asked excitedly.

"He can't talk, stupid," Addie said from my belly.

I nodded toward Lou and attempted to smile, but realized my respirator completely covered my mouth.

"Don't move, Dad. I get it. Isn't Angel amazing?" he asked excitedly and pet Angel.

I nodded.

Annie walked in and came to stand next to my head.

"Please tell me you are okay, babe," she said and glared into my eyes.

I nodded and again started to cry.

"No more tears, babe. Between the three of us, we have leaked so much from our faces over the past couple months the world has three new lakes," she smiled and wiped my face.

"So, my husband was murdered, and then somehow came back, and then was murdered again. This is fun, Olaf. So, so fun. Has anyone told you why those asses at the other place tried to kill you and invoked the anger of the US Special Forces?" Annie asked intently.

She continued, "Okay dead husband, it goes like this... they called you a witch and intended to kill you slowly to appease some god or goddess or something. You crashed at the house, and the team there called an ambulance, thinking you would be brought here. Instead, they went to that awful place and told no one where you were. A search started immediately and Iokua—bless him—found out where you were, doing some kind of dead people juju. He calls Joe, who calls his buddy in the Army, and they agree to go in and get you—Joe and these commandos. Joe's buddy classified you as being kidnapped and labeled the whole thing as domestic terrorism with the government. In my book, that just gave them free reign to shoot people and break stuff, but that's just my opinion. Anyway, the guy there was doing something to your heart machine when a commando goes and shoots him in the head twice, a 'double tapper' as he called it. That place was *destroyed*, Olaf. I think Joe and your pals from the gym had a blast. They are still talking about it. Your heart was cooked and failing, so you have a new one. The docs aren't sure you can talk *or* reason yet, so I can't wait to see if blinking and crying is all I get forever more."

"Mommy! Behave! Daddy's fine!" Addie yelled from my belly.

"Peanut, your father may be mute for all you know," Annie dismissed.

"No, Mother. He made noise when I woke him up," Addie said, looking squarely at her mother.

"Were your father not as fragile as he is presently, I would completely destroy you, child. You woke your dad up? Why have you done such a thing?"

"The doctor told me to. You were there. You could have, but weenied out. So, I did it. *Remember?*" Addie asked, glaring through squinted eyes.

"Maybe so, now that you mention it. Anyway... Olaf, the doctors seem to think you are much better. Can you tell if you are? If so, blink," Annie said and leaned in.

I blinked.

"So, no pain in your chest?" she implored.

I blinked.

"The docs said if you didn't hurt, the new 'blessed' heart is working the way it should. No pain?" she asked again, every bit the investigator.

I blinked.

"Okay. Next, your head. Any headaches? Blink twice if yes, okay?" she clarified.

I softly chuckled and blinked. Just once, dear Reader.

"Dreams. First, are you dreaming?"

I blinked twice.

"Mommy, he just woke up today. He probably hasn't had a chance to dream," Lou said studiously.

"You're right, my son. Thanks, smarty-pants," Annie smiled. Annie refocused her eyes into mine. "Do you have any pain you feel right now, babe?"

I blinked twice. Angel seemed to be picking up on the dialogue and moved closer to my torso after I blinked.

"Looks like the pup is making his presence known. I'm so sorry, Olaf. Losing Doc just about ripped the heart out of my chest. I was so sad. I mean, like, not able to function sad. Then, this little critter shows up and turns out to be Doc's kid, and all of a sudden, I had a reason to believe. I knew you'd be okay. Lou was the one who knew how to make this happen, though. Tiny Angel couldn't see your face while he was on the ground when you finally got here. Lou told Addie to put him up on the bed and the game changed. He's got you, babe. He's barely three months old at this point, or at least that's what the vet thinks. Just look at him, Olaf! He's watching your eyes, he's listening to you breathe. He's got you, and his daddy has to have something to do with it all," Annie said sentimentally and kissed my cheek.

She continued, "I really thought you were gone, babe. We all—the kids, me, our parents, Joe, Nol, Coach—felt you go. I didn't know what to think when Daddy called me the day he found you conscious. I mean, seriously Olaf, the doctors—independent, non-related doctors—gave you a two percent chance at recovery. Our fathers gave you a *zero* percent chance at recovery. Is our singing lady the one we should thank for you being here? Did you spend all kinds of time with her and other dead people?"

I blinked twice.

"Wait… What? Were you with any of the dead people you've seen in the past several years?"

I blinked twice.

"Mommy, remember? The singing lady told me she only talked to Daddy once, and she knew he couldn't see her," Addie interjected.

"Yeah okay, but then how is your father alive, Peanut? Solve *that* riddle for me," Annie retorted sarcastically.

"He's my Daddy. *That's* how, Mother," Addie jabbed.

Almost as if on cue, a nurse came into the room, pet Angel, and looked over both my chart and two of the machines I was connected to.

"This is such a beautiful family. You are truly blessed, all of you. Mr. Waniglia, any pain? Blink once if yes, two if no," the nurse asked.

I blinked twice.

"Excellent. Are you ready for a couple more visitors?"

I blinked once.

"I'll send them in," she said and left my room.

The parade that followed included Mother, Mrs. Glaush, Nol, Sadie, Joe, Stan, most of the members at Joe's, and Iokua at specific intervals.

"Thanks for helping me find you, my friend," Iokua said warmly.

I found myself exhausted after all the visitors. This unfortunately complicated the testing the doctors wanted to do, because I could hardly remain awake through the procedures. Regardless, they were ultimately able to get everything done despite my droopiness. As promised, after the testing was complete, I had time to myself. The quiet was comforting, and my eyelids sure appreciated the rest. Incessant blinking is not the most fun thing to do, dear Reader.

I don't believe I was awake for much of that hour. I woke up the next morning to find Angel at my side, watching me unnaturally closely. When he saw my eyes open, he disappeared. A short time later, my doctor returned with Angel happily trotting behind him.

"Our canine friend here is quite something, Mr. Waniglia. I mentioned yesterday I wanted to catch you when you woke up, and apparently, this little guy understood me. You slept and woke on your own, correct?" he asked, putting Angel back on my bed. He immediately went back to his spot by my legs and laid down facing me.

I blinked.

"Excellent. This morning, we are going to begin slowly disconnecting your appliances. We have to do this in a specific order, Mr. Waniglia. So, one machine will be decommissioned, and you will be watched for about an hour in a couple cases—two to three in others. When your body proves that it is able to function without assistance over that time, another machine will be disconnected. We're going to start with the oxygen. Your lungs were in interesting shape when you got here, so this is your first test. I'm keeping your visitors limited today. It was obvious that yesterday was hard on you. For sure, your wife and children will be with you most of the day," he said and smiled.

Two nurses walked in, pet Angel, and began disconnecting my oxygen mask. It differed from a conventional mask in a couple ways. It wasn't a respirator, per se, but it was sending pulses of air at specific times. The mask itself went in my nose and covered my mouth. One nurse disconnected clasps that held the mask in place and carefully removed it. This effectively meant I no longer needed air to be artificially pumped into my body. The other nurse then removed the strap that wrapped around my head. Both nurses were both so precise, yet incredibly delicate in their movement, smiling the whole time. It was quite something, dear Reader.

When the mask was first removed, I immediately had trouble breathing.

"Just relax, Mr. Waniglia. Your body needs to re-learn how to do this for itself. Give yourself a minute to adjust. Try not to panic," my doctor said.

I did, and gradually, I found it easier to breathe. My lungs definitely felt different, in a sense. Previously, I couldn't have told you my lungs were even there; I just breathed. Now, I felt them with each breath in and each breath out. It was quite an unusual feeling, dear Reader.

"That's right, Mr. Waniglia. I'm not going to ask you to speak just yet. Please sip water for the next twenty minutes or so. Your feeding tube should not interfere, but if it does, please notify the nurses," he said kindly.

I nodded and leaned forward to get a drink. That water felt so good going down my throat, dear Reader. I am quite confident I have never before cherished a simple sip of water nearly as much.

Angel had been watching the whole show and took interest in my drinking. I got to thinking maybe he was thirsty, so I grabbed my jug of water and a Styrofoam cup someone had left the day prior. I filled the cup three-quarters of the way, making sure there was at least one ice cube in the cup. I picked up the cup and snapped my fingers. Angel carefully made his way next to me, and I pet him for the first time. Like Doc, there was something undeniably special about him; I could see it in his eyes. I was rewarded with a thank you lick, and then like a hawk, he surgically removed the ice cube and returned to his spot by my legs and shredded it. His tiny tail wagged furiously back and forth during this destruction.

Yep, that's Doc's kid alright, I thought.

I could not believe my sidekick was gone, dear Reader. Angel was indeed a miracle in the way he appeared, and certainly in the way he was watching over me. Regardless, he wasn't Doc. Maybe in time he would be just as special, but our bond was just forming. I knew this creature was in my life for a reason, and if it was in any way due to Doc, I owed it to him to pour my energy into our connection.

Once the ice cube shards had either been ingested or melted, I again snapped, and Angel walked over to me. I offered him a drink out of the cup, and he did a distinctly Doc move. He took two sips, then dunked his whole muzzle into the water. When he pulled his head up, water poured from his jowls both into the cup and all over me. I chuckled and gave him a pat.

He laid back down next to me and put his head on my thigh. I put the cup down and slowly dragged my hand down his silken coat, from head to tiny tail. His eyes drew heavy, and he soon fell asleep. He snored ever so gently, and if you've ever witnessed a puppy snore, dear Reader, you know just how much fun it was to watch the little guy sleep.

He actually slept so soundly, he didn't wake up for my next nurse review. This prompted the medical staff to speculate that he hadn't slept hardly at all during his time at the hospital. So, a blanket was fetched, and the critter was tucked in. This apparently deepened his slumber, as he did not wake up when Annie and the kids arrived.

"It seems our soldier here needed a rest, babe," Annie said smiling.

"He is the cutest thing I've ever seen, Daddy," Addie said.

"Wait until you hear 'im snore," I said through a whispery, gravelly voice.

"You're not mute! Peanut, you win! I had my doubts, babe. How are you?" Annie asked intently.

"Mommy, I told you he was fine," Addie flatly retorted.

"I'm getting there, love. My lungs feel weird, but I can breathe and drink water. I guess they are disconnecting more today if I can handle it, but I don't know what else they plan to do," I said with my scratchy voice.

In the middle of my response, my doctor walked in.

"You're talking, Mr. Waniglia! This is wonderful! How are your lungs feeling?" he asked.

"Okay, but it feels strange to breathe. I can actually feel my lungs when I breathe."

"This is normal, honestly. We did a fair amount of work on them to correct the issues we saw. I'd imagine you will continue to feel this way for a few days. Beyond that, you should no longer feel the sensation. How do you feel about moving on to the next step in our process?" he asked as he pet the still-sleeping Angel. The little guy was dreaming about something; his ears and jowls were twitching like crazy!

"Yep! What's next?" I asked.

"Well, this is up to you. If you're up to it, the feeding tube *and* IV can go away. The sole item to consider here is this means you will need to become mobile within the next three days. Are you willing to do this?" he asked, furrowing his brow.

"You tell me. Is it smart? I'll be honest, doctor. I don't want to do anything to compromise my progress. If removing both is logical and risk is low, I'm willing to do it," I replied, admittedly nervous.

"Well, bear this in mind, we are monitoring you closely with every change. This change is one where monitoring will take place over the next two hours. After two hours, all of us will know where you stand. As it is, you are on track with my expectations. You should feel very good, Mr. Waniglia. Your body has accepted your heart. This was the biggest challenge you faced, and you met it," he said encouragingly.

"So, this means, essentially, you have no concerns about Olaf returning to a normal life, right doctor?" Annie asked.

"For the most part, yes, Mrs. Waniglia. We still have to get Mr. Waniglia up and moving before we truly know where he stands. I have every confidence, though, that he is on his way to being back to his old self," he replied.

"If you're comfortable with me moving forward with the two changes, I trust you."

"Excellent. I will send in the nurses," he confirmed.

"Can you even begin to imagine surviving what you have, babe? I mean, honestly, you've cheated death three times now. This last time… Babe, you were gone. I lost you. We all did. Then somehow, you were back. When you woke up in Charleston, I was already making funeral plans. Your mom and I cried so hard while we were trying to figure out how you'd want to be buried. We'd decided to have you and Doc buried next to each other somewhere near Grandpa when we got the call you were awake. Babe, that morning, you were being kept alive by machines and were less than an hour from having them turned off. Do you remember anything?" Annie asked, amid a constant battle with tears. Addie was crying too, and Lou simply bowed his head.

As if on cue, the nurses came into the room and saw the emotional carnage. Both smiled, and without a word, made their way to Annie and the children, hugging them tightly.

"You mustn't focus on the fact that this wonderful man is *not* dead. Your family means so much to many of us just because of what Mr. Waniglia has done for an incredible number of our family members and friends. Life is a gift. Focus on the gift of this moment together and believe in how special each one of you are!" one of the nurses pontificated happily.

"I agree. You see, we are sisters, Mr. Waniglia, and you saved her life not all that long ago. I don't focus on the how or the why. I simply cherish every word, every smile, every laugh, every moment we are still able to share. It so happens we are all going to witness the next step forward for this wonderful man. Shall we get you one more step closer to going home, Mr. Waniglia?" the other nurse said.

I gently grabbed the first nurse's hand and said, "I can't believe it. Anna?"

"Yes, Mr. Waniglia. It's me," she said, smiling brightly.

Anna was in this very hospital; her body was unresponsive. At the time, I diagnosed and assisted in treating her, she was over three-hundred pounds. The person I was looking at couldn't have been but a tiny bit over a hundred pounds soaking wet in a velour sweat suit four sizes too big.

"I couldn't wait to tell you who I was! I knew you wouldn't recognize me," she said happily.

The two then went about their work, removing my feeding tube and IV.

"You're going to be incredibly tired as your body adjusts to the change. Sip water often. You'll be on a gelatin and liquid diet with your first semi-solid food being soup tomorrow. We will be back every fifteen minutes for the next two hours. If you need us in between, please call. Any questions?" Anna asked kindly.

"No, and thank you for everything. I truly appreciate it," I said, my voice raspy from the feeding tube.

Both smiled and left the room.

"You treated that nurse? Do you remember her?" Annie asked.

"I did after I really looked at her face. She was easily over three-hundred pounds the last time I saw her. I cannot believe the change. But, Annie, to answer your earlier question, I had no major event when I woke up in Charleston. It wasn't like the shooting where I had this crazy sequence of events helping me heal. I just woke up and opened my eyes. I don't know how or why, but I'm glad I'm here. I have a question for you, though. How come you guys didn't come see me at all when I woke up?" I asked carefully.

"I couldn't watch you die again, Olaf," Annie began intensely. "I was there twice when your heart stopped. I had umpteen consultations with doctors forcing me to make impossible decisions. When you woke up, none of the doctors thought you would even survive the hour. Then, they didn't think you'd survive being transported even just out of the room. Then, there were the car and plane concerns. Somehow, you survived all of it."

Her tone softened and she continued, "The honest to God reason you're here is Akamu. He felt you had the best chance of survival with the energy of the islands. If you didn't survive, you and Doc were going to be buried at the house together, here. I still have his ashes, babe. I think it's your call where he will be buried. So, to sum it all up, that's why. Your daughter positively destroyed me verbally on a daily basis as a result. I am so completely and utterly disgusted with myself. I prayed that our absence wouldn't in any way hurt you. It's all on me, babe. I can't speak for anyone other than those in the room. We lost Doc, then we lost you, then we got you back, then we lost you, then we got Angel, and then we got you again. Here we are. I promise you, with the same love and devotion of our wedding vows, that I will not leave your side again. I was selfish, and you deserve better. I love you, husband, and I love our family. You are owed a better me, one who is there no matter what."

Annie grabbed a tissue and dabbed at her eyes. She then walked over and kissed me. "I'm not good at this, Olaf. I admit it. I'm getting better, and the next time someone tries to kill you, I'll be by your side from start to finish. Just please promise me something, okay? From now on, take your cane whenever you go somewhere unfamiliar. That would have been a game changer at the funny farm."

"Mommy, stop it," Addie pouted. "This isn't going to happen again."

"But if it does, Dad should have the killer cane. I agree," Lou stoutly responded.

"It's not a bad idea, y'all. Just hear me when I say this, I need range time if I'm carrying that thing. I would imagine my shooting acumen is anything but accurate at the moment. And, y'all have been through too much as it is. I owe it to you to not put myself in compromising situations," I said, losing my grip on my emotions. I knew all too well that I had put my family through too much in such a short amount of time. I made it my mission to not only recover from this, but to improve from what I was before. This was my goal, anyway.

By the end of that day, I only had heart monitors attached to me. Twelve hours later, I took my first steps, to the bathroom.

A day after that, I began using a walker. I had quite the entourage, dear Reader. The cutest member was Angel, who walked proudly beside me. He carried himself with his chest held high, steps solid. Three months old looked more like years, or lifetimes, of maturity wrapped in a tiny package. The other consistent members of this entourage of mine included Annie, the kids, Vickery and Olivia, any or all of my nursing staff, Susan, Joe, and my dear friend Stan, who had just celebrated his 77th birthday.

The walker was discarded after four days. Well, I should say I no longer used the walker. Addie carried it for me 'just in case' on every walk for a week.

Once walking was no longer an issue, I was transferred to the physical therapy department, who agreed to allow Joe to assist as often as he wanted. This occurred daily; he warmed me up with the Thai Chi fusion movements he introduced me to the first time I was in Hawaii. The goal was to do a stress test on my heart within two weeks.

Instead, one was done in three days, and somehow, I wasn't all too stressed. My new ticker was like a fine sports car, dear Reader. It took quite a beating and still purred like a content tiger licking a ribeye. It became obvious I needed a greater challenge, so I was handed over to Joe as long as a nurse was present throughout.

He put me through the paces for two solid days. My resting heart rate never rose above forty-two BPM from that point forward. I was evaluated for a week in the hospital afterward, with daily sessions at Joe's. I was released from the hospital after that week. Akamu insisted on doing a separate evaluation at the beach not far from our office.

"I think we're close to having you back, my friend. Thing is, I doubt you've heard a single voice since waking up. Am I right?" he asked intently, every bit the healer.

"That's true, Akamu. I hadn't realized that until now. Can you see what's wrong?" I asked, upset with this new wrinkle. With no *vox corporis*, my ability to help people was severely compromised.

"I think so, but something's different. Let's see what we find," he said playfully. I could tell he already knew something he wasn't saying.

"Olaf, please close your eyes and listen. Become the observer, my friend," he preached.

I did this, and to my surprise, I was standing with five additional individuals: three men and two women. They, along with Akamu, formed a half-circle. I was on the edge, next to Akamu.

"Olaf, we all share similar talents. My name is George. I can communicate with animals," the first man said.

"My name is Juanita. I can communicate with plants," one of the two women said with a thick English accent.

"I'm Henry, Olaf. I can communicate with our planet," the second man said happily. He had an accent similar to Juanita's, but definitely not the same.

"My name is Sarah. I can communicate with water. It's so nice to meet you finally!" the second woman said excitedly.

"Last, but not least, or so I hope anyway, people call me Po. I can communicate with the spirits of those who have passed, no matter when they lived. It's nice to meet you, Olaf," the final man said, sincerely. He too had an accent, but I couldn't place from where.

"Olaf, these are the people I told you about years ago. They each have helped me to heal you from the beginning. It's taken all of us, and this is the final step. After we do one more round, you should be back to normal. All, shall we begin?" Akamu asked intensely.

All nodded and bowed their heads. I was pulled into the center of the half circle and lifted off the ground. I could feel something like pulses of energy flowing through every part of my being. An odd, black, cloudlike substance wafted from every part of my body and drifted below me. I seemed to get lighter as this occurred and had no sensation otherwise. No one said a word during this process.

After maybe two minutes, I began to hear my singing lady. She sang the same beautiful song she always had. She never spoke; she just sang. As she did, the black cloud was ripped apart and folded into itself. It was violent to watch, dear Reader; I had no idea what that stuff was, but it was being destroyed.

When the singing lady's song finished, the air around me was clear. I was gently lowered, and the people in front of me each raised their heads and looked at me through weighty eyes.

"This has been quite a journey, Olaf. I am eternally grateful for this moment. It is truly a blessing to be a part of this. Thank you for allowing me to help," Po said emotionally.

"How do you feel, Olaf?" Sarah asked, wiping tears from her eyes.

"I feel wonderful! Thank you all for that! But, I can't escape the feeling that something's wrong?" I was extremely perplexed. It felt as though something bigger was at play.

"Olaf, this has been quite a process. We have worked tirelessly to get you here, but we are all now exhausted both physically and emotionally. For me, it goes deeper, though. That heart of yours has special meaning to me. It's my son's heart. He was murdered by someone who felt I was evil because of what I do. I am grateful he lives on as part of you," Sarah said, struggling through tears as she spoke.

"Oh my God, Sarah… I don't know what to say," I could not believe what I had just heard.

"I still see him, and Po has been wonderful for me and my husband. Please just know how special that heart is. I will be connected to you for the rest of your life as a result. Promise me you will come see us. We could use your talent and would love your cooking. We would love to hug your kids and your wife too. They are wonderful people," she said, gaining composure as she spoke.

"I think we just did it, Ak. All the nasty stuff is gone," George said to Akamu, who stood before us like a proud papa.

"We did. I could not be more proud of each of you. Your parents, grandparents, greats, all of your lineages would be incredibly proud of you all. Know this," Akamu praised.

"Where do y'all live?" I asked the group.

"Georgetown, Kentucky," Sarah answered.

"Bangor, Maine," George said.

"Johannesburg, South Africa," Henry responded.

"London, England," Juanita said.

"Perth, Australia," Po said, grinning.

"Thank you all so much for helping me! I cannot wait to meet each of you in person!" I was elated to feel as good as I did, but was still shaken by the revelation that my heart had once belonged to Sarah's son. This proved to me that being one who practices something counter to what people understand is often dangerous. My life had echoes of this, and it was terribly sad to know it had impacted one like me with the loss of a child.

"Trust us, Olaf, you will pay us back in spades. Your talent will help us more than you know," Henry responded sentimentally.

The rest of the group nodded in agreement.

"Thank you, all. We will be in touch soon. Be well, and be proud of yourselves!" Akamu beamed. As soon as his last word had left his mouth, he and I were standing alone on the beach. "Well my dear friend, I believe you to once again be whole. It took all of us, together, to fix you. Remember this. It may come in handy someday."

"I'd help any of those folks in a heartbeat, Akamu. Especially Sarah. I cannot fathom the loss she and her husband have endured," I lamented.

"Olaf, think about something for me. What is the difference between Sarah's experience and Annie's experience? Both suffered tremendously as a direct result of their, or their spouse's, abilities. In our own ways, each of us has been hurt, certainly some more than others, simply because of what we are able to do. The difference, though, is that we serve a greater purpose. In truth, the whole of humanity does. We just have a refined responsibility to those who seek us. This is true across the board. It matters not what each of us are able to do."

He wiped his brow and continued, "Sarah was the one who offered her son's heart to you without even a blink of hesitation. He hadn't been gone for even an hour when she did. She saw it as her responsibility. Annie, as time has gone, has accepted her role as your wife and what this means, good and bad. Po has a particularly interesting charge, as he is often asked to settle disputes between loved ones that were not resolved in life for one reason or another. George, Juanita, Sarah, and Henry each help the parts of our world few pay attention to, but in their way, are vitally important. The whole of life works together as one, Olaf. Sometimes one's loss is another's saving grace. I tend to believe you would not have survived a minute longer unless you had that heart. So, when you see her, hug Sarah tightly. Let her feel your heartbeat, then listen to her and her husband's truths. You will offer a tremendous benefit to all of the people who you just met."

"I... I didn't realize this, Akamu. Thank you. You've given me perspective I in no way had before," I responded, hugging him.

I led Akamu back to Rupert's house, where the rest of the family was getting ready for dinner. That night, I looked at everyone differently. I saw them more clearly, without needing to hear a single word out of their *vox corpora*. I hugged every person at least three times each that night, dear Reader. I felt that the more the heart Sarah's son gave me could feel loved, the better.

The next day, we returned to the Dolby house with Angel so he could run through the hallways. Instead, he stayed next to me. So, I ran through the hallways and he followed, with his tongue flapping the whole way. Yep, just like Doc.

Ah, Doc. A couple days later, I took his ashes to the pier close to where he had first smelled the Pacific air. Annie, Addie, Lou, and I stood there for a moment, sobbing. Angel seemed to understand and stood with his head bowed sadly. In the end, Doc was returned to a place I knew he loved. Dammit, dear Reader. I still miss the guy.

Our heavy hearts stayed with us until we returned to South Carolina later that day, but certainly did not last! We were met with quite the surprise when we got home, dear Reader. Sitting on the deck was a large dog, slightly emaciated, but a happy tail wagged wildly as we approached. Angel tore toward her and rubbed his head against her shoulders. She licked him like only a mother could. With no hesitation whatsoever, Annie opened the door, gave her a bath, gave her a cooked meal, prepared Doc's beds with fresh blankets, and welcomed Penelope into our family.

Starting the second we welcomed Penelope into our tribe, we deliberately and selfishly celebrated every aspect of our family. For two solid weeks, Annie, Addie, Lou, Penelope, Angel, and I sequestered ourselves at home, dear Reader. We had all of the expected members of our inner circle as visitors during that time, of course, but we did not leave our home. Best I can explain, we took every possible second of every day in those two weeks to heal, to laugh, to love—to be thankful—at home. I appreciated every moment I spent cooking. I took an extra two to three seconds from every hug. I felt the sunshine on my skin with a specific dedication to feeling it. I smiled at every living thing I saw in the Intracoastal as though each had helped me heal. Ultimately, in some way, I believe they did to this day.

As soon as the two-week sequester completed, we each took deep breaths and started our "normal" lives again. Annie returned in earnest to the farm, the kids returned to school, and I returned to my practice. It so happened that our two weeks aligned with the kids' spring break, so the damage to their schooling wasn't furthered by our deserved selfishness.

One of the first patients I put on my schedule was the Crawsnatch family. When I last saw them, they were embracing amid the chaos in the nut house. Their story unacceptably ended with all the violence that brought us to this point, and that simply was not right. We resumed our sessions, and they remained my clients for almost fifteen years. In that time, I heard the story from the nut house hundreds of times, experienced "ha-ha" time thousands of times, and had more conversations than I could count that made no sense whatsoever. I also saw a connection between them I've never found in two others. Please don't get me wrong, dear Reader; I've seen many people who adore one another. Jeb and Jolene had the very fabric of time and space pulling them together and wrapping their hearts in a common thread.

Sadly, Jolene got very sick when she was 36 years young and passed away as a result. Jeb then died at her funeral, holding her hand as she laid in her casket. They were buried together, where they belonged.

Their passing was a loss to be true, dear Reader. I learned more from those two people about love and perspective than anyone I have ever met—with the exception of my wife. Jeb and Jolene shared a connection so profound that it controlled their well-being. Their brains were irreparably damaged when they entered this world, but this didn't matter when they were together, dear Reader. Their connection was so deep—so special—it allowed their lives to function in a way that enriched their every moment. It allowed joy to flow unobstructed from one to the other and back again. All of this allowed me to see what love looked like in its purest form, and I am eternally grateful to Jeb and Jolene for that gift.

They may have been fit n' borned out a crawsnatch, but they were mighty special people.

Those like Me

We settled back into "normal" life when we got back home. Penelope was a welcome, calming influence on all of us. I wished like anything I knew the start of her story, but I knew the rest of it would be full of love, travel, and comfort with us and her pup. Knowing she had some sort of relationship with Doc was so special to me, and having Angel's mom in the house was a blessing to him too.

My mind turned to the people I had been introduced to during my final healing session in Hawaii, and I was determined to see as many of them in the next year as I possibly could—starting with Sarah and her husband. I talked to Annie, who understood my urge to see them. In turn, she thought the experience of traveling to different places would be good for the kids. It was May, and the kids were due to be out of school in mere days. The time of the year was right, but my schedule was a mess after being away for almost six weeks. Fanny was positively unbelievable in terms of scheduling gymnastics; she figured out a way, with Vickery's help with the dogs, to get us to Kentucky to see Sarah, and then to Maine to see George—for a week each. She did all of this without impacting a single appointment. I have no idea how she did it, dear Reader. She also figured out a way for me to see Juanita in London and visit all my clients in the area too—including Vickery's brother, Owen. This was timely, as he had just won several awards for his photography and had recently become engaged. The dear man took years to allay the guilt of finding someone new, but he did, and boy did he fall hard. I knew this would be fodder for a fun, but potentially challenging, session (or four).

We were going to be able to see Po in Perth at the very end of the kids' summer vacation, after leaving England. Then, we'd have a break until finally seeing Henry in Johannesburg during spring break of the next school year. Fanny also built in more time for me in Hawaii. As much as I didn't prefer to travel alone, I went for a week every month to help Akamu and as many families as I could while there. I saw the benefit from our work all around me when I was in the hospital, and was not willing—for a second—to let my support for that group drop whatsoever. And, Akamu was becoming much more frail in his older age. He could no longer travel to South Carolina for our shared practice. It took weeks for him to recover after my latest endeavor with death. I therefore forbade him from traveling east, which was seconded by Fanny, Gerard, and each of their children independently. We all agreed Akamu needed our combined attention to provide him the best care, and I took lead in that cause.

Our visit with Sarah and her husband, John, was a rollercoaster ride for my soul, dear Reader. Both welcomed us with open arms, but the pain I felt in them was almost overpowering. I can't imagine for a moment what meeting the man who possessed your child's heart might feel like, especially because that son was murdered. I was determined to help them any way I could, but I knew this one fact would not be easy for either to settle, potentially ever.

In our first session, Sarah and I began to unravel the layers of pain and guilt she carried, both subconsciously and consciously.

"Hello, Olaf. Thank you for coming here. Both Sarah and John are in such profound pain. You will be able to help them, but don't expect it all to resolve during your time here. They will help one another once you show them the path. One thing you must know before proceeding, Christopher's murderer could not handle what Sarah said to him. He completely lost his mind, not because of Sarah's ability, but because of her kindness. I hope this helps you," Sarah's *vox corporis* said sadly.

This hit me like two tons of concrete, dear Reader. I was determined to help Sarah. However, she was not willing to allow me to help her. In fact, John was exactly the same, but he had a layer of anger that hid his pain. Neither wanted to consciously feel better. So, my time focused on this detail. I knew that, without addressing this first, improvement was impossible.

"Sarah, can you tell me how you feel right now?" I asked, hoping to get her to open up.

"Empty. Honestly Olaf, I just don't know who I am anymore. Healing you after your horrible accident was everything to me. Not just because of Christopher's heart, but because of who you are to the rest of us. You are better, and I'm right back to the dark place I was in once he was killed," she answered.

"Can you tell me about your ability?" I asked in an effort to shift her mind to something else.

"I can communicate with water, Olaf. Typically, I do this with big bodies of water, but I also have been called in to certain municipalities who have issues with their water being unclean or tainted. Lastly, I can communicate with the water vapor in the air, or in the body. It gives me insights into how healthy our planet, or a person, is." Her tone had completely changed. It was as though a switch had been thrown in her personality.

"You are still using your ability, right?" I asked carefully. I knew this might be part of the problem.

"No, Olaf. I haven't since Christopher died. I just can't do this knowing it's why my son is gone," she said as tears careened down her cheeks.

"Sarah, your ability is not the reason your son was murdered. He was killed because the monster who did this couldn't accept what you said to him. Your ability and the cause for Christopher's murder are not parallel. You must be able to accept this truth, my friend. Y'all will not be able to get better unless you do," I said strongly.

She cried for a minute or so, then stared down at her hands.

"Hi," she said sadly. She then seemed to get a response that changed her. I saw a shocked look on her face, and knew she had just heard something important.

"I… I cannot believe…" she began.

"What happened, Sarah?" I interjected, hoping to hear her truth.

"My tears just told me that my hopelessness is hurting the world," she answered, her voice shaking.

"Nicely done, Olaf. Thank you," her *vox corporis* said sincerely.

The rest of that session focused on getting Sarah back to being comfortable with her ability and her responsibilities. It also was the first time I learned that my sweat, saliva, tears, and the rest of the water in my cells could communicate independently. Sarah's ability to communicate with water was fascinating, dear Reader. It's hard to imagine anyone could find her to be anything but genuine, even if they found her ability strange. If one really listened to her, deeply profound lessons could be learned. I learned more about the impact to my body—from both the shooting and the needle attack—than I ever thought possible, from a vastly different perspective. The way in which I was hurt was shown to me in such vivid detail that the scope of the injuries seemed more real to me in a sense. It was incredible, if not profound, dear Reader.

John's session wasn't nearly as easy, dear Reader. Christopher was John's pride and joy. They shared many of the same interests and were planning a trip together when Christopher was murdered. His anger, directed at the world and all of its inhabitants, hid a sorrow that had depth like the Mariana Trench. It was cold, dark, and full of pressure.

"Hello, Olaf. Christopher's murder has changed the way John looks at life. Until this changes, he won't be able to get better. Be careful. He's already dismissing you and not one word has been spoken," John's *vox corporis* said.

"John, thank you for allowing me to speak to you today. I know this isn't easy for you," I began, measuring my words down to the millimeter.

"You are able to do what, Olaf?" he asked sternly.

"I can hear a person's truths, John. I can also heal those who allow me to do so, and every so often, I can have personal conversations with those who have passed," I answered, keeping my tone light. In no way was I going to match his intensity here.

"Have you heard my truths?" he asked, his voice cracking.

"Yes John, I have. Is this okay?" I responded softly.

"How in the hell do you heal people? That's lunacy," he said, his voice cracking more.

"I can see areas in the body that are damaged or failing. Many times, I am able to heal damaged tissue or bone, but it's the body that shows me what I need to fix," I said, trying desperately to keep him from completely tuning me out.

"Dead people. You can have conversations with zombies. How?" he said, tears forming in the corners of his eyes.

"Yes John, I can. It's usually something that happens in the healing process if need be." I was gaining some confidence.

"You have his interest, Olaf. Don't stop," his *vox corporis* interjected.

John sat silently, measuring this. Tears began to fall along his nose, which were swiftly wiped away when they met his lips.

He took a deep breath and said, "So, the Po guy has helped us talk to Christopher, but I couldn't see him"

"John, please close your eyes," I instructed.

He did, and we found ourselves in what looked like a baseball field.

"This is where Christopher hit for the cycle. I can't believe it!" John said excitedly.

"Yep, that's right Dad," a voice said above us.

"Christopher? Where are you?"

"I'm close, but I need you to promise me something," the voice boomed.

"Anything. What?" John asked in a panic.

"Promise me you will listen," the voice said.

"Of course, Christopher. Anything. Please, I need to see you," John begged.

Across the field, a figure approached. He was young, maybe in his twenties, and had a smile identical to Sarah's.

"My boy! Oh my God, my boy!" John yelled and ran toward him. He feverishly wiped his face as he ran. They embraced on the pitcher's mound for a good minute and a half before walking together back to me. I was standing at home plate.

"Olaf, thank you. I absolutely cannot say that enough," Christopher began. "This was essential."

"I believe I owe you the thanks, sir," I said smiling, placing a tender hand to my chest.

"We'll be mutually in thanks then. So be it!" Christopher said triumphantly.

"How are you, son? My God, I have no idea how this is happening, but I am so happy right now. Do you remember the game you played here? You pitched a complete game with only one hit, and then *you* hit for the cycle. It was unbelievable, son," John reminisced, smiling so wide his whole face had wrinkles.

"Dad, I'm here because you need me to be. I certainly remember the game, and my accomplishments. But, the reason I have you here is that I need you to hear a couple things. Okay?" Christopher asked, his tone serious.

"Of course, son. Anything," John answered, his eyes widening.

"Olaf, would you tell Dad what you told Mom earlier? I think you say it better than I do," Christopher asked.

"Well John," I began, "Christopher's death was not the result of Sarah's ability. Instead, it was caused by someone who failed to accept what she told him. He couldn't resolve it, and in a sense, lost his mind. The two are mutually exclusive."

"What did she tell him? That had to have something to do with it," John said, his tone becoming agitated.

"She told him he was loved, Dad. That's all," Christopher said, taking over the conversation.

"*What?!*" John demanded, putting his head in his hands.

"He hated himself so much that hearing he was loved was too much. What I will not accept is you blaming Mom in any way, shape, or form for what he did. It essentially makes you the same as the man who took my life. You're not that person, Dad. She needs you, badly. Do you hear what I am saying?" Christopher pontificated.

"Oh my God," John said, allowing this to seep into his mind. I could practically see his thoughts moving a million miles a minute through his mind.

"I promise you. I promise both of you. No more. I had no idea that's what happened," John said emphatically.

"You never asked. Dad, please. You can be the healer here, with a little bit of Olaf's help. She needs you," Christopher said, putting his hand on John's shoulder.

"I promise you, son. I am so completely sorry, Christopher. Please tell me I'll see you again," John said, embracing his son.

"I'm always close, but you need to be okay with me not being around. Okay?"

"I understand. Olaf, thank you. This has been a blessing unlike any other," John said sincerely.

As quickly as it started, we were back on the patio.

"You did it, Olaf. I cannot believe this! I never thought this to be possible! Thank you!" John's *vox corporis* gushed.

"Where's my wife? I have to find Sarah!" John said and ran out of the room.

A few minutes later, they returned to the patio, hand in hand, their faces wet and red with emotion.

"I don't know what you did, but thank you Olaf!" Sarah said, then hugged me tightly.

"This is what y'all needed to start healing. We ain't quite done with either of ya, but I won't leave until we are. I promise y'all that," I said and gave in to the emotion of the moment.

That night, I cooked up some tasty barbecue, and we had a nice dinner. John played catch with Louis afterward and seemed to smile bigger with every throw. Annie had Sarah tell her and Addie about the tears in their eyes, which seemed to be fascinating to both.

Annie's tears were proud of the person she was, and at the same time, sorry for all the pain she'd experienced. Addie's tears just simply said she was special and among the strongest people in the world. Sarah coyly did not share the details of the message, but rather just delivered the message itself. Incidentally, both my and Louis' tears were consulted with. Mine said I wasn't done, and Louis' said he needed to have more fun.

Two days later, I had second sessions with both John and Sarah. John and I dove deeper into his pain, which still remained. He also was curious about my ability, and we spoke for quite some time about his *vox corporis*. The outer layer of anger was removed when we spoke with Christopher, and though I no longer had a crevasse of pain to remove, it was still a moderately sized valley to address. So, we focused on the good, and we focused on his health as we spoke. By the end of that session, I could tell that the world was maybe a shade or two lighter in his perception. His smile was brighter, both in his mouth and his eyes.

In Sarah's session, I hadn't even formed a "Hello" in my mind before I heard Christopher's voice.

"Olaf, could I see Mom?" he asked kindly.

"Sarah, would you close your eyes please?" I asked.

"I guess so… sure," she replied reluctantly. She did, and we found ourselves in a park, by a relatively large lake.

"Where are we, Olaf? This looks like the park where we had Christopher's first birthday party," Sarah said sadly.

"It was the location of my first six birthdays, Mom," Christopher chuckled. His voice was behind us.

"Christopher? Where are you?" Sarah nervously said, her voice shaking.

"Swings. Come visit!" he responded happily.

We turned and indeed saw the man sitting on a swing, swaying back and forth slowly. Sarah saw him and sprinted over to the swings. He met her half way, and they embraced for a couple minutes. I walked over, and we all went back to the swing set. We each sat and... well, started swinging.

"How is this happening?" Sarah demanded.

"You needed this as part of your healing process, Sarah. This is part of what I do. The mechanics of it aren't really important, and truthfully I could not give you an answer as to the how anyway," I said, swinging slowly.

"Mom, you heard everything you needed to hear except one thing. I'm *okay*. I know you are worried about this constantly. Please hear me when I say this," Christopher said, stopping his motion on the swing.

Sarah stopped swinging too and started crying. She took a minute to find her response. Ultimately, she wiped her eyes and said, "Son, I know you are. I just can't stand the fact that in some way, I took your life. I lost you. I don't know how to get passed that."

"You didn't lose me, Mom. You never will, either. You just stopped listening to me. If you listen, you will know I'm always close. *Always*. You will see my smile everywhere if you pay attention. You will feel me if you allow *yourself* to feel. I am not lost, Mom. Maybe this isn't a conventional situation, but both you and Olaf touch the part of life that is anything *but* conventional. As you told Olaf, you and I are always connected. He may have my heart, but you and I are connected in a different way. You have to choose to realize this, and when you do, your sadness and guilt will disappear. You are not to blame for me losing my life. You *are* to blame for choosing to see me as lost, however," he responded, his voice heavy and unyielding.

Sarah's eyes widened, and her breath became agitated. The truth of what Christopher said slowly dripped into her soul like sand in an hourglass. With each piece of sand, her recognition of it became clearer. She had made a choice that countered her own experience, and the weight of this grew.

"I cannot believe I did this," she began, her voice laden with disappointment. After a brief pause, she continued, "I knew better. I heard and saw the truth all around me, but my grief made me dismiss all of it. Christopher, I am grateful you're okay. I promise you, I will listen, and I will allow myself to feel. I am blessed to have had you in my life, son. Still, you have to forgive me for being sad that you won't have the experiences every mother wants for her son. I wanted to dance with you at your wedding. I wanted to hold your babies and babysit every day for the rest of my life. I wanted to love your wife as my own daughter. I'm being selfish—I know. I of course realize what you've told me is an absolute truth. But, there is another truth I need to be allowed to mourn."

Christopher hugged Sarah tightly.

"I understand, Mom. I do. Please though—don't allow your mourning to keep you from living your life. What you do is too important. Okay?"

She nodded sadly.

"Olaf, thank you again for your help. I'll look forward to seeing where my heart goes. I already know the adventure is far from over," he said, grinning widely.

"I agree, Olaf. This has been a blessing unlike anything I could imagine. Thank you, my friend," she added.

I smiled, knowing this was critical to Sarah reclaiming her life.

"I'm more than happy to help. Christopher, I hope your heart has fun, but I've had plenty of adventure so far. I'd like good n' boring from here on out if that's okay," I said, allowing everything that led to me having Christopher's heart to ooze out and then crash around me like emotional meteors. Poor me—right, dear Reader?

"You and I know that's not true, Olaf. Please tell Addison the horse's name is Sam, okay?" Christopher asked.

"I've no clue what that means, but okay," I responded, shaking my head slightly.

"It's time for both of you to return home. Thank you for this wonderful time together!" Christopher said and slowly backed away.

"I love you, Christopher," Sarah called after him. The space around us returned to Sarah's living room. "I don't know how, but thank you," she said as she dabbed at tears in her eyes.

"You're more than welcome, Sarah. I'm always available to you. Please know this implicitly. Y'all are family to me," I replied and gently held her hand in mine.

Addie appeared in the doorway and asked us about dinner. After that was settled, with hot dog and cheeseburger counts established, I told her the message Christopher had asked me to relay.

"Sweetheart, the horse's name was Sam," I said, completely unaware of what this was in regard to.

She giddily bounced up and down after learning this detail, smiled in her eyes, and left the room. I never found out what the heck that was about, dear Reader. To this day, it's a mystery that's more fun to leave unsolved.

We left the next morning, the relationship between our families strong. Both kids, and each of my grandkids (who you will meet later), get birthday cards every year from Sarah still to this day.

A week later, we ventured off to Maine to see George. He could communicate with animals, so we brought our doting pups with us with the hope we could learn a little more about them.

We had purchased a decently sized vehicle for Doc, replete with a dog bed and a bevy of blankets in the back. Both dogs fit pretty well, with room to stretch out. Angel was still a puppy, but was growing, what seemed like, every minute of every day. By the time we were at speed on the freeway, we had two sleeping pups—much to our amusement. You see, dear Reader, Angel was a hysterical snorer. His jowls would fill with air, and he would breathe it out as though he were saying "Poof." It was a fun car ride, just listening to the sound effects coming from the backseat.

We arrived in Maine a day after we left, after a stopover in Boston. A psychiatrist colleague of mine lived just outside of town and invited us to stay—so long as I made him a fresh strawberry pie. I swear, the way I make them things must form some drug or something in people's guts as they digest. I dunno, dear Reader.

George's house was a gorgeous historical home not far from the coast. We could hear the Atlantic in his backyard. He had two dogs himself—both Dobermans—that sat like statues even when Angel and Penelope said their puppy hellos. There was an emotional strength in them pups like nothing I had ever seen. They looked through your soul and evaluated your dreams, dear Reader—felt like it anyway.

"Olaf, welcome to Maine! I'm so happy you're here! Thanks for introducing me to your dogs! We have some fun conversations coming our way," George said evasively.

"Should I be worried, George? What am I in for?" I responded, trepidation woven into my words.

"Special, my friend. Just very special. Have you met mine yet? They can be a little intense when you first meet them. It's a breed thing, but I love 'em. Can I get you a drink? I brew my own beer and would love for you to try it," he said happily.

"I'd love to try it! Absolutely! I did meet your dogs and could not believe how calm they are. Their gaze is absolutely piercing."

"They're harmless, but are devastatingly smart. I'm guessing you will see a different side of them the next time they're around. Offer 'em a hand and watch what happens. I'll be right back!" he said and vanished into the house.

Both of his dogs approached me, almost as if on cue, and sat within my reach. I stuck out both hands, and almost in unison, they put their heads into my palms and closed their eyes. I could not believe this; it was positively surreal, dear Reader.

George returned, and neither dog flinched.

"See, Olaf? The emotion in these two runs deep," he said proudly.

I used my thumbs to gently rub the sides of each pup's head, which resulted in each pressing deeper into my palms. I had certainly felt deep emotion from Doc, Angel, and Penelope. This was different, an innocence absolutely misplaced in the outward intensity of these creatures. When I moved, they stayed next to me. In fact, they stayed close as George and I headed to a couple chairs near the fire pit in the corner of his yard.

Annie, George's wife Pam, and the kids joined us. Pam was head chef at a five-star restaurant in town, and she and I were to craft a dish with just our brains for that night's dinner.

"You up for some cooking creativity tonight, Olaf?" Pam asked, smiling.

"I can't wait, but I gotta be honest, y'all. I can cook, but it's a feeling thing. I'm not trained at all, and I'm a bit afraid I may do something you find to be completely wrong," I answered honestly.

"The best kind of cooking is by feel, Olaf. Rules only apply when one is tied to a menu. I cannot wait! George doesn't like to cook, which makes no sense given his love of creating beer. Honey, why?" she asked and produced a light but notable glare.

"I don't know food, sweetheart. I know fermenting. That's all. Olaf, what do you think of this batch?" George asked, completely deflecting his interrogation.

The beer was a scotch ale, aged in a genuine scotch barrel from Ireland. It was literally the best beer I had ever tasted, dear Reader.

"Best suds ever, hands down," I offered, showering praise to who I now knew was a brew master.

This prompted Annie to grab my glass and take an uncomfortably large gulp.

"Yep," she said, wiping her mouth, "that stuff is amazing."

"I'll get you a glass Annie! Looks like you need a top-off too, Olaf. I'll be right back," George said and disappeared across the yard.

"He's been looking forward to this for weeks, you two. Thank you so much for coming! Your kids are adorable, and so polite. Do you beat them into conformity?" Pam asked, chuckling.

"Well, their father has ushered a few people to their graves with his hands. He himself is something of a zombie, so I think the abject fear of him keeps them in check," Annie suggested, and fixed her eyes into mine. There were times I felt she was genuinely looking at me, wondering if I were really there. This was one of those times, dear Reader.

"Yep, and in fact, I was committed too. So, I think the crazy murderer thing basically keeps those around me in a vail of fear and submission," I added, playing into Annie's sentiment.

"Outstanding! I love a challenge and complicated people! Olaf, all kidding aside, I've been looking forward to you and your family's time here almost as much as George. I cannot wait to cook tonight!"

"I love meeting everybody. It's so great for the kiddos too. Thanks for inviting us to your house!" Annie said sentimentally. "What are you two cooking tonight?"

"A meat, a starch, a veggie, and a salad. That's as far as we've gotten thus far," I said.

"Could I make a request for the starch? You remember those potatoes you made with the sour cream stuff? Could you two make a version of those? I've been craving them for months, Olaf. Months. Do the wife a solid, yeah?" she asked, her glare returning to my eyes.

"Looks like the starch is settled," Pam said and laughed.

"Addison Grace will thank you. She shares my pain," Annie lamented.

"I had no idea. We'll make a version of those for sure," I responded reassuringly.

George returned with our beers. "What did I miss?"

"We have the starch settled. Oh—and we've resolved that people around Olaf are scared into submission due to his status both as a murderer and a zombie," Pam recounted.

"Well okay then. Good to know! Can I make a request for the meat? You know that beef thing I always ask you for, but you say is a pain in the ass to make so you always change it? Could we have that? I love that," George asked hopefully.

"The modified beef wellington. I promise nothing, Dear. We may start down that path and head somewhere else in the eleventh hour. One can't know these things when cooking collaboratively," Pam responded, much to George's chagrin.

After the shared beer and some more light conversation, Pam and I made our way into the kitchen. The kids were interested in how this all was going to "go down," so they came with us. The four dogs did too, but the reason for this is speculative at best. Maybe they sensed opportunity for "gifts from Heaven" to appear on the floor as we cooked. Aw heck though, they probably just followed the kids, dear Reader.

In the kitchen, Pam put her hands on my shoulders, looked me in the eye, and said, "No rules. Let's make something yummy!"

"I'm in!" I said excitedly.

The kids were fascinated by this exchange.

"We're going to like this too, right?" Louis asked, nervousness obvious in his voice.

"Sweetheart, I promise. If you don't like this, I will make you anything you want before I eat tonight. Deal?" Pam offered.

"Yeah. Thank you, Pam. So, what are you making anyway?" he asked.

"Well, my husband thinks he loves beef wellington, but he doesn't. It's a ruse I pulled a while ago, hoping he'd forget. Let's start down that path, but do what feels right. We're making your fun sour cream potatoes, Olaf. I have some really nice, fresh broccoli I'd like to serve, and I'm thinking a salad with homemade dressing the kids can assist with. How does that all sound?" Pam said, every bit the chef.

"Amazing! It all sounds amazing! I can't wait—I love those potatoes!" Addie said happily.

Cooking with Pam was nothing like I imagined, dear Reader. I thought for sure my means of feeling my way through dinner prep and cooking would be counter to her methods as a chef. Instead, she did the same thing; there was a notable part of the experience where we complimented one another's contributions just by feel, nonverbally. The beef went about as far from wellington as one can imagine. The taters were a derivation of what I made in the past. The broccoli was served with a sauce we made, but neither of us could remember what half the ingredients were. The salad was prepared by the kids, Annie and George, and Pam and I made a dressing. By the end of this, a dinner was served that all—yes all—of those present that night *still* speak of decades later.

The next day, George and I took turns giving sessions to one another. My first session focused on pain he had in his back, which I felt was similar to Gerard's when I first met him. It didn't take me long to find three discs in his back that were in mild disrepair, and over two sessions I was able to remove his damage and his pain. George's session with me was not quite as easy though, dear Reader.

"Olaf, your dogs aren't just pets. You know this, right?" he began.

"Well, I guess if I look at it, they all found us, but I've never tried to figure out why. Doc found me first, and then both Angel and Penelope arrived almost as soon as he passed away. In what way are they not pets, George?" I asked, my curiosity rising.

"Well, just tell me this… did both Doc and Angel do something to protect you?" he asked and leaned in.

I found myself becoming both incredibly introspective and also a touch sad, dear Reader. Doc's passing was not something I really ever got over. Yes, I completely realize this is counter to most of what I have written in the book to this point, but it was true. Doc was bonded to me in a way complimentary to Annie. He was both a protector and a conspirator in my debaucheries. Angel had taken his dad's place in every way but one: he wasn't Doc.

I gathered my thoughts and said, "Yes, Doc and Angel have protected me. Both did so in hospital settings and Doc took bullets protecting me. Why do you ask?"

"Well, the first thing Penelope told me was about Doc, and how his place was by your side. This is similar to what my pups say. It's their analogy to protection. She also said that Doc specifically told her that she and Angel were to take his place, but instead they would serve to protect the whole family. Here's the thing though, Angel told me when he first saw you, he knew his only responsibility was to you, in a protective way. He also said his favorite memory was when you accepted him and let him nap next to you in the hospital," he began, a big smile on his face.

George took a deep breath and said, "Olaf, it seems shortly before he died, Doc told Penelope of your passing, and as a result, he felt as though he'd failed," George said, and offered me a tissue.

I needed it, dear Reader. Hearing this was like an atom bomb going off in my heart. I lost control of my emotions and almost immediately soaked through that tissue with eye leaks. This elicited a response from Penelope, who was napping across the room. She slowly approached me and put her massive head on my knee. As soon as she did, my tears slowed, and I looked at her deeply expressive eyes. It was almost as though she was taking my sadness from me, something I hadn't ever seen her do with me, Annie or the kids.

"She's right where you need her to be, Olaf. She keeps saying, 'It's okay. It's okay.' This is my point. Your dogs aren't just pets. They are bonded to you in a way that goes beyond the typical master-pet relationship. They feel responsibility for your life, for your emotions, and for your health. You are the center of their existence. They certainly have relationships with Annie and the kids too, but it's different. From what I have seen, Angel has also bonded tightly with Annie and the kids, but in a more typical pet way. Penelope and Angel have a known responsibility to you first, Olaf. Penelope has a version of this with Annie, but it's nowhere near as strong. My hunch here is that your dogs will always be a part of your existence, and you will never have to seek them. They will always find you.

Losing Doc was tragic in the way it occurred, but he was old and had lived a good three years longer than Ridgebacks typically do. I can appreciate how hard it is to hear this, but you need to in order to understand. Both Angel and Penelope feel the same way. If you die, they fail. In all my years as a practitioner, I've never heard animals say this in the way your dogs do. My pups are guard dogs, but they aren't tied into our health in any way. I can't explain why they are in your life, but Penelope told me you would find out, 'The next time you see the singing lady.' Any idea what that means?"

I blew my nose into the tear-soaked tissue and gave Penelope a hug. She thanked me with a tiny lick on the cheek, and returned to her napping place across the room.

"Yeah, the singing lady is another part of my existence I couldn't explain if I tried, George. So, you're telling me that my dogs today look at me the same way Doc did? I guess I never allowed myself to see that. Losing Doc still hurts," I said and leaned forward, resting my elbows on my knees.

"Can you help me, George?"

"Absolutely not, Olaf. They can, and they will. My job was to bridge the gap and let them do the rest. You just saw the first step. I'd imagine the next time you see Angel, it will be different too," he said and patted my back.

"Now then, you have miraculously healed my back, I did what I needed to do, and we have no beer. This is a problem that must be rectified immediately. To the back yard we must go, kind sir. Please join me!" George said enthusiastically.

We indeed headed to the back yard, suds in hand.

We hadn't been sitting two minutes when Angel sauntered over to me, moved next to my chair, and leaned into my side. I wrapped my arm around him, and allowed myself to see and feel him differently. I allowed myself to see him as I had Doc. In that moment, my world changed. I no longer mourned Doc, but in truth I would always miss him. I saw both Angel and Penelope differently from that point forward, and realistically did the same with every dog I have had up to the point of applying these words to these pages.

Our visit with George and Pam ended the next day. We got to enjoy Pam's favorite dish to cook, a lasagna that she had refined over the years. I think we ate two full pans of the stuff that night.

As a side note, Pam and I enjoyed cooking together so much that twice a year, we held a "Creative Cooking" night at her restaurant. The menu was abandoned, and Pam and I would blindly pick base ingredients from an array of refrigerators. We then did what we did that night, adding other ingredients (spices and sauces primarily) as our combined cooking souls dictated, and prepared the whole lot by nothing but feel. We conducted the whole thing in front of the diners, so it was a show from the beginning. After the first event, reservations were made for years in advance in some cases. We had to move the whole event to the convention center after year three as a result, simply because of the demand. The line outside the building extended across town every time. Folks never knew what they were getting that night, but we ruled out common allergens and had independent hawks keeping track of every ingredient in case any of the diners became nervous. By far, this was one of my favorite things. We did it for thirty-five years. Our last one, in year thirty-five, allowed us to cook for generations of our families and friends. Great, great memories, dear Reader.

I left George's with a completely changed vision of Angel and Penelope. I also now had an expectation to talk with my singing lady about the dogs. In true form, I got anything but specifics when we talked two days later.

"Dear one, they are a part of your experience. They always will be," she said on the topic.

I never got clarification, dear Reader, not a why or a how. I've reasoned it's a synchronicity I need in life, and life rewards me as a result. It's a reach, yes, but isn't a ton of what I've written a tiny bit out there, dear Reader?

Interestingly, my time with Juanita and Po was much more conversational. They weren't bad meetings in any way, but the conversations were much more akin to colleagues comparing notes than anything else. Juanita spoke of the work she did on behalf of the planet, which was interesting in that she referred to our planet as "she" more often than not. Po spoke of "those who have departed" in regard to his work. Both were in good health mentally and physically, and more than anything just wanted to get to know me better. I certainly shared that sentiment!

In both cases, cooking was the highlight for me given my time with both people. I cooked for Juanita and her girlfriend, Jill, over the three days we were in London. Po insisted on sharing cooking duties with me, and his wife, Mary, enjoyed watching "the boys" cook while she and Annie sipped white wine.

While I was in London, I got to see Owen, Vickery's brother. As I expected, I conducted four sessions with him, allaying the guilt he felt for falling in love again. He returned the favor by taking pictures of our family. One picture of Addie won three awards, dear Reader. It's a beauty for sure; she is looking toward the sunset, and her hair is the same color as the rays of light. Her soft features reflect the warmth of the setting sun. I have a huge print of it in my office. There's also a picture of Annie and I looking at each other, almost as though we're trying to talk with our eyes. I don't know how Owen captures what he does, but the end result is profoundly beautiful.

In the end, I had a wonderful, emotional journey when meeting Sarah, George, Juanita, and Po in person. I've kept in contact with all of them through the years, and they each have contributed to what has been an absolutely amazing life for me. I look back on the memories we made together often, and smile every time.

Children, Gifts of the Heavens

Children. This word has an interesting effect on people. In some, it creates a sentimental, loving response. In others, it creates a shuttering that results in a sick feeling. I lean more to the first group in this example, though given my very tepid inclusion of these wonderful offspring of mine in this memoir, one might think the opposite. So, among quite a bit of other fun, this is my kid chapter, mostly because they were the center of the next few decades of interestingness.

To give a bit more structure, dear Reader, the following pages detail the time from my mid-forties through my late seventies. Indeed, though this is a notable amount of time, there were but a handful of major events worth documenting as part of my little story. One such event was a phone call that, to this day, makes me cry.

"He's gone, Olaf."

That's all I heard, dear Reader. I dropped the phone to the floor, and sobbed uncontrollably for the better part of an hour. Akamu had died, and the effect on me emotionally was akin to colliding black holes.

Akamu lived a wonderful life despite being blind for almost ninety percent of it. He helped thousands upon thousands of people in his care. His ability to heal saved my life at least twice, and improved the lives of countless others too. He was a mentor and partner to me for decades and was family to Fanny, Gerard and their sons, and certainly a surrogate to Annie, the kids, and me. "Akkie" was a rock for Lou and Addie beginning when they were in diapers, and continuing all the way into their respective college careers. In the same way, he was the eye of the hurricane for Annie when chaos was swirling around her. So, this wonderful man was a fixture for all of us and losing him was about as hard a loss as anything we had experienced as a family. Akamu was ninety-eight when he passed.

Death is such a complicated topic, dear Reader. One the one hand, it's extraordinarily black and white. The grey area seems to evolve in the shadow of the deceased's life as details are learned and impacts are felt. In this case, I had lost a person who taught me something almost every time we spoke. Akamu had an uncanny way of communicating both ideas and truths in a way that hit home well after they are spoken. This was indeed the case with our last conversation, but I in no way realized it until months after the fact.

"Olaf, the people we help, in turn help us. After all, we're the ones asking them to do so."

That, dear Reader, was the last example of an Akamu pontification. He had a habit of saying things that outwardly made little sense, but under the surface, carried an ocean of meaning. The little item above was not just commentary about our patients. It was Akamu reminding me that every life is connected, and this connection creates the actions and conversations that serve both people in correlating ways. This was the one thing Akamu drilled into me every chance he got, and this last example hit me as I held a hysterical Addie who mourned Akamu so much that she left school that quarter on bereavement leave.

"Daddy, I just… I can't… I…," she stammered.

I tightened my grip around her. "Sweetheart, it would break Akkie's heart to know you're this sad. He loved you so very much."

"I know Daddy. It's just that he did so much for me, even up to the week he died. I talked to him almost every day," she said, feverishly wiping tears away from her cheeks. "I just don't know how to do this without him."

"How to do what, Addie?" I asked, confusion weaving its way into my melancholy mind.

She paused for a couple moments and said, "Life, Daddy."

In the immediacy of the moment, this did two things: it broke my heart, and it disturbed me in a way I found hard to resolve.

"Life, Addie? Help me understand, sweetheart," I imparted, finding myself desperately wanting to resolve this.

"It's just that he was such a big part of my weeks, Daddy. He called me every Tuesday at 3:00 and Friday at 1:00 because he knew that's when I was in my room studying and needed a break. I never told him that—he just knew. I don't know how I'm going to be able to do this knowing he won't be part of my weeks," she said and wiped more tears from her eyes.

This made more sense to me. Akamu indeed had this uncanny ability to find holes in one's day and call. It was remarkable every single time.

"Her heart is hurting, Daddy. I have every confidence you know how to fill this void in Addison's life. It's important you do," Addie's *vox corporis* said.

Yes, dear Reader, my kids', and then my grandchildren's *vox corpora,* addressed me in the same manner they did physically. Remember that first time I heard Addie's voice when I was coming out of my coma? It's special every single time I hear it.

I considered this new wrinkle, and wondered if indeed I had the same talent Akamu had. If I did, I intended to have some fun with it. In the immediate moment, though, I had to calm my daughter down.

"Addie, how do you think Akamu would feel if you told him what you just told me?" I asked, a strategic thought forming in my mind.

She sniffed and replied, "He'd be really sad, I think."

"Well, do you remember Iokua saying the distance between life and death is but a breath? And, do you remember all the times the singing lady was with you? Sweetheart, Akamu will be a part of your days for the rest of your life. You just have to listen. The phone isn't likely to ring, but you will still hear his voice if you just listen," I said, copying a message I'd told hundreds of people by this time.

"Perhaps you should listen to your own word, my friend. Tell your daughter to close her eyes, and then you do the same. We must talk, the three of us," Akamu's voice bellowed.

My immediate thought, dear Reader, was akin to a child waiting for a verbal assault from a parent. Regardless, I did as I was asked, and we found ourselves in Addie's apartment near the college campus. Akamu was sitting at her desk.

"Why... How are we here? How are *you* here, Akkie?" Addie asked, astonishment apparent in her voice.

"We are here thanks to your father's ability. I am here because I choose to be, child. I must admit, however, that I am disappointed in both of you. You tell me right now, young lady, why you are not in school," Akamu scolded, his arms crossed.

"I... I... I was so sad I couldn't study. I just cried, Akkie. I miss you so much," Addie said, ran to Akamu, and hugged him.

"Addison Grace, what was the last thing I told you, the last time you sat in this chair?" Akamu asked, his voice more calculating than scolding.

"You told me I was never alone, Akkie," she replied.

"Well, do I need to say this again, child? My dear heavens, Addison Grace, I am connected to you, your father, your mother, and your brother. When you need me, I am here. This will be true until time ends. Do I need to say this again?" Akamu asked intensely, alternating his laser-like eyes between me and Addie.

He continued, "Olaf, I understand not one of the tears that has fallen from your eyes. Not one. You know this truth, and still you mourn. Tell me why."

"Well, because I'm allowed to be human, and mourn the loss of my friend. Yes, I know the truth you speak of, but it's still not easy," I replied, searching my soul for answers.

"Yes, you are allowed to be human, my dear partner. However, it is your charge to be the rock of this family, bearing truth. Can I trust you to stop this nonsense and get back to work? And Addison Grace, I want your aft end to be in this chair next week. You have much to catch up on. The two of you are such special people to me, and I just can't understand how you could ever feel that I would vanish from your life. Iokua said it perfectly, and by damn Olaf you found a way to ignore a very simple truth. I am not gone from your life, and I never will be. Please, get back to your responsibilities. No more tears should fall from your precious eyes. If I need to, I will tell Sarah to come to your house to tell you what those tears are saying, and it's nothing good. No, not good at all. So please, hug me, then start your days. I will be with you every step of the way. Oh, and yes, Olaf, what you heard today is true, and I indeed expect you to have fun with it. Now hug me, please," Akamu demanded.

Addie hugged him tightly. "Okay Akkie. I promise."

I then took my turn in embracing my dear partner. "Message received, but I don't regret a single tear shed, my friend."

He smiled, and we were back on the couch. Angel and Penelope studied us intently, almost as though they had witnessed the whole exchange.

"I think you need to get back to school, kid. I'll make you a nice, yummy dinner tonight, and you get back to school tomorrow," I said, hugging her.

"Okay Daddy. I think you're right," she replied and went up to her room.

Almost immediately after she left, Annie joined me on the couch.

"So, I'd guess you just got yelled at. Yeah?" she asked, her voice akin to a child knowing a sibling had just been caught doing some nefarious childhood crime.

"Yep. Got a fairly stern talking to," I said, shame apparent in my reply.

"I did too, babe. I think the boy is the only one of us who escaped judgment," she exasperated and collapsed into my arms.

Indeed, Lou escaped Akamu's wrath. Thing is, Akamu apparently spent a copious amount of time talking to my son after his passing. So, all in all, it wasn't terribly fair. Well, to me it wasn't, but that is the immature part of my brain talking, dear Reader.

So, after Akamu set us all on the straight and narrow, we got back to our lives. Annie and I returned to our responsibilities, and the kids went back to school. To begin the stories of their young adulthoods, I'll tell you about Addie's collegiate life... Now.

Addie went to school for business management, and went all the way through Master's studies on the topic. I found it fascinating to talk to her about business simply due to my success in that realm. Turns out, dear Reader, that I should have never had the success that I did based on her textbooks. This resulted in some of the most intense discussion with my daughter I ever had. She would argue, based on case studies all through her course book, that my deals should have never been possible. I would calmly go to my office, grab a couple folders, and hand them to her. Her face would get varying shades of red as she reviewed the details. Ultimately, she would calmly hand me back the folders and disappear someplace upstairs without saying a word. We often would not speak for several hours afterward.

Our last such exchange ended with me suggesting I talk to her professor. She agreed. So, I contacted the professor, who excitedly invited me to the class. I knew I was walking into a minefield, so I brought some protection in the form of my deal folders. Indeed, dear Reader, I was shelled by the professor and that whole class over a two-hour lecture time. By the end of that lecture, the professor and class agreed with me on one core principle: business was not formulaic. From what Addie told me, their study changed radically after my time in class.

In fact, the professor contacted me toward the end of that semester and asked if I would be willing to co-teach a lecture with him, and then help him both write and grade the final exam. I agreed. The class was astoundingly fun; the discussion was lively and the debates were intense. The creation of the exam was interesting too, simply because forming questions for topics that were not black and white was challenging. Grading them... I've never done anything so maddening in my life. By the end of the twelve-hour meeting I had with the professor to accomplish the task, he finally and formally relented that business, in principle, didn't have one answer or approach. When we finished grading the exams, he asked if I would consider coming back the next semester. I agreed, and helped that class every semester for twenty-two years, until the professor's retirement.

Lou decided to study agriculture. I never in a million years saw that coming, dear Reader. I thought he was on the medical train, but he got the farming bug instead. He had a love for the orchard starting when he was a small child. My parents loved walking with him through the fruit trees. Father, bless his soul, taught Lou about every single aspect of the trees and how he went about caring for them. The Rodriguez family put Lou to work in the fields starting when he was ten. He found the process involved with farming to be fascinating—from soil considerations to hydration, to the notion of organics. So, my boy went to school and graduated with a knowledge of farming that literally changed the farm. When he was done imposing his influence, the entirety of our farm became organic and yields increased by almost forty percent in a single year. Neither I, nor José, ever thought this possible. Even through droughts, our crops have remained healthy—thanks in large part to Lou's suggestions and leadership.

José retired three years after Lou's first successes. As a result, Lou took a primary role in the farm's day-to-day management. The rest of the Rodriguez family wholly accepted this. One person in particular seemed to be his champion, for good reason. Julia Rodriguez was madly in love with my son. Julia was the daughter of Carla and Jorge Rodriguez, born two years after my Lou. If you remember, dear Reader, her parents and brother—Manny—were brought to America by my grandfather.

I can truthfully say, though, the flame of this love was not lit until Lou came back from college. The two worked together frequently as kids, and then adolescents, but their relationship was passive at best. Both I and the Rodriguez family were wary of Lou when he first returned from school simply due to what he was recommending. I proudly let him present his ideas and use a crop to test them—even though Lou's methods were such dramatic departures from processes we had refined for decades. It was Lou's work ethic, I think, that earned him acceptance. It was his results, though, that earned respect. My boy was working so hard at the time that he didn't see Julia's affections. However, there wasn't a person on that farm, between both families, that didn't see it. Ironically, it was Sadie who opened Lou's eyes.

One hot afternoon in July, Lou came into the office from the fields to talk to Annie and me about the corn yield. Sadie had joined us as she and Annie were going to head off to do some birthday shopping for both Nol and Jonah, whose birthdays were but two days apart. Julia came in just a minute or so after Lou did and offered him some lemonade. She smiled shyly before she left, and Sadie couldn't keep her mouth shut. I'll tell you why in a minute dear Reader; this was a retribution thing.

"Well I'll be damned if that girl isn't head over heels for you, Louie. I saw that same look in your momma's eyes every time she looked at that dead father of yours," she said devilishly.

"Dammit Sadie! Leave my son alone. That was mean," Annie playfully replied.

"Wait… What? Julia?" Lou stammered, trying to understand.

"Dad, Lou has been infatuated with Julia for a long time. He's too shy to do anything about this, especially after April. Can you help?" Lou's *vox corporis* asked.

I got up and ushered him outside. We walked into the shed, which was empty for the moment. I knew Carlos was going to be back any minute as he was working on one of the newer tractors we desperately needed for the soybeans. When there was a rush like this, Carlos only took breaks if his bladder or stomach complained too much, and even at that, his breaks were tiny at best.

"Son, I'm so sorry about that. You doing okay?" I asked, trying desperately to contain my emotion. Lou had his heart ground up in a meat grinder about two years prior by his college girlfriend. April admitted to cheating with Lou's best friend for the biggest part of a year. Mind you, dear Reader, Lou had bought a ring and was days away from proposing. So, to say my son had walls up was putting it mildly. He had walls, barbed wire, and a no-fly zone around him.

"I don't know, Dad. I… Julia's gorgeous, but I just… I can't… I don't know what to do," he said, and hung his head.

Well, dear Reader, I did the only damn thing I could. I hugged him tightly and said, "Trust yourself. I know April hurt you badly son, but not every woman is April."

Dammit if my son then didn't break my heart clear in two. He started crying.

"Louis, tell me what these tears are about," I said, still hugging him.

He took a step back, angrily wiped the tears from his eyes, and said, "I just don't trust anyone anymore, Dad."

No sooner did he finish his sentence than Julia walked right up to him out of nowhere, closed her eyes, and kissed his lips.

"Try," she whispered, kissed him again, and left the shed.

My jaw hit the floor, dear Reader. I was speechless. I gave my boy a pat on the back, a nod, and went back into the office. I was peppered with questions from Annie and Sadie, but simply said, "Ask Lou."

Both Lou and I were tight-lipped on the whole thing for a couple months, and that drove Annie nuts. It was too much fun to watch my wife squirm, dear Reader. Lou loved it too. But, eventually Julia told her parents what she did, and eventually Annie got the scoop from Carla. When Annie heard what happened, she immediately found Julia and hugged her. Annie's heart broke almost as bad as Lou's when April disappeared from our lives. Carla and Annie have been inseparable to this day, and gossip constantly about the family.

Lou and Julia got married two years to the day after that kiss in the shed, and they have three children. Victor José is thirteen, Gabrielle Sierra is sixteen, and Nicolas Luis is eighteen. I'm so proud of my boy. I love Julia dearly and those grandkids are among the most driven people I've seen in recent memory. Nick is heading off to college on a full ride. Gabby graduated high school by age fourteen and started medical school. And Victor has been an apprentice under Uncle Carlos since he was a toddler and is planning to go to the same technical school the Rodriguez boys attended. He was able to change the oil in the tractor before he could color in the lines with crayons. Vick, at age ten, changed the engine out of his dad's car for fun—with an engine he made by *hand*. Carlos watched intently, but said not one word during both the engine build and the replacement. I'll be damned if that thing don't purr like a kitten, dear Reader—a monstrous, man-eating kitten.

Remember just a few paragraphs back when I mentioned Sadie's retribution? Good sweet damn, dear Reader, but that fiery woman got mad as sin at Annie when it came to *her* son. Yes, her six-foot-five, cannon-armed, sweeter n' sweet tea quarterback son, Jonah. Ah yes, dear Reader, Jonah was an athlete, just like his father. But, unlike Nol, he was not a defender, and this broke his dad up like nothing else.

"A QB? My flesh n' blood is a QB? 'The hell I do wrong?" he would ask many, many times. This diatribe was quite a show when alcohol was introduced.

Jonah was such a good kid. He's an even better man, despite his success in football. Oh, and there is the infatuation with my daughter that furthers my feelings for this person. Thing is, he told not one soul about this infatuation in the beginning. Neither did my daughter, who *also* had an infatuation for him.

Addison Grace was accomplished in her own right, dear Reader. Remember a while back me mentioning that Addie was one of the best junior tennis players in the South? Well, she took that just a tad bit further, reaching the international stage at the ripe old age of fourteen. My little girl was a ranked player on the world stage well before she could vote. She also had a relationship with one of the nation's most sought after quarterbacks…. For *years*, they were together romantically and not one person knew outside of those two beautiful souls.

Addie and Jonah started their relationship during their sophomore year of high school. They went to different schools, but just like Annie and I when we were kids, they were together frequently due to our friendship with Nol and Sadie. Indeed, there were many barbeques, fishing trips, dinners, mini-vacations, and a host of other one-off occasions when we were together as families. When he was a boy, Jonah first developed a love of baseball, and then he outgrew baseball by a good two feet. That kid, like his father, was north of six feet by the time he was in middle school. He was breaking catchers' hands with his fastball at age twelve. His parents were asked not to allow him back on the diamond, so Nol encouraged him to play football, hoping with his lean but powerful frame, he'd play linebacker or safety and hit people. Well, that didn't exactly happen as planned. Jonah could throw from the back of one end zone, through the opposing goal post at age thirteen. He was accurate to within a ten-inch square throwing window on a moving target by fourteen. He also could do this with two or three kids attempting to tackle him.

Jonah set a national record for passing every year of high school. As a result, he was the most coveted quarterback in the nation on the pro stage. Curiously, he decided to go where Addie went, though he could have gone anywhere but South Carolina University. We all figured he wanted to stay close to home to be near his mother, who he absolutely adored. Conversely, there was not one person on this planet good enough for Sadie's son. Not one. Sadie was so infatuated with her son that she summarily dismissed any female who dared to show interest in him through high school *and* college alike, saying not one potential suitor was good enough.

One sunny afternoon, just after the kids graduated from SCU, we had gathered for a joint graduation party. There was light conversation. A few families had joined us, along with our parents, Akamu, Fanny, Gerard and their boys, Stan, (boxing) Joe, Joe Lating,

Coach, Rupert and Michael, Iokua and a couple families from the village by the Dolby house. It was a day of celebration, and also one of discovery.

I recall Annie pulling me aside and saying, "Babe, seriously. I need you to look at our daughter right now."

I did, and aside from her looking happy, I saw nothing out of the ordinary.

"Look closer," she said, her voice accusatory.

I did as I was asked, and I didn't see anything.

"Olaf, Annie believes Addison and Jonah are in a relationship, and something major is going on. If you want the truth, you should talk to your daughter," Annie's *vox corporis* said calmly.

Astonished, I agreed to talk to my daughter about this. So, a little bit later, I pardoned myself, found Addie, and asked her to join me in my office.

"Sweetheart, is there anything you maybe haven't mentioned that, might be significant? Please bear in mind that it's super easy for me to get the truth on my own, but I'd much rather you tell me."

Addison studied my face for an uncomfortable couple seconds as a knowing feeling grew in my heart.

"Come on," she said and grabbed my hand. She dragged me to her room, where Jonah was in absolute hysterics. He was panicking in a way only a very large human can. He was rolling back and forth on the floor.

I rushed to him, thinking something was truly wrong.

"Olaf, he is afraid you are going to murder him," Jonah's *vox corporis* said.

"Addison Grace, here now. Jonah, up," I demanded.

I may have been nudging fifty-three, dear Reader, but damned if I didn't still have a hell of a temper and a willingness to break my hands if the occasion called for it.

"I'm so sorry, Olaf. I didn't..." Jonah began, but I cut him off.

"I need truth, now. Both of you calm down and give me truth. One at a time," I said, my anger taking over.

The look on both of their faces was something I will never forget, dear Reader. They were caught and nervous to reveal the truth.

"I'm in love with him, Daddy," Addison said, her voice shaking. "I have been for a long time."

"I love her too, sir. I think I need to ask you something though," Jonah said, tears falling from his eyes.

"Okay... I understand the need for secrecy, but I don't understand why you're both losing your minds. Jonah, I know your mom is going to be upset, but you're twenty-one. You can make your own decisions about life. What do you need to ask me, Jonah?" I asked as I started to calm down.

"Olaf, do I have permission to marry Addie?" Jonah asked, grabbing my daughter's hand.

"What? You're only kids," I gawked, my mind completely avoiding what was more than obvious.

"Daddy, I'm... I'm pregnant," Addison said.

I heard no sound. Not my own breathing, not my heartbeat, not the kids.

"You're what?" I asked, my voice barely more than a whisper.

"I'm pregnant with Jonah's baby. We've… we've been together for almost six years, but this wasn't something we planned. I'm so sorry Daddy," Addie said, then ran over and threw her arms around me.

"Sweetheart, you know this means tennis is done for about a year, right? I don't believe you can compete while pregnant as a pro. This is not just an impact to tennis, though. This is a major life event. It's going to impact your Master's work too," I said and stepped back before continuing. "You both have some huge decisions to make, and make quickly, because this is not trivial. You are not two people in the countryside. You are both well-known athletes on the world stage. Jonah, you're off to the pros in a few months. Addie, you are in the tournament rotation and are due to leave for London next Month. You have got to carefully consider when and how this is communicated out of consideration for both of your futures."

I took a couple breaths, trying to keep my head straight. Fact was, dear Reader, this was incredibly trying for me. My daughter was pregnant. The colors of emotion I felt were many and all over the place.

"I will not kill you, Jonah, so get that damn thought out of your head. I will get close, though, if you ever lay a hand on my daughter with anger, or if you dare to hurt my grandchild. Are we understood?" I asked, my voice was the exact opposite of my last sentence; it was cold and calculating.

"Yes, sir," Jonah said, his voice shaking.

"Okay then. Figure out what, and when you are going to tell your mothers. It will not be today. Am I clear?" I said, thinking of the abject spectacle that would erupt if this news weaved its way through the crowd downstairs. I also knew I needed to get myself right because there was a very real possibility Sadie would attempt to harm, threaten, or kill my daughter. This is not an exaggeration, dear Reader.

Having gotten the kids' acceptance, and calmed myself as much as I could, I went back to the party. I was intercepted on the way by Annie, who was hell bent on finding out what the situation was.

"Okay babe. Dirt—now!" she demanded and grabbed my hands.

I pulled my wife close and hugged her tightly. I didn't know what to say, dear Reader.

"Babe... I can't breathe," Annie gasped.

"I'm so sorry, love. That wasn't an easy conversation," I said, withdrawing from my embrace.

"What the hell is going on? Are they together or not?" she asked. Her voice was laced with frustration.

"Annie, is this something we can talk about as a family once the party is over? You know how Sadie is going to take any sort of news that involves her son. Please, love," I implored.

"So, they *are* involved," she said as though a great mystery had been solved.

Annie took a second and thought. After careful consideration, she agreed with me.

"You're right, Olaf. She gave that one girl a black eye and ripped her hair out for kissing Jonah on the cheek," Annie recalled.

After a few deep breaths and a less bearlike hug, we returned to the party.

I tended to my smoker and threw some more grub on the grill. I tried desperately to appear normal to my guests, but Annie, bless her, took a slightly different road after having a couple (or four) glasses of whiskey sours over the next couple hours.

The crowd had dissipated, but still a small contingent remained with Nol, Sadie, their kids, Rupert, Michael, and Joe Lating.

Annie, in front of the whole group, said, "Jonah my boy, I think you have a crush on my daughter."

Jonah's face turned sheet white. Sadie's face turned a deep shade of red.

"Annie, why would you say that? Jonah doesn't like her like that," Sadie dismissed.

"Oh no? What say you quarterback?" Annie pressed.

I shot Jonah a look that probably could have bruised him. I was praying he did the right thing and deflected the conversation. Problem was, Nol saw me do this.

"Somethin' goin' on y'all? I don't think I like this," Nol growled.

"Dad, I…" Jonah started.

"What, son? My lord, people. Someone fill me in. This is lunacy!" Nol said, his voice a mixture of concern and nervous laughter.

"Well, I do like Addie. In fact, um, we've been together for a few years. I… I am in love with her," Jonah said nervously.

"Well, that's one bit of truth. Why the hell did you shoot my son that look, Olaf? Damn near coulda' taken 'is dome off wit' it. What's the rest?" Nol answered, his words calculating.

"You've been in a relationship with *her*?" Sadie began condescendingly, shaking her head. "Son, you can do so much better."

Addie ran into the house. I followed her—and so did Jonah. He beat me to her. I found them in a deep embrace, Jonah looking as though he was trying to pull the sadness out of her.

"Aw kid—I'm so sorry," I said and turned to leave.

"Olaf, what do I say?" Jonah asked, obviously upset.

"Jonah, I think this is the first time you are allowed to be honest about your feelings with your mother. Be careful, but understand who you are representing when you do," I said, and turned to head back toward the group.

Annie met me before I left the room, the look in her eyes unlike anything I had ever seen. Even in an inebriated state, she was hell bent on protecting Addison.

"How could she?" she asked angrily.

"Could have been anything, love. We need them to work it out the way they need to, while we support our daughter any way she needs. Right now, though, it's important that *he* be her rock. We're playing second chair from now on," I said, leveling my eyes into hers.

"I still don't know something. This isn't just a relationship, is it?" she asked pointedly.

"That is not a question for me to answer, my love. I believe they will address this when they are ready, in a manner they deem appropriate," I said and hugged my wife.

Nol came in and observed the scene. He was masterful in situations requiring levity, and this was one such occasion. He walked over to the still-embracing Jonah and Addie and put his hands on both of their backs.

"Y'all heard somethin' today. Addie, sweetheart, you are a big 'ol dream for this lug of a son I have. You're a nine to his six. My wife is extremely protective of this idiot as a first born, and what you heard was the lunacy of a person possessed because they know only that protection. I am so completely sorry you heard such hurtful language, but y'all have got to realize the buffoonery of it. You're a damn supermodel who plays tennis at the highest levels. J is a step down for *you*. So look, I understand you getting hurt by these silly words, but please child, understand how completely empty they are," he said, constantly moving around the still-embracing couple as he pontificated.

Sadie arrived toward the end of Nol's speech, and got a tremendously cold reception from the room. Everyone glared at her.

"Addison, I…" she began.

"Mom, that was wrong," Jonah said sternly, interrupting her. "Addie and I have been in a relationship for over six years. She's an amazing person, and I love her. I think you owe her an apology."

I was shocked, but also so proud of him, dear Reader. Jonah was one of the most respectful kids I had ever seen around his mother. The thought of interruption was unheard of.

Sadie's reaction reflected the same shock I felt.

"Jonah, how dare you," she said angrily.

"No, Mom. How dare *you*. I suggest you start making this right, because Addie is everything to me. It's time you realize that I am an adult, and I am allowed to make decisions for myself. This includes the people in my life. Addie is one of those people," he responded calmly, his voice resolute.

"Six years? How could you have been in a relationship for that long? I don't believe this at all. You never said a word about this to me," Sadie responded.

"Well Mom, that's because he talked to me," Jonah's sister Lizzie said, entering the room. Lizzie Glassburé was someone who absolutely took not one bit of grief from anyone, especially her mother.

Jonah was this tall, handsome quarterback, right, dear Reader? Well, Lizzie was two inches shorter than her brother, had her father's wit and character, her mother's fire and had been in photoshoots around the world starting at age twelve. Liz was the model in the family, exotically beautiful and unnaturally tall. She was also viciously smart, having graduated high school by age fourteen. The things I heard from her *vox corporis* starting at about ten could fill a novel unto themselves. To say she was complex is disappointingly inaccurate.

"What are you talking about Lizzie? You were almost never in the country over the last six years," Sadie responded dismissively.

"Jonah called, Mom. He wrote. For that matter, Addie called and wrote too. I spent time with her when she played in London last year. I spent time with her in Australia two years ago. She's an amazing woman—someone I'm certainly proud to call my friend. I cannot believe you would suggest another human not worthy of my brother, especially when that human has been in every memory I have going back to my childhood. Set aside the history, consider her accomplishments on the world stage alone, and she's a special person. You owe her an apology, Mother—a *damn* good apology," Lizzie spoke powerfully.

Sadie stood silently, shocked at what she was hearing. Lizzie kissed Addie on the cheek and wrapped her arms around her proud father. Nol loved that huge daughter of his almost the same way Sadie loved Jonah. He was extremely aware, though, that controlling her, or the people around her, was not a possibility. So, he taught her everything he knew, and coached her to be a strong person. Yes, she was a supermodel. She also could fish better that anyone except her father.

"How could you say that about my daughter, Sadie?" Annie asked angrily. "We've been family for years."

"Annie, I…" Sadie stammered.

"You have been like a sister to me since way before we were both hitched. We were pregnant together, and we supported each other's kids through everything possible together. Tell me how my daughter is anything but perfect for your son, please," Annie said, the hurt she felt obvious in her voice.

"There's one other thing you should know, all," Jonah said.

In the breath between the end of that sentence and the start of his new one, the panic I felt was unlike anything I had experienced ever before in my life.

"Addie is pregnant with my child," he said stoically, and my panic reached a fever pitch.

"Well no wonder you shot that look, y'all," Nol said to me. "You knew."

The whole room looked at me with furrowed brows.

"I did. Here's the thing, y'all. I'll remain a steadfast guardian of my family and of Jonah. When I know to protect them, I will. This is one time that my silence was extraordinarily warranted to serve that purpose. I don't need to be a part of this, in this room, any longer. Please excuse me," I said politely and went back to the deck. I knew beyond a shadow of a doubt my anger would show itself verbally, dear Reader, and I wanted to avoid this in any way possible.

Michael, of all people, met me first, with a full glass of whiskey in hand.

"You need this, grandpa. We should talk," he said, smiling.

I smiled, given this overture. "Of course, Michael," I said happily and sat down.

"Olaf, I've known you for quite a few years," he began and took a sip of wine. "The one thing I have always admired about you is your dedication to your family. Today is a wonderful example of this. Hearing that your daughter is pregnant could not have been easy. You were there when both she and Jonah needed you. You are such a good man, Olaf. I am privileged to call you a friend."

I was shocked, dear Reader. Michael had been Rupert's right hand as long as I had known him, and was mostly known to me for both exquisite cuisine and questionably appropriate conversations loaded with sexual accoutrements. I found myself unable to respond as a result. So, I got up and hugged Michael tightly. When I let go, I still had no words. I think Michael understood; he sat down and smiled at me.

Angel was an old pup at this point, and Penelope was the definition of geriatric, but both knew I was a mess. I stood on the edge of the deck, looking out passed the Intracoastal to the Atlantic, where the sun had started to set. I stood there flanked by my dogs, allowing that sunset to take my anger. I let the distant waves pull my emotion, and the Intracoastal to bring me lazily back to normalcy.

"Y'all know I don't allow y'all to drink solo, son. We talk this out?" Nol asked, cracking a beer.

"How 'bout we just watch the sun for a bit?" I asked. I wasn't ready to talk yet.

"Y'all watch the star. I talk. This is how we do," he began and took a swill of beer. "We gonna be granddads y'all. Togetha'.

We gonna fish, we gonna grill, we gonna teach this grandchile' everythin' 'bout life. Ain' no life neva' befoe' got two granpops like us, and damned if I ain't excited as anything to do this thang wit y'all. I know we got laundry that ain't clean. I think it be gettin' close though. The ladies talkin' n' cryin' back in 'ere. We good y'all?"

I nodded.

"Okay then," he said, finishing his beer.

After maybe ten minutes, a pair of familiar arms wrapped around my chest. A second pair wrapped from the right. A third pair surrounded me from the left. Both pups pressed against my legs. I closed my eyes and allowed that moment to soak into my soul.

"Thank you, Daddy," Addison Grace whispered to my right.

"I cannot thank you enough, Olaf," Jonah said to my left.

"I'm here babe," Annie said behind my neck.

"Y'all, we do this together, as a family. That's what we are and forever will be," I said, smiling.

Eight months later, my first grandchild, Lawrence Carolas Glassburé was born.

Sadie spent the entirety of the pregnancy apologizing to Addie and Jonah. By month four, she and Addie began shopping together. By month eight, Addison honestly and thoroughly forgave her.

They've been married for thirty-four years now, dear Reader. They got married in a small, but elegant, ceremony two months before their son was born. Consequently, that was also about three months before Jonah set the football world on fire with his arm. To hear Nol and Jonah go back and forth all throughout Jonah's career was priceless, dear Reader. Nol ate quarterbacks for his job; Jonah made defenses look like fools. Dream away, my dear Reader, and I promise the craziest trash-talk you can imagine happened between father and son.

Addison and Jonah have two other children—a daughter, Dylan Elizabeth and a son, Paul Christopher. Larry is thirty-four, Dylan is twenty-eight, and Paul is twenty-five. Oddly, the younger children were born on years Jonah's team won the championship. He played twelve seasons of professional football, and owns several records that are not expected to ever be broken.

Larry, interestingly, took an interest in architecture and worked with Mr. Toth for the rest of the latter's career. He's but a part in that business, but he has learned from the best. He got married three years ago to the offspring of two people I mentioned about two-hundred pages ago. You remember Mitsy Brock and the Tackle Dummy? Well, turns out that Misty and the Tackle Dummy got married, had twelve children and raised them all in a five-hundred square foot double-wide on the back of some guy's chicken farm. Larry married child eight, Blue April, who told us some of the most insane stories about growing up I think I've ever heard. Their wedding was something else, dear Reader. Tackle Dummy, a bald, nearly toothless mess of a human, was still scared of Nol. The spectacle was positively unbelievable.

Dylan, like the person whose middle name she bears, both has the intelligence of Lizzie and the looks of a supermodel. While she didn't graduate early, she did graduate as valedictorian and has graced the cover of many fashion magazines over the past couple years.

Paul came to me when he was six at his mother's urging, saying he was hearing things. Indeed, dear Reader, Paul has an ability similar to mine, but he also can see and participate in what I can only describe as dimensional shifts or anomalies. I urged him to go to college, and he did a dual major in both psychology and astrophysics.

I tend to believe his mark on the world is going to be both profound and transformative if he truly lives up to his potential, and remains true to himself. He's three years into his career at this point, and is unlocking our understanding of life. It ain't just breath, y'all—holy hell no! Suffice to say, the lessons my grandson has taught me in his life have changed the way I look up at night, and makes me look at my dreams much more closely. There is so much of our existence that is pliable, in a way that one can observe if one so chooses. This is a story for another day, dear Reader.

****

As I prefaced at the start, this chapter covers over thirty-five years of my life. I hate to talk to the sad side of this time, but it's as important as the wonderful experiences with my family after all. I apologize in advance, dear Reader, as some of this sad stuff overlaps the time I've just written about. Let's just put that in the "me being selfish again" bucket and call it even, okay?

Akamu's passing created a template of sorts when it came to death. I hate to think of it in this light, but it's true, dear Reader. You see, six months after Akamu passed, Stan died. Then, over the next twenty-five years, we would experience the death of both my and Annie's parents. Nol's parents passed in that timeframe too. Rupert died the year after Nol's Dad, and Michael died two weeks later, seemingly of a broken heart. Mr. Toth and Joe Lating died within two years of one another, starting one year to the day from Stan's death. Both José and Maria Rodriguez passed away within five years after Joe did. The circumstances of each person's passing were all so completely different, and the losses significant in their own unique ways. Regardless, each was mourned until their funeral ended. Should mourning extend beyond this, interventions were held in the same way Akamu intervened with Addie. This was especially true when the person's mourning disaffected life in a notable way.

Please don't get me wrong, though, dear Reader. "Template" or no, losing a parent or a significant person in one's life reverberates for, potentially decades, after the person's death. I felt a weighty sadness every time I cooked years after Mother died. The same was true if I saw, ate, or smelled shepherd's pie. Hospitals were at times extremely hard to be in without Father or Dr. Glaush, even though they both had retired a decade plus before either man died. Annie and Gill drifted extremely far apart after their parent's passing, and to this day, I still try to reconnect them with absolutely no success whatsoever.

I felt such sadness when I was in Hawaii, especially when I saw Joe at the gym or when I was anywhere on Maui. Stan's and Rupert's echoes were everywhere on the islands. I couldn't be in any building Mr. Toth and I had worked on jointly without being sad or deeply reflective for six months after he passed. This included both the farm and the Dolby house and about a hundred places around town we had collaborated on together. Joe Lating had transitioned his business to a colleague almost two years prior to his passing, but all things legal and financial were dripping with sadness irrationally for a good year after he died. I will admit that, though I know these truths about life and death, I allowed death to color my reality whether it made sense or not.

When José and Maria passed, it created a ripple in the fabric of time and space for their entire family. It took months of appointments to get their family back to functioning with the rest of humanity. The way the boys, in particular, mourned displayed the most immersive emotion I'd ever seen. Carlos, who was married and had an eight-year-old son at the time, stopped speaking to everyone in his life for *weeks*. Julio passed out, and was hospitalized for about a week when they each died. Though their deaths wrought me with sadness, I put the entire Rodriguez family in my care. In time, I made them whole again, but only after a couple intense conversations with their parents, oddly similar to the one I had with Akamu. When Carlos came out of that experience, he hugged his son and cried harder than I thought possible by a human being. Julio, on the other hand, got out of his funk and immediately went back to work. Interestingly, he proposed to his girlfriend of three years the day after having his scolding from his mother. I understood maybe every third word of that conversation, but I did not hear anything about a proposal in that exchange.

I almost hate to write this, but this time period also brought us the deaths of our dogs. Angel had brought me back among the living after the attack at the nut house. He and I had grown our connection to one rivaling my relationship with Doc. Penelope was Annie's rock in dog form, and losing her was devastating. Immediately after losing both dogs, though, two new puppies found their way into our lives. I still have no idea how this is the case, dear Reader, but it remains true even today.

Mind you, dear Reader, I lost Doc over fifty years ago as I write this. I have been without a dog somehow related to him genealogically or by breed for a grand total of ten hours since he bound into my life. After Angel died, we were handed Poco by Carlos, who found him on the farmhouse porch that same day. Poco is Spanish for "a little" and he was anything but. As a puppy, he was a spitting image of Doc. As an adult, he was the biggest, though most gentle, dog I ever owned. He was joined by Daphne, who we found sleeping on our deck an hour after saying goodbye to Penelope. She was no more than two months old when we found her.

I have no explanation for this, dear Reader, but every female dog we have ever had appeared on our deck within hours of the death of another. This pattern has repeated *four* times in total if I count Penelope. The male dogs appeared in a myriad of ways. The females always appeared on the deck, in the same place, and in every case, they attached themselves to Annie immediately. Perhaps the appearing puppies is a cosmic anomaly, perhaps it has a significance beyond what I understand, and perhaps it's all chance. Whatever the reason, I am grateful for every dog we have been fortunate enough to have in our lives.

Lou brought us our male puppy after Poco tragically passed, who he found on the front porch of my parents' house one day he was there gathering apples at harvest time. That pup was aptly named Red due to Lou picking Red Delicious apples at the orchard the day he found him. That pup was ironically the brownest ridgeback I ever owned, dear Reader. I found our next male pup, Gale, two hours after I painfully said goodbye to Red. This happened right after a minor hurricane made a mess of my neighborhood, so his name had to be storm-related. As expected, we found Violet chewing on a violet from one of our planters, sitting on the deck about forty-five minutes after we said goodbye to Daphne. If I remember correctly, Annie passed out briefly after Daphne died. She was so, so close to her.

We said our farewells to Gale two years ago and Violet one year ago. Annie found our current male, Stone, ironically sitting on a rock on the side of our house ninety minutes after Gale was laid to rest. I found our current female, Andi, soundly sleeping on that spot on our deck about four hours after tearfully saying goodbye to Violet. As a side note, Violet is the reason we currently have no planters on our porch, and why the majority of the wildflowers in our beds have to be replanted. Damn dog was the most destructive creature ever when it came to pretty things in nature.

Stone is sleeping at my feet as I write this, dear Reader. He's such a good dog, and is patient with me as an old man. Andi is about a sweet a creature as I can remember knowing. She, like the other females, bound to Annie immediately. They are sitting out on the deck with Sadie having wine and conversation. I guess Nol is stopping by with dinner tonight, which should absolutely excite the Bo jangles out of Stone. My big guy has a thing for Nol for sure; I think primarily because he gets fed an overabundance of food Nol catches in the ocean. The pups get the most exercise from our grandchildren these days.

****

I am so very proud of my grandchildren, dear Reader—their parents too for that matter! Lou remains the steady hand of the farm, and is the primary caretaker of the orchard. Addie, after retiring from tennis, transitioned the business portion of the farm to her leadership when Annie chose to retire. Addison still runs the farm to this day, and continues to find new opportunities to grow the company. Jonah, after retiring from football, helped Nol with the Richard Carolas Glassburé Schools. He took his father's place on the board when Nol decided to retire. Julia, last but not least, took over half of Fanny's time over the past six years as an assistant to me. She is as much an asset to me as Fanny has been, which is saying an awful lot about her abilities!

Two children, two kid-in-laws, and six grandchildren, dear Reader. I am a blessed man to have such love in my life.

Thank You, Dear Reader

Well, if you've traveled this far with me, dear Reader, I believe some thanks are in order. Indeed, you have read about my life. There have been ups, downs, the unexplained, and the unbelievable. No matter how insane this book has gotten, you stayed. I promised you a trip down a road of both intrigue and tragedy. I promised you laughter and tears, and I hope by this point, you will perhaps view your own physical self differently than you have in the past.

Thank you, dear Reader. See, as much as I've written this for you, it was wonderful remembering the life I've lived. I've certainly laughed and cried along the way, and have truly enjoyed all the conversations that have been had as I wrote. There were little details Annie, Nol, Sadie, and I talked through together. The same is true with the kids, who were a tremendous help to me in so many ways.

I have lived a profound life. Thank you for allowing me to share it with you. Find blessings in every moment, dear Reader, even in chaos. They are there so long as you look and listen closely enough.

****

The last words you read were the last my father wrote. None of us had any idea he was writing this book, even though he credited us with helping him do so. If anything, we thought he was just enjoying remembering certain things that we all experienced. Regardless, finding this book has given us—all of us—something to smile about. You see, I discovered this manuscript in his office shortly after his passing.

Olaf Waniglia was an unbelievable man. In his lifetime, he treated generations of people all over the world. He was the best father to me and Louis we could have ever hoped for, and his grandchildren were the light of his eyes. We have been blessed to have had him in our lives.

He loved my mother so much you could feel it just being around them. He honored and respected her in all she did, and enjoyed her flaws as though she were perfect in every way. I have to believe, to him, she was.

Mom died peacefully holding my father's hand out on their deck one Thursday afternoon. She was not sick; Dad explained that it was "just time" through some exceptionally heavy tears. I have to believe her passing was too painful for him to write about, simply because she passed away while he was writing this book. Much of what Dad wrote, in particular about his grandchildren, is current as of this year. Mom passed away just over two years ago.

I am writing this one month after Dad's passing. I will admit that despite all he taught us, losing my father has created a "ripple in the fabric of time and space" for our family—to borrow his words. For that matter, his loss is being felt around the world. There are an awful lot of sad people in Europe and Hawaii, in addition to the wet eyes here in America from coast to coast. Olaf Waniglia was a great man, and I thank you from the bottom of my heart for reading his story.

I will leave you with something my dad told me and my brother frequently, something I believe he would want his story ended with.

"Trust the words not spoken and the truths felt within above all else."

Blessings, Addison Glassburé

Acknowledgements

I was privileged to work with two wonderful editors during this project. Alex Larson and Courtney Lindemann, thank you from the bottom of my heart for both keeping me honest and helping me to make this book into something greater than I ever thought possible.

Larry Smithmier, thank you for everything. You are a gem, sir.

There are countless others I need to recognize… I'll simply say this: there were many people who I spoke to as I wrote this, both in airplanes and on terra firma, who reconfirmed this project as sound over and over again. I am eternally grateful to this grand population of folks; I hope you have enjoyed the project you heard about but were forbidden from seeing *until now*…

Lastly, thank you—the holder of this book—for spending your time reading my words. This is perhaps the greatest gift you can give me. If ever you find me out an about in the world and happen to have this book in hand, I'll gladly sign it, butchering some part of what otherwise would be a nice piece of paper.

www.ingramcontent.com/pod-product-compliance
Lightning Source LLC
Chambersburg PA
CBHW071729110726
47908CB00006B/1542